STOUT CORTEZ

When Colin Fairbright finds himself in a snowbound train a short distance from home, he befriends a young lady called Rosita. She tells him she is on her way to visit her father who lives at a nearby Country Club. Battling through deep snow, Colin and Rosita reach the Club, where they find that Rosita's father is very ill. When he dies overnight, they learn that he has lost a fortune gambling. Colin feels that something is not quite right at the Club. Then another resident dies under suspicious circumstances . . .

Books by George Goodchild
in the Linford Mystery Library:

THE DANGER LINE
McLEAN DISPOSES
THE LAST REDOUBT
NEXT OF KIN
McLEAN INVESTIGATES
SAVAGE ENCOUNTER
FALSE INTRUDER
LADY TAKE CARE
THE BARTON MYSTERY

GEORGE GOODCHILD

◆

STOUT CORTEZ

Complete and Unabridged

LINFORD
Leicester

First published in Great Britain in 1949

First Linford Edition
published 2003

British Library CIP Data

Goodchild, George, *1888* –
    Stout Cortez.—Large print ed.—
    Linford mystery library
    1. Detective and mystery stories
    2. Large type books
    I. Title
    823.9'14 [F]

ISBN 0–7089–9479–2

Published by
F. A. Thorpe (Publishing)
Anstey, Leicestershire

Set by Words & Graphics Ltd.
Anstey, Leicestershire
Printed and bound in Great Britain by
T. J. International Ltd., Padstow, Cornwall

This book is printed on acid-free paper

1

The English scene as it presented itself at the latter end of December was not displeasing to the man from Malaya. All through the 'Bay' it had been a toss-up whether the ship would berth in time for its very mixed assembly to reach their homes before Christmas, for already a day had been lost in the wildest of weather, and the cold, green seas and fifty-mile head-wind were still as rampageous as ever. The radio spoke of exceptionally wintry conditions in northern Europe with graphic descriptions of delays in transport from London to Aberdeen, and the passengers, staggering along the decks found the warmest of their clothing far from adequate in the changed conditions.

More precious hours were lost as the ship beat her way up the western Channel, and now it became a real race against time, with the odds against the ship. But during the night the wind eased off and by morning the ship was well up the English Channel, forging ahead at her maximum speed. The steward who burst into Colin Fairbright's cabin, with an early cup of tea, was as cheery as a bird in spring.

'Nice morning, sir,' he said. 'Bit of a sea still running, but no wind at all. We're timed to dock at eleven o'clock. That ought to get you to London by two. Depends upon the customs examination. But as we're thirty-six hours overdue I reckon they'll hustle things a bit.'

'I hope so,' yawned Colin. 'Why, it's snowing.'

'Just a few flakes. Gosh, I'll be glad to get home to my wife and kids. I'm lucky to live in Southampton. Gives me time to do a bit of Christmas shopping. They'll have their stockings hanging up to-night. The missus as well. She's never grown up, my missus hasn't. Still believes in Santa Claus.'

'Very nice too,' said Colin. 'I'll bet you've managed to come by some nylons.'

The steward winked, and left the small

tray. The occupant of the comfortable deck cabin was an impressive figure. He was over six feet tall, with a face the colour of a new penny and long supple limbs. The wide-set, blue-grey eyes were thoughtful — the lean jaw square and purposive. One would have guessed his age to be slightly over thirty, but actually he was two years younger. He drank his cup of tea reflectively, smiling from time to time, as he allowed his mind to reach back into the past. This was natural enough for he had not seen England for over seven years, and the sight of the distant land was something he had dreamed about hundreds of times.

Breakfast this morning was an occasion. The dining-room was a hubbub of sound — cross conversation and laughter, jokes about contraband and all the well-known swindles. The sun rose out of a low mist and the snow-clad uplands of Dorset and Hampshire came to full view. The decks became alive with passengers . . .

At Southampton the business of getting through the customs, and on to the waiting train was not lengthy, but to Colin it seemed an eternity. At last he found himself in the corner seat of a first-class compartment with several of his shipboard companions. The journey to London was uneventful, but at Waterloo there was the usual struggle for porters and taxis. Then the good-byes to people, most of whom he would never see again, and the taxi ride across London to King's Cross in a mad rush to catch the two-forty-five to Lincolnshire. Now it was snowing again, and the streets were ankle deep in brown slush which was flung up in murky fountains by the mass of traffic. Colin would have liked to see some of the shopping centres, with the inevitable crowds, but the driver was obeying the injunction to 'make it snappy' and drove his ancient vehicle through a maze of side streets to avoid the main crush of traffic. Ultimately Colin found himself at the railway terminus with a quarter of an hour to spare.

'There you are, sir,' grinned the taxi-driver. 'After this, I'm going to knock off. Got my bit er shopping to do — if there's anything left in the shops. Thank Gawd termorrer's Christmas Day. Trains are all running a bit late, so you'll be all okey-doke.'

He took Colin's ten-shilling note, and looked his fare between the eyes in a way which spoke volumes. Colin laughed and waved his hand.

'Thank you, sir. Merry Christmas to yer!'

Colin bought his ticket, and waited while his considerable baggage was labelled to his destination. The train steamed in as it was finished, and the porter pushed the loaded truck down the platform to the luggage van. Colin retained only one small suitcase for the compartment, and in due course he found himself a very uncomfortable seat.

The taxi-driver proved to be right, for the train did not pull out until nearly three o'clock, by which time there were three passengers standing in the compartment and many more in the corridor. Once free of the London suburbs Colin was able to appreciate how severe the weather conditions were on the eastern side of England. The fields and trees were deep in snow, and occasional open water was frozen. Frost was again forming on the windows, and fine snow piling up in the corners of the window-frames.

'Good old-fashioned Christmas,' said his opposite neighbour. 'It's nice enough when you're young, but not so good afterwards. This damned carriage is like an ice-well. Time they got some heat going.'

Colin did not join him in his lamentation. Truth to tell he was rather enjoying it all. A few hours ahead of him there was a comfortable house with, no doubt, some festive decorations. By this time his mother and sister would have received the telegram which he had sent from the port of arrival, and he could well imagine the excitement there. If he could have chosen the weather he would have chosen just such conditions. One had to stew for months and years in tropical heat to appreciate the falling snowflakes, the lovely effects of the snow on the branches of trees, and the frost on the window-pane.

But very soon the wintry scene outside was blanketed out by the fading light, and he gave himself up to reading, and dreaming alternatively. Then, after about an hour, he stood up and offered his seat to an elderly man who was standing and who graciously accepted the offer. After about half an hour the train stopped and he heard a voice bawling the name of a station. Four of the passengers then grabbed suitcases and miscellaneous baggage and left the compartment. It enabled the rest of the passengers to comport themselves with greater comfort. Colin who took over his recent seat next to the corridor went outside for a moment and cleaned a small area of frosted window. He caught a glimpse of a platform deep in snow, and of a myriad snowflakes drifting past a solitary lamp. A whistle blew and the train resumed its journey.

'Still snowing?' asked his opposite companion.

'Yes — heavily.'

'I thought it would. Never known such weather since I was a kid. I doubt if I'll get a taxi at Peterborough, with all this snow on the ground. That will mean a nice walk of over two miles.'

'Has this weather been on long?' asked Colin.

'A week now. Before that it was like an Indian summer. You never know what will happen next in this country. Going far?'

'Just short of Roxton.'

'You'll have a slow journey after Peterborough. I heard there were deep drifts further north.'

'Well, as long as I get home to-night I don't mind very much. Lord, I hope there's a dining-car on this train. I forgot to find out.'

'There is.'

Colin resumed his reading, but very soon it was noticeable that the train had reduced speed appreciably, and when, finally, they reached Peterborough the man who was getting out looked at his watch and said that already the train was twenty minutes late, not counting the half-hour wasted at King's Cross. Two others followed him, and a new passenger arrived and took the corner seat opposite

Colin. She was a girl whose age might have been anything between twenty and twenty-four, and she carried one suitcase which Colin lifted into the rack for her.

'Thanks very much,' she said.

'Not at all.'

The train now never attempted anything more than a crawl, and Colin had to change his ideas about the time he would reach his destination. A ticket-collector appeared and clipped the tickets.

'Are we going to lose more time?' asked Colin.

'I'm afraid so, sir. There are some big drifts further on, and in places we are only working a single line. That means hanging about. But dinner will be on in half an hour. Have you got a dining ticket?'

'No.'

'I'll send the man along.'

'Thank you.'

Colin read for a while, but spent some time 'taking in' the girl opposite. She was attractively — even expensively — dressed, with a mink coat, which Colin guessed must have cost a lot of money.

Her hat was of similar fur, trimmed with a kind of short, black veil, which set off her classical features admirably. Her behaviour intrigued him, for unlike his other travelling companions, who had composed themselves for a monotonously tiring journey, she appeared to be as restless as a caged linnet. She dived into a handbag and produced a gold pencil and proceeded to solve a crossword puzzle in the daily newspaper, but after she had written in a word or two she put the paper aside and turned over the pages of a magazine, merely scanning the illustrations until she came to the end. Then she lighted a cigarette, smoked for a few minutes, and stubbed out the cigarette in the adjacent ash container. Once more she tried the crossword puzzle, and Colin smiled to himself to realise from the newspaper heading that it was one which he had almost completed on his journey from Southampton to Waterloo. Then the slowly-moving train stopped, and the passengers began to moan. The girl threw the newspaper aside as if exasperated, and tried to light a second cigarette, but the petrol lighter refused to function.

'Permit me,' said Colin, and had better luck with his own lighter.

Again she thanked him in her curious soft voice. It seemed like an opening to start a conversation, but at that moment the dining-car attendant entered.

'Any dining tickets?' he asked.

'Yes,' replied Colin. 'When will dinner be on?'

'Very soon now, sir. I'll call you.'

'I should like a ticket, please,' said the girl.

He produced two tickets and gave one to each of them.

'Why have we stopped?' asked Colin.

'Waiting for the signal. We're on a single line now — or shall be when we get the signal. I expect the down express is late. Rather a bad journey this evening. It's snowing like mad outside.'

'Not enough snow ploughs,' growled a man in the far corner, who had just dragged himself out of a sleep.

'Snow ploughs wouldn't help,' said the attendant. 'It's men with shovels that are needed, and about a hundred of 'em at

11

that. There's about two feet of snow out there, with six feet or more in the drifts. It's a miracle that trains can run at all.'

'Hm!' snorted the passenger. 'They do these things better in Canada.'

'Oh, I don't know, sir,' said the attendant, half in and half out of the compartment. 'The last train I caught in Canada — at Regina — was two days late, so we've got a good bit in hand.'

Colin could not help smiling at this ripost, and he noticed that the girl was as amused as he was. Then the train gave a jolt and started to crawl forward again.

'Thank goodness!' sighed the girl.

'It's bad enough for the passengers, but it must be ten times worse for the driver and his mate, and the signalmen whose job it is to get trains through,' said Colin.

'I agree.' She picked up the newspaper again, and the gold pencil hovered in her lovely fingers. 'Oh dear, I wish I knew who it was who looked and saw. Saw what and where?'

'From a high peak in Darien. He saw the Pacific.'

A pair of beautiful eyes regarded him.

'So you know?' she said.

'Yes. His name was — But perhaps you would rather I didn't say.'

'I ought to be ashamed, but the fact is I don't know.'

'It was the conqueror of Mexico. Actually I believe the poet was wrong, but he was referring to Cortez.'

'Of course! How stupid of me.'

She wrote in the word, and then put the newspaper aside.

'I'm really no good at these things,' she said. 'But they do help to pass the time on a journey.'

'Especially on a journey like this, when there's no knowing just how long we shall be cooped up here. Are you going very far?'

'No. Only to Roxton.'

'My destination too. At least it's about four miles from Roxton. A little place called Apsley.'

'I don't know it,' she said. 'As a matter of fact I've been abroad for many years, and have forgotten most of the scenes of my childhood. You look as if you had come from abroad.'

'Yes — Malaya.'

'Good gracious. This must be a change.'

'It is,' he laughed. 'Oh, that sounds like the dinner bell. Sooner than I hoped.'

A few moments later the attendant opened the sliding door and announced that the meal was ready.

'Two coaches forward,' he said.

Colin waited for the girl to leave the compartment and then followed her down the corridor to the dining-car, which was about twenty degrees warmer than the rest of the train, and looked very inviting with its white table-cloths and red-shaded table lamps. The waiter showed her into a seat at one of the smaller tables, and Colin, reading an invitation in her eyes, occupied the opposite seat.

'This is better,' he said.

'Very much.'

The meal which followed was sparse enough, but at least the soup was really hot, and the service excellent. At intervals the train passed through small stations, and, with the windows free of ice, Colin caught glimpses of falling snow and piled-up platforms. On the station lamps long icicles hung like stalactites, then again all was merged in a wide field of grey-white.

'Is Apsley your home?' asked the girl.

'Yes. I last saw it seven years ago when I went out to Malaya. There was a leave due to me after three years, but by that time the Japs had occupied the territory, and I had managed to get a passage to India. There I got a temporary war job, and when the Japs were beaten I was urgently wanted back. So I missed the leave which was due to me. That means I'm getting a double dose now, and it's rather nice being in time for Christmas.'

'It must be. Did you arrive only this morning?'

'Yes. I came straight through from Southampton.'

'Malaya indicates rubber,' she said.

'Usually, but I happen to be an engineer.'

'That covers a multitude of activities.'

'You're right. My job is to look after a

generating plant. The dear little Japs made a mess of it before they put up their hands, and getting it working again was a major operation. But I'm talking too much about myself. Are you on your way to indulge in seasonal festivities?'

'Partly. It's a kind of reunion with my family. I've not seen much of England since I was a small child. I was educated in France, and went to a finishing school in Switzerland. After that I took up music as a career.'

'Singing?'

'Oh no — the piano. The war restricted my movements, but I was able to give a few concerts in Berne and Zürich. I left Zürich only yesterday, and I'm very anxious to get home.'

A cloud seemed to pass across her face, and Colin recalled the restlessness which she had displayed previously. He could not help feeling that the family reunion was not expected to be all festivity and unalloyed joy.

'Where do your people live?' he asked.

'Alton Hall — but only since the war started. Before that we lived in Lincoln.

I've never been to Alton. Do you know it?'

'Yes. It's quite a large place, with a park. You can actually see it from the railway train — in daylight. I believe it was occupied by the military during the war. I suppose that as the crow is reputed to fly it isn't more than two miles from my home. So in a sense we are neighbours.'

'That sounds — rather nice.'

'But tell me about your music. Do you mean that you are a professional solo pianist?'

'In a humble kind of way. Don't imagine I live by music — yet. That takes a long time. But the critics were kind and the audience generous. The concerts were all for charity, and that probably disarmed the critics — and the audience — in advance.'

'You're just being modest.'

'Not unduly. I've a tremendous lot to learn.'

'I envy you. I always wanted to follow an artistic career, but my father was against it. He drew horrible pictures of starvation in a garret — burning my precious manuscripts to warm my frozen hands. I'm quite mad on music and poetry, but I doubt very much if I have any talent on the creative side. Tell me — what sort of things do you play?'

'The well-established classics. Chopin, Beethoven, Brahms, Debussy and Ravel — occasionally Scriabin and Rachmaninoff. I once did the Schumann Concerto, but it wasn't very successful. I was scared by the orchestra and the conductor.'

'Wonderful!'

'Not much more wonderful than being able to run an electric generating plant. That's where I envy you.'

'Oh, but the arts are different. They are the eternal verities — the gifts of the gods. In the presence of great music, painting, or poetry I feel like that chap whose name eluded you in the crossword puzzle — stout Cortez.'

'You're making me feel shockingly ignorant. I remember that Cortez conquered Mexico, but who was the poet you mentioned?'

'To my mind the greatest of them all

18

— Keats. I think you must have read the lines, but have forgotten them. How do they go?

'Then felt I like some watcher of the
　　skies
When a new planet swims into his ken;
Or like stout Cortez when with eagle
　　eyes
He stared at the Pacific — and all his
　　men
Look'd at each other with a mild
　　surmise —
Silent, upon a peak in Darien.''

'That's lovely,' she said. 'I wish I could remember things like that.'
'You remember other things no less lovely. I suppose it's a good thing human beings are so diversified, or we might all die of utter boredom.'
The train which had been going very slowly now stopped with a harsh jolt, throwing people back in their seats. Through the window Colin could see nothing but that grey expanse, unrelieved by any light. A minute or two passed and

then the waiter came with the coffee.

'Signal against us?' asked Colin.

The waiter made a wry face, and shook his head.

'Wouldn't surprise me if we've had it, sir,' he muttered.

'Had what?' asked Colin.

'Run into a deep drift. It's snowing cats and dogs — fine driving stuff that piles up in the wind.'

'What will they do — dig us out?'

'If they can get a labour gang here. But, of course, I may be wrong, sir.'

'I certainly hope you are.'

'Is he just being pessimistic?' asked the girl, when the waiter had passed along the car.

'He looked serious enough, and it certainly is snowing hard outside. Anyway, we are cosy enough here, and we can't be very far from Roxton.'

They drank their coffee in leisurely fashion, but there was no further movement of the train. When the attendant came with the bills Colin questioned him about the position.

'I know nothing yet, sir,' he said. 'But

20

it's pretty clear that we are going to be here for some time. I believe the guard has gone along the track to the next signal-box. When he comes back he'll probably know just what the position is.'

'How far are we from Roxton?'

'Only about six miles — but it's six miles of very deep snow. Ah, here comes the guard.'

The guard looked like Father Christmas himself. He was coated with snow from head to feet, and looked most unhappy.

'I'm sorry to say there will be some delay, ladies and gentlemen,' he said. 'We're in a big snowdrift, but help is coming. Please return to your seats when you have finished, as we want to conserve the lighting.'

'Why can't we stay here?' asked a passenger.

'For the reason I have just given, sir.'

Everyone looked depressed, and after a few minutes the diners began to file back to their compartments. In the compartment which Colin and the girl re-entered only the fat man in the opposite corner remained. He was sleeping soundly, presumably ignorant of the realities of the situation. Colin opened the corridor window for a moment and looked outside. A man was walking along the line, with a lantern in his hand. The snow came up to his knees, and the whirling flakes seemed to be smothering him.

'Where are we exactly?' asked Colin.

He held up the lantern.

'Hey?' he bellowed.

'Where are we?'

'Just short of Alton signal-box. We're stuck fast, and are likely to be here for hours. Better close that window, sir.'

'Did he say hours?' asked the girl.

'Yes — and all the time the snow is getting deeper. So near home too. What a pity.'

They sat and talked — about a number of things. Music, books, the state of the worried world, and soon it became noticeable that the compartment was getting colder and colder.

'Conserving heat as well as light,' said Colin. 'Wouldn't surprise me if we find ourselves in darkness soon. By the way

22

it's time I introduced myself. My name is Colin Fairbright.'

'Mine is Rosita Paston. I should like to see just where we are. At Peterborough I bought a map of the neighbourhood.'

She pulled her suitcase from the rack and delved into it, to produce a one-inch Ordnance Survey map. Colin came and sat by the side of her.

'That's where we are,' he said. 'Just about at that point. Oh look — there's your objective. It's marked Alton Hall. Less than three inches — say two miles and a half in a straight line.'

'What's in between?'

'Chiefly fenland, but frozen hard I expect.'

Her eyes came round — looking into his, and somehow he knew what was in her mind.

'I don't think it's possible,' he said. 'Heaven knows how much snow there is out there, nor how much ice on open water. One could easily get drowned.'

'But I must get home to-night,' she said. 'There's a reason.'

'You may achieve that by less dangerous devices.'

'If I could only be sure.'

The lights flickered and then came on
again. The sleeping man gave a thunder-
ous snore, and opened his eyes.

'Where — where are we?' he growled.

'Stuck in a snowdrift,' replied Colin.

'Nonsense!'

'Have it your own way,' said Colin,
sweetly.

The late sleeper got up on his feet, and
opened the window wide. It was the
windward side, and a cloud of snow blew
into the compartment.

'My hat!' he ejaculated.

'Would you mind closing that window?'
asked Colin.

The fat man did this, and collapsed
into his seat.

'What are they doing about it?' he
demanded.

'Why not go and find out?'

'I will. Damned inefficiency — being
stuck in a bit of snow, and people wanting
to get home for Christmas. Excuse me,
sir!'

Colin slipped the door back and let him pass through it.

'Disgruntled old scoundrel,' he said. 'But unless I am mistaken he is due for a ticking off very shortly. B-r-r-r! It's getting cold.'

The girl pulled her fur coat around her and drew on her thick gloves. Colin sat reflecting upon the position. Already they were hours late and he had no doubt that his mother and sister would already have been put to considerable worry and inconvenience. He felt sure they would have gone to the railway station with the family car — presuming that was possible. If the worst should happen he might have to spend the night in this chilly compartment instead of in a warm bed. His companion might be some compensation — but not quite enough to balance such discomfort. He couldn't help wondering what was the urgent need to get home in her case — more urgent than his own to judge by her attitude. He was still cogitating when suddenly the lights flickered again and then went out.

'Just what I expected,' he muttered.

'Mr. Fairbright?'

'Yes.'

'I — I must get home. There's no sign of anything happening here. Please tell me how to get to Alton Hall — after I leave the train.'

'But I told you it was dangerous.'

'Yes, but I must take a chance.'

'But you're not clad for such a feat. Your thin shoes and stockings — '

'I'm going,' she said determinedly. 'The suitcase isn't very heavy and my other baggage is labelled and in the guard's van. I've got a small pocket torch, in case — '

'You really mean that?'

'Yes.'

'All right. We'll go together.'

'But I don't want to bother you — '

'I'm as keen to get home as you are, and perhaps two heads are better than one in this business. But we had better not be seen, or we may be stopped. Give me that suitcase.'

'No — you've got your own to carry.'

'Give it to me!' he said almost fiercely.

They went sneaking along the corridor

until they came to the door of the coach. It was very dark, but on opening the door there was a slight amount of illumination from the white surface of the snow. Colin jumped first and was cushioned by the deep snow. He reached up for the girl and she was soon beside him. Then he picked up the two suitcases.

'Follow close behind me,' he whispered.

2

The darkness and the driving snow soon swallowed them up, but before they had gone a hundred yards Colin was brought to realise just what they had undertaken. Before them was a wide stretch of open country, intersected by many deep dykes, all now under snow and in the main impossible to distinguish from the land itself. He knew that about a mile and a half ahead there was a narrow road running approximately parallel with the railway track. On the further side was another open stretch, with more dykes, but which rose gradually to the higher land on which was Alton Hall.

'This is ghastly,' he said, as the snow blew into his face. 'Our first objective is the road. Just let me have one look at that map. We may have to cross a couple of the main dykes, but I want to avoid as many as possible.'

Rosita handed him the map and the

torch, and Colin dumped the suitcases while he mapped the course. He believed he was headed in the right direction, but he wanted to strike the bridge across the main dyke, rather than risk a crossing of the ice, and the bridge, marked on the excellent map was not quite in their line of approach.

'All right,' he said at last. 'Here we go.'

The torch was switched off and the suitcases picked up. Away they went, sinking at every step up to their knees. Colin found this most unpleasant, for the snow forced itself up his trouser ends and froze on his skin. Rosita was in a worse plight, and was compelled to keep her skirt permanently raised, but she raised no word of complaint and trudged on manfully.

Then at last came the first dyke. It was unmistakable by the slight rise of the bank and the dip on the other side. Colin brought the torch into action but could see no bridge. He shone the torch right and left, but the whirling snowflakes reduced visibility to a few yards.

'We've missed the bridge,' he said.

'There was always that risk. If we start looking for it we may not last out. Wait here! I'm going to try the ice.'

'Oh, be careful,' she said, with chattering teeth.

He descended a few steps and put one foot on the snow-covered ice — then the other. There was a loud creaking, but the ice held. The succeeding steps raised fresh creakings, but at last he was safely across.

'All right,' he called. 'No need for you to worry. Come on!'

He shone the light across, and Rosita made the passage.

'Good!' he said. 'The second big dyke is about half a mile ahead — running slightly at a tangent. There's a bridge there too. Let's hope we may be luckier this time. Are you all right?'

'Yes,' she gasped, trying to keep her teeth from chattering. 'My feet don't feel to be there — that's all.'

Colin deliberately increased the pace to the second dyke, believing that it would mitigate the cold to a certain extent, hard as it might be on muscles and lungs. It was, he reflected, like walking in glue, and

30

every step was equal to a dozen taken on unencumbered land. But at last the second dyke was reached — and again there was no bridge by which to cross. He shone the torch and saw that Rosita was completely encrusted in snow, and breathing heavily. She was able to beat it from her fur coat, but it had frozen on her silk stockings and was immovable.

'Well, we crossed the other one,' he said. 'No reason why we shouldn't cross this. Here goes!'

He put a foot on the ice, with but half his weight on it. Then he raised the other, and instantly there was an alarming crack and he was in water up to his waist. Rosita gave a little cry and hastened to him. He waved her away.

'It's only waist-deep,' he gasped. 'I — I can clamber out.'

Putting the suitcases on the snow, with the torch on top of them, he managed to get to the bank, in a half-frozen condition, drenched from the waist downwards.

'Can't hope to get across there,' he said.

Rosita reached out for the torch and shone it to the right. There was a momentary pause in the driving snow, and something loomed up in that direction.

'The bridge!' she cried, and before Colin could look the snow had blotted it out again.

'Are you sure?' he asked.

'Yes — yes.'

They plodded along the bank and came upon the ancient bridge.

'No more big dykes,' said Colin. 'Only an occasional ditch, and we can't be far from that road.'

They found the road a few minutes later, and here the snow lay less deep. Colin took another look at the map.

'We can follow the road for about a quarter of a mile,' he said. 'Then cross it to the fen. Alton Hall must be less than a mile away. Cheer up!'

But that mile was equal to ten, and the two suitcases felt as if they were full of lead. Both of them were now near exhaustion, and their chattering teeth made speech almost impossible. At last

Colin was sensible of a rise in the land, and suddenly he saw a hedge, and beyond it the indistinct shapes of trees.

'We're there!' he mumbled. 'The road which skirts the park is beyond the hedge, and the drive to the house lies to the right — I think.'

Crossing the hedge was quite a major operation, but at last it was done. They came out on a road bordered on the further side by a high stone wall. Colin moved to the right and very soon found an entrance gate to a drive. The drive was lined with huge trees, and recently the old snow had been swept from the centre of it, leaving a hard surface under the new fall of about nine inches. Here he put the suitcases down, and stamped his painful feet. Then he noticed that Rosita was swaying as if she would fall.

'Steady!' he said, placing an arm round her. 'You've been marvellous. It's practically over now. Look, you can see a light in the house. Can you make it?'

'I'll — try.'

'Good! It's easier going here.'

Slowly they mounted the slight rise,

and at length arrived at an imposing portico. It was still snowing hard and the details of the large house were vague, but Colin got the impression of a huge mansion with innumerable windows, many of which were lighted. The outer hall was decked with holly, and round the blue antique lamp was a spray of mistletoe.

'Home to a Christmas atmosphere,' he said. 'Certainly better than waiting in that cold train all night. Where's the bell?'

He found a button and pushed it. Very soon one side of the great double door was opened, and a servant came to view, and gazed incredulously at the snow-encrusted figures, and Colin's drenched lower parts.

'I'm Miss Paston,' said Rosita.

'Oh, yes, miss. We — we weren't expecting you. We heard a little while ago that the train was snowed up. Please come inside, and I'll inform Mr. Stockforth.'

'I'd better go now,' said Colin.

'Oh no — you can't. You'll catch your death of cold unless you change into dry clothing. Please — please wait.'

The servant led them to the inner hall, where a huge log fire was burning, and then vanished along a passage. The warmth from the fire was delicious, and they crouched before it, thawing their frozen limbs and dripping water on the carpet.

'We're making an awful mess,' said Colin.

'Who cares?'

'Your family might. Are your parents here?'

'Only — my father. My mother died a few years ago. And my father is seriously ill. That's what brought me here. Oh, why doesn't somebody come?'

'I didn't know,' said Colin. 'Now I can understand your haste. I'm very sorry.'

There came the sound of hilarious laughter from some part of the house, and then a man and two women came down the stairs. They were all most correctly attired, and one of the women wore a mass of jewellery. They shot interested glances at the odd-looking couple by the fire, and then vanished through a door to the right of the stairway.

'Guests,' said Colin.

Rosita looked very worried and anxious, and Colin was puzzled by the whole thing — the cold reception, the mention of Mr. Stockforth, whom Rosita took no steps to explain, the long delay, and the peals of laughter which came at short intervals. Then, at last, came a dapper fellow of about forty years of age, wearing evening dress, and a flower in his buttonhole. He looked from Rosita to Colin, and then smiled at Rosita.

'My name is Stockforth,' he said. 'I am a friend of your father. You, of course, are Rosita?'

'Yes. This gentleman is Mr. Fairbright, who helped me to get here. You see, the train was snowed up — '

'I heard that. It was only a little while ago that I telephoned to the station and was told there was little likelihood of the train being able to move until morning. I don't understand — '

'We left the train and came across the

fields. Mr. Fairbright lives near here. But how is my father?'

Stockforth shook his head slowly.

'Not too good, I'm afraid. But he's sleeping at the moment. I will explain everything when you have got out of those wet clothes. I had no idea it was possible to get across the fields. For days we have been almost isolated. And you, Mr. Fairbright — '

'All I need is to use your telephone to speak to my home, and then the opportunity to change some of my garments. I have some slacks and socks in my suitcase.'

'Then I suggest you lose no time. Better change first and use the telephone afterwards. Forbes will take your case to your room, Rosita, but what about the rest of your luggage?'

'It is on the train, but I can manage out of the suitcase.'

Stockforth pushed a bell, and the man who had opened the door came into the hall.

'Oh, Forbes, show Miss Rosita to her room. I'll see you, my dear, later. Mr.

Fairbright, if you will come with me I'll fix you up.'

'Don't leave until I see you,' said Rosita to Colin. 'I haven't had time to thank you properly.'

'That's all right,' said Stockforth. 'Mr. Fairbright will be with me in my office. Come down as soon as you can, and I'll have some hot drinks ready.'

Rosita smiled at Colin, and then went up the stairs with Forbes. A moment later Colin followed Stockforth down several passages and up a secondary staircase to a comfortable room that appeared to be a compromise between a sitting-room and an office. Here a large electric fire was burning.

'There's a bathroom two doors along the passage,' said Stockforth. 'I should advise a hot bath. I'll leave you to it, and go and round up some hot punch. Can I do that telephoning for you?'

'No, thanks. I've been away from home a long time, and I rather think my people would like to hear my voice.'

'Of course. But how do you propose to get home?'

'Isn't there any possibility of a hire car?'

'Not the slightest. They won't turn out on a night like this. In fact I doubt very much whether a car could get here.'

'In that case I can walk. But I rather think my sister will manage to get to me. I know she had a set of chains.'

'Good! Now you get a move on. Won't do you any good to stand about in those wet things.'

He left the room, and Colin latched the door and quickly got rid of his saturated garments. From his suitcase he took a pair of flannel slacks, a shirt and socks, and using his overcoat as a dressing-gown he had his hot bath, and changed into his warm, dry garments, thrusting the wet things into his suitcase. A little later Stockforth returned carrying a tray on which was a large glass jug, three glasses, and some sandwiches.

'There you are!' he said cheerily. 'I saw Rosita just now. She will be with us in a few moments. Rather marvellous effort that, for a pretty girl. They usually take hours over their toilet. Curious creatures

39

women! Now I've got some good news for you. I spoke to the chauffeur about your predicament. We've got a shooting brake with a high ground clearance, and some chains. Rupert — the chauffeur — says he thinks he can get you home. That should save your sister a very nasty journey.'

'That's very good of you,' said Colin. 'While we are waiting may I use the telephone?'

'Certainly. There is an extension here. Just a moment.'

He removed a beautifully made doll from the receiver, and then pushed a button.

'Oh, Forbes,' he said. 'Put me through to the exchange.'

A moment later he handed the receiver to Colin, and politely left the room. Colin put the call through and soon heard the voice of his sister at the other end.

'Colin!' she gasped. 'Where on earth are you talking from? I've just got back from the railway station — my second trip there. They told me your train was snowbound.'

Colin explained the situation, and then waited while his mother was brought to the instrument. It was good to hear that soft beloved voice after so many years, and he detected in it her uncontrollable emotion.

'Don't keep us waiting long, Colin,' she begged. 'But it will be a nasty journey for you. There are over two feet of snow in places.'

'I know that well enough,' he laughed. 'With any luck I'll be with you in about half an hour. Keep the home-fires burning.'

'We will. Good-bye, darling!'

As Colin hung up the receiver the door opened, and a young man with sandy hair staggered in. He was evidently under the influence of drink, and for a moment he didn't realise that Colin was a complete stranger.

'Looking for you — everywhere,' he hiccoughed. 'Lot of hard-baked card-sharping — Oh, beg pardon. Thought you were my — hic — friend Stockforth — '

'He was here just now,' replied Colin. 'Ah, here he comes.'

Stockforth entered the room, and the half-tipsy man swung round on him.

'Hullo, old bean,' he said. 'I'm right this time anyway. They've stung me down there. You'll have to cash me — cheque.'

'Yes, Charles — presently. I'll see you downstairs. This gentleman is — '

'Oh hang, I can't wait. Let me have fifty, and I'll give you cheque presently. Come on — cough up.'

Stockforth sighed, and then smiled at Colin.

'The news that it's Christmas Eve seems to have gone round,' he said. 'All right, Charles, but be careful. Actually I should advise you to go to bed but that would be a waste of breath. Here you are.'

He drew a wallet from his pocket and counted out ten five-pound notes, which he handed to the youth, who touched his forelock in a mock salute, and then staggered to the door.

'Sorry,' said Stockforth. 'There are times when the line of least resistance is the obvious one. I suppose the Christmas spirit is responsible. He should be a wiser man to-morrow. Did you get your message through?'

'Yes, thank you.'

'You certainly look better for your clean-up. Rupert will be ready when you are.'

There was a tap on the door, and then Rosita entered. She wore a very simple frock, with a single string of pearls round her throat, and was completely transformed. But in her attitude was unmistakable nervousness and apprehension.

'Sorry to have been so long,' she said.

'But you haven't. Are you feeling better now?'

'Oh yes — thank you.'

Stockforth poured out the hot punch, and offered it and the sandwiches. Colin accepted but Rosita declined.

'I'm not a bit thirsty or hungry,' she said. 'When can I see my father?'

'When you wish, but it seems a pity to wake him now,' replied Stockforth. 'At any rate, do take a little punch. It will do you good after your ordeal.'

Rosita looked at Colin, who made no attempt to persuade her one way or the other.

'Very well,' she said. 'Just a sip.'

She took the steaming glass and echoed Stockforth's toast of a 'Happy Christmas.' Colin found the grog very potent, and very pleasant. He ate a sandwich in order not to appear unappreciative, and then felt his overcoat and hat which he had placed on a chair in front of the stove.

'Comparatively dry,' he said.

'Have you telephoned your home?' asked Rosita.

'Oh, yes. And Mr. Stockforth has kindly fixed up a car for me. I really ought to be leaving.'

'Have another glass for the road?' asked Stockforth.

'No thanks. Well, Miss Paston, I do hope that your father will soon recover. I really have to thank you for missing a night in that train.'

'On the contrary. Without your help I could never have got here. I am most grateful.'

Colin offered his hand and she shook it warmly. Then, as a last thought, he found a visiting-card, and gave it to her.

'I should like to hear any good news,' he said.

'Thank you.'

'I expect the car is waiting,' said Stockforth. 'Will you wait here, Rosita? There are quite a lot of things I have to tell you.'

Rosita nodded, and the two men left the room. On passing through the hall Colin saw a man and a woman sitting by the fire. They were not those he had seen previously. Stockforth nodded at them, and then led Colin to the outer hall where the chauffeur was waiting.

'Ah, Rupert!' said Stockforth. 'This is Mr. Fairbright. I hope you'll manage to get him to his home.'

'I think I can promise that, sir,' said Rupert in a curious thick voice. 'It's not snowing quite so hard now. Your suitcase, sir.'

A few moments later Colin was in the front seat of the large box-like car. Stockforth stayed at the door, and waved a hand as the car began to move down the drive.

'It's very good of you,' said Colin to the chauffeur.

'That's all right, sir. I can understand anyone wanting to get home on a night like this — Christmas Eve and all. Will you direct me?'

Colin did this, and once the car was out of the drive the trouble commenced. It was certainly snowing less heavily, but there were deep drifts where they were reduced to a crawl. In the town itself it was not quite so bad, but there was a complete absence of traffic, and vast banks of snow piled up near the pavements.

'Is Mr. Stockforth related to Mr. Paston?' asked Colin.

'No, sir.'

There was an air of finality about the crisp answer, and Colin refrained from asking any more questions. Again they were in narrow lanes where progress was painfully slow and, but for the chains on the wheels, would have been impossible. Finally they entered the short drive to the house. Colin's heart bounded to see the familiar gables, and he produced a pound note from his wallet and pressed it into Rupert's hand.

'A thousand thanks!' he said.

'Glad to be of service, sir. Merry Christmas!'

'Same to you.'

The car moved away at once, and the door opened before Colin could reach the latch. His sister, a merry-eyed girl, three years his junior, gave a squeal of delight and kissed him under the mistletoe. Then came Mrs. Fairbright, almost over-wrought with emotion.

'Oh, Colin!' she said. 'To see you again — after all these years. But where's your baggage?'

'On the train — except for this one case. I'll have to collect it to-morrow. As I told you on the telephone, I've had quite an adventure. I say, you have made the place look nice.'

'All done with my own fair hands,' said Rhoda. 'Had an awful job getting holly with berries. The weather has been so vile the birds must have eaten all the berries. What are you doing in those ghastly grey slacks?'

'All I had in the suitcase. I fell into a dyke and had to change a few things.'

'Shove the bag anywhere,' said Rhoda. 'I've got some drinks poured out. I think you said you had had a meal?'

'Yes — on the train, before it gave up the ghost.'

They passed into a very comfortable lounge, and Colin was pushed unceremoniously into the deepest chair by his unruly sister.

'Drink!' she said, giving him a glass.

'I've already been drinking. But here's to both of you, and a Merry Christmas.'

'Now all the news,' pleaded Rhoda. 'I couldn't make head or tail of what you said on the telephone. What were you doing at Alton Hall?'

'I told you. I decided to leave the train, rather than risk getting frozen to death in it.'

'But why Alton Hall?'

'For the simple reason that there was a girl in my compartment who wanted to get home as quickly as I did. Alton Hall was a kind of mid-way halt. I stayed there to have a hot bath and a drink, and then the chauffeur drove me here.'

'But did the girl live at Alton Hall?'

'Not exactly. Her father lives there, and she had hurried from Switzerland to see him because he is very ill.'

'What was she like?' asked Rhoda.

'Oh, very nice — but rather upset.'

'It's a curious place for her father to live.'

'Why?'

'It's a club.'

'A club?'

'Yes. Two years ago it was bought by a syndicate, and turned into a club. Hasn't got a very good reputation.'

Colin expressed surprise at this information, but it explained the presence of the queer people he has seen there, including the drunken young man.

'I never thought of that,' he said. 'What is wrong about it?'

'There may be nothing wrong at all,' said Mrs. Fairbright. 'You know how Rhoda loves a bit of scandal.'

'That's not fair, mother,' protested Rhoda. 'You know very well that a man committed suicide there, less than a year ago.'

'That's true, but it doesn't follow that anything is wrong with the club. At the inquest it was proved that the poor man was an ex-officer in the R.A.F. who had been badly shot-up, and had not been long out of hospital. There was nothing to suggest that the club was not a perfectly respectable place.'

'I've heard quite a lot of rumours.'

'You shouldn't listen to them.'

'Is it a residential club?' asked Colin.

'Yes,' replied Rhoda. 'I think the people who bought the property leased part of the big house, and nearly all the grounds to the club. There are a number of bedrooms at the disposal of club members — frightfully expensive I'm told. But you can be a non-resident member if you like. All very luxurious — tennis, and golf, and fishing in the lake. All the drink in the world and bridge at a pound a hundred.'

Mrs. Fairbright smiled and shook her head.

'I shouldn't take Rhoda too seriously,' she said. 'She has the richest imagination

50

and her geese are always swans. I would much rather hear about your own exploits. Seven years is a very long time. Tell us about your work, and what happened to you while you were in India.'

Colin related his experiences between drinks. It was very pleasant to feel warmed to the marrow, and to know that he would wake up in his own bed the following morning, with the joyful prospect of months of leisure before him — months in which he could roam over all the old playing grounds and recapture the joys of the past. It was past midnight before he went to bed, and snuggled down between the clean white sheets. But there, curiously enough, his thoughts were not of the distant past or the alluring future, but of the incidents of that night — the girl in the train, the wretched journey in the snow across the frozen fenland, and the big house in the park. Even in his sleep he carried with him the lovely features of Rosita Paston who had come into his life like a bolt from the blue, to intrigue and fascinate him as nothing ever had before.

3

Christmas day broke clear and cold, and Colin was awakened by the intrusion of his sister, with early morning tea.

'You shouldn't!' he protested.

'Orders are you are to have your breakfast in bed — later.'

'I certainly am not. What do you take me for — an invalid.'

'But mother's set her heart on it. Now be a good boy and do as you are told.'

'I absolutely refuse. Thanks for the tea old girl, but I'll be up and downstairs in half an hour. Draw the curtains, darling.'

Rhoda did so, and the first light of the sun stole into the bedroom. Colin sat bolt upright and stared at the lovely scene. All the trees in the garden were carrying a full load of virgin snow and the sunlight caused a million frosty jewels to scintillate.

'Quite a Dickensian Christmas,' he said. 'Now why didn't I hang up my stocking?'

'We hung it up for you,' laughed Rhoda. 'An old golf stocking, and I had to darn a hole in the toe before it could be used. Here it is.'

She detached the bulging stocking from the foot of the bed, and heaved it into his lap.

'Well, I'll be — What's in it?'

'That's for you to find out. You're not serious about coming downstairs for breakfast?'

'Of course I am. Immediately after breakfast I want to go to the railway station and collect my baggage. By jove, Rhoda, you have improved.'

'What do you mean by 'improved'?'

'You ought to know. Seven years ago you were rather a plain Jane, with skinny legs — '

'You leave my legs alone. How's the tea?'

'Delicious. We talked a terrible lot last night, but it was all about me. What about you?'

'Well, what about me?'

'Still completely fancy-free?'

Rhoda's eyes twinkled.

'Not so free as I was. He's a young doctor at the hospital. Neale by name, and nice by nature. He's coming to lunch.'

'Good! I hope you told him you've got a very critical brother.'

'I told him more than that. I told him you were a big bully, and the worst correspondent on earth. That you kept mother and me waiting months on end for a letter of one page, and excused your deplorable silence on the plea that no news is always good news. But I must get downstairs. Mrs. Hacking is bound to be late this morning.'

'Who is Mrs. Hacking?'

'The lady who breaks the china. This snow is a lovely excuse for her to arrive round about lunch-time. Sure you won't have breakfast in bed?'

'I've told you twice.'

'Good! That saves me toiling up those stairs.'

Colin threw a slipper at her as she departed, and then turned out the contents of his stocking. There were nuts and oranges and most of the things he

54

had loved when a child, including some lead soldiers and denizens of Noah's Ark. With them were two packages wrapped in tissue paper. One was a silver cigarette-case, bearing an inscription from his mother, and the other a wrist-watch — from Rhoda.

'Bless you both!' he muttered.

Within the half-hour he was down-stairs, and in time to receive a fair-sized mail from the postman — cards and packages from various friends and relations.

'Oh, Colin dear,' said Mrs. Fairbright. 'What a lovely lot, but it would have been nice for you to lie in a bit this morning, after your long journey yesterday, and that awful experience.'

'It wouldn't, mother. Nothing could be nicer than breakfast together. I don't feel a bit the worse for last night. But can I help you?'

'Oh, no. Breakfast is all ready.'

The newly-arrived parcels were added to many others which had arrived earlier, and Colin managed to include his own contribution while both the women were absent. After breakfast all the parcels were opened and there were various exclamations of surprise and appreciation. Suddenly Rhoda opened the one which Colin had introduced to the pile.

'No postage stamps,' she said. 'Just my name. Oh, it's from you Colin! Silk stockings — lovely ones. Why, there are a dozen pairs, and I haven't a single decent pair to my name. You darling! But how did you know I had no stockings!'

'My dear innocent. I happen to know that there isn't a single woman on this earth who isn't willing to sell her soul for those quite silly leg coverings — with the possible exception of mother.'

By this time Mrs. Fairbright was wrestling with yet another parcel bearing no postage stamps. The contents brought tears to her eyes, for there were yards and yards of lovely hand-made lace, and Mrs. Fairbright had a weakness for lace only equalled by her daughter's mania for 'leg coverings.'

'Oh, Colin!' she said. 'You shouldn't — you shouldn't.'

'That's exactly what the man at the

customs said,' laughed Colin. 'But I was able to convince him that I should, and finally he let me off quite lightly on both items. Thanks to both of you for the stocking and contents.'

Mrs. Hacking arrived after breakfast, with thrilling stories of cars snowed-up, and of her personal Christmas gifts, a large proportion of which appeared to be contained in bottles. Colin got one glimpse of her and wrote her down as a very hard case.

'Now you won't be needed to wash up,' he said to Rhoda. 'What about running me down to the station?'

'I am at your service, sir. Heaven knows what the roads will be like, but I've got chains on the old bus.'

'Still the same car?'

'You bet. It cost us under three hundred pounds in the dim and distant past, and only last week I was offered five hundred for it. We do live in crazy times.'

The subsequent trip to the station turned out to be not unpleasant. There Colin heard that the snowed-up train had been dug out at five o'clock in the morning, and he thanked his lucky stars he hadn't been in it. He found his luggage, and very soon they were back at the house again.

'That's a good job done,' he said. 'I think I shall ring up Miss Paston.'

'Paston?' asked Rhoda. 'Oh, the girl you met in the train.'

'Yes. I hope she isn't unwell.'

'Why should she be?'

'She was almost frozen by the time she reached Alton Hall.'

He looked up the telephone directory and found the place listed as Alton Country Club. He dialled the number and asked if he could speak to Miss Paston. The man at the other end didn't appear to know the name, so Colin explained.

'Oh yes, sir,' he said. 'The young lady who arrived last night. Hold the line please.'

Colin held the line for a long time, and finally the man came back and regretted that he couldn't find Miss Paston. He then rang off unceremoniously, before Colin could ask any questions or leave a message. Half an hour later Colin tried again, with exactly the same result, except that on this occasion he was able to make the request that she should be informed that Mr. Fairbright had telephoned.

'Any luck?' asked Rhoda.

'No. They say they can't find her. I don't think they tried very hard. What about a walk?'

Rhoda was agreeable, and got into a ski-ing outfit, which was most suited to the conditions.

'If we can't go to Switzerland we can pretend,' she said. 'But we must be back in good time, as Neale should be here by half-past twelve.'

'That gives us nearly two hours. What's his other name?'

'McKinnon. He's Scotch.'

'I should think so with a name like that. How long have you known him?'

'About a year.'

'And not a word about him until this morning.'

'He was my little secret.'

They walked through the countryside for nearly two hours, going round in a wide circle, and taking in many spots dear to Colin. On a small pond some enthusiastic skaters had cleared a section, and were trying a few turns, while nearby some children in colourful woollen jumpers were screaming with delight as they tried out home-made luges on the side of a hill. The bright sunshine and the clear blue sky enhanced the beauty of the scene, and stirred Colin deeply after his long absence.

'I had hoped for an old-fashioned Christmas,' he said. 'And here it is. Did you manage to wangle the traditional turkey?'

'We did — and don't ask me how. Oh, Colin, it's so good to have you home.'

'It's good to be home. I know things are bad just now in this war-scarred old country, but you have to be abroad for years on end to appreciate all this.'

They got back in time to welcome Dr. Neale McKinnon. He was the typical Scot — fair and tall and somewhat lean, and he spoke with the most delicious accent. At first he gave one the impression of being grave to dour, but suddenly there would appear a twinkle in his blue eyes, and he would reveal a rich fund of humour. The Christmas dinner was an unqualified success, and afterwards Alton Hall came up in the general conversation.

'Oh, Neale,' said Rhoda. 'I've been trying to convince Colin — and mother — that Alton Club isn't a very respectable place, and am accused of being prejudiced. What do you think?'

McKinnon shrugged his shoulders.

'Why drag me in?' he asked. 'I've never set foot in the place.'

'But you know Major Kent who was a member — until he resigned. You told me that he said it was nothing better than a gambling hell. Or was that supposed to be confidential?'

'It was,' replied McKinnon, with a smile.

'Oh, I'm sorry. I didn't know — '

'Och, it doesn't matter. The major has told hundreds of people the same thing. But he's no a guid bridge player, and lost more than a few bawbees to much better players. It's an expensive place and I'm thinking the major couldn't stand the pace.'

'Now you're going back on me,' said Rhoda.

'Not a bit. Maybe you painted it a little too black, and I a little too white. Shall we compromise and call it a dull grey?'

But later, when McKinnon was alone with Colin for a few minutes, he referred again to Alton Hall.

'Yon place was bound to get a bad reputation after the suicide there,' he said. 'I knew the poor chap slightly, and was called to give evidence. His name was Alan Devlin. I could only say what I knew. It was true he did suffer from melancholia, and was capable of taking his own life, but I've often wondered whether he did.'

'How did he do it?'

'It was found he possessed a service pistol and some ammunition. The weapon was found beside him, with his finger-prints on it.'

'Inside the club premises?'

'No. In the garden.'

'Why was there a doubt in your mind?'

'Because he was found to be almost penniless. But about a week before I had met him, and he told me he was sick of living at the club, and was looking round for a small cottage to buy. Now to buy a cottage a man has to have money. Question — what became of the money which presumably he possessed?'

'I see,' mused Colin. 'Was that point brought out at the inquest?'

'No. I was only asked questions in respect of his alleged melancholia, and I had to admit that I found him prone to deep depression. At that time I did not know that he was penniless.'

'Perhaps he knew where he could raise money?'

'That's possible. But he had no parents. There may be nothing in it, but — '

He left the sentence unfinished, and then Rhoda came and joined them, and the subject was abandoned. Colin rather expected that Rosita would telephone him, in view of his two attempts to speak to her, but he heard nothing that day.

On the following morning he wondered

whether he should ring her again, but finally he put aside the idea. If she wanted to talk to him she had his telephone number. In all probability the Christmas Eve adventure was but a minor incident in her life, and was now in the process of being forgotten. Or her sick parent might have monopolised all her attentions. But whatever the cause it was disappointing.

'I've just heard there is good skating on Loveton pond,' said Rhoda. 'Quite a large area is open. Admission six-pence, for the benefit of the Red Cross. Shall we dig out our old skating boots?'

'But Loveton is eight miles away.'

'The car still goes.'

'But some of those back lanes will be feet deep in snow.'

'What are you two up to?' asked Mrs. Fairbright, as she entered the lounge.

'I'm trying to persuade Colin to take me skating, but he thinks Loveton is too far in this snow.'

'So it is,' said Mrs. Fairbright. 'Why not go to Alton Park? The milkman has just told me the pond is open to the public, but they are charging half a crown.'

'What a swindle!' ejaculated Rhoda.

'Not really. It's for some fund.'

Rhoda looked at her brother, and saw at once that he was deeply interested.

'What do you think, Colin?' she asked.

'Well, it's miles nearer, and is quite shallow if we should go through the ice. Let's go.'

'Right. I'll get the boots. They'll need a clean up, but fortunately the skates are covered with vaseline. Colin, you be getting the car out. Oh, this is grand!'

4

In the meantime Rosita had been facing
some hard facts. After Colin had left
Alton she had been taken by Stockforth
to a bedroom only a few doors from the
one which had been reserved for her own
use. Here, lying in a very old-fashioned
bed, was the man she had not seen since
she was a small child — her father. She
could only recognise him by the photographs which had come to her from her
dead mother, and since those were taken
great changes had taken place. The face
was thin and lined, and the hair scanty.
The eyes were deeply sunk beside the
rather large straight nose, and he was now
sleeping — a sleep which looked very like
death itself.

'How — how long has he been like
this?' she asked.

'Two days.'

'You mean — unconscious all that
time?'

'Not quite unconscious, but unable to recognise anyone.'

'What is the matter with him?'

'Heart. It was always his weakness.'

'When did the doctor see him last?'

'Yesterday. He would have come this evening but he rang up to say it was impossible. He said he would come to-morrow morning.'

'Did the doctor say — if there is any hope?'

Stockforth hesitated and then shook his head.

'It wouldn't be kind to mislead you,' he said. 'The doctor takes a very grave view of his condition. Your father appears to realise that, otherwise I don't think he would have sent that telegram. Now I suggest you seek your bed. To-morrow I will have your room changed to the one next door.'

'I don't quite understand the position,' said Rosita. 'Is this my father's house?'

'Oh, no. I and a friend own the property. Your father has been living here for the past two years. You see, the place is mainly a country club — all except this western wing. There are a limited number of bedrooms for such members as wish to live here. Until recently your father occupied one of the best suites, but when he was taken ill we moved him here. It was more convenient, but to-morrow my partner will be back from a trip, and then we can go into a lot of details which will need clearing up. Now you go and have your rest, and try not to worry too much.'

Rosita went to bed perplexed and anxious. She could not pretend to be heart-broken, since her personal memories of her queer parent were so vague as to be almost non-existent. All she knew was that her parents had separated when she was very young, and that until her mother's death her father had made them a certain allowance. After her mother's death she had been informed by a solicitor that it was her father's wish that she should continue her studies, and that the previous allowance would now be reduced to the sum of four hundred pounds a year. It had hurt her a little to realise that her father had no great wish to see what sort of a girl she had grown into, and that the only letters he had written to her were devoid of any real affection. Why had he behaved like that? She hoped that when he was able to speak he would explain much that called for explanation.

Early the next morning she knocked on the door of the sickroom but received no reply. Softly she turned the handle and crept inside. Her father was lying exactly as she had seen him the night before. She went closer to him, and saw that he was breathing.

'Father!' she whispered, but there was no reaction of any kind from the still form.

It was the first time she had seen anyone so clearly on the portal of death, and the experience was most disturbing. It brought a curious lump to her throat, and a smarting to her eyes. Slowly she turned away and made towards the secondary staircase, the descent of which brought her to a wide passage, at the end of which was a large lounge, full of nice antique furniture. There were two outlets, and she chose the one on the left. As she closed the door behind her she noticed that it bore a notice — 'Private'. Now she realised she was in the part of the building reserved for the club, and it was here that everything was different. Unlike the rest of the place it had been recently decorated — in somewhat garish style. The carpets were new and luxurious and the ornaments rather vulgar. Room followed room — a regular maze of a place, and here and there were servants, dusting and polishing, and laying tables in a magnificent dining-room, which led into a winter garden that displayed some wonderful chrysanthemums. From here — through the wide modern windows she could see the snow-clad expanses of the garden, and the park beyond. A man who looked like the head-waiter bowed to her in a surprised way.

'Can I help you, madam?' he asked.

'I — I was looking for Mr. Stockforth,' she stammered.

'I doubt if he's down yet, madam,' he said. 'It's very early.'

'Yes, I know.'

'If you wish to give him a message they

70

can telephone him from the main office. Along the passage and then the first to the right.'

Rosita found the reception office, but did not raise any inquiry there. Instead she went into the reading-room, and sat in a chair by the newly-lighted fire. After a little while there were signs of increasing activity. Going out into the splendid hall she saw a waitress taking two trays up the stairs, and two middle-aged men gave her a glance as they made their way to the dining-room. Then suddenly she saw Stockforth.

'Ah, Miss Paston,' he said. 'You're up betimes. Have you seen your father yet?'

'Yes. He was still sleeping.'

'Good. I expect Dr. Bredding will make an early call, so the best thing for you to do is have some breakfast. I'll introduce you to the head-waiter.'

He took her into the dining-room and introduced her to the man she had already seen.

'Breakfast is now on, miss,' said the head-waiter. 'I have rather a nice single table by the window. This way, please.'

'I'll see you afterwards,' said Stock-forth. 'My partner has just arrived, and is anxious to meet you.'

Rosita nodded and was then led to her seat. The table was decked with chrysanthemums and evergreen, and the menu, when she consulted it, had an amazing variety of things from devilled kidneys to eggs and bacon, which she scarcely expected in this land of severe austerity. There was a choice of tea or coffee, and she chose the latter. The large room contained only the two men she had seen earlier, but by the time the first course arrived other guests began to file in. They were a curious collection, and one or two of them gave her a 'good morning' in purely conventional tones. The young man with the fair hair, who sat near her, stole a glance at her from time to time. She thought he looked rather dissipated, for although he was obviously young there were already little lines about his eyes, and he sat in tired fashion and tapped his fingers on the table until the waiter brought his food.

The place was astonishing in many

respects. It was equal to any first-class hotel that she had ever been in, and the china and table silver were of the highest quality. Everywhere there were flowers and evergreen, and the table-cloths were of the best linen, and in excellent condition. No doubt was left in her mind that its guests and *habitués* were persons of considerable wealth, and that the management had very reliable connections with the black market.

'Lovely day!' said the young man suddenly.

'Yes,' she agreed. 'Rather different from yesterday.'

'I don't think I've seen you before. Are you a new member?'

'No. I came last night — to visit my father.'

'Oh, you must be Miss Paston?'

'Yes.'

'Stockforth told me he was expecting you. I'm sorry your father is so ill.'

'Thank you.'

'May I introduce myself? My name is Charles Simbourne.'

'I'm pleased to meet you,' she said.

An elderly man, with a face like a hawk, entered the room and stopped by Simbourne.

'How's the Honourable Charles this morning?' he asked.

'Just a little bent.'

'So I should imagine. You got a bit pickled last night.'

'Don't be ridiculous.'

'I'll bet your head feels like a balloon this morning.'

'Yours looks like one, which is much worse. Now may I have my breakfast in peace?'

Hawkface cackled and moved down the room. Simbourne looked at Rosita.

'Colonel Rooke,' he said. 'He has the deplorable habit of trying to be funny early in the morning. Actually he isn't a bad sort, if you can tolerate his jokes, none of which are ever new or decent. I do hope you'll have a better report on your father when the doctor sees him again.'

'Thank you,' said Rosita. 'I am expecting him very soon.'

Despite her anxiety she enjoyed the

excellent meal, and then went out to do some more exploring. On the north side were several games rooms, and leading from the largest of these was an ancient ballroom, with a musician's gallery at one end. There was also a grand piano on a slightly-raised platform under the musician's gallery. She was drawn to this fine instrument, and raised the heavy top. It was a nearly new Steinway. She sat down on the stool and ran her fingers over the keyboard, bringing forth lovely ripples of sweet music. Then she played a few chords, and was satisfied that the instrument was perfectly in tune. One thing led to another, and in a few moments she was completely immersed in the thing she loved most — music.

The accoustics of the large room were perfect, and the brilliant Chopin study surged and rippled like a woodland river. She forgot her surroundings — everything that belonged to the more mundane world and played on and on like one possessed. And then suddenly she realised that she was not alone. Sitting in a chair to her left, and slightly behind her was one of the strangest persons she had ever seen. Her hands went dead on the keys, and she swung round on the stool.

Her solitary auditor was a man of about fifty years of age. He was as swarthy as a Spaniard, with a body as thick as a gorilla. The great head seemed to rest on his shoulders, without need of a neck, and the features were large and coarse.

'Very good!' he said in a sepulchral voice. 'Very good indeed. Your father told me you were a musician of talent, but I never expected anything like that.'

'I — I thought I was alone. I couldn't resist — the piano.'

'I don't wonder. So you are Rosita?'

'Yes.'

'I am your father's old friend, and Stockforth's partner. My name is Mark Grandison, and I regret I was not here when you arrived last night. I came to find you just now because the doctor is here.'

Rosita rose from her seat and lowered the top of the piano. Grandison also rose, and she noticed that he was taller than he had looked in a sitting position — a great bull of a man, almost frightening in his aspect.

'I will take you to your father, and the doctor,' he said.

'Thank you.'

He led her to the sick-room by a route new to her, for the whole place was intersected by corridors and staircases. When at last they entered the room she found an elderly man consulting a thermometer. He gave a little grunt and then turned round.

'Here, my dear doctor, is Miss Paston,' said Grandison.

The doctor nodded and smiled rather gravely. Rosita gave a glance at the man in the bed.

'How is he?' she asked.

The doctor did not speak for a few moments. He shook down the thermometer, and placed it in the glass on the side-table.

'I'm afraid, Miss Paston, that your father is slowly sinking,' he said.

'Oh! Is there no hope?'

'I wish I could say there was. He is in a

77

coma and I doubt very much if he will come out of it.'

'You — you mean he may not — be able to speak to me?'

'That is very doubtful. I wish he had sent for you earlier, but he took a more optimistic view of the position than was warranted. There is nothing more I can do now, but if you need me I shall come as quickly as possible. Otherwise I will look in this evening.'

Rosita thanked him as he took his departure. Grandison spent a few moments outside with the doctor and then came back into the room.

'I rather expected that,' he said. 'His health has been failing for the past six months. Do you wish to stay here, or would you rather come to my quarters and talk things over? There are certain matters I should like to discuss. If you feel in the mood I will get Stockforth.'

'I think I should like to know what the exact position is,' said Rosita.

'Yes, of course. Come with me then. I have a quiet apartment far from the madding crowd.'

He led her along a passage, and through a door, beyond which was a self-operating lift. The lift ascended to the top of the big house, and here Rosita was surprised to find herself in a most luxurious apartment. The main room was an enormous lounge, equipped with all the latest modern inventions. On one side was one of the largest radio sets that Rosita had ever seen, and in the centre was a colossal table-desk, on which were a lot of clever devices. One of them was a lacquered image of a squatting Buddha, with a gaping mouth. Grandison pressed one of the bulging jewel-like eyes, and both orbs came alight.

'Are you there, Harry?' he asked.

Stockforth's voice came back, loud and clear.

'Yes, G.'

'Come up, will you? I've got Miss Paston here.'

'In two minutes. I'm in the middle of a trunk call.'

'As quickly as you can.'

He pushed the other eye, and the lights went out.

'Like it?' he asked.

'It's very ingenious.'

'I'm fond of gadgets. I had a friend who was an electrically-minded genius. Unfortunately, he is now in a mental home. He lived here for a time and paid for his keep by keeping me supplied with toys. You will notice there are no lights here.'

Rosita looked round the amazing room, and had to admit this seeming fact, but it was well lighted by the clear sun outside. Grandison pushed a button at the side of the table and almost instantly the room was plunged into complete darkness.

'Oh!' she ejaculated.

Grandison laughed in his guttural voice.

'Don't be nervous, my dear. Watch this,' he said.

The room became brilliantly lighted, and Rosita, staring at the many wide windows, saw that all of them were now completely covered by draped velvet curtains. Not a glimmer of daylight was visible.

'Concealed lighting,' said Grandison. 'It's reflected down by the ceiling which is treated with some kind of chemical substance. I don't pretend to understand it. The mercury vapour tubes which are chiefly responsible are cleverly hidden behind that ornamental frieze. A pity poor Michael went crazy. I think we will have the natural sunlight.'

Rosita saw the heavy curtain drawn up in a twinkling, and the sun once more threw shadows across the room. Then came Stockforth, very apologetic and effusive.

'Sit down!' said Grandison curtly. 'I want Miss Paston to know the position — so far as we know it. You too, my dear.'

Rosita sank into a deeply-upholstered arm-chair, facing the table, and Stock-forth brought up a small chair. Grandison now took complete charge of the meeting, and Mr. Stockforth seemed quite content to sit and listen.

'I understand that you have not seen your father for a very long time, Miss Paston?' he said. 'I mean, of course, before you came here.'

'Not since I was about five years of age.'

'What a shame! I did not know your father in those days. When I first met him, fifteen years ago, he told me he was married, but living apart from his wife. He did not mention a daughter until years later. I was associated with him in America, and for some years I lost touch with him. Then, about three years ago, I met him on a trans-Atlantic crossing from New York. I was surprised to notice how he had changed in those years, but he would never admit to being in poor health. He told me that his wife had died the previous year — in Switzerland, I think.'

Rosita nodded.

'I asked him about you, and he said that you were studying music — and still in Switzerland. I asked him if he now proposed offering you a home with him, but he was not disposed to discuss the matter, and I never mentioned it again. When we reached this country I kept in touch with him. He seemed to have no permanent home, and went from one hotel to another. When I bought this place I met him again in London and had a meal with him. I told him what I proposed to do here, and he seemed very interested. He admitted he was unhappy and lonely, and was tired of big cities. To cut a long story short he joined the club as soon as it was formed, and rented one of the apartments. I think the change did him good spiritually, if not physically. I knew he was gambling on the Stock Exchange, but had no idea how he was faring. Then, after about a year, he grew much worse in health, and had to stop playing golf. He hated doctors but at last I persuaded him to see Dr. Bredding. Well, despite a strict régime, he continued to get worse, and then one day he was unable to meet his weekly bill. I paid no attention to this, as I believed him to be very comfortably off. But the weeks went by, and the club secretary brought up the matter at a meeting of directors. I undertook to speak to him about the matter, and did so the next day. He told me that he had lost a great amount of money playing the markets, but that he had assets in America which he would be able to realise very shortly.'

'He told me that, too,' put in Stockforth. 'But he was always very vague about it.'

Grandison nodded and then resumed his narration.

'About two months ago, when he was bed-ridden, he asked to see me. It was about you.'

'Me?' asked Rosita.

'He said he was unable to continue your allowance unless I could help him. He assured me about the American securities, and I lent him fifty pounds, and later another fifty pounds. Stockforth, did you bring those I.O.U's?'

Stockforth produced an envelope from his pocket, and drew two sheets of paper from it. They were two I.O.U's for fifty pounds each, and signed by Joseph Paston.

'I'm sorry to bother you with all this,' said Grandison. 'But it's as well that you should know the position. If anything should happen to your father these claims would be made on his estate. The point is — can you help us at all? Do you know anything about the American securities which he mentioned?'

'No,' said Rosita. 'I don't think my mother knew very much, but she always gave me to understand that my father was a wealthy man.'

Grandison looked at Stockforth, and Stockforth shrugged his shoulders.

'How much is owing to the club?' asked Rosita.

'What is the bill to date, Harry?' asked Grandison.

'Four hundred and thirty-two pounds,' replied Stockforth, referring to his note-book.

'If your father is able to speak to you — later, I should like you to raise the matter of the American securities — in fact the whole question of his personal assets. It would save a lot of trouble in the event — You do understand, don't you?'

'Yes, of course.'

'Good. Now may I ask you a personal question?'

'Yes.'

'Have you any private means?'

'None at all. I had to spend what money I had to get here. I had no idea that — that my father's position was so bad.'

'It may not be so bad as it appears. But if it is, there is no need for you to worry about these bills. In law you are not responsible.'

'But I am morally. Whatever happens I'll find a way to — '

'Oh, no — please. That is not the reason why I spoke to you. Some bad debts are inevitable in this life, and we can stand them — if need be.'

'But I must settle my father's debts.'

'Not at all. If I may say so, he should have had you live with him after your poor mother died, and then perhaps he would not have indulged in reckless gambling. But let's hope things will turn out not so badly. That's all, my dear.'

Rosita thanked them, and then left the room, with her brain whirling. Here was a situation she had never dreamed of. Only two years ago her father had sent her the expensive fur coat, with an accompanying curt note to wish her many happy returns of her birthday. Now, unless the story of the American securities were true, he was hopelessly bankrupt.

What a fool's paradise she had lived in! The eight pounds a week had been sufficient for her comparatively modest needs, for since her mother's death she had lived in a small *pension*. But now this had come to an end, and the future was indeed ominous. There were some things she might sell — the fur coat, some bits of jewellery. But how long would the proceeds last? If her father died there would be other expenses, and probably accumulated bills for medical attention. It was a blow to her pride too, to realise that for the past few months her personal income had actually been paid by Grandison. That sum at least must be returned.

She crept back to the sickroom and took a glance at the still form. Then she commenced to open drawers, and various suitcases that were on top of the large wardrobe. She found masses of documents, most of which bore the printed heading of a firm of London stockbrokers. She could not understand the typewritten details. In a briefcase she found some bank statements — equally involved. There were sales slips of all kinds of stock, but nothing in the shape of securities. A letter from the bank dated only a few months back requested her father to deal with the matter of his overdraft. Then she found some letters from her mother, tied up with pink tape. She hesitated and put them aside, feeling that at the moment at least there was no justification for reading them.

All the clothing in the wardrobe was very worn — indeed quite shabby. She was delving into a large trunk which contained many souvenirs of foreign countries, when suddenly there came a curious little sigh from the bed. She went to it and saw that her father's jaw had dropped a little. Then she uttered a cry as she realised that there was no visible movement of the chest — nothing but complete immobility. It had come at last — swiftly and mercifully. Her eyes were hot and smarting, but no tears came. Staggering to the door she closed it behind her and hurried through the building to Stockforth's office. He was talking on the telephone — laughing at some joke, until he saw her pallid face. He placed the receiver on its rest, and came to her.

'My — my father is dead,' she gasped.

'Oh — no.'

'Yes, yes. Please ring up the doctor.'

'I'd better see him first. You sit there. I won't be long.' He was back again in a few minutes.

'You're right,' he said sympathetically. 'Was he able to speak to you?'

'No. I've been looking through his things for any documents in connection with the American securities. I — I found nothing. Oh, please get the doctor.'

Stockforth used the telephone, and was successful in speaking to Dr. Bredding. Then he spoke to Grandison.

'Paston has gone,' he said. 'Please come down, if you can. Miss Paston is here.'

Grandison entered the office, with his huge ungainly head thrust forward.

'I'm sorry, Rosita,' he said. 'But it was best that way. Better go and rest until the doctor gets here.'

'No. I'm all right,' she said. 'I'd rather

wait here, please.'

'As you wish. This is a very sad experience for you. I presume he passed away in his sleep?'

'Yes.'

Bredding arrived in quick time, and was not in the least surprised. He and Rosita went to the bedroom, and Bredding was occupied only a minute or two with the dead man.

'I expected this within a few hours,' he said. 'I will send on the death certificate. I suppose you have no friends in the neighbourhood?'

'No.'

'Then leave things to me. It's a little awkward being Christmas Day, but I'll do what is immediately necessary. I presume you want a simple funeral.'

'Oh, yes.'

'Is there a will?'

'I don't know. I haven't seen one.'

'Are you the sole living relative?'

'So far as I know.'

'Well, I'll do all I can. Now you go and rest.'

But Rosita did not feel like resting.

There was so much to occupy her mind — so many problems. She put on her hat and coat, and trudged through the snow in the park. Her thoughts switched from one thing to another, and finally concentrated for a few moments on the man who had helped her the previous night — Colin. He had invited her to telephone him, and in the ordinary way she would have done this, but now it was different. Much as she needed a friend her rather foolish pride prevented her from calling him. No, this was no time for her to inflict her woe upon a comparative stranger — charming as that stranger might be. So she spent the rest of the day, going through her father's personal effects, hunting for a will, and those alleged American securities. Before she went to bed the kindly doctor telephoned to tell her that he had made the necessary arrangements for the funeral at the church of St. Giles on the following Thursday.

The next morning she felt better. After all, she had received scant affection from her dead parent. Certainly he had maintained her, but never had he shown any desire to play the part of a real father — even after her mother had died, and she had felt lonely beyond description. The receptionist told her that Grandison had been looking for her, and had left a message to the effect that he would like to see her. She found the lift which went to his lair, and was soon sitting in a chair in front of the colossal table.

'Bredding spoke to me last night,' he said. 'I understand that he has fixed up everything?'

'Yes. It is to be on Thursday.'

'You have not found a will?'

'No. Nor anything else of value.'

'I don't think there is anything. It's better to accept that. But what are you going to do — afterwards?'

'I don't know. But I can't stay here very long. I must — '

'I'm coming to that. Rosita, I have a suggestion. You have quite remarkable musical ability. Why not commercialise it?'

'That is my only hope. But I scarcely know where to start.'

'Why not start here? Listen. For some

time past I've been thinking that the club needs developing, especially at the present time, when outdoor sports are so few. We could throw a first-class concert one night a week. I could hire a good vocalist to help you out, and I'm absolutely certain we could make a go of it. What do you say?'

'It's all so — sudden. I hadn't thought of anything like that.'

'Sudden inspirations are sometimes the best. You could live here and over and above your board I would pay you a fiver a week. I'd also wash out those claims upon your father's estate, whether or not you find he has hidden securities.'

'But how do you know I should be good enough?'

'My dear child, I was brought up in a musical family. My mother was Italian, and had a voice like a nightingale. Believe it or not I am a passably good violinist. The moment I heard you play I was enraptured. There's a good bedroom going, with a private sitting-room attached — not the hovel you are in now. And later — if you find you can do better elsewhere — I won't stand in your way. But in the meantime you would have ample time for practice, and plenty of time for leisure. The piano can't be improved upon. I bought the very best, and you are the person who can justify the expense. Is it a deal?'

Rosita was overwhelmed by the offer. It was indeed a solution to her major problem of her immediate maintainance. Grandison was looking at her intently — waiting for a decision. She would have preferred to think it over, but clearly he wanted the matter settled.

'Yes,' she said. 'I accept the proposal, and I'll do my best to make the idea a success.'

'Fine! Just a moment.'

He operated the squatting Buddha again, and Stockforth's voice was heard.

'I want you to come here, Harry. Bring Paston's bill to date, and also those two I.O.Us.'

Stockforth was not long putting in an appearance. He smiled at Rosita and then handed Grandison the bill and the two I.O.Us.

'Harry, we're going to inaugurate something new,' said Grandison. 'I have engaged Miss Paston as concert organiser and chief executant. This place is going to have some real music. Don't stare as if I were mad. I know what I'm doing. Miss Paston is engaged from to-day. I'll tell you the details later. Have her things removed to the lilac suite.'

'But I've just let it to Sir George — '

'Then unlet it. Ring him up and say you made a mistake.'

'Very good, G.'

'Now I want you to receipt this bill. Sign it as being settled by contra. Here's a pen.'

Stockforth took the pen and signed the bill. Grandison handed it to Rosita, and then took the two I.O.U's, tore them into a dozen pieces and consigned them to the waste-paper basket.

'That matter is off your mind, Rosita,' he said. 'Now about the first concert. Shall we say Saturday week?'

'Yes,' replied Rosita.

'Then you'll need a vocalist. Better be a

man. I'll get on to an agency. What I want you to do is to make up your programme of pianoforte solos, and indicate where you want the vocal numbers to come. I'll ask the singer to supply the details, and we'll get in touch with a quick printer.'

'If there is one,' put in Stockforth.

'You'll jolly well find one. We want programmes and some show-bills. It will give the place a tone, and that's what we need just now. Some of the non-resident members need a kick in the pants, and this should do it. Harry, how is the rink progressing?'

'I've got three men clearing the snow. Should be ready in half an hour.'

'Good! Do you skate, Rosita?'

'Yes, but I've no skates here.'

'Stockforth can fix you up. We're opening the lake for skating this morning. Free to club members but outsiders will have to pay. Now you run along and try to forget about things — but not about your concert.'

'I'm scarcely likely to forget that,' said Rosita. 'I am very grateful to you,

Mr. Grandison, for the chance you have given me.'

'I'm the one to be grateful. Harry, take Rosita back with you and try to fix her up with a decent pair of skating boots.'

5

Rosita made her way through the extensive old-world garden to the park, with a pair of quite good white skating boots under her arm. The snow which had encumbered trees, bushes, and topiaries had thinned since the heavy fall, and a roller had been run over the paths, rendering walking comparatively easy. As she walked in the dry keen air her mind was busy with the latest development, and for the first time since her arrival she was conscious of the lifting of the damper upon her normally bright spirits.

From one of the terraces she could see where the skating was in progress. There seemed to be few skaters at the moment, but between her and the frozen lake there were sundry walkers, all going in the same direction, one of them dragging a luge on which a person was sitting. Beyond the lake she could see another entrance gate, with some cars parked just inside it, and as she looked more cars arrived.

The lake itself was some acres in extent, and its setting was magnificent. As she approached it the vista improved, and looking back she was able to appreciate Alton Hall itself. It fitted into its surroundings like a jewel in its setting, with its ancient cedar trees lending additional beauty to what was one of the most stately country mansions.

Some garden seats had been dragged to the edge of the ice, about a quarter of which had been cleared of snow, and which seemed to her to be of excellent quality. Of the persons skating she saw few who cut a good figure, but one or two were certainly first class.

She sat down and got into the skating boots. They were rather on the large side, but she had put on an extra pair of socks to take up the slack. Finally she got on to the ice, and began to cut a few simple figures. She was at her ease at once, for already that season she had skated in Switzerland, but with a different type of skate. A gramophone was playing on the further side of the cleared space, and she moved closer to it, with the grace of many years of experience. A figure flashed past her at a great pace — far too great she thought. It was a man in a yellow pullover, and she wrote him down as a public menace on a comparatively small skating area. A few minutes later she saw him again, bearing down on her still at about the same speed. But he stopped before he reached her, with a rather clever toe break, and she recognised the Honourable Charles.

'Good morning!' he said. 'Grand, isn't it?'

'Yes.'

He skated closer, but now in more civilised fashion.

'May I offer you my condolences?' he asked. 'I heard the bad news — about your father.'

'Thank you.'

'He and I were quite friendly, for a bit — before he had to keep to his room. Such a shame. He was no end of a good sport.'

'Do you live at the house?' she asked after a pause.

'On and off — more on than off. I go home at times, but it's a devilish dull place in the middle of nowhere. Where did you learn to skate?'

'Switzerland.'

'You must have been there a lot.'

'I was brought up there. I went to school at Lausanne, and every winter the school moved up the mountains.'

'I see. But you've got a home in England, of course?'

'No. I lived with my mother — until she died.'

'And now — are you going to stay in England?'

'Yes.'

'Lousy place just now.'

Rosita looked up at the sun, and then round the lovely park.

'Do you call this lousy?' she asked.

'Just a flash in the pan. To-morrow it will probably thaw, and rain like hell. Too many restrictions, and prohibitions. No servants, no civility, no anything worth having. My family keeps a barn of a place — all going to rack and ruin, because my father can't even get a permit to stop the rain coming through the roof, nor a few tons of coal to keep it decently warm. What a life!'

'And you escape from reality by living here — off and on?'

'Why not? Old Grandison knows the ropes, which is more than my respected parent does. We used up our cellar years ago, but here the stuff comes in in cartloads. All black market, of course, but what's the odds.'

'From which I gather that your father doesn't use the black market to further his comfort?' asked Rosita.

'My father would rather die in the gutter. I've tried to reform him but it's no use. He lives in a past that is dead for ever. It's the past of high integrity, firmly held religious principles, and family honour.'

Rosita looked at him sharply, to see if he was really serious, which he appeared to be.

'You don't mean that,' she said sharply.

'Oh, but I do. You see, the rules of the game have been altered, and the sensible person plays to the new rules.'

'What are the new rules?'

'Look after yourself first, and those near to you. Close your ears to all the claptrap about equality, and your mind to pipe-dreams about earthly arcadias. Everything that has been done in this world has been achieved by a handful of brilliant individuals. When you see the mob armed with full power, spread your wings and fly.'

'Is that what you have in mind?' asked Rosita coldly.

'As a matter of fact it is.'

'And who will feed you then — when you alight?' asked Rosita.

The Honourable Charles met her gaze without flinching.

'I am hopeful of feeding myself,' he said quite soberly. And then he laughed in gay abandon. 'What started us on that tack? It's too good a day to talk politics. Oh, there's the 'Skater's Waltz'. Shall we?'

Before Rosita could make up her mind he had placed himself in position, and taken her hand. She found him a little awkward on some of the turns, but on the whole he was a good partner.

'You're marvellous!' he said. 'You aren't Sonia who-is-it in disguise, are you?'

'I'm just my poor self. Get over on that edge. Why are you afraid of it?'

'It's my gammy leg. I hurt it baling out of a plane, and haven't been able to trust it since.'

It silenced Rosita effectively, but thereafter she noticed he put a little more faith in his injured leg, and did very much better. Then the music stopped and the Honourable Charles thanked her prettily and skated across to the red-faced colonel who was making slow and imperfect revolutions round an orange.

'Good morning!' said a voice from behind her.

She swung round and came face to face with Colin.

'Oh — good morning!' she stammered. 'I certainly never thought of seeing you here.'

'I had rather hoped to see you,' said Colin. 'No ill effects from our adventures?'

'None at all.'

'Good! I wish I could skate like your

last partner, but I'm a complete novice. I think I saw him when I was at the Hall.'

'Oh, did you? He's living at the Hall. His name is the Honourable Charles Simbourne, so I presume he is connected with the peerage. I — I was going to ring you up, but finally I decided not to.'

'So you got my message?'

'Message? No.'

'I rang you twice, and was told you were not available. So I asked the person who spoke to tell you I had telephoned.'

'Nobody told me. I'm so sorry.'

'It's all right. I merely wanted to find out if you were all right, and to know how you found your father.'

Rosita winced and Colin knew he had dropped a brick.

'My — my father died the following morning,' said Rosita, in a low voice. 'I never even spoke to him.'

'I'm dreadfully sorry. I had no idea it was so serious.'

'Nor I. It may seem callous — me skating out here, but I felt I had to get some exercise. It was a terrible shock, but to me he was a stranger. I had hoped that he might explain many things, but it wasn't to be.'

They had skated away from the main crowd, and Colin got the impression that the girl was really glad to see him, and that she was troubled.

'Shall we sit down for a minute or two?' he asked, indicating a vacant seat.

'Yes.'

With the sun on their faces they sat on the seat, and watched in silence for a few moments the movements of the diversified skaters.

'When is the funeral?' asked Colin.

'On Thursday.'

'Can I help in any way? It must be an ordeal for you.'

'Dr. Bredding has been most helpful, and is arranging things. But you are very kind.'

'Have you any relatives handy?'

'No one at all.'

'That's bad luck — at a time like this. I hope your father's affairs are all in order.'

Rosita shook her head.

'My father died in debt,' she said. 'I

— I knew nothing about his circumstances, but had reason to believe he was very well off. Had I known the real position I should have taken more care of my allowance. But he so seldom wrote to me. Oh, I oughtn't to be telling you all this, but in a way it helps.'

'Yes, I can understand that. I suppose in the circumstances you won't go back to Switzerland?'

'No. I don't know what I should have done but for Mr. Grandison.'

'Who is he?'

'He's the business partner of the man you saw — Mr. Stockforth, and was a friend of my father. He discovered I could play the piano, and made me a proposition which came as a godsend.'

'A business proposition?'

She nodded and then told him of her interview with Grandison and the outcome of it.

'That was thoughtful of him,' said Colin. 'But are you sure you are doing the right thing?'

'No, I'm not. The right thing might be something quite different, but you see I'm not everybody's money. All I can do is play the piano — and perhaps give music lessons. But I can't see myself as a music teacher, and should hate it. It seemed to me that as a temporary stop-gap this offer had a lot to recommend it, and it has the effect of washing out a debt.'

'But it wasn't a debt so far as you are concerned.'

'Some of it was — the part which my father incurred in order to continue sending me my allowance. I had that money, and it was a relief to be able to liquidate the debt.'

'Yes, of course. I suppose you have committed yourself?'

'Oh, yes — absolutely.'

Colin was silent.

'You don't think I've done the right thing?' she asked.

'I've no right to think anything about it.'

'But you are thinking all the same.'

'Well, to be brutally frank, Alton Hall doesn't appear to enjoy a very good reputation in the neighbourhood.'

'What — what is said against it?'

'Some people say it is just a gambling hell, with a veneer of respectability.'

'You know it's a club?'

'Yes.'

'A club is bound to provide bridge and other games for its members, isn't it?'

'Naturally. But there are clubs and clubs. It's really no business of mine, but I think you should know what people think.'

'Couldn't it be just spiteful gossip?'

'It could, but it's very widespread. Still, I don't want to be a dismal Jimmie. Tell me about the concert. Can anyone buy a ticket?'

'I'm not sure, but I suppose members can bring friends — as guests. Would you like to come?'

'Very much.'

'I'll arrange to have a ticket sent to you.'

'Thank you.'

'But please don't expect too much.'

'I shall expect you to play at least as well as you can skate. There's my sister, wondering where I have slid off to. Do come and be introduced.'

Rhoda had already seen them, and as they skated towards her she came to meet them.

'Meet my sister Rhoda,' said Colin. 'Rhoda this is Miss Paston whom I told you about.'

'Glad to meet you,' said Rhoda. 'I have to thank you for getting Colin home earlier than otherwise would have been possible. I think it was your idea to abandon that uncomfortable train.'

'It was, but without your brother I wouldn't have risked it. It's not the sort of thing I would care to do again. I suppose you have been here before?'

'No, never,' said Rhoda. 'But Colin has. He used to trespass in here and catch fish in the lake. Once he was caught by a keeper and my father had to guarantee his good behaviour in future.'

'You would drag that up,' said Colin. 'But it's a marvellous place — like something out of a fairy book. Miss Paston is staying here — for a bit.'

'Really!' said Rhoda. 'In that case I do hope you'll come and see us. What about New Year's Eve, when we shall make the most preposterous resolutions.'

'I should love to,' said Rosita. 'Oh, that won't be a Saturday, will it?'

'No,' replied Colin.

'Then I shall be free.'

'That's a promise then,' said Colin.

'Yes. Now will you excuse me? I've got quite a lot of things to do at the Hall.'

'Of course.'

Rosita skated across to a chair, with all the grace of a professional. Rhoda's gaze followed her.

'No wonder you went on a nocturnal trip across the snows,' she said. 'You didn't tell me she was like that.'

'Like what?'

'A beauty prize winner.'

'Is she?'

'You know darn well she is. I forgot to ask after her father.'

'It's as well you did. I suddenly remembered that, when I brought her across and hoped you wouldn't mention him.'

'Why not?'

'He died the morning after she arrived here.'

'Oh, I say! That's bad luck. But she behaved just as if — everything was all right.'

'She hadn't seen her father since she was a small child. There was some trouble between her parents.'

'And she lived with her mother — in Switzerland?'

'Did I tell you — ? Oh, yes, of course, I did.'

'But Colin, why is she going to stay here? You ought to tell her that the place has a bad name.'

'I did.'

'And she wouldn't listen?'

'I was too late. Her father died in debt to the club, and she was offered a job. As she was in an awful predicament she accepted the offer.'

'What sort of a job?'

'Music. She is going to organise a weekly concert. Alton Hall is going in for culture with a capital C.'

'H'm!'

'Why do you say 'H'm'?'

'I think it's a pity she was so impulsive. There is something sinister about this place, you know, in spite of it looking like a picture from a fairy book. You can pick out the club members by their faces. They're rather like some of the men and women I once saw at Monte Carlo — '

'Oh, come and skate,' interrupted Colin.

Colin and Rhoda finally drove home with their ankles aching from the unusual type of exercise. When Mrs. Fairbright was told of the meeting with Rosita, and the impending visit of Rosita to the house she expressed her pleasure, and looked at Colin somewhat shrewdly. On the following day the weather changed completely. The wind went round to the south-west and it commenced to rain, with most unpleasant results.

'I knew it wouldn't last,' said Rhoda. 'But now that the rain has come I hope it won't leave off until all this fearful slush has vanished.'

Her hope was fulfilled, for the downpour continued for twenty-four hours, and the post-card Christmas vanished as completely as the snows of yester year. It was then that Colin put into practice an idea which had been in his mind ever since the meeting with Rosita. He telephoned her, and on this occasion managed to speak to her.

'Oh,' he said. 'I just wondered whether you would be all alone at the funeral this morning.'

'That is good of you,' she said. 'But Mr. Grandison is coming. Of course I'm very glad, as I hated the idea of being alone.'

'That's fine. You won't forget about New Year's Eve?'

'I'm glad you rang up because I was going to write to you — about New Year's Eve. I didn't know we were to have a special party here, and Mr. Grandison wants me to be present. I do hope you'll excuse me. I couldn't very well refuse him in the circumstances.'

'That's perfectly all right. Perhaps you'll come along some other time?'

'I'd love to. Isn't the weather dreadful?'

He felt slightly rebuffed as he hung up the receiver, but tried to look at it from her point of view. The rain having stopped he walked into the town, and did a little shopping. Then he found a coffee-shop and went inside and sat down. He was ordering coffee when Dr. McKinnon entered.

'Hullo!' he said. 'I had to call at a chemists', and caught the whiff of coffee. Is that seat vacant?'

'Yes.'

'Rhoda isn't with you?'

'Oh, no. She's learning to cook. Have you seen her since we went skating?'

'No. Where did you skate?'

'Alton Park.'

'Oh, yes, I heard they had opened the lake. Nice gesture to charity.'

'Doc, do you know Grandison, who seems to run the place?'

'I've met him once or twice.'

'What's he like?'

'He's an atavism — repellant to some people — attractive to others. A man of many parts, I should say.'

'Good parts?'

'That's an interesting point. No one knows a great deal about him, for he seldom comes into the town, or interests himself in any social functions. I shouldn't have known he existed but for the death of the young man I told you about.'

'The suicide?'

'Yes. I told you I was called upon to give evidence at the inquest. I met Grandison there, and on two or three occasions afterwards. I must say he behaved quite well, but I got the feeling that it was all window-dressing — that his flowery language had been rehearsed, to create an impression. Are you interested in him?'

'Not really.'

'Indirectly perhaps?' he asked, staring at Colin.

'Yes,' admitted Colin. 'You see, Miss Paston, the girl I met in the train, is now in his employ.'

'You mean in the club?'

'Yes. Her father died the morning after her arrival. He is being buried this morning. Rosita — the girl — was persuaded to stay on and organise some concerts. She happens to be musical. I don't feel very happy about it.'

McKinnon was silent for a few moments.

'Does that mean she was left unprovided for?'

'Yes. Her father actually died in debt.'

'To Grandison?'

'As a matter of fact — yes.'

'It rather fits in with the pattern of things,' mused McKinnon. 'That young man I told you about also died penniless. Perhaps two suicides would have looked a bit too nasty.'

Colin winced at this remark.

'What am I to make of that?' he asked.

'No more than is intended. What doctor attended Paston in his illness?'

'A Dr. Bredding I think.'

'I know Bredding. He's a highly-qualified man, and is not likely to make a mistake. I presume he had been attending Paston for some time?'

'Oh, yes — some months at least.'

'I must try and introduce the subject when I next see him, and risk a severe ticking off. Sorry to have to rush off, but I'm in a very under-manned profession. Better treat what I said as mere idle and irresponsible gossip. If you want to get the low-down on Alton Hall, and Mr. G., why not join the club? You've time on your hands, and certain interests there. Good-bye, old chap!'

Colin smiled at McKinnon's last minute suggestion, but as he sat and smoked and drank his coffee he began to wonder if it was so foolish a suggestion after all. There would be the concerts, and he was not averse to a game of bridge at moderate stakes. It was certainly an idea worth thinking about!

6

Several days passed and then came a letter from Rosita. Enclosed was a complimentary ticket for the opening concert, with regrets that the programmes were not yet printed. While waiting for the great night Colin saw McKinnon again at the house, where he had a drink while waiting for Rhoda to beautify herself prior to going out to dinner.

'I saw Bredding yesterday,' said McKinnon, 'and casually mentioned the name of his lost patient.'

'What did he say?' asked Colin.

'He was most annoyed, and told me that his patients were his own concern. Then he added that if I thought he could make a mistake with a straightforward case of valvular trouble I must be a bigger idiot than he had imagined.'

'That was certainly straight from the shoulder.'

'I asked for it. He's a crusty old devil,

and I expect he'll apologise the next time I see him. Ah, here comes Rhoda — at last.'

On the night of the concert Colin borrowed the car and drove out to Alton. He had cut the time rather short, and when he was shown to his seat in the imposing music-room he found almost every chair occupied, and the great central chandelier beautifully decorated. Most of the audience were in evening-dress, and they looked as if they had dined extremely well. The programme which had been given him was very elaborate, and printed in silver and black, and he noticed that the vocalist — an Italian tenor — had his own accompanist, Rosita presumably being considered above such things. He also noticed that it was Mr. Mark Grandison who 'had the pleasure to present Miss Rosita Paston in a pianoforte recital (in large lettering) assisted by Signor Arturo Rossi (in smaller lettering)'.

Rosita's programme of music was an ambitious one, including some of the more difficult of the Chopin Studies, two

Brahms Rhapsodies, and, after some incursions into the modern French school, the hackneyed but none the less lovely 'Moonlight Sonata' by Beethoven. Rossi was down for the ever-popular arias from Italian opera.

While waiting for things to get started Colin gazed around at the persons who comprised the audience, and found them an interesting collection. They did not look like a typical cross-section of the music-loving fraternity such as one would normally see at a musical recital, but exhibited impatience, as if they had a strong suspicion their time was being wasted. Then Colin noticed that the seat beside him which had been empty was now occupied by a young man in evening-dress, with a mass of fair hair. He had come in at the last moment, and was without a programme.

'I wonder if you would be good enough to let me glance at your programme,' he said.

'Pleasure.'

As Colin handed the young man his programme their eyes met. Then the young man consulted the items.

'Thanks awfully,' he drawled. 'But have we met before?'

'Yes,' replied Colin.

'I thought so, but for the life of me I can't recall where.'

'It was in Mr. Stockforth's office late on the evening of Christmas Eve.'

'By jove, so it was. I was slightly binged I seem to remember.'

'That was the impression I got,' replied Colin.

'How right you were. But I thought I knew all the club members.'

'I'm not a member.'

'Oh, I get it now. You're a friend of Rosita.'

'Shall we say — an acquaintance?'

'Or even an admirer?'

'Why not?'

'Why not indeed? And I think I saw you talking to her on the ice a few days ago. In which case she probably told you that my name is Charles Simbourne, and that my chief occupation is drinking?'

'She told me the first part but not the second.'

'How remiss of her. Do you enjoy this sort of thing?'

'I shouldn't be here if I didn't.'

'I should — and am.'

Colin stared at him in mild astonishment.

'Then why on earth are you here?' he asked.

'To look at Rosita. That's a good enough reason isn't it!'

'She'll be interested to know she is worth a guinea a look.'

The Honourable Charles slapped his leg and burst into hilarious laughter, which caused fifty heads to be turned in his direction.

'Damned good!' he said. 'It isn't often one meets someone with a sense of humour. Regard all those stuffed owls, pretending to be patrons of the Arts. They wouldn't laugh if they saw Old Nick with his pants down. I suppose one may smoke?'

'One may not,' said Colin, indicating a note on the programme.

'You're right, brother. Lord, I do hope you're not going to turn out to be one of those insufferable persons who are always right.'

As he finished Rosita made her appearance. Grandison led her on to the stage, and introduced her in his basso profundo voice. Rosita, obviously a little nervous, gave a smile and a little bow, and then went straight to the piano. She was most beautifully turned out, from her lovely flame-coloured hair to her dainty silver sandals, and the shimmering frock which she wore was cut well away at the shoulders to reveal the sinuous curves of her admirable figure. The audience continued to clap until she was actually seated at the piano. Then there came dead silence — except from Colin's neighbour.

'A guinea a look,' he whispered. 'Oh boy!'

'Shut up!' hissed Colin.

Then the music started, and Colin sat well back and drank it all in. To him the brilliant work seemed faultlessly played, and as ever it held him completely in its spell. The details of his surroundings disintegrated into a kind of nebula, and even the attractive figure of Rosita became vague and evanescent beside this river of lovely melody. Exactly what the Honourable Charles was thinking was anybody's guess, but he was quite as silent as Colin, until the end of the piece when he clapped rapturously, and even stamped his feet. Rosita was recalled several times, and then at last the applause ended.

'Now I suppose we shall have to endure old macaroni,' yawned the Honourable Charles. 'Lord there'll be a smell of garlic.'

But the Italian tenor proved to be quite young and immaculate. He gave a very sound performance and was suitably rewarded by the audience as a whole, although Charles appeared to have worn out his hands already.

'Was that Grandison who introduced Rosita?' asked Colin.

'The great man himself. Do you know him?'

'No.'

'Oh you should. He's the veritable cat's whiskers.'

The programme went on with no

undue delays. There was no interval — a fact deplored by the Honourable Charles who had his usual evening thirst.

'That's all G's doing,' he complained. 'He knows that if he lost his sheep he'd never get them together again.'

At last came the Beethoven item, and in this Rosita was at her best. When she had finished it looked as if the over-sophisticated audience really had enjoyed it. They clapped and called until she was compelled to give an encore. She chose a small thing by Bach, and had the ovation all over again. Then bouquets were tendered, and Rosita found herself surrounded by expensive flowers. Grandison appeared by her side, and waved his big hands for silence — that Rosita might say something. She appeared to be too overwhelmed by her very obvious success to say more than 'Thank you all — very, very much,' and the curtains were drawn, and the crowd began to disperse through the door which led to the club proper. Colin deliberately loitered, so did Charles.

'Two minds with but a single thought,'

he said. 'Of course you want to see Rosita. You'd better come with me.'

'No thanks. I'll wait here. I think she may come along presently.'

'What a hope. Old G. will whisk her away, and fill her up with champagne. He regards her as his particular discovery. You go through that door and into the first room on the right, and I'll tell Rosita you're there.'

Without waiting to hear what Colin thought about this he hurried off. As the music-room was now almost empty Colin acted on the suggestion and found himself in a small writing-room. He had only been there a few minutes when the door opened and Rosita came in. Her face was flushed and she wore a single orchid on her frock.

'So you did come,' she said. 'I'm so glad. Was — was I all right?'

'More than all right. You were magnificent, and so amazingly self-possessed.'

'I felt dreadful — at first.'

'You looked as composed as a Greek statue. Tired?'

'Yes. Not tired from playing, but tired

from all the preparations. It won't be so bad next time.'

'Is Grandison satisfied?'

'He seems to be. He has been awfully good to me over this. He and the other directors are expecting me back to a little supper they are giving. I would much rather go to bed, but can't very well refuse.'

'Of course not. By the way, I sat next to the Honourable Charles Simbourne. He also seems to be your champion.'

'Poor Charles!' she sighed. 'I never know what to make of him. At times he can be quite charming, but at others — '

'Not so charming apparently. I too found him a bit of an enigma. He pretends he doesn't care for music.'

'That's what he told me, but I never know when he's telling the truth.'

'Rosita, are you going to be happy here?'

'I think so. Now that the funeral is over I can devote myself to my job.'

'What are you doing about your father's estate?'

'There is no estate. I can't find any

trace of the American securities which he was believed to have had. I think he must have realised them and spent the money.'

'You could save yourself a lot of trouble by putting the matter into the hands of a solicitor.'

'I had thought of that. Do you know a good firm?'

'Yes. There's our family solicitor. The head of the firm is a Mr. Ryburn. You would like him. Shall I speak to him and ask him to get in touch with you?'

'Thank you. I should like that. I've piles of Stock Exchange notes, and bank statements, which are Greek to me.'

'I'll see him. Now what about coming to tea one day next week?'

'I could come to-morrow week.'

'That's fine. I'll pick you up at half-past three.'

'I'll be ready. Now I must fly. I think Grandison will be waiting for me. Take this as a souvenir.'

She unpinned the exotic orchid and thrust the stalk through the buttonhole of his coat.

'Good-bye!' she said. 'To-morrow week

then at half-past three.'

Colin went home with snatches of the music ringing in his ears and Rosita's exquisite form vivid in his mind's eye. Rhoda was quick to spot the flower in his coat.

'Just do for me to-morrow night,' she said.

'You buy your own flowers. This is a souvenir.'

'How did it go, Colin?'

'Very well indeed. It's an amazing place — inside. Marvellous furniture and carpets. Perhaps just a bit flashy in parts. Queer people too. Some of them live at the Hall, but heaven knows where the rest came from.'

On the Monday Colin rang up Mr. Ryburn, and saw him an hour later in his office in the town. He was a small shrewd man, bordering on sixty years of age, and he remembered Colin immediately.

'I heard you were home,' he said. 'How are your mother and sister?'

'Very well, indeed. But I came to see you about a friend whose father has recently died at Alton Hall.'

130

'Alton! I heard someone had died there. That's a strange place.'

'I know. The daughter of the dead man is Rosita Paston. All her father left were some debts. It was a great blow to her because she imagined he was wealthy. There is no will that can be discovered, and she is the sole surviving member of the family. It may be that there are some undiscovered assets, as Paston was believed to have property in the United States. Would you be willing to look into the matter?'

'Certainly. I presume there are letters and documents?'

'Yes.'

'What do the debts consist of?'

'I think they were debts to the club where Paston lived for two years. But they have now been liquidated.'

'You mean Miss Paston has settled them herself?'

'In a sense.'

He then explained what had taken place, and shrewd Mr. Ryburn shook his large bald head.

'A curious way of doing business,' he

said. 'It rather looks as if Mr. Grandison was certain there are no assets, to have made such a sacrifice.'

'That's what I thought. Do you know Grandison personally?'

'No. But I remember a case of suicide up there. It caused a certain amount of gossip.'

'So I understand. I have no sort of interest in this matter — except that I want Miss Paston to have a square deal. She is absolutely ignorant in these matters, and would be easy prey to any unscrupulous persons, although I am not suggesting there has been any dirty business.'

'Well, I shall be pleased to look into the matter. Shall I write and make an appointment?'

'I wish you would.'

Ryburn made a note on his memorandum block, and then began to talk golf, at which pastime he was an expert.

'You used to be a promising young player,' he said. 'Have you kept it up?'

'I don't suppose I've played a dozen games in six years. Are you still plus something?'

'No. Old age creeps on apace. They've pushed my handicap up to four. But we've got two new and very difficult holes on the course. You must come and give me a game. What about Wednesday afternoon? I always take Wednesday afternoons off.'

'You'll beat my head off,' said Colin. 'But I should like it.'

'Good! See you at the club-house at half-past two.'

Colin kept this appointment, and was glad to find the course almost deserted, for he was nervous about his driving. But after the first two holes — which he lost — he recovered his old nerve and skill. On reaching the ninth they were all square.

'You're not doing so badly for a man who has only played twelve games in six years,' commented Ryburn. 'By the way, I saw your lovely young friend yesterday. She brought with her a suitcase full of odds and ends, and I spent last evening at home going through them. This morning I saw the bank where Paston kept his account and some interesting things have emerged.'

They drove off the tenth tee and then Colin asked what the interesting things were.

'When Paston came to live at Alton he had assets to the value of fifty thousand pounds at his bank,' said Ryburn. 'I've traced a lot of that money to his broker. For over a year he gambled madly, and lost over half of it. But what I haven't been able to trace is just how he lost the rest. There were regular drawings of thousands of pounds in cash, almost up to the time of his death, and nothing to account for it. I can only assume that that money was used for gambling — and not on the Stock Exchange.'

'You mean at Alton Hall?'

'That's a reasonable guess, but there is nothing to prove it.'

'But if he drew cash from the bank it must have been in notes of large denomination.'

'Yes. Mostly ten-pound and five-pound notes.'

'Can't they be traced?'

'Very doubtful after this long time.

Most of them will already have found their way back to the Bank of England. But I am going into that matter. You must realise, however, that even if we knew he had lost a vast sum of money to Alton Hall — or to Grandison himself — nothing could be done about it. Still, I agree, it would be satisfactory to discover just what became of the money.'

'Have you told Rosita yet?'

'No. Naturally she realises that her father must have gambled away his fortune, but it's doubtful if she suspects that Grandison may have been a recipient. She seems to take quite a good view of him.'

Colin rather expected that, in view of what had happened. He was so intrigued by what he had been told that he played the last holes indifferently and was well beaten before they reached the eighteenth.

On the following Sunday he called at Alton for Rosita, and found her quite ready.

'How did last night's concert go?' he asked.

'Quite well. Not quite so packed as the opening night, but Grandison was pleased. He has doubled the cash part of my wages.'

'That was nice. Will he make anything out of the innovation?'

'Oh, yes. Most of the members who come to the concerts dine there first, and drink very expensive wines. He's a very extraordinary man.'

'So I should imagine.'

'He told me he used to play the violin, and three days ago he went to London and came back with a lovely old fiddle. For two complete days he practised almost without stopping, and last night he asked me if I would accompany him. I said I should love to, and he gave me the pianoforte part of the Kreutzer Sonata. I was ready for anything, but he amazed me by playing it with the greatest ease and correctness. It was my turn to applaud. I told him he would have to play at the next concert, but he turned that down flat.'

'How do you find the people there?'

'That's a hard question.'

'Why?'

'They're so mixed. They're all very nice to me, but I don't get much out of them. I think they're mostly lonely people, with no homes of their own, and they get a kind of club habit and club look. Sometimes they pass one by as if they had not seen you, but I'm sure they don't mean to be rude.'

'Isn't there a lot of card playing.'

'Yes, I think there is. But I don't play any card games, and so never go into the card-rooms. These weekly concerts keep me very busy too, but I rather like it.'

'I hear you saw Ryburn about your father's estate.'

'Oh, yes. I must thank you for that. He is a charming man, and I handed everything over to him. But I don't expect to get anything out of it. The clothing was all dreadfully old so I gave it to the gardener to burn. I'm left with several rather good travelling trunks, some ornaments, and a pistol.'

'A pistol!'

'Yes. I meant to have brought it along for you to see.'

'I'm not a collector of pistols. The best thing you can do with it is to take it to the police.'

'I'll do that,' she promised.

Rosita was given a warm welcome at Colin's home, and McKinnon dropped in to swell the tea-party. The conversation was of the light order, and after tea Colin suggested they should take the car and have dinner together at a road-house. But Rosita begged to be excused as she had work to do in connection with the concerts. So instead they took a walk through the lanes in the dusk of evening.

'What do you do with yourself these days?' asked Rosita.

'Laze and play — and read a good deal. I find it all a very nice change. Perhaps in time I may get bored with it — but certainly not yet.'

'Is your sister engaged to the nice young doctor?'

'S-sh! We never mention that. But I think it's very near. The trouble seems to be housing. I'm quite sure that when they are together they talk of nothing but houses.'

'Then they must be engaged.'

'My opinion is that they will cut the engagement, and simply announce one evening that they are going to be married, and that will mean they have found some hovel for about five thousand pounds. It's all very difficult unless one has tons of money.'

'The trouble is that the wrong people seem to have it. There are a number of people at the Hall who wear enough jewellery to buy a dozen houses.'

'How is the Honourable Charles getting on?'

'As usual. It's such a shame he drinks so heavily.'

'Is that his only vice?'

'The only one that is obvious. I don't think you like him very much, do you?'

'No. How can one like a healthy young man who spends his time guzzling and gambling, when he might be doing a job of work? I looked him up in a reference book. He is heir to a Viscount, and presumably he is waiting for his father to die — '

'That's very unkind, Colin,' she said. 'He's difficult to understand. I made the mistake of thinking he was just a waster, but I discovered that he was awarded the Victoria Cross.'

'What!'

'That's what the colonel told me, and he ought to know.'

'Then I apologise. But I still think he should get a job.'

'So do I. But it isn't easy for these young men to readjust themselves after years of horrible experiences. Now, I must get back — really.'

'I have an idea I've offended you.'

'Oh, no. I like you when you are forthright.'

'Only then?'

She gave him a glance in the darkness, which made him wish it were daylight, so that he might read what was in her eyes.

'No — at all times,' she confessed.

'But your work first?'

'I'm not sure. Are you trying to make me say that I am a career girl?'

'Well, are you?'

'Yes. I want a career of my own. All my life I've been dependent on others for every bite of food, every scrap of clothing. Now I want to stand on my own feet. Do you blame me for that?'

'Of course not. I was merely fishing in deep waters. Are you aware that Charles Simbourne is quite crazy about you, so infatuated that he is prepared to forsake the American bar and endure two hours of music merely to look at you.'

'You're absurd.'

'But it's true.'

'It's just nonsense that you are inventing.'

'Was he at last night's concert?'

'I — I think he was.'

'You know he was, and who can blame him? Not I at any rate.'

'You're embarrassing me dreadfully,' she said. 'I can't help it — can I?'

'You could, by being less lovely.'

'But Colin — you don't think that I have encouraged him to — to come and ogle me?'

'No, of course not. Forget what I said. I don't know what is happening to me.'

There was silence after that, but as they walked briskly side by side, her hand touched his, and then he was aware that she had caught him by the fingers, and that her hand was full of warmth and tenderness.

7

It was some days later that Colin had a surprise meeting with the Honourable Charles. He had dropped in at an ancient hostelry in the town, which had a very comfortable, old-fashioned bar, and an open fire which burned huge logs. He was just ordering a drink when Charles came through the swing door, with the energy of a young bull.

'Hullo!' he said. 'I didn't know you patronised such dens of vice. Lord, what a lousy day!'

'Not too nice. What will you have to drink?'

'Thanks. I'll have a whisky — I hope.'

The hope was borne out.

'Say when,' said Colin.

Charles waved his hand after Colin had introduced about a teaspoonful of water into the diminutive dose of whisky.

'Good health!' he said.

'Same to you. Do you often come here?'

'No. I just trickle in on occasion.'

'How's the club going?'

'As usual — except that some of the staff have staged a strike. I left Grandison wrestling with them. They won't get much change out of him.'

'So he's tough?'

'Tough and clever — and prosperous. Grandison is always about two steps ahead of most people. But the trouble with people who keep ahead is that they are liable to trip up. Good Lord, these drinks are short. Drink up, and let's have a refill.'

Colin was interested in the conversation, and had his beer-can refilled.

'Have you been a member of the club long?' he asked.

'Not very long. It's really a hell of a place, but has some obvious advantages.'

'Such as liquid refreshment at all times?'

'Yes, and oodles of food — good food. But G. is clever enough to avoid getting into trouble. Most of the food is of the unrationed kind. Poultry and kidneys and fresh salmon. At Alton you can live like a prince, but it costs money, and what's money?'

'It used to be something one worked for.'

'You're one of the world's workers, aren't you?'

'Yes.'

'On leave?'

Colin nodded, and watched the curious play of emotions on the face of his companion.

'Engineer?' he asked.

'Sort of. Hydro-electrics.'

'Lucky man. I wish I had been brought up in some interesting profession. But I'm thinking of going to Kenya and starting a farm.'

'What about the family estate?'

'Mortgaged to the hilt. It will belong to the Government soon, for my father is a sick man, and two lots of death duties within ten years will be just too much. For me there loom two alternatives — spivery or farming. I expect I shall decide on farming, preferably in some sunny place, where men can call themselves free.'

'In the meantime Alton Hall must be a drain upon your resources?'

'I hope I shall not grace Alton Hall much longer. It depends upon certain eventualities.'

Colin had no idea to what he was referring, but he could not help thinking of Rosita in this connection. Was it possible that Charles had ambitions in that direction? If his sick father died he would become a peer — a somewhat dazzling prospect to some girls.

'I wonder you don't join the club,' said Charles, after a long silence.

'What on earth should I find to do there?'

'I should have thought — '

He stopped as if he did not like to express exactly what was in his mind.

'Go on,' said Colin.

'There might be advantages. It might be worth while keeping an eye on a certain person.'

Colin stared at him almost resentfully.

'What person?' he asked.

'You know. Life at Alton can be a constant temptation to a young and inexperienced girl — especially when a man like Grandison takes her up.'

'I don't quite like that expression,' said Colin.

'Well, put it another way. Grandison acts the part of Fairy Godfather. Butter won't melt in his mouth when Rosita is on hand. But I happen to have been friendly with her father. He was weaker than I am — but in a different way. He squandered a fortune at Alton — everything he possessed — on the turn of cards.'

'Are you sure of that?' asked Colin.

'Surer than I am of most things, but I've no proof if that is what you need. It's difficult to get proof where Grandison is concerned.'

'Have you spoken to Rosita about that?'

'No. She would resent the imputation, and I have no proof. Yes, I think it wouldn't be a bad idea for you to join the club. I am on the committee, and to-morrow evening we have our monthly meeting. If you were put up for membership by me, my friend Colonel

Rooke would second the proposal, and it would go through because I happen to know that Grandison will not be present at the meeting.'

'If he were would he vote against me?'

'He might.'

'Why?'

'Because you are a friend of Rosita. He doesn't like people to be too friendly to Rosita.'

Colin drew in his breath with a little hiss of surprise. Here was a situation he had never dreamed of. Why was Charles saying these things? Had he some personal axe to grind? What exactly was going on?

'Think it over and give me a ring,' said Charles. 'But it must be before six o'clock if you want to become a member forthwith.'

'What is the subscription?'

'Ten guineas. Of course you needn't live at the club. In fact there isn't any accommodation left. Do think it over.'

'I think I will,' said Colin.

'Good. Now I'll have to buzz off. Cheerio!'

Colin sat on for some time pondering over the conversation, which had shown

Simbourne in a completely new light. Hitherto he had regarded him as a mere sycophant of the man behind Alton Club, and there was no doubt at all that he was strongly addicted to drinking, but he had been sober enough that morning — and sober with a strange kind of determination in his habitually carefree face. What he had said about Grandison was a strong corroboration of what Ryburn already believed. Yet there was always the possibility that he was putting on an act for some purpose not immediately comprehensible. The remark that Grandison didn't like people to be too friendly to Rosita was particularly telling, for Colin found himself in just that frame of mind. He walked back home across the fields, which were wet and soggy, but yet pleasanter than some of the muddy lanes where the water had lain since the thaw, and by the time he had entered the house he had accepted the challenge thrown out by Charles.

'Why so thoughtful, brother mine?' asked Rhoda.

'I'm thinking of joining Alton Club.'

'Doing what?' asked Rhoda, flinging round on him.

'Joining the club. But don't say a word to mother — yet, or she may draw wrong conclusions.'

'What are the right conclusions?'

'A desire to meet some of the queer people who haunt the place.'

'I — see.'

'You don't, old girl. But don't worry. I'm not likely to become a dipsomaniac, or to squander my substance over the card-tables. As a non-resident member I can drop in when the mood takes me.'

'Don't let it take you too often.'

'I won't.'

He thereupon rang up Simbourne, and finally spoke to him.

'Good!' said Simbourne. 'In a couple of days you should receive a letter from the secretary informing you that on payment of the subscription you will be entitled to enjoy all the amenities of this comfortable and somewhat exclusive retreat from the world.'

8

Rosita found her time fully occupied at Alton, for in addition to the weekly concert it was essential that she should keep up her practice, and this alone used up several hours each day. Then there was Grandison, wanting to play duets with her on his newly-acquired violin, and to talk music at every opportunity. Also she was still busy reading her father's old letters, of which there were thousands. From these she was able to build up a fairly broad picture of his movements over the years, and to realise what a strange rolling stone he had been.

Her mother's letters were a drama in themselves. They revealed a human soul racked with doubt and repression. They dated back to the time of the separation, but gave no real clue as to the cause. But reading between the lines she devined that her mother suspected her father of living a double life, but no other woman was named. There were many references to herself as a young girl, and always in her favour. Her mother had been quick to sense her daughter's gift of music, and had begged for extra allowance that she might be enabled to secure for her daughter the best tuition possible. It was to her father's credit that this appeal was not made in vain. How sad it all was — that the marriage had gone astray, that she — Rosita — had never had a chance of possessing a real father, nor her mother a real husband.

She had had time now to form some opinion of the club and its resident members, and there was much which gave her food for reflection. Of the twenty-odd persons who made the club their permanent abode at least half were foreigners, ranging from Dutch to Cypriots. They were all polite — too polite in fact — but curiously detached from any real friendliness. Most of these had their breakfast in bed, in Continental fashion, and only one or two used the private nine-hole golf-course, or the excellent Badminton court. Card-playing seemed to be the order of the day, and this went on from early afternoon until midnight and after. Non-resident members came by car in the evenings and then the bigger bridge-room was packed. What stakes they played she had no idea, for she gave the place a wide berth. But she could not help noticing that Grandison seemed to hold a little card party of his own, in that sumptuous apartment of his, for she saw champagne and cold chicken, and other delicacies being taken up there in the lift almost every night. The party usually comprised the same persons — Grandison, Stockforth, a wealthy old Jew named Isaacs, and two middle-aged hags with unpronounceable names. On occasion Charles Simbourne would join this party. As there were too many for bridge she gathered it was some other game they played.

The relationship between Grandison and Stockforth puzzled her. At times they seemed almost brotherly, but at others Grandison displayed animosity towards Stockforth — almost hate. Rosita has seen him treat Stockforth as if he were the lowest underling, and Stockforth would take the insults as quietly as a well-trained dog would take a lashing from his master.

She tried to overlook the sinister atmosphere of the place, and to give herself wholly to her own job. In this matter Grandison was her loyal ally. Everything she did in that respect was right with him. The man really did care for music. He would come into the music-room while she was practising, and sit for an hour on end, saying nothing. At first she found this embarrassing, but she got used to it. Several times she dined with him alone in that huge lounge, and his behaviour was unimpeachable.

'You've brought some light into this place,' he said. 'Stockforth thought I was mad, but he is being proved wrong. The concerts are a financial success as well as artistic. We are clearing thirty to forty pounds a week over them. You've got a big future, Rosita.'

'I wonder.'

'I'm sure of it. Not here, of course. But this is all good practice. One day you'll leave me, and I shan't like it. But I won't stand in your way.'

'That's very kind of you.'

'Not at all. Shall I tell you something? I hate this place — and most of the people here. What are they but a gang of useless parasites? I'd rather be a good fiddler in a first-class symphony orchestra any day, but a man must live. Rosita, tell me frankly, am I improving?'

'As a violinist?'

'Yes.'

'You are better every time you play.'

'You really mean that?'

'Sincerely.'

His dark eyes gleamed with pleasure.

'It's you — your influence,' he said. 'Years ago I broke up my old violin in disgust. I had stagnated. But all I needed was someone to lead me through the forest — someone who could set an example too. Of course I'll never be anything but a novice — not in your class, but I get a hell of a kick out of it. It's a cheek me asking you to play with me, but there's no one else who cares a damn. Queer, how people differ — how some are deaf to tonal beauty. Take young Simbourne. His idea of music is something you can jig to. If he was a son of mine I'd put him through his paces.'

He said this with the deepest emphasis, and clenched his big hands as if they were itching to carry out his threat.

'I don't think Charles means half he says,' she said. 'He rather likes to appear a cynical man of the world. After all, he is one of your best customers.'

'I don't need his custom. Half the time he's drunk, and I have no patience with men who lose control of themselves. It's people like him who get a place a bad name. Take my advice, Rosita, and give him a wide berth. One of these days he'll come a terrible cropper. Wish I could get him out of the club.'

Rosita was quite surprised at this sudden revelation of his real feelings about Charles, especially as she had believed that he liked titles, and had himself put Simbourne's name forward when there had been a vacancy on the committee. It was immediately following this conversation that Simbourne burst a surprise upon her.

'Got a new member coming this afternoon,' he said. 'I shall have to introduce him to the few members who are worth talking to.'

'Why you?' she asked.

'Oh, I proposed him. He's not a bad chap.'

'Not another member of the nobility?'

'I wouldn't inflict that upon you. But I particularly want you to meet him. Do join us at tea, will you? Four o'clock in the winter garden?'

'I'll try.'

'The table at the eastern end.'

'I'll try.'

'You'll come, and you'll like it.'

Rosita kept the appointment a bit late. It was a lovely afternoon with the setting sun shining down the whole length of the long glazed winter garden. She saw Simbourne facing her as she went through from the lounge, and his companion had his back towards her. Simbourne waved a hand, and Rosita went forward to the vacant chair. It was then that she saw Colin as he rose from his chair.

'Why!' she gasped. 'You — you can't be the new member?'

'I'm afraid I am.'

She knew not whether to be glad or sorry. Somehow she had never dreamed of this possibility, for Colin and Alton Club seemed like two opposite poles. But she did her best to conceal her discomfiture, and was not very successful.

'It's nice to see you,' she said. 'Do sit down.'

'All my idea,' said Charles. 'Grandison told me I never did a thing for the club, and so I thought I'd find him a new member or two. Here's the first, and I ought to draw a commission. Toasted scones or bread and butter?'

It was during tea that Grandison came into the winter garden to have a word with Colonel Rooke. As Rooke was at the further end of the place Grandison did not see Rosita's table until he left the colonel. When he did so Colin had his face turned to Rosita, and Grandison stared and then came forward.

'Excuse me,' he said. 'I should like to see you when you are free, Rosita. I'm in

158

trouble over the singer for next Saturday.'

'Oh, Mr. Grandison,' said Charles. 'May I introduce you to the new member — Mr. Colin Fairbright. Mr. Fairbright — Mr. Grandison, our chairman and administrative genius.'

Grandison bowed stiffly.

'Welcome to the club, Mr. Fairbright,' he said. 'I hope you will have many happy times here.'

'Thank you,' said Colin. 'I'm sure I shall.'

Grandison smiled and walked away.

'I shall have to hurry,' said Rosita.

'But why?' asked Charles.

'If the singer has let us down we have to find a substitute.'

'Singers are four a penny. If you pay me enough I'll take his place. Don't gulp that tea down. You'll get indigestion.'

'I really must go,' said Rosita. 'I'll see you again, Colin. In the lounge in about half an hour.'

'I'll be there,' promised Colin.

She hurried off and Charles gave a little laugh. The situation was not quite clear to Colin. He got the feeling that Grandison was deeply annoyed, and that Charles was enjoying himself very much.

'Didn't he know about me?' he asked Charles.

'Not a thing. I told you he would be absent from the meeting. The fact is that Grandison has had the club too much under his control. Some of the members feel raw about this, and were glad to put a new member through without Grandison having the final word.'

'Do you think he would have objected to me?' asked Colin.

'Yes.'

'On social grounds?'

'Oh, no.'

'You mean because — because I am a friend of Rosita?'

Simbourne nodded very seriously.

'I don't feel very happy about this.'

'You may think it was a dirty trick on my part to score off old G.,' said Simbourne. 'But I had other reasons.'

'What reasons?'

'One reason is that Rosita is too nice a girl to be here at all. A lot goes on here that isn't nice. You'll see as time goes on

— if you keep your eyes open. And don't be lured into playing poker up in Grandison's den. I've had some.'

'If it's as bad as you suggest why do you stay here?'

'Perhaps it's because I like living dangerously. Now come and see the billiards-room and the library.'

They went upstairs and entered the billiards-room. It was lavishly equipped, and the table itself was excellent. Hanging on the wall were a number of cue-cases, with padlocks on them.

'What sort of a game do you play?' asked Charles.

'Oh — just medium.'

'If Count Zadlo wants to give you a game be careful. He'll let you win, and will then suggest playing for a fiver. Somehow he'll just manage to beat you.'

Colin laughed at the grim picture which Charles was presenting, and they passed through a door into the library. Here there were shelves full of books, and a large central table on which there were many magazines. Through the large end window there was a pleasant view of the garden, now almost in darkness.

'Quite a good collection,' said Charles. 'But nobody reads them — except Colonel Rooke. He's busy reading *The Decline and Fall*, and hopes to finish before he dies of a surfeit of fiery cocktails.'

As they turned to leave Colonel Rooke entered. Colin had already been introduced to him.

'Well met, Mr. Fairbright,' he grunted. 'Don't tell me we have another member who can actually read!'

'Only very simple works,' replied Colin.

'That's a start anyway. No one in this damned place is interested in anything except straight flushes and three of a kind. But Charles is making progress with comic strips. Charles, what have you done to Grandison? He's as mad as a wounded bear.'

'I thought he might be,' said Charles.

A little later Charles asked to be excused and left Colin in the lounge, talking to Mrs. Widdens, who had made a dead set at him. She was a somewhat faded beauty, laden with many rings and cosmetics, and rumour had it that she had killed three husbands — all wealthy, but by what means was not divulged.

'You look as if you might ride,' she said.

'I have — on occasion.'

'Oh, goody-goody! So difficult to get anyone to ride with, and there are three hacks in the stables dying for exercise. Oh, here's Rosita. Quite a charming girl, and so talented. But I believe you know her?'

Colin nodded as Rosita came forward. The three chatted for a few minutes and then someone came and called Mrs. Widdens for bridge.

'Thank goodness!' said Colin. 'That woman is going to be a bit of an ordeal.'

'Making love to you?'

'Not quite that, but proposing riding excursions.'

'She's horse-mad and bird-mad. Keeps two parrots and some canaries in her rooms. The place sounds like the zoo when you pass it. Shall we go into the grounds, while there is still some light? They are rather lovely.'

'I'd like to. There's too much heat in here.'

They went on the terrace, coatless and hatless, and found the air not unpleasantly cold after the sunshine of the day. The stars were appearing and in the west a clear new moon was floating above the tall trees, whose silhouettes looked most beautiful against the dying glow of the western sky.

'Why did you do it?' asked Rosita suddenly.

'Join the club?'

'Yes.'

'Well, in the first place I was at a loose end.'

'But you could have joined the town golf club.'

'You talk as if I had done something wrong.'

'Nonsense! But really I can't see that this place has much to offer you, with your comfortable home and all that goes with it.'

'Use your imagination, Rosita.'

'I am. What I fear is that you will get drawn into card-playing and heavy drinking — '

'What about you?' he asked with a laugh.

'Are you immune to such temptations.?'

'I've work to do here.'

'You are talented enough to find work elsewhere.'

'I doubt it.'

'Never doubt yourself, Rosita.'

'But I do. Not everyone would be so generous as Grandison.'

'Is he generous? I thought he was doing quite well out of the concerts — selling hundreds of meals and drinks at enormous profit. Charles thinks — '

'For Heaven's sake don't quote Charles,' she begged. 'I don't understand him at all, and no one else does. I can't help thinking that his war experiences have affected his mental health. At times he does and says the strangest things. Yesterday —'

She stopped suddenly.

'What about yesterday?' asked Colin.

'I don't think I had better tell you.'

'Don't tell me if it's a secret.'

She was silent for a few moments, and then she caught his arm and turned him towards herself.

'I don't know that it's a secret. Colin, I trust you implicitly. You've been my best friend all along. I must tell you about Charles. It's all very silly, and yet it troubles me. He came to me when I was practising, looking as if he was drunk. But he wasn't. He gave me a small key with a tag on it, and said it was the key of a little flat which he had in London.'

Colin's mouth twitched.

'Oh, wait!' she begged. 'He asked me to do something for him in an emergency. I asked him what he was talking about, and he said he had a premonition that something might happen to him. I told him not to be absurd, but he persisted. If something happened to him — would I go to his flat at once, open it with the key, and take a lacquered box to Scotland Yard. He said the box was hidden in the top of a riding boot in his wardrobe.'

'Amazing!' gasped Colin. 'Did you accept this commission?'

'Yes. I couldn't very well do anything else.'

'He must have been drunk. Why couldn't he take the box to the police himself — before something happened to him?'

'I don't know. Look — here's the key.'

166

She opened her handbag and produced a Yale key with a tag attached to it. On the tag was written '27 Palting Street, Knightsbridge'. Colin wrinkled his brows as he tossed the key in his hand. The thought came to him that this might possibly be a cheap trick to get Rosita to enter the flat, but he put it aside at once, since Rosita would not be expected to act unless something happened to Charles, and by 'something' he obviously meant his own death.

'Why not give it to him back?' he asked. 'Tell him the whole idea is so repugnant and macabre that you won't have anything to do with it.'

'That would hurt his feelings.'

'Doesn't he deserve to have his feelings hurt when he behaves in such a manner. If there is any threat to his life he should go to the police — not inflict his morbid premonitions on you.'

Rosita, whose expression had been serious, now conjured up a smile.

'There's really nothing to it if we refuse to take it seriously,' she said. 'I think in a day or two I'll give him the key back and tell him to go easier with his drinking.'

'Probably that's the best thing to do. Tell me, what part does Stockforth play in this set-up?'

'He appears to be just a kind of stooge. He's only an honorary member of the club, and takes his orders from Grandison. I don't have much to do with him. I think his chief job is to look after the staff, and usually he does it very well. But a few days ago there was a strike, and all the kitchen staff threatened to leave at once, unless they got a big advance in pay. Stockforth found it too much for him to handle, but Grandison settled it in half an hour.'

'By giving way?'

'Partly. He had them all up in his lounge, and talked to them. They were soon back at work again. He offered them half the increase of pay they were demanding, or as an alternative to pack their trunks and leave the premises in half an hour. He's very clever.'

'So I should imagine.'

They had walked down several terraces to the lower garden, where there were many evergreen shrubs and trees to give the lie to winter. As two huge cars rolled up the drive the lights from their lamps shone full on the imposing mansion, flood-lighting it effectively for a few moments.

'It's all rather wonderful, isn't it?' murmured Rosita. 'The oldest part of the fabric is fifteenth century, and sometimes I imagine the people of those days strolling about in their colourful and elaborate dresses, and others in the house making music on weird instruments. I wonder what they would think and say if they could come to life and see what has happened to their late abode?'

'Something not very complimentary, I should think.'

Rosita laughed and led him by devious paths, in the gloaming, to strange arbours where ancient statuary loomed out of the darkness like sentinels.

'It might be summer — so mild,' said Rosita. 'I shall never understand the English weather.'

'No one ever has understood it. Mind that step.'

'I have cat's eyes. Here's my favourite

urn — brimming over with lovely jasmine. Even the snow did not kill it.'

'A nice replica of a Greek original,' said Colin. 'It might have been the veritable specimen which helped to immortalise Keats.'

'The poet who wrote about 'Stout Cortez'?'

'The one and only. But as a lover of heard music you shouldn't regard it so highly.'

'But why not?'

'Don't you know what Keats said of it:

'Heard melodies are sweet, but those
   unheard
Are sweeter; therefore, ye soft pipes,
   play on;
Not to the sensual ear, but, more
   endear'd,
Pipe to the spirit ditties of no tone:' '

'Go on,' she said enthusiastically. 'That was beautiful. Oh, Colin, I love you when you quote poetry.'

'Then I'll go on quoting:

'Fair youth, beneath the trees, thou
   can'st not leave

Thy song, nor ever can those trees be
    bare;
Bold lover, never, never can'st thou
    kiss,
Though winning near the goal — yet,
    do not grieve;
She cannot fade, though thou hast
    not thy bliss,
For ever wilt thou love, and she be fair!''

Rosita stood quite still, except for one hand which moved aside the trailing jasmine that she might see dimly the piping demi-gods and the fleeing face-averted nymphs.

'Any more?' she asked.

'Quite a lot, ending as everyone knows — or should know:

' 'Beauty is truth, truth beauty' that is
    all
Ye know on earth, and all ye need to
    know!'

'I must really buy you a copy of Keats.'

'Do, and inscribe it 'To the girl who didn't know'.'

'I think you do — all the time, or you couldn't be what you are.'

Another car rolled up the drive, and Rosita gave a little sigh.

'Life is a very mixed affair,' she said.

'Mixed and marvellous.'

'Good and evil.'

'But always a little more of the good.'

'You believe that?'

'If it were otherwise we should have destroyed each other by now.'

'Bless you for that, Colin. Now I must get back, as I have my evening practice to do. If we go round this way I can get to the music-room by the side door, and save going through the club.'

They came at last to the side door.

'This is where I vanish,' she said.

'May I come and listen to you?'

'The music-room isn't part of the club premises. Besides I should find you a disturbing element.'

'But not Grandison,' he blurted.

'Why did you say that?' she asked plaintively.

'I don't know. Forgive me.'

'Just this once,' she said with a smile.

'Good-bye, Colin!'

'Good-bye!' he said, taking her warm hand.

He stood there a moment or two after she had gone, wondering why he had let her go like that, when he might so easily have taken her in his arms and told her just what she had come to mean to him. How easy it was imagining himself doing this, and how hard it was to do so when an opportunity offered. He made his way round to the main entrance and got his hat and coat. A few minutes later he was driving through the dark lanes.

9

The days passed and Colin visited the club at intervals. It was inevitable that he should see Rosita on most of these visits, but his times with her were never so lengthy as he would have wished. Always there was something she had to do, connected with her work. He attended two more of her concerts and found her playing as brilliant as ever — even more brilliant, for now there was no sign of nervousness, and it really looked as if she had scored a lasting success. Charles as usual was present, as was Grandison, and Colonel Rooke.

'I know nothing about music,' growled the old colonel. 'But the bridge-room is empty while the concerts are on. Nothing a fellow can do but run with the pack.'

'That seems to be the case with Simbourne,' commented Colin.

'That young man puzzles me. If I didn't know him as I do I'd say he was

174

turning over a new leaf. Hasn't been drunk in weeks. Can't think what's come over him.'

'Economising perhaps.'

'He's no need to economise. His mother left him a lot of money in his own right. Three or four thousand a year, I believe. It's as well she did for he won't get much from the estate when the viscount dies. Talks about emigrating to Kenya, but what the hell would he do in Kenya? Why, a fellow has to go a hundred miles to get a drink.'

'That may account for his sobriety.'

'You mean he's in training for a more austere life?'

'Why not?'

'Couldn't be done — not in Charles's case. He'll break out again soon, and the sooner the better because it isn't doing him any good.'

Later Colin saw Charles, and found him very quiet and reflective. All his old facetiousness had vanished, and Colin could scarcely believe he was the same man.

'A bit under the weather?' he asked.

'A bit perhaps. Bad news from home.

The old man has taken a turn for the worse, and can't last very long. He and I never got on very well together. My fault no doubt. I'm going up in a day or two to see him. I know what it'll mean. He'll want me to promise to stay and rot at Lockleys, just as he has done all these years.'

'And you don't want to?'

Charles shook his head.

'I simply couldn't knuckle down to it,' he said. 'I don't want the title nor anything that goes with it. I couldn't even run the place after the estate duties are paid. There has always been a wild streak in my family. It missed my father, but came down to me. I've never been any good, and six years in the army didn't improve me.'

'I've been given to understand you did very well in the army.'

'Not really. I won a decoration, but that doesn't prove anything. The best friends — in fact the only friends — I ever had were nearly all killed. There are some matters I want to clear up, and then — '

'Then what?'

'New lands, new experiences, new friends. It's my only chance of happiness. God, why am I talking so much?'

'Nothing like getting things off your chest.'

Simbourne looked at him warily.

'You think so? Sometimes it's the first step towards becoming the perfect bore. How are you liking this place?'

'I find it — interesting.'

'Have you had much to say to Grandison?'

'No. He seems to take a pleasure in avoiding me.'

'That's not your loss. Look — may I ask you a personal question?'

'If it isn't too personal.'

'That's the rub. But here goes — is there anything between you and Rosita?'

Colin winced at the question but faced it out.

'There's a great deal,' he replied. 'I like her, and I rather think she likes me.'

'That's no answer. Have you asked her to marry you?' Colin here showed resentment.

'Oh, come — I mean no impertinence.

You see, I've already asked her.'

Colin stared at him, as if he doubted his ears.

'You — you asked her that?' he said.

'Yes. It was the maddest, damnest impulse. Of course she declined the doubtful honour of being my wife. I expected that.'

'Then why did you ask?' demanded Colin.

'Because I wanted to get down to basic facts. I want to know what the future holds for her.'

'What the hell has that got to do with you?' asked Colin angrily.

'A great deal. More than you can guess. I've loved her since she first set foot in this ghastly place, and I'd have told her to get out of it as quick as possible if it hadn't been for the fact that it enabled me to be close to her. Not very altruistic, eh? She's the only girl who has meant anything to me — and I've met packets of them. But she's playing with fire, and doesn't realise it.'

'I don't get this.'

'Then you're more obtuse than I

thought. This musical ambition of hers is all-absorbing. How could it be otherwise considering her talent for it? Who's helping her — encouraging her — driving her onwards? Who smooths out the path — gives her marvellous bouquets — whispers the glad tidings into her ear. She's human — and like most humans, and all the plants in the garden, she turns naturally to the sun that warms her. God, can't you understand?'

'Are you suggesting that Grandison — '

'Ah, you've named the beast. In the Bible he is given merely a number.'

'Charles, are you crazy?'

'Never more sane than at this moment. Why do you think Grandison passes you by? Why do you think he was so annoyed with me because I proposed you for membership, and sneaked you through in his absence? He didn't want you here, because he sees in you the deadly rival. You may think he is too old to stand a chance in a straight fight, and not physically attractive enough to seduce any lovely young girl. But don't overlook the other attributes. He's as cunning as a snake, and a consummate actor. He is giving her what she thinks is the most desirable thing in the world — a career. Think what money can do in that connection. It can hire the biggest concert hall in London, Paris or anywhere else. It can overcome most obstacles in this world, and I happen to know that Grandison has stacks of money. There is nothing that can dazzle and blind an ambitious young woman as much as early success. There are various ways of wooing, Colin, and Grandison knows them all. If you love Rosita as I believe you do, go in and do something about it, before it is too late. Now if you would like to crack me on the head with that vase you may do so.'

Colin was momentarily dumbfounded, but all his resentment had gone, for at least here was sincerity beyond doubting. But the substance of it was so unpalatable — the more unpalatable because at the back of it he saw logic and reason. Rosita undoubtedly was at Grandison's beck and call. He had experienced many instances of that. Also it was significant that she invariably referred to Grandison in terms of gratitude and admiration. His surprise at Simbourne's admission of a marriage offer was quite out-balanced by the grimmer aspect of Simbourne's warning.

'I appreciate your candour, Charles,' he said. 'Maybe I will do something — and quickly.'

On the following day he met Mr. Ryburn in the town, and the old solicitor dragged him into a coffee shop, and stood him a coffee.

'I think I've cleared up the Paston estate,' he said. 'The claims upon it were inconsiderable. The value of the personal effects is just about sufficient to pay the few bills and the cost of the funeral. I have not been able to discover any securities of any kind, nor any will.'

'What about those heavy drawings in cash?'

'I'm afraid there is nothing to be done about it. The bank was willing to give me a complete list of the note numbers, but even if some of the notes are still in circulation it wouldn't help matters to trace them, since theft is not in question.

I am convinced that Paston lost the money in gambling on a very large scale, and over a fairly long period. But he is dead and buried, and it looks as if the matter is finally closed. I'm sorry for Miss Paston.'

'Have you told her the result?'

'I wrote to her last night. How is she getting on up there?'

'She seems to be a big success.'

'That's a pleasure to hear. Of course, I said nothing about our suspicions, in view of the complete lack of proof.'

Colin nodded as he sipped his coffee.

'Now what about a game of golf to-morrow afternoon?'

'Sorry,' said Colin. 'I should like to, but I'm booked up.'

'Well, another day. How are you enjoying your leave?'

'Very much,' replied Colin, with little sign of enthusiasm.

'Is it true you have joined the Alton Club?'

'Yes.'

'Queer place, isn't it?'

'In a way. But the concerts are rather enjoyable.'

'So I should imagine. Well, I'll look forward to that round of golf when you are less busy.'

Colin had no engagement for the following afternoon, but his mind was not in a state to enable him to give the redoubtable golfer any sort of a game. Simbourne's sinister suggestions were still buzzing in his brain like a swarm of angry bees. Clearly the thing to do was to see Rosita without undue delay, and to attempt to discover what place — if any — he occupied in her affections. He took his courage in his hands that afternoon and motored over to Alton. On reaching the vestibule he heard the hall porter speaking on the telephone, telling some caller that Mr. Grandison was not available. He was away for the day, and was not expected back until late in the evening. It occurred to him that this was a splendid opportunity to speak to Rosita, outside the heavy atmosphere of the club. They could run out in the car some-where, and have dinner in a quiet hotel. Rosita would be unable to plead club business with Grandison as an excuse.

'Is Miss Paston about?' he asked the hall porter.

'I saw her about half an hour ago, sir, but I rather think she was going for a walk. Shall I ring her apartment?'

'Please.'

He used the telephone again, and then reported no reply.

'I'll have a look round the grounds,' said Colin. 'If you should see her please tell her I am looking for her.'

'Certainly, sir.'

Colin went out into the gardens and spent the best part of half an hour in a fruitless search. Coming back he opened the side door of the music-room, but found the piano closed. Impatient to get his business off his mind he went back into the club, and took tea with the colonel.

They had finished their tea and were engaged in an argument about Singapore which both of them knew very well, when Stockforth came along to them.

'Excuse me,' he said. 'Can I persuade you two gentlemen to make up a bridge four. There's Mrs. Watling dying to play and no spare players in the bridge-room.'

'Certainly!' said the colonel.

'I'm sorry,' said Colin. 'I rather wanted to speak to Miss Paston.'

'Don't let that worry you,' said Stockforth. 'Rosita went out some time ago. I think she must have gone into town. At any rate she told me she wouldn't be back until about seven o'clock.'

'That lets you out, young man,' said the colonel. 'Who's the fourth, Harry?'

'I am.'

'Good! There's nothing I should like better than to take your pants down. What do you say, Fairbright?'

It put Colin in an embarrassing position, but in view of Stockforth's statement, he concurred, and he and the colonel followed Stockforth to the bridge-room, where some half-dozen tables were full, and Mrs. Watling was sitting alone, looking bored. But her eyes brightened as she saw Stockforth and his companions.

'Oh, how nice!' she said. 'Shall we cut in each rubber, or stick to the same partners?'

'Stick,' said the colonel. 'I'm out for Stockforth's blood.'

'Suits me,' said Stockforth. 'If Mrs. Watling will put up with me.'

'I should warn you I'm a complete rabbit,' said Colin.

'I seem to have heard that one before,' laughed Stockforth. 'Well, are we all happy?'

The colonel and Mrs. Watling nodded, and the cards were shuffled and cut.

'Stakes?' asked the colonel, glancing at Colin.

'A shilling a hundred and no more,' said Colin.

'A shilling it is, but I'll have a fiver with you on each rubber, Stockforth.'

Stockforth nodded, and the cards were dealt. After that it was ding-dong all the way, with heavy scoring above the line, and the colonel over-calling his hand in his determination to skin Stockforth. But it was Colin who won the rubber, not so much by his play, but by the cards he held.

'The colonel is splendid at bidding on his partner's hand,' said Stockforth.

'Intuition, my lad,' said the happy warrior. 'That's one to me. Deal 'em, Colin.'

The second rubber went much the way of the first, and the colonel was in transports of delight. Colin would have liked to sign off then, but it seemed ungracious after winning two rubbers. So a third was started. It was interrupted by a boy who came along with a plug-in telephone.

'Excuse me, Mr. Stockforth,' he said. 'It's Mr. Grandison on the line, and he wants to speak to you.'

'Damn!' muttered Stockforth, and laid his cards face downwards on the table. 'Hullo!' he said. 'Yes — speaking. Oh, I see. Yes, that's all right. I'll tell Rupert.'

Stockforth gave the instrument to the waiting boy.

'Tell Rupert that Mr. Grandison can't catch the evening train, and that he will arrive at one-fifteen to-morrow. Is that clear?'

'Yes, sir. He's to meet Mr. Grandison at one-fifteen to-morrow.'

'Good! And don't interrupt me any

more. Take messages in future.'

Stockforth made his excuses and picked up his cards again. That third rubber looked as if it would never end, but finally Colin pulled off his 'hat-trick' with a little slam redoubled, at which the colonel looked as if he would burst with glee.

'No credit to you, Colonel,' said Stockforth. 'Your partner held all the cards. I make the score twenty-six hundred. Sorry we had such bad luck, partner.'

Mrs. Watling was at least a good loser, and paid Colin his winnings with a smile. Stockforth handed the colonel three fivers and the odd money with equally good grace.

'I'll get it back,' he said. 'Now I must vanish.'

'Are you going too, Fairbright?' asked the colonel.

'Afraid I must.'

Mrs. Watling had already seized upon two new arrivals, so Colin was able to beat a retreat without more ado. It was now nearly seven o'clock and he went downstairs to see if he could find Rosita. But there he was informed she was still absent, and he had to make up his mind whether he should go home for dinner or stay on. He had a drink in the bar to celebrate his victory, and then decided to stay on. He rang up his home, and then went into the dining-room, where dinner was now being served. While he was waiting to be served he looked round for Simbourne, and finally asked the head-waiter if Simbourne had already dined.

'No, sir,' he said. 'I haven't seen Mr. Simbourne since breakfast. He told me he wouldn't be in to lunch, but he said nothing about dinner. I expect he'll be in later.'

It was the first time that Colin had dined at the place, and he was most agreeably surprised at the choice of food, and the excellent cooking and service. The price charged was utterly inadequate, and it was obvious that he was expected to take wine. This he did, at a cost of forty-five shillings, which went to corroborate his former suspicion that the real cost of the meal was included in the price of liquid refreshment. He had reached the coffee stage when the colonel staggered in and took the seat opposite him.

'Hullo, Fairbright!' he said. 'I lost the next two rubbers. Funny thing I'm such a bad card-holder. Seen Charles?'

'No.'

'Missed him at lunch. He's been queer lately. Quite hit about his father's illness. A bit surprising that.'

'I should have thought it was a natural reaction.'

'But they've never got on together, and it wasn't all Charles's fault. Mother died when Charles was a youngster, and His Lordship is a hard character — too hard for a sensitive fellow like Charles. Wrong sort of handling altogether. Kept the boy short of cash — even short of clothes. It was natural that Charles should sow a few wild oats when he came into the money his mother had left him. Now the old man is on his last legs, and Charles is going to see him to-morrow. Within a week or two, if I'm any judge, he'll be the new Viscount Simbourne. That ought to please him but it doesn't.'

190

'Probably he doesn't like the responsibility of looking after the family escutcheon.'

'That's about it.'

A minute or two later Colin paid the bill, and went again in search of Rosita. But she was nowhere to be found, and so he wandered into the billiards-room and watched a very fierce match between two middle-aged men, whom he had not met before. It was nearly nine o'clock when he was informed that Rosita was in the music-room. Ignoring the notice on the door which intimated that the room was private, he went inside and saw her playing the piano. It was a tremendous piece of music — a transcription by Lizst — and the full-toned piano sent volumes of sound through the large room. Without indicating his presence he sat down and waited for her to finish. Finally it ended with great crashing bars. He clapped his hands and Rosita swung round on the stool.

'Oh!' she gasped. 'I didn't know. But you're trespassing, Colin.'

'I know. But I've been here since before

tea hoping to see you.'

'I'm so sorry. I had to run into town to keep a hair-dressing appointment. It took an awful time, and then I discovered it was nearly seven o'clock. I — I decided to have a meal in the town, instead of waiting half an hour for the next bus.'

His glance went to her hair, which, he noticed, was done in a new style, and which suited her splendidly.

'I like it,' he said.

'I'm sure you wouldn't have noticed it if I hadn't told you.'

'Oh, yes, I should.'

'You're a gallant prevaricator. Men never notice women's hair.'

'But women must hope they do or surely they wouldn't spend so much time and money on it.'

'That's the incurable masculine fallacy. We do it all to please ourselves. But why did you want to see me?'

'In the first place I wanted to take you out to dinner.'

'That was nice of you. But we had better get out of here, before there's any trouble.'

'Who would make trouble?'

'Stockforth wouldn't like it. He hates members coming into the private rooms.'

'Then put on a coat and come into the garden. There's nearly a full moon.'

She hesitated for a moment and then said she would.

'I'll wait for you in the outer hall,' said Colin. 'But don't be long.'

'I won't.'

Colin found his coat and then walked into the entrance hall, where he paced up and down, rehearsing in his mind what he intended saying. He wished he could have seen Rosita earlier, and carried out his programme as planned, reaching the matter at issue by gradual steps, rather than this storming method. But it had to be done, whatever the result might be.

He heard a car draw up outside, and then the door opened and three men entered. To his surprise one of these was in the uniform of a police sergeant, and all of them looked very grim and business-like. One of the men in plain clothes approached the hall porter, and after some inaudible conversation the hall porter hurried away, and returned a few moments later with Stockforth.

'What is it, Inspector?' asked Stockforth of the man who had spoken to the hall porter.

'Have you a gentleman staying here named the Honourable Charles Simbourne?'

'Yes. He is a resident member of the club.'

'When did you last see him?'

'This morning — about half-past nine.'

'Does he own an Alvis car with the registration number GPH 175?'

'He has a car of that make, but I can't swear to the number. Has there been an accident?'

'Yes.'

'Good God! Not serious, I hope?'

'Yes — fatal. The car was found in Lott's Wood, about three miles from here, about half an hour ago. It has been taken to police headquarters, but the body is in an ambulance outside. It will save you some inconvenience if you can identify the body now.'

Stockforth looked pale and terribly

shaken. He took out a handkerchief and mopped his brow. Then he looked appealingly at Colin, who was close by and must have heard the conversation. Colin read what was in his mind and came forward.

'Excuse me, Inspector,' he said. 'I was a friend of Simbourne, and if it's merely a question of identification — '

'You will do equally well, Mr. — ?'

'Colin Fairbright.'

'Thank you, Mr. Fairbright. Please come with me.'

Colin went outside where the ambulance was pulled up. The door was opened and on a stretcher he saw the still form of Charles Simbourne. The face looked like wax and there was nothing to show from what injuries he had died.

'That's Simbourne,' he said.

'That's good enough. Do you know his next-of-kin?'

'He is the elder son of Lord Simbourne, of Lockleys in the county of Westmorland, but I understand his father is seriously ill.'

'Thank you. I want to get the body

away now for medical examination, but shall need to take some evidence here. Please don't leave.'

The inspector spoke to the driver, and the other plain-clothes officer came from the hall and entered the ambulance. The inspector gave him some whispered instructions, and then the ambulance moved away. Colin went back into the entrance hall, and there saw Rosita talking with Stockforth. She looked almost as pallid as Stockforth.

'Mr. Stockforth,' said the inspector. 'I want to take some evidence here. Can I have the use of a private room?'

'Certainly!' said Stockforth. 'I'm sorry — I behaved so badly just now, but I've never seen a corpse — '

'That's all right. There seems no doubt he is the person we believed him to be. We found some letters in his pocket addressed to this club. Now the room.'

Stockforth led him along the passage, the uniformed sergeant following. By this time a number of members had gathered in little groups, and Rosita came to Colin.

'What has happened?' she asked in a whisper. 'I know it's about Charles, but is — is he dead?'

'Yes.'

'An accident?'

'So the inspector said, but I've no idea what sort of accident it was, except that his car figured in it.'

'How terribly tragic! To-morrow he was going to see his sick father. Shall — shall we be wanted to give evidence?'

'Yes. Do sit down. You look so upset.'

Rosita did so, on one of the long upholstered seats, and Colin removed his coat and sat beside her.

'Will — will they want me to give evidence?' she asked.

'I really don't know. It will, I suppose, depend upon the circumstances in which Simbourne met his death. Ah, here comes Stockforth.'

Stockforth was besieged by various people, but he waved his hands and shook his head.

'Dammit!' snapped Colonel Rooke. 'You must know what has happened.'

'Well I don't. Inspector Parsons told

me practically nothing. He is going to take some evidence — '

'Hell of a lot of good that will do — when we are completely in the dark. I knew Charles better than anybody — '

'That's exactly what I told him,' said Stockforth. 'You will probably be the first to be called. Now I must go and telephone G. He'll be horrified.'

The colonel grunted and came and sat down next to Colin.

'Do you know anything, Fairbright?' he asked.

'Practically nothing. I was asked to identify the body because Stockforth didn't like that experience.'

'He wouldn't,' growled the colonel. 'From what I can gather the poor boy's dead.'

Colin nodded, and Rosita gave a little shudder. Then the sergeant came along and asked for the colonel.

'That's me,' said Rooke.

'Inspector Parsons would be obliged if you would answer a few questions, sir,' said the sergeant.

The colonel stood up and then went off

with the sergeant. The low hum of excited conversation restarted immediately and continued for a full quarter of an hour after which the colonel returned. Several persons drew near him, but the colonel shook his head.

'I've been asked not to say anything,' he explained. 'Fairbright, the inspector would like to see you now — in the writing-room.'

Colin asked Rosita to excuse him, and went to the writing-room. He tapped on the door and was asked to come in. When he entered he saw that a large table had been drawn into the centre of the small room, and on the longer side — facing the door — sat the inspector, while the sergeant occupied a chair on the shorter side next to him. The latter had a notebook open in front of him, and a fountain-pen in his hand.

'Do sit down, Mr. Fairbright,' said the inspector, and Colin occupied the vacant chair facing his interrogator.

'Your full name and address, please.'

Colin supplied these and the sergeant wrote in shorthand.

'How long have you been a member of the club?' asked the inspector.

'Only a month.'

'But you knew Charles Simbourne fairly well?'

'Yes.'

'Have you seen him at all to-day?'

'No. The last time I saw him was yesterday evening.'

'Did he tell you what he proposed doing to-day?'

'No. I understood that he proposed visiting his home in a day or two, but he was not very specific about that.'

'Did he appear to you to be quite normal?'

'He was a little disturbed about his father's illness.'

'Was he not given to heavy drinking?'

'Yes, but recently he gave that up. He was perfectly sober last night, and I have not seen him the worse for drink for quite a time.'

'Do you know if he was in possession of an automatic pistol?'

'I have no knowledge of any such thing.'

'Has he at any time, while in your company, threatened to — or hinted at taking his own life?'

'Never.'

'Has he ever expressed, or displayed, any great dissatisfaction with life?'

'At times I found him cynical — but not more than a great many people are at this time.'

'Mr. Fairbright, you needn't answer this question if you don't want to. But would you say that Mr. Simbourne was a person likely to take his own life?'

Colin thought for a moment. His first impulse was to give a flat negative, but he recalled what Simbourne had told him about his proposal to Rosita, and it seemed to him that the question was best left unanswered.

'I don't think I knew him long enough, or well enough, to answer the question,' he said finally.

'I can appreciate that. Was Simbourne popular in the club?'

'Yes, I think he was.'

'Do you know any person at all who bore him any ill-will?'

Colin thought of Grandison, but decided that it would be indiscreet to raise this matter.

'No, I don't,' he said.

'Had he any love affair to your knowledge?'

This was the question which Colin feared. It would have been easy to say 'no,' but the occasion was not one for untruths or evasions. Charles was dead in obviously mysterious circumstances and the need for truth was now paramount.

'I think he loved Miss Paston,' he said.

'Is she a club member?'

'She's an honorary member, and is employed here to organise concerts. She is a brilliant pianist.'

'I see. Did you gain this knowledge from your own observation?'

'No. Simbourne told me himself.'

'When?'

'Yesterday.'

'Was that feeling returned by Miss Paston?'

'No.'

'What makes you think that?'

'Simbourne told me he proposed

marriage, and was turned down.'

The inspector was silent for a few moments, and Colin thought he could see the workings of his mind. He hated this situation, and yet believed that he was right in not attempting to conceal the facts. The sergeant was waiting, pen in hand.

'I don't think I need keep you any longer at the moment, Mr. Fairbright,' said the inspector. 'Thank you for your evidence. But I shall be obliged if you will refrain from discussing it with anyone. Of course you are a free person, but it would not be in the interest of this inquiry if witnesses — '

'I understand,' said Colin.

The inspector turned to the sergeant.

'Show Mr. Fairbright out,' he said. 'And then try to find Miss Paston.'

10

Colin could not help feeling that the sergeant had been sent to get Rosita at that particular moment, to make sure that no conversation passed between him and her, but he was far from taking offence at that precautionary measure. Rosita was still waiting, and she looked nervous when told that the inspector wished to see her.

'I'll wait,' said Colin.

'Yes — please do,' she murmured.

The inspector greeted her with a pleasant smile, and begged her to be seated.

'This is a very unpleasant business, Miss Paston,' he said. 'But I'll try not to keep you very long. What is your full name?'

'Rosita Mary Paston.'

'How long have you known Mr. Simbourne?'

'Just over a month.'

'When did you last see him?'

'At nine o'clock this morning.'

'Did you speak to him?'

'Only to say 'good morning'.'

'And you haven't seen him since?'

'No.'

'Did he appear to be quite normal?'

'I think so.'

'Have you any idea where he has been to-day?'

'None at all.'

'During the time that you have known Mr. Simbourne did he make any sort of advances to you?'

Rosita hesitated.

'I should like you to answer that.'

'Yes,' said Rosita. 'He proposed to me.'

'When was that?'

'Two days ago.'

'What was the upshot?'

'I told him I — I did not love him — in that way.'

'Was he much upset by your answer?'

'No. He took it very well. He said he rather expected that answer — in view of his habits.'

'He meant his intemperance?'

'Yes.'

'Had you any cause at all to believe that he might do something foolish?'

'Oh, no. He made a joke, and said he would probably finish up by marrying a barmaid.'

'Have you ever seen him deeply depressed?'

'Not depressed, but cynical. I don't think his cynicism went very deep — that it was only a pose. At heart he was very kind and charming.'

'Has he ever caused you to suspect he had an enemy?'

'No.'

'No one who might wish to do him some injury?'

Rosita looked perturbed at this question, and the inspector was quick to see it.

'I advise you not to keep anything back,' he said gently but very firmly.

'I was thinking of something which happened some days ago. He — asked me to do him a favour, and handed me a small key with a tag on it. He said it was the key of a small flat in London which he sometimes used, and he asked me to go

206

there in the event of something happening to him, and find a small lacquered box which was hidden in a riding-boot in his wardrobe. I was to take the box to the police without delay.'

The inspector's eyes were now very keen, and the sergeant appeared to be pricking up his ears.

'Did he give you any hint of what this 'something' which might happen to him might be?' he asked.

'No. But he said he had premonitions.'

'Did you take the key?'

'Yes.'

'And agree to do as he asked?'

'At the time — yes. He was so serious and I didn't want to hurt his feelings, and a few days afterwards I gave it back to him.'

'Why?'

'It all seemed so foolish. I told him he was silly to entertain morbid premonitions, and that I had decided to have nothing to do with it.'

'What did he say to that?'

'He said 'Perhaps you're right. I get in that mood sometimes'.'

'But you told me you never saw him depressed.'

'That's true. He was not depressed when he gave me the key — only serious. He was a difficult man to understand, or to describe.'

'Was there an address on the tag attached to the key?'

'Yes.'

'What was the address?'

Rosita thought for a few moments and then shook her head.

'I'm sorry,' she said. 'I can't remember. In fact I hardly glanced at it, because I found it impossible to take the thing seriously.'

'Can't you even remember the name of the street?'

'No.'

'Do try.'

Rosita did try, but again shook her head.

'But it's possible that Mr. Fairbright may remember,' she said.

'Oh, did he see it?'

'Yes. I showed it to him. He agreed with me that it was foolish to take the thing seriously, and suggested I should give it back to Mr. Simbourne when he was in a brighter mood.'

A glance appeared to pass between the inspector and his recording sergeant.

'Mr. Fairbright didn't mention it,' said the inspector. 'The matter would appear to be important, in view of what has happened. If that box exists it may throw much light on this affair. You see, Miss Paston, we have to decide whether Mr. Simbourne committed suicide or not. That box may give us the answer.'

Rosita winced and an unbidden tear welled up in her eye, so that she was compelled to seek her handkerchief. The inspector looked at his notes while she mopped up the tear.

'I know this must be very painful to you,' he said. 'But if it was suicide you have nothing to reproach yourself with. I won't trouble you any more now, but please do try to remember what that address was on the key tag.'

'I'll — try,' she promised.

The sergeant let her out, and then the

inspector took a few paces up and down the room.

'Strange that Fairbright said nothing about that key,' he said. 'He must have realised it was important. Very strange.'

'Any use seeing him again, sir?' asked the sergeant.

'Not at the moment. I'm anxious to get back and hear the medical evidence. At first light I want to examine the site where the car was found. I think we'll pack up now, and take more evidence to-morrow. See if you can find Mr. Stockforth.'

The sergeant went out and came back with Stockforth, who looked as perturbed and worried as ever.

'Did you succeed in getting in touch with Mr. Grandison?' asked the inspector.

'Yes. It was too late for him to catch a train, so he has engaged a hire-car and is coming at once by road.'

'Good. I should like to see him first thing in the morning.'

In the meantime Rosita had rejoined Colin, and the pair went to a quiet part of the club. Colin looked unusually tense, as he was, for everything that afternoon and evening had gone wrong. The thing which had been uppermost in his mind was now snowed under by the tragedy which had taken place. Who could talk of love when such issues were at stake?

'They — they think it was suicide,' said Rosita. 'Oh, Colin — Colin, I feel so miserable.'

'Oh, come — there is no blame attaching to you.'

'No blame perhaps, but I can still be the cause. There's something I must tell you. Charles made love — '

'I know.'

'Who told you?'

'Charles himself.'

'Poor Charles! He seems to have taken too much for granted. I had no idea that — that he felt that way. It's terrible to think — '

'Don't think about it. Declining a man's proposal of marriage is no crime. A million men are turned down every year, and manage to get over it. You look tired, and it's very late. The best thing is to go to bed, and get some sleep.'

'Yes, I will. Oh, Colin, I told the

inspector about that key which Charles gave to me. He seemed very surprised, and very interested. You must have forgotten to tell him.'

'As a matter of fact I did. You told me you gave it back to Charles.'

'Yes, I did. But the inspector wants to know the address that was written on the tag.'

'Did you tell him?'

'I couldn't. I can't remember it. Can you?'

'No, I'm blessed if I can. Of course I see his point. What on earth was that address?'

'Oh, wasn't it somewhere in Knights-bridge?'

'I believe it was. Perhaps it will come by to-morrow. Go now, my dear. I'll come along to-morrow morning.'

'Do. Good night, Colin!'

'Good night!'

Colin watched her go up the stairs and then sought his car, and drove home. His mother was in bed, but Rhoda was waiting up, surprised by his long absence. The moment she saw his face she knew that something important had happened.

'What is it?' she asked. 'You look like a ghost.'

'I've had bad news. Get me a drink, old dear. A strong whisky and soda.'

Rhoda did this and then sat down opposite him.

'Something at the club?' she asked.

'Not actually at the club — but within a few miles. I think I've mentioned Charles Simbourne to you?'

'The son of Lord Simbourne — yes.'

'His dead body was found in his car this evening. Suicide is suspected. I had the horrid task of identifying the body, and I had to stay to give evidence.'

'Oh, Lord! What a dreadful experience. But what happened to make him do that?'

'It's a long and rather confused story, and I've more or less promised not to discuss the matter while the evidence is being taken. Actually there isn't much I could tell anyone with any certainty.'

'I'll bet it's to do with the club. No wonder the place has such a rotten name. There was that other young man too.

Colin, I wish you hadn't got mixed up in it.'

'I'm not mixed up in it. But I mustn't talk about it — yet. In a day or two there is bound to be an inquest, and then it will be everybody's secret. Don't say anything to mother.'

'But she'll certainly want to know why you returned home at close on midnight. She's not been at all happy since she knew you had become a member. I — I suppose Rosita Paston was the reason?'

'Yes.'

'You're in love with her, aren't you?'

'Yes.'

'And she — '

'I don't know. I might have known but for this ghastly happening. There's a lot I don't understand.'

'The death of her father, for example?'

'That was natural enough. He was ill for a long time.'

'So are lots of people who don't die natural deaths. But I won't worry you, darling, with my particular phobia.'

When Colin got to bed he felt about as near to sleeping as when he woke up that morning. His mind would persist in reaching back to the day when he had met Rosita in the train, and had been fascinated by her looks and conversation, and then it would perform a series of endless spirals wherein he seemed to get nowhere at all. The queer business about the key bothered him. Was it simply a morbid obsession based on nothing, or had Charles grounds for his expressed fear? One knew so little about his past, except that he had been a wild character at loggerheads with a stern parent. Of course the suicide theory was the logical one, especially in view of his failure with Rosita. But if it was ultimately proved to be suicide there were other possible causes. He might easily be in debt, despite the fact that he ran a very expensive car. It might be that his failure with Rosita was but the climax to a long series of disappointments and frustrations. But in the meantime Rosita was undoubtedly torturing herself with the belief that she had been chiefly instrumental in bringing about this tragedy.

Only a few miles away the chief object

of his thoughts was no nearer sleep than he was. She had not even attempted to undress, but lay on the bed and walked about at intervals, while the hands of the mantelpiece clock moved round the hours with painful slowness. It was about three o'clock when she heard the sound of a car coming up the drive, and on going to the window she saw the car pull up outside the main entrance and Grandison step out of it. He paid off the driver and hurried up the steps. Rosita moved away from the window and rested in the chair for a few minutes. Then there came a rap on the door.

'Who is it?' she asked.

'Me,' said Grandison's gruff voice. 'I've just got back. Are you up?'

'Yes.'

'I should like to talk to you — and Stockforth — in my apartment. Are you too tired to spare me a few minutes?'

'No. I can't sleep. I'll come now.'

'Good!'

She opened the door and saw Grandison outside.

'Ah!' he said. 'I must know just what

has happened. This is a terrible business. I couldn't believe my ears when Stockforth told me over the telephone. Why should Charles take his own life? It doesn't seem to make sense. But let's get up to my apartment.'

They went to the private lift and were soon inside Grandison's magnificent lounge. Stockforth was already there, clad in a dressing-gown.

'Thank God you're back, chief,' he said. 'This is going to be a bad thing for the club.'

'Why say the obvious?' snapped Grandison. 'What is the exact position? I could scarcely hear you on the telephone, except that you made it clear that Charles was dead. What did he do, and where, and how?'

'I think he shot himself — in his car.'

'You think? Don't you know?'

'No. The police said so little, but they mentioned a pistol, and that seems to indicate suicide.'

'But why should he do that? So far as I know he had no financial trouble, and his father, the Viscount, is at death's door.

Why should a young man commit suicide when he is on the point of inheriting a famous title?'

'I have no idea.'

'Where was he found?'

'In Lott's Wood — in his car.'

'When?'

'About half-past nine, I think.'

'How long had he been dead?'

'The inspector didn't say. Did he tell you, Rosita?'

'No,' replied Rosita.

Grandison turned to her with an expression of sympathy on his great face.

'So they questioned you?'

'Yes.'

'Damned shame! Why should they come here and worry you, just because a fool has taken his life miles away? Harry, do you know anything about this — I mean any reason which might have caused Simbourne to — to act like that?'

'None. The inspector asked me the same question. I told him that Simbourne was very popular here, that his bills were paid regularly, and that the whole thing was a mystery to me. He questioned a number of persons, and then left. But I don't think we have done with him yet.'

Grandison wagged his head, as he invariably did when Stockforth spoke at any length. It was as if Stockforth's method of speaking irritated him. Then he turned to Rosita.

'What sort of questions did he ask you, Rosita?'

'He asked me if I was in love with Charles,' said Rosita.

'In love with Charles?' asked Grandison incredulously. 'Is the man mad?'

'No. I think the matter cropped up when he questioned Mr. Fairbright.'

'But I don't understand.'

'Colin had told him that Charles had proposed to me, and been rejected.'

'But — but that wasn't true — was it?'

'Yes. Charles told Colin himself.'

'Good God! The impudence! I had no idea he harboured such ambitions. I suppose he thought you would fall easily for a prospective title, and a lot of cheap sentiment — '

'Please!' begged Rosita. 'He's dead and I — '

'Sorry, my dear. But you're not to blame in any way. He was always an unpredictable character, as wild as they make 'em. I'll admit I was rather flattered when he came to live here. After all the son of a viscount is a pretty good advertisement on the face of it, but his intemperance was rather disgusting. What I deplore is that you should be dragged into this business. Why on earth did Fairbright have to tell the inspector about that incident?'

'Because he was asked. Colin isn't the sort of person to make untrue statements.'

'But he might have had some regard for you, and for the club.'

'I'm not so sure that he wasn't right,' said Stockforth. 'The police want to be sure that it was suicide, and the coroner's verdict must depend a great deal upon motive. It looks as though they have the motive.'

Grandison waggled his head again.

'Bad for us, all the same,' he said. 'Just when we were doing so well — creating a nice atmosphere with the concerts.

220

Though no one is to blame people will gossip and throw some mud. Anything else, Rosita?'

'They asked me if Charles had any enemies, and I said I knew of none. Then I remembered a key which Charles had given me. It had a label on it, and he said it was the key to a flat which he had in London. He asked me to go there if anything happened to him, and to get a box that was hidden there, and take it to the police at once.'

'What an extraordinary thing to do,' muttered Grandison.

'Yes. I accepted the key at the time, but a few days later I returned it to him, and said I wanted nothing to do with it. The inspector wanted to know where the flat was situated, but I couldn't remember. He asked me to try and remember, because the box might contain evidence that would help the inquiry.'

'Of course,' said Grandison. 'Can't you remember anything of the address?'

'Only that it was somewhere off Knightsbridge. That only came after the inspector had gone, and I was talking to

Colin Fairbright.'

'You mean — he knew about the key?'

'Yes, I told him earlier. But like me he took very little notice of the address on the tag.'

'And he can't remember either?'

'No.'

'What a curious situation! It certainly looks as if Charles had already contemplated taking his life, and probably left a letter in the box giving all his reasons. Perhaps we should look in his room for the key.'

'We can't,' said Stockforth. 'The inspector took away the key of the door.'

'Well, let us hope he finds the key of the flat, and the hidden box,' said Grandison. 'It might do away with the necessity of Rosita attending the inquest.'

'That's true,' agreed Stockforth. 'It's all very regrettable.'

'Ghastly!' said Grandison. 'What about notifying Charles's family?'

'The inspector asked me not to. He said they would deal with the matter direct — in view of His Lordship's serious condition.'

'Very thoughtful,' mused Grandison. 'I think we had better drop the subject until the morning. I wish I had known that Charles kept a pistol. Well, try to get some rest, Rosita. You too, Harry. Good night!'

Rosita and Stockforth went down in the lift, and parted at the bottom. Rosita went to her room, with her head aching badly. But one of Grandison's final remarks rose above the confusion of her thoughts. She remembered that she had failed to take Colin's advice in the matter of her father's pistol, and on reaching her room she opened the bottom drawer of the dressing-chest, and felt for the leather holster in which the automatic had been contained. It was no longer there!

11

During the night there were some developments in the case of Charles Simbourne, some of which sprang from the medical evidence, and the Chief Constable of the area, who had cogent reasons for disliking the set-up at Alton Hall, decided to ask Scotland Yard for assistance. His own people liked this decision none too well, for they liked to solve their own cases in their own way, but when Chief Constable Staverton made decisions it was always better to accept them without argument. Staverton suggested a man he knew personally at the 'Yard' and the suggestion was complied with. By ten o'clock the following morning Inspector Laurance Ogilvie, and Sergeant Harris, stepped out of an aeroplane some miles from the headquarters of the County Constabulary, and were welcomed by Staverton, who was waiting in an official car. They drove straight to Staverton's office, where Staverton introduced both Ogilvie and the sergeant to the inspector who had had temporary charge of the case.

'Now to details,' he said. 'On the face of it this case seems fairly straightforward, but I have certain doubts. Better read Inspector Parsons's report first. It's not quite up to date, but will give you a pretty clear outline.'

Ogilvie took the rather lengthy report, thrust out his long legs, and began to peruse it. He did this with such rapidity that one would have imagined that he could not possibly have taken in the many details. But Staverton knew his man, and when finally Ogilvie gave a little grunt and raised his eyes from the last sheet Staverton had no doubt that everything in the four closely-typed sheets were registered on that big brain behind the wide brows.

'That all seems very clear,' he said. 'Now bring me up to date.'

'It means going back a little. A year ago there was another suicide — actually in the grounds of Alton. The victim was a young R.A.F. pilot — a man named Devlin. He, too, shot himself with an automatic. But in his case there was evidence of mental trouble. He had been shot down over enemy territory, and spent some years in a prisoner of war camp. For over a year after his release he was in hospital and a mental home. Then he came to live at Alton. There is evidence that he gambled heavily, and lost a lot of money. But the pistol was his own, and the medical evidence was strongly in favour of suicide. Position of wound, scorching around the bullet-hole in the coat, all corroborated the medical finding. At the inquest the obvious verdict was returned, and the case closed. Just over a month ago another man died at Alton. He was fairly old, and had been sick for a long time. His name was Paston. Just before his death he wired his daughter who was living alone in Switzerland. She came but was unable to speak to her father, who died a few hours after her arrival. In this case the doctor in attendance gave a perfectly clear certificate of death from natural causes, and the daughter, who had considerable musical ability was induced by Grandison to stay on, and organise some concerts. She is still there. But, of course, she is mentioned in the report. I am mentioning this event because Paston, who was believed to be a wealthy man, died in debt. But it is in evidence that when he came to live at Alton he possessed tens of thousands of pounds. We have no doubt where that money went.'

'To the club?'

'Yes — or to certain members of it. I have been looking into matters there — checking up on Grandison and the general running of the place. I have tried to catch Grandison out in breaches of the law but he's very clever. He operates in the black market in a big way, but is much too wise to touch rationed goods. But this is by the way. Now to Simbourne. The medical evidence is that he died from a single gunshot wound between five o'clock and seven o'clock last evening. His body was found in the back seat of his saloon car, in Lott's Wood — just off the road. The place is three miles from Alton, and offers good cover for a car. As a result the car was not discovered until nine-thirty. The pistol lay on the floor at his feet. It is a nine millimetre Luger. There were five live rounds left in the magazine.'

'Has it been examined for finger-prints?'

'Yes, it carries finger-prints of Simbourne. The bullet was taken from the body by the county pathologist, and its direction charted. Here arises an interesting point. The pathologist demonstrated to my satisfaction that the wound could only have been inflicted by the weapon being held in the left hand, yet — and this is the important point — the finger-prints were of the *right* hand.'

Ogilvie saw at once the significance of this. It seemed to indicate that Simbourne had been shot by some other person, who, later had wrapped the victim's hand round the butt of the weapon.

'Any sign of scorching?' he asked.

'Yes. Parsons, hand me that suitcase.'

From the suitcase the Chief Constable produced several garments all of which bore a bullet-hole, and dried blood. Ogilvie was chiefly interested in the tweed overcoat, which showed scorching round the hole made by the bullet.

'Consistent with a self-inflicted wound,' he said. 'But I agree that the position is suspicious, but the body itself should give a much more definite picture.'

'It does.'

There was a rap on the door, and a man from the police laboratory entered, with the pistol and other oddments. One of these was an almost perfect nickel-covered bullet.

'We've finished with the weapon, sir,' he said. 'I have checked the bullet with the pistol grooving, and am satisfied that it was fired from this weapon.'

'Thank you, Watson.'

The pistol, bullet and loose magazine were passed over to Ogilvie.

'Very popular killers,' he ruminated. 'I presume you've taken the serial number?'

'Oh, yes, but I'm rather afraid that isn't going to help. So many of these things are war souvenirs, and are unlicenced. But I have taken the usual steps. This one dates back to the first world war.'

Ogilvie nodded and deftly slipped the five live cartridges from the slim magazine.

'You might take the number, Harris,' he said to the sergeant. 'It is 576389.'

Harris used his note-book and Ogilvie handed the exhibit back to the Chief Constable.

'Unless you have anything more to tell me I should like to see the body,' he said. 'Then the dead man's car.'

'There's the business of the key which Simbourne gave to Miss Paston, and which she returned to him. Inspector Parsons had no time to examine Simbourne's room at the club, so he locked it up and brought away the key of the door. You'd better have that now.'

Parsons handed over the key, and then the Chief Constable and Ogilvie and the sergeant walked to the mortuary, which was only a few minutes away. Here they found the pathologist, still fussing round the corpse.

'Morning, Inspector!' he said to Ogilvie, whom he knew by sight. 'I've taken a few more checks and am satisfied that my estimate as to time of death is correct. Want to see the wound?'

'Please.'

The covering was removed from the lower part of the body, and Ogilvie examined the blue puncture to the left of the heart. The pathologist then gave him a sheet of paper on which he had made a drawing showing the direction of the wound, and Ogilvie was very quickly convinced that he was right in his conclusions.

'It was murder,' he said quietly.

'That's what I thought,' said the Chief Constable. 'I'm rather glad you're here, Ogilvie, because I have an idea it isn't going to be easy to nail down the murderer. Shall we see the car now.'

They went back to headquarters and found the car inside a locked garage. Ogilvie was assured that nothing had been taken from the vehicle except the corpse. It was a very fine car, with excellent bodywork and leather upholstery, and on the back seat, where the body had been found there was a little blood. In the other corner was a luxurious car rug, with the dead man's initials embroidered on it.

Ogilvie then examined the two bucket seats in front, but appeared to find nothing which interested him. He lifted an ash-tray from the dashboard, and found in it four cigarette-ends. Three of these were fairly clean at the unburnt ends, but the fourth bore traces of lipstick. He handed them all to Sergeant Harris, who placed them in a small box.

'Now we'll have everything out of the car,' he said.

Harris removed the cushions one by one, and then detached the carpet from the floor. In the door-pockets there were a number of oddments, including a few road maps, the car registration book, and some old car licences.

'All clear now, sir,' said Harris.

Ogilvie entered the car, and looked in every corner. Then he pushed forward one of the bucket seats, and found what he had expected to find. It was a small brass cartridge-case.

'The ejected cartridge-case,' he said.

'That would appear to support the suicide theory,' said Harris.

'No. It merely suggests he was shot inside the car. Even that supposition may be untrue, for presuming he was shot by someone else — a person cunning enough to wrap his dead fingers round the butt of the weapon, we should credit that person with enough sense to realise that for the evidence to accord with suicide the ejected cartridge-case must be found in the car.'

The Chief Constable nodded his head.

'What I don't quite understand is why his body was in the back seat,' he ruminated. 'If he was shot while in the car you would imagine he would be at the driving-wheel. If out of the car you would expect the murderer to put him back at the driving-wheel.'

Ogilvie shook his head. There seemed to be nothing in the argument, since a man determined to take his own life might easily have preferred the greater space available in the rear part of the car. There was too the possibility that Simbourne had left the driving-seat to sit in comfort with someone else — someone who left lipstick on the butt of a cigarette. But at the moment he did not feel like theorising. He examined the carpet and the rubber on the running-boards of the car, and then raised the two front windows which were in the 'down' position. Both were perfectly clean, and free of finger-prints.

'You can put everything back, Harris,' he said. 'Then we'll go to the site, and have a look round there.'

They were at the place where the car had been found half an hour later. The tracks where the car had been driven off the road were quite clear on the damp ground up to the spot where it had finally stopped, and it was easy to see where it had been reversed and driven away by the police.

'The few footprints were made by my men,' explained the Chief Constable. I am assured by the man who found the car, and reported the matter that there was not a sign of a footprint anywhere near the car. But quite obviously anybody could have got away by choosing his ground on the drier patches.

Ogilvie and Harris spent some time in a search round about the site, but they found nothing that helped the inquiry in the least, and finally they gave it up and were driven back to police headquarters. Here there was another short discussion, after which a car was put at Ogilvie's disposal, and he and Sergeant Harris were driven to Alton Hall, accompanied by the local inspector.

12

Colin, after an almost sleepless night, went down to breakfast early the next morning. Rhoda was not down, but his mother was.

'Good morning, Colin,' she said. 'I scarcely expected you up so early, after your late night.'

'Sorry, mother. I — I was detained.'

'But it must have been nearly midnight?'

'Yes.'

'Not Rosita by any chance?'

'What made you say that?'

'She rang up a little while ago. I told her you were not up, and she asked me to ask you to telephone her as soon as possible. I thought she seemed rather anxious. But perhaps that was my imagination.'

Colin was silent for a few moments. Then he realised how foolish it was to leave matters at that pass when, very soon, everyone in the neighbourhood must know the truth.

'You weren't mistaken, mother,' he said. 'Last night a dreadful thing happened. You've heard me mention Charles Simbourne? They found his dead body in his car, not very far from Alton. The police came and I had to give evidence — also Rosita.'

Mrs. Fairbright almost dropped the plates she was carrying.

'Oh, Colin. How terrible! Did — did he do something — to himself?'

'It looks rather like it.'

'But why should they question you — and Rosita?'

'To find out if we knew why he did it. But we weren't the only ones, and I expect that before they are finished almost everyone at the club will be questioned.'

'What a shocking state of affairs! Two suicides in one year. Oh, Colin, I wish you had never had anything to do with the club.'

'I don't,' said Colin. 'I may be of some service to Rosita — at least some comfort.'

'But she can know nothing about it. She told me that all she did was organise the concerts.'

'That's true, but she could not help coming into contact with Simbourne, and he — he got very fond of her.'

'I see.'

'You don't — quite, mother. But it means that her name will be associated with this —'

The telephone-bell rang again, and Colin hurried to the receiver. On lifting it he heard Rosita's voice at the other end.

'Oh, Colin,' she said. 'Are you coming here this morning?'

'Yes.'

'Come soon, please. I've made a most unpleasant discovery.'

'What is it?'

'That pistol which my father left with his other personal things — I forgot to take it to the police as you suggested.'

'That was foolish of you, but you can still do it.'

'I can't. It isn't here any longer.'

'What!'

'I've searched everywhere. Somebody

must have taken it.'

Colin drew in his breath hard.

'Are you there, Colin?'

'Yes — yes. What you say is incredible, and yet — I'll come along at once.'

'Thank you. Meet me by the Grecian urn in the garden.'

'I suppose you haven't told anyone?'

'Not yet.'

'Well don't until I see you.'

Mrs. Fairbright entered the dining-room with a tray full of plates and cutlery.

'Was that Rosita?' she asked.

'Yes. I have to hurry to Alton. Shan't have any time for breakfast.'

'Colin!' she protested.

'Sorry mother, but the matter is urgent.'

'It can't be so urgent that you have to starve yourself. Oh, here's Rhoda. Rhoda talk to him. He wants to rush off to Alton without any breakfast on a cold morning. Make him wait. I'll have something ready in ten minutes.'

Rhoda closed the door after her mother, and looked at Colin.

'Does she know?' she asked.

'Yes. She told me that Rosita had rung up and then I told her the truth.'

'I'm glad. But why must you rush off to Alton?'

'Something quite unexpected has happened.'

'Please — please stay and have some breakfast. Rosita may be upset, but so is mother. She's been worrying about your associations with that beastly club ever since she knew you had joined it. Mother pretended that I was prejudiced, but I think she knew all the time that it was the resort of gamblers and drunkards. Don't make her pay for your impulsiveness. Sorry if I have to hurt your feelings, brother.'

'You haven't,' said Colin. 'But I'll wait.'

'Good!'

It was half an hour later that Colin took the car and drove swiftly to Alton Hall. He drove the car past the main entrance and finally parked it round by the garages. Then he hurried to the rendezvous, where he found Rosita, walking up and down to keep herself warm.

'Sorry to keep you waiting,' he said.

'That's all right. It's too bad to worry you about all this.'

'I'm glad you did. What you told me is astonishing, to put it mildly. You're quite sure the pistol is gone?'

'Absolutely.'

'Have you seen it since you spoke to me about it?'

'No. I had so much on my mind that I forgot every word about it.'

'What persons knew it existed?'

'No one so far as I know.'

'Could Simbourne possibly have known?'

'Not unless he knew my father had it.'

'He was quite friendly with your father, wasn't he?'

'Oh, yes. Colin, do you think he — he took the pistol and then — then used it?'

'It looks rather like that. But if someone else took it — '

He stopped and Rosita stared into his eyes.

'Go on,' she said.

'No. It's too grim.'

'But — he had that premonition. Perhaps it wasn't merely a premonition but a fear that his life was in danger.'

'We're leaping ahead too fast. Even if the pistol was stolen, it doesn't follow that it is the same weapon which killed Charles. The two things may not be related at all. It's for the police to sort things out.'

'You mean I must tell them?'

'Without a doubt. They are almost certain to come here again this morning. If there's any delay about that, telephone the inspector and tell him.'

'I will. Oh, why didn't I remember to do as you told me?'

'Don't worry,' he begged. 'As things appear at the moment I can't think it will make much difference. Charles could have got the pistol presuming he knew it was there. You can never guarantee that your door is locked all the time, with the cleaners going in at all times. Do you usually leave your key at the desk?'

'Not always. Sometimes I have left it in the door. I'm rather careless about such things. Oh, I forgot to tell you, Grandison is back. When he heard the news over the telephone he hired a car and arrived early this morning.'

'What does he think about it?'

'He's terribly upset. Thinks it will do the club a lot of harm.'

'There's no doubt about that. Two suicides in one year are a bit too much.'

Rosita stared at him in surprise.

'Two?' she ejaculated.

'Didn't you know?'

'No.'

'There was another man who shot himself in the garden just on a year ago.'

'But you didn't tell me.'

'How could I? You had just taken a job here. I didn't want to cast a gloom over the place.'

'And yet you joined the club?'

'Yes. I had my reasons.'

'What reasons?' she asked, in a tone which compelled an answer.

'You,' he said. 'I was seeing too little of you, and I wanted to see more. You came here knowing practically nothing about this place and — '

He stopped suddenly as he became aware of footsteps behind them, and then he turned his head to see the thick-set figure of Grandison, hatless and breath-less.

'Good morning!' grunted Grandison. 'Sorry to interrupt, but I must speak to Rosita.'

Colin stood his ground, resenting the intrusion, and making his resentment clear.

'What is it, Mr. Grandison?' asked Rosita.

'About my business in London yester-day, in reference to the concerts. I have to make a decision this morning and it's rather necessary that I discuss the matter with you.'

'Will ten minutes' time do?'

'Yes — yes, of course. In my apartment. Well, Mr. Fairbright, this is a pretty bad state of affairs, isn't it? I understand they dragged you into the inquiry.'

'I was asked to give evidence, but that's natural enough in the circumstances.'

'I suppose so. But if everyone who knew Charles is to be questioned the police will be here for days. Unpleasant as the facts are they seem to be pretty clear — '

'How can any of us say that — knowing practically nothing about the circumstances. Suppose the police have cause to believe it wasn't suicide?'

'You can't be serious.'

'Why not?'

'Because Charles wasn't the sort of man anyone would want to murder. He was friendly with everybody.'

'Was he? I'm not so sure.'

'I really don't follow you. I understand that he was found in his own car with the pistol at his feet, and the police are inquiring about the state of his health. We know — I think — why he took that crazy step. The fact is he was a damned bad loser.'

'At cards?'

'No. At love. See you in ten minutes, Rosita.'

He marched off with his big head projected forward and was soon lost amid the plants and shrubs.

'You — you spoke as if you really thought there — there was a doubt,' said Rosita.

'Well, he seemed so cocksure. It was as

if he were gloating over the fact that Charles had lost the game of love, as he calls it. Oh, my dear I'm sorry. But I simply can't stand him.'

'Do you really try, Colin?' she asked. 'He's doing his best for this place. The concerts were his idea, and he works as hard as I do to make them a success. He hates the gambling which takes place here, and also the heavy drinking. If he's a little bitter about poor Charles it's because of the effect of this tragedy. This morning he told me that he believed the police would publicise this sorry affair to the utmost, with a view to having an excuse to cancel the club licence.'

'It might be a good thing if they did,' blurted Colin, and then regretted it, for Rosita's eyes flashed as if it were a personal attack upon her. She made a hurried excuse and strode off, leaving Colin anxious and ill at ease.

He went into the club and found the place exceptionally lively. People who seldom came downstairs until half the morning was over were as busy as bees collecting the latest bits of news — or rather gossip, for there was no news. A newspaper reporter, with no authority at all to enter the club premises, accompanied by a Press photographer, was doing his best to get the 'lowdown' from the hall porter, but was most rudely interrupted by Grandison, who had come into the vestibule for some purpose.

'What the hell is this?' demanded Grandison, pointing to the huge camera. 'Don't you dare take photographs here.'

The reporter thereupon introduced himself, by handing Grandison a small card. Grandison gave one look at it and then tore it to pieces.

'I'll give you just one minute to get out of here,' he said.

'But, sir — '

'One minute, and if you are not gone I'll throw you out personally?'

He looked so capable of carrying out this threat that the reporter shrugged his shoulders and, with a jerk of his head at his companion, made his way out.

Colin avoided the gossiping groups, and made his way to the dressing-room where he kept a bag of golf clubs. He took out a mashie and a couple of balls, and went out to the golf course where he killed time by practicing approach shots. As he played he cogitated over Rosita's warm defence of Grandison. In her eyes, apparently, he could do no wrong, and any criticism of him, even by her nearest friends, was resented. Now he knew that Charles's recent warning was well-founded. Here was Grandison set upon winning the high regard of the daughter of the man, whose friend he professed to count himself, but whom he had almost certainly ruined. How well he was succeeding was painfully obvious. In view of his unattractive physical attributes this was amazing. But Colin thought he saw the means he employed — subtle flattery, the tributes to her undoubted musical gift, the promise of great opportunity under his championship, his personal protection from any undesirable approaches from admiring club members, the pretence that he hated the way of life of the curious collection of persons out of whom he derived large profits. No doubt it was all beautifully done at moments when he and Rosita were alone. No doubt he never for one moment caused her to believe that his motives were not absolutely altrusitic — all sacrifices made before the altar of true Art.

He found himself hitting the little ball savagely, and over-running the green by dozens of yards. One ball he sliced away into a copse, and stood cursing it, until he pulled himself together and regained control. He was on the ninth green, pocketing his remaining ball, when he saw a car arrive at the portico and three men emerge from it.

'The police,' he muttered, and made his way back to the house where he put away the mashie and ball, and tidied himself. The colonel ambled in as he was washing his hands.

'Hullo, Colin!' he said. 'Here for the second act? Things have been happening.'

'What do you mean?'

'Scotland Yard is taking a hand.'

'How do you know?'

'They're here. A shrewd-looking chap named Ogilvie is in charge. Mighty quick work that.'

'Very. But that can only mean one thing.'

'You mean that they suspect dirty work?'

'Well, would they call in Scotland Yard in a pretty obvious case of suicide?'

'Shouldn't think so. By jove, this is going to cause a stir. But I wonder what they've found out.'

'Whatever it is they're not likely to tell us.'

'Grandison barged in in his rhinoceros fashion. Wanted to give his evidence straight away, but was nicely snubbed, and told he would be called when required. They've gone to the same room as last night, and Rosita is the first witness. The new man — Ogilvie — asked everyone to be on hand, so it looks as if he means business.'

While they were talking Rosita found herself on the mat for the second time. The man who now faced her was very different from the last. His personality was enormous, despite his comparative youth. Yet the wide, cold, intelligent eyes could be kindly when he smiled.

'I called you first, Miss Paston,' he said. 'Because a message was brought to me at another place. I understand that a pistol which was in your possession has vanished.'

'Yes,' replied Rosita. 'It was with my father's effects. I meant to hand it over to the police, but in the worry of the funeral and — and other things — I forgot. Late last night I discovered that it was no longer where I had left it.'

'Didn't you think about the pistol when you gave evidence yesterday?'

'No. I was so nervous at the time.'

Ogilvie nodded and opened a small case, from which he took an automatic Luger pistol.

'Was the weapon like that?' he asked.

Rosita looked at the pistol as it lay on the table.

'Pick it up,' he said. 'Don't be afraid. It isn't loaded. Was the pistol left by your father like that?'

'Yes. But it was in a leather holster.'

'Is the holster also missing?'

'Yes.'

'When did you last see the pistol?'

'About a fortnight ago.'

'Where did you keep it?'

'In the bottom drawer of my dressing-chest.'

'Was the drawer locked?'

'No.'

'Miss Paston, did Charles Simbourne ever enter that room?'

'Never — to my knowledge.'

'Did he know you had that weapon?'

'No. At least I didn't tell him.'

'Did anyone else know?'

'Yes. I told Mr. Fairbright, and he advised me to take it to the police.'

'I do not want to go over the former evidence again. I presume there is nothing in it which you wish to withdraw?'

'No.'

'What did you do yesterday say from noon onwards. Try to give me the details.'

Rosita told him of her visit to the hairdressers, and then of her decision to stay in the town and have dinner there. Sergeant Harris took the times, the name of the hairdresser, and also the name of the restaurant, and the starting time of the bus which she had finally caught home.

'Oh, one thing more,' said Ogilvie. 'When you had the pistol did you look inside the magazine?'

'I didn't look anywhere. I hate fire-arms.'

'Quite right,' said Ogilvie, with a smile. 'And you never saw Simbourne after you said good morning to him yesterday?'

'No.'

'Nor his car?'

'No.'

'That is all at the moment. No, there's still a point. It's about that key which Simbourne gave to you — have you remembered the address that was on the tag?'

'Not the full address, but I'm sure it was some street off Knightsbridge.'

'That may help, in the event of our failing to find the key in Mr. Simbourne's room. It was certainly not on his person. Thank you, Miss Paston.'

Rosita stood up and left the room. The sergeant then read back her evidence to Ogilvie, and Ogilvie nodded.

'Before we resume taking evidence I want to examine Simbourne's room. The key may well be there, also other evidence which may help the case. Better come now.'

They opened up the dead man's bedroom, and found it very tidy. It was one of the best rooms, and Ogilvie stopped for a few moments to admire the view over the grounds. Then they got to work on the drawers, and suitcases, also coats with pockets in the wardrobe. But the key with the tag on it never came to light, and such documents as they found did not promise to throw any light on the tragedy. But a number of letters were taken away for careful reading.

'Question — where is that key?' asked Ogilvie. 'Harris, get on to Simbourne's home. It is possible they have sent letters to this alleged flat, and may know its whereabouts. I'll speak to them when they are on the line.'

The telephone call was soon proved to be fruitless. It was not known there that Charles Simbourne had a flat in London. His father, who might possibly have known, was too ill to be questioned about the matter — in fact unconscious.

'Well, we must adopt other means,' said Ogilvie. 'I want Miss Paston's statements about her movements checked. Now we'll take some more evidence. Yes, I think we'll see Mr. Grandison.'

13

Grandison entered the room still smarting under the rebuff which he had
recently suffered at Ogilvie's hands. He
was not used to that sort of thing,
especially from a man years younger than
himself. The chair creaked as he put his
heavy body into it, and he sat with his
great hands on the table, head forward, as
if sizing up the man opposite. To his
surprise Ogilvie was now adopting an
attitude of extreme civility.

'I'm sorry to have kept you waiting,
Mr. Grandison,' said Ogilvie. 'But I had
first to see Miss Paston on an important
point which has arisen, and then to
examine Mr. Simbourne's bedroom. I
hope I shan't keep you long. I understand
you were in London yesterday, and
unable to give evidence.

'That's true. My partner telephoned
me, and as there was no convenient train
I engaged a hire-car and arrived here very

early this morning.'

'When did you last see Charles Simbourne?'

'The night before last. I did not see him yesterday morning, as I caught the early morning train to London.'

'How long had Simbourne been staying here?'

'Just over three months.'

'Did you think it unusual that a young man — the elder son of a viscount — should live in this kind of club?'

'What do you mean by 'this kind of club'?' asked Grandison.

'I mean the kind of club that is chiefly devoted to the playing of card games.'

'But it isn't. We have every kind of entertainment here. Our own golf course — '

'Yes — yes, but my information is that the club is chiefly used by card-players. Let us leave that for the moment. Did you know Simbourne very well, personally?'

'Yes.'

'Would you say that he was the sort of man who, under some emotional strain might take his own life?'

'In certain circumstances — yes.'

'What circumstances?'

'Frustration, or deep disappointment.'

'Did you know that he was in love with Miss Paston — and that he had proposed to her and been rejected?'

'I didn't know until Miss Paston told me this morning. But I had observed that he was paying her a lot of attention.'

'Did you think he might seriously offer her marriage?'

'No. I thought his social position and hers were too far apart. I was amazed when Miss Paston told me.'

'Do you think she was telling the truth?'

'Yes. She was deeply distressed, and blaming herself for this dreadful tragedy.'

'So you believe that Simbourne killed himself because he was rejected?'

'I do. It's the only thing that makes sense. I know of no other reason why he should do it. He has a very comfortable income from his dead mother's estate, and before very long he must have inherited the family estate, with the title. He was a brave man — a V.C. in the war

— but he was passionate by nature, and a heavy drinker.'

'Did you know him before he joined the club and came to live here?'

'No. He wrote to say he would like to become a member.'

'From what address did he write?'

'His home up north.'

'Had he any London address to your knowledge?'

'No.'

'Are you aware that he told Miss Paston he had a flat in London, and that he gave her a key which he said was the key of that flat?'

'Yes. She told me that, but I know of no such flat.'

'Miss Paston probably told you that Simbourne had asked her to go to the flat and take a box from it, which she was to hand over to the police in certain eventualities?'

'She did.'

'What do you think about that?'

'I don't know what to think. Perhaps all along he had that morbid idea of suicide in his mind, and that Rosita's rejection of him caused him to lose control of himself. But why he should have a secret flat and a secret box I can't imagine.'

'It might be that Miss Paston's rejection of his offer of marriage had nothing at all to do with his death.'

Grandison thought for a moment.

'It might be,' he agreed. 'There could be other reasons — such as some incurable disease.'

'The medical evidence does not bear that out, nor does Miss Paston's evidence. According to her Simbourne accepted her rejection quite calmly. Afterwards he goes and tells Mr. Fairbright that he has been turned down. Does that sound like a man who is contemplating taking his own life?'

'I don't quite follow you,' said Grandison. 'Are you trying to make out that he didn't kill himself?'

'That is exactly what I am trying to do.'

'But that would make it — murder!'

'Yes,' said Ogilvie quietly. 'Nothing less.'

'Good God! It can't be as bad as that.'

'I think it can,' Ogilvie turned to the

sergeant. 'Harris hand me Exhibit A.'

Harris opened the suitcase and produced the automatic.

'This is the weapon which killed Simbourne,' said Ogilvie. 'Have you ever seen such a weapon on these premises?'

'No.'

'Are you not aware that Miss Paston's father, who died here, left such a weapon among his effects?'

'I certainly am not.'

'Well, he did, and that weapon was stolen during the past fortnight from Miss Paston's room.'

Grandison pushed his hand through his bushy hair. Then he seemed to have an inspiration.

'That's it,' he said. 'I saw Simbourne at the door of Rosita's room two days ago. He looked as if he were coming away from it. When he saw me he hurried away. He must have known about the pistol and have gone there.'

'Miss Paston has stated that he didn't know.'

'That is only her belief. He was friendly with her father, and Paston may have

261

shown him the pistol at some time. Doesn't it all fit in with suicide?'

'It does not,' said Ogilvie. 'Because I have evidence to the contrary, whether or not this pistol is the one that was stolen.'

'What evidence?' blurted Grandison.

But Ogilvie had not the slightest intention of divulging all he knew, and he merely shook his head.

'Is it your contention that someone stole that pistol from this house, and shot Simbourne with it?' asked Grandison.

'Isn't that a reasonable deduction?'

'No. It's preposterous. It — it is tantamount to saying that we are harbouring a murderer.'

'You find that incredible?'

'Yes. Suicide is one thing. That may happen anywhere — '

'It seems to me equally incredible that it should happen twice here,' put in Ogilvie. 'And within one year too.'

Grandison's heavy brow became corrugated into hard ridges, and the big hands closed until the knuckles grew white.

'I take exception to that remark,' he growled thickly. 'A clear verdict of suicide was returned by the coroner. The poor fellow was a mental case. I can't help thinking that great prejudice is being shown. Next you will be telling me that that other man was deliberately shot by the same murderer who inhabits this house.'

Ogilvie was completely unmoved by Grandison's passionate protest. He turned over some papers.

'Let us confine ourselves to the present,' he said. 'You say you left here yesterday morning on the early train. Tell me the time of your arrival in London, and what you did throughout the day until you hired the car and was driven back here.'

'What the hell are you getting at?' snarled Grandison.

'I hope I am getting towards the solution of this affair,' replied Ogilvie. 'Why should you object to telling me what you did yesterday when the cause is the cause of justice?'

'I'm not objecting,' roared Grandison.

'Then I beg your pardon.'

Grandison bit his lip in his vexation, for

in his normal experience he usually managed to get the best of an argument by bull-rush tactics, but a vastly different technique was required with a man like Ogilvie, who never in any circumstances lost control of himself, and who invariably weighed every word before he uttered it. He was now waiting for Grandison, calm and perfectly immobile.

Grandison started with his arrival in London, and told of his first appointment with a concert agency, and the lunch which followed. He had a similar programme for the afternoon, and this was followed by dinner and the attendance of a concert at which was a vocalist he was thinking of engaging for a series of concerts at Alton. He gave times and names, and finally finished up with the receipt of Stockforth's message, and the subsequent hire of a fast car to get him to Alton quickly. When he had finished Ogilvie had it read back to him.

'Is that correct?' he asked.

'Yes,' replied Grandison. 'Anything more?'

'No. That's all for the moment — thank you.'

Ogilvie was only now getting into his stride. One after another the witnesses came in, and some of them were dismissed after a few questions. But it gave Ogilvie a chance to have a good look at everyone, including the servants. One of these — the chauffeur and garage attendant — was able to add a little to Ogilvie's knowledge of events. He gave his name as Rupert Zanfeld, and said he was a Balt and a displaced person, who had been permitted to take his present job. He was in the habit of washing and cleaning Simbourne's car, and on the day before the tragedy Simbourne had asked him to give the car a wash and polish as he was going on a trip the next morning.

'Did you do that?' asked Ogilvie.

'Yes, sir,' said Rupert in his rich accent.

'Did you clean out the ash-trays on the car?'

'Yes, sir — everything.'

'At what time did Mr. Simbourne leave the next morning?'

'At half-past nine.'

'Had you any idea where he was going?'

'I think he was going to Manchester, because I saw a map of the Manchester district on the seat, and there was a slip of paper on which some of the towns in between were marked. When I had finished cleaning the car I put the map and slip of paper on the driving-seat where I had found them.'

'You never saw him again?'

'No, sir.'

Sergeant Harris knew why Ogilvie had asked about the emptying of the ash-trays. There was still that cigarette-end with the lipstick on it to be explained. It suggested a woman. But what woman?

All this time Colin had been hanging about, waiting to be called and to find out what was happening. When Rosita emerged she looked pale and anxious, and Colin drew her away for a few minutes.

'Was it a fresh inspector?' he asked.

'Yes. I think his name is Ogilvie, and that he's from Scotland Yard.'

'I heard that too. Did you telephone about the missing pistol?'

'Yes. He had got the message, and

266

asked me all about it. He showed me a pistol and asked me if it was like the one which my father left.'

'And was it?'

'Yes — exactly.'

'Then it means that they suspect that pistol. Rosita, could Charles possibly have taken the pistol?'

'I don't know. I'm so — so worried. I was asked what — what I did yesterday — questioned me as if they didn't believe it was suicide. I believe they think that I — I might — '

'Nonsense!'

'Oh, but it isn't. They asked me about that key. I told them I couldn't remember the address on the tag, except that the last line was Knightsbridge.'

'I can't either. But that key may well be in Charles's room. Why the devil don't they go and look?'

Almost as he spoke the two officers came out of the writing-room and went up the stairs. Then there was a delay, and Grandison came snooping round. He shot Rosita a glance, and then Rosita discovered she had a bad headache, and wanted to lie down.

Later, when the questioning was resumed, Colin overheard remarks from various witnesses which left no doubt in his mind that the whole aspect of the case had altered. This highly experienced sleuth from Scotland Yard was no longer concentrating on the dead man's personality but on the movements of persons between certain hours. It could only mean one thing, and that horrid thing was murder.

At last his turn came, and he found himself again in that chair facing Ogilvie. The first question was about the key with the address on it, and he had to admit that he was still unable to remember the full address.

'That's a pity,' said Ogilvie. 'I understand that you were on fairly intimate terms with Simbourne?'

'Yes.'

'What is your opinion about this matter, Mr. Fairbright? Do you believe that Simbourne shot himself because he was rejected by Miss Paston?'

'I don't know.'

'Have you any reason at all for that doubt?'

'Yes.'

'What is that reason?'

'When Simbourne told me that he had proposed marriage to Miss Paston he was perfectly calm. He showed no sign of bitter disappointment, and even admitted that he had expected to be turned down.'

It was clear that Ogilvie considered this remark as important for he waited a moment while the sergeant wrote the shorthand version.

'Why should Simbourne tell you of his failure?' he asked. 'It isn't the sort of thing that a rejected lover likes to talk about — so soon after the event.'

'I think he told me because he knew I was very fond of Rosita. He advised me to — to try where he had failed.'

'And have you?'

Colin shook his head and Ogilvie referred to Colin's former evidence and to some other notes which he had.

'You haven't been a member of the club for long,' he said. 'Was Miss Paston the chief attraction? That's a very personal question, but it is not entirely irrelevant. You need not answer it if you would rather not.'

'I've no objection. Miss Paston was the only attraction. Her father died here, in poverty. I knew nothing about the club then, but later I heard a lot of gossip, and I became a little concerned about her welfare.'

'Did the gossip concern another young man who took his own life here?'

'Yes. But that wasn't all. Right or wrong I got the impression that her father was swindled out of his money. I advised Miss Paston to put her father's affairs in the hands of my family solicitor — Mr. Ryburn. He discovered huge drawings of cash from the bank, with no clues as to where it finally went. The matter had to be dropped because there was no proof of my suspicions.'

'And then you joined the club?'

'Yes. It was Simbourne who proposed me, and my name went through while Grandison was away, otherwise I think he would have blackballed me.'

'Why should he do that?'

'I don't know. I want to be fair. It was Simbourne who dropped that hint. He may have been prejudiced.'

'Then he didn't like Mr. Grandison?'

'He did not. But I think he was successful in concealing that from Grandison.'

'Did he show an equal dislike for Mr. Stockforth, who appears to be Grandison's partner in this enterprise?'

'He seldom mentioned Stockforth.'

'It is in evidence that you were playing bridge with Stockforth and some others when Grandison telephoned to say he would not be back until the following morning.'

'Yes.'

'Was he engaged at bridge between five and seven o'clock?'

'Yes. I left the table just before seven, but I saw Stockforth downstairs at about quarter past seven.'

Ogilvie took a few paces round about the table, and then came and sat down again.

'What was the address on that key-tag?' he asked quietly.

Colin stared at him, and then shook his head.

'It's all right,' said Ogilvie with a laugh. 'Sometimes these things come when you are not searching for them. There was to have been an inquest to-morrow, but unless I can find that alleged flat and can satisfy myself about the alleged box, I shall have to postpone the inquest. Harris, make a note to phone London to try Rating Authority, Knightsbridge area, also post office for flat in occupation of Charles Simbourne. Well, Mr. Fairbright, I am grateful for your evidence, but I may have to ask you to attend the coroner's inquest when it takes place.'

'I shall be pleased,' said Colin. 'But I hope it won't be the day after to-morrow, because I have rather an important appointment in London, with the head of my firm.'

'I don't think it can be as soon as that.'

14

During the rest of that day and the next Ogilvie did a vast number of things. The evidence now occupied a huge file, and it included a great number of non-resident members of the club, as well as persons outside the club. Rosita's evidence regarding her movements was checked and found to be true. Grandison's were similarly checked, and almost every minute of his time was accounted for. Ogilvie looked for any gap in the latter and found none.

'It's queer,' he said. 'There's the lack of a motive too, except in the case of suicide. Of course it could be a motive which none of us dream of — something to do with the past. But even so it looks as if Grandison must be ruled out. I've never seen a tighter alibi. Then there's this additional medical evidence. I'm up against Dr. Reynolds who is quite sure that the wound could have been self-inflicted by the right hand, by a small wiry man such as Simbourne was. Perhaps it could — at a pinch, but what Reynolds lacks is a good dose of common sense. Why should a man, intent on shooting himself, engage in body contortions? He may have had æsthetic objections to blowing out his brains, but he could have shot himself through the heart without almost dislocating his right wrist. I smell trouble at that inquest, unless we can produce something of a clinching nature. What news about that flat?'

'No trace of any flat in the occupation of Charles Simbourne in the whole area. But, of course, sir, that only applies to unfurnished flats. If he took a furnished flat he wouldn't be rated separately.'

'What about the G.P.O.?'

'No reply yet. They are still searching. Mightn't Simbourne have taken the flat under another name?'

'He might, but I hope he didn't because that might make for considerable delay. When did Fairbright say he was going to London?'

'To-morrow, sir.'

'He may be able to help us. See if he's in the club. If not try to get him on the telephone.'

Colin was not in the club. He had telephoned Rosita to learn that she still had a bad headache, and was keeping to her room. What truth there was in this he had no means of knowing, but he could not help feeling that for some reason she had no great desire to see him, and again he saw the hand of Grandison, and liked it not. Then came the telephone call from Sergeant Harris, and he was asked to wait while the sergeant fetched Inspector Ogilvie. Ogilvie was heard on the line a few moments later.

'Oh, Mr. Fairbright,' he said. 'How's that memory of yours?'

'No better I'm afraid,' replied Colin.

'So far my inquiries about that flat have produced no results. I have an idea which might be fruitful if you will collaborate. At any rate it is worth trying.'

'What is it?' asked Colin.

'Are you going to London to-morrow

to keep that appointment?'

'Yes.'

'Good. If you can spare time to drop in at my office and ask for Detective-Sergeant Owen he will show you a large-scale street map of London, which includes the Knightsbridge area. All the streets are clearly marked, and it may well be that you will see and recognise the street which was on the tag of that missing key. It won't help you with the number, but we can quickly make a house to house inquiry. Will you do that?'

'Yes,' said Colin. 'Of course. I shall have an hour or two to spare.'

'Good man! I'll telephone Owen to say you are coming.'

Colin found this mission not uninteresting, and he caught the early train the next morning, with a view to keeping his eleven o'clock appointment before going to Ogilvie's office at Scotland Yard. On the way up in the train he turned his mind to that elusive street, and wondered why he could not recall it, when as a rule his memory for details was quite good. But apparently Rosita was no better, and he supposed the reason was that in the pale moonlight the writing on the tag had not been very clear, and that he had really been more interested in the significance of the thing.

He reached London dead on time, and had a very pleasant meeting with the chairman of the company which employed him, during which it was made clear to him that the directors had voted him a bonus for his work in the reconstruction of the damaged plant. He left with a very substantial cheque in his pocket, and took a taxi to Scotland Yard. Upon inquiry there he was immediately taken up in a lift to an office on the third floor, overlooking the river, and was welcomed by a bluff middle-aged man.

'The chief informed me you were coming, Mr. Fairbright,' he said. 'He's mad to look into that flat, and so far we haven't been able to help him much. Well, there's the map on the wall. Take your choice, and if you score a bull's eye you'll deserve a prize. It's a pretty big area.'

Colin went across to the map, and ran his eye along the main thoroughfare and the streets which abutted on it. Then suddenly he saw a name which rang a loud bell in his brain. There it was, in very small type — Palting Street.

'That's it,' he said excitedly. 'Palting Street. Why on earth couldn't I remember that? Do you know it?'

'Quite well,' replied Sergeant Owen. 'It's only a short street. I've instructions to proceed there without delay. Would you like to come along? If there's any trouble in locating the flat you may be able to describe Simbourne.'

Colin was quite ready to take a hand in the business. Owen used the telephone, and then slipped on a coat and hat and escorted Colin downstairs to where a police car was waiting, with a driver at the wheel.

'Know Palting Street, off Knightsbridge, George?' he asked the driver.

'Sure.'

'Okay then. Get her going.'

The car had gone barely five hundred yards when Colin's memory tried to make up for arrears.

'Well, I'm damned!' he said. 'I've

remembered the number now. It was twenty-seven.'

'Good for you. George, the number is twenty-seven.'

Colin was finding this new experience quite thrilling. Would they find the lacquered box, hidden in the riding-boot as Simbourne had alleged? Would it contain information which would account for his sudden death? Every second of that swift journey was packed with tension.

'There's just one thing,' he said to Owen. 'It is bound to be locked up. What then?'

'If I am reasonably assured it is the flat we are looking for I have instructions to force an entry.'

'You mean break down the door?'

'There may be other ways.'

At last Palting Street was entered. It was as Owen had said a very short street, and Number 27 was a hairdresser's shop, with a side entrance leading to two flats overhead. They entered the doorway and saw on the wall 'First Floor — Mr. A. E. Matthews'. Second Floor — '

'Looks as if the second floor flat is unoccupied,' said Colin.

'There may be a card on the door. Let's go up and see.'

They climbed the first flight of steps and passed the door of the first flat, and then proceeded up the second flight.

'Can't see any card on the door, or wall,' mused Owen. 'Lord, I hope this isn't going to prove a wash-out.'

When they reached the door there was nothing to indicate who occupied the flat, but there was evidence that a card had been attached by four drawing-pins of a rather uncommon type, and only two of which now remained. Under this was a small fragment of pasteboard.

'We'll try the bell,' said Sergeant Owen, and pushed the button.

Colin could hear the bell ringing inside, but there was no response of any kind. Owen tried again with no better result. Then he tried the handle of the old-fashioned lock, and to his surprise the door opened.

'That's a bit of luck,' he muttered. 'Somebody was mighty careless. Must be something inside to indicate who lives here.'

'There's the box inside the riding-boots,' said Colin.

'Well, we'll see.'

Owen opened the door on the right of the small hall. It was a bedroom, with blankets folded and stacked on the single bed. The room contained no more than the bare necessities, which included a wardrobe of fumed oak. Inside the wardrobe was a dressing-gown, several old coats, some shoes and — most welcome of all — a pair of brown leather riding-boots.

'So you were right,' said the sergeant.

He dived for the boots, and thrust his hand deep down into one of them. It encountered nothing, so he tried the other.

'Anything there?' asked Colin.

'Nothing at all.'

Everything in the room was examined, but there was no sign of a lacquered box, and nothing in the shape of documents. They left the bedroom and opened the door of the sitting-room. The first thing that Colin saw was a small red box lying on a table by the settee.

'There it is!' he gasped.

Owen swooped on the box and opened the lid. It was empty

'Blast!' he muttered. 'He must have come here.'

Colin caught his arm and pointed to the fireplace. In it was a pile of black ashes.

'Burnt paper!' ejaculated Owen. 'Why the blazes did he do that, after what he said — '

He stopped suddenly in the middle of stirring the ashes with his index finger.

'Here, feel the brick,' he said.

Colin did so and found the hearth appreciably warm.

'That paper can't have been burnt more than half an hour ago,' said Owen. 'It couldn't have been Simbourne who came here. It must have been someone else. He found what we were after and then got away in such a hurry that he forgot to lock the door after him.'

'That's it,' agreed Colin. 'And there's this too to be taken into consideration.

He could have got the key with the tag on it from the dead body of Simbourne.'

Owen nodded almost in agony.

'To think that we've only missed him by minutes,' he said. 'It was he who probably tore down the name on the door.'

'But who?'

'Search me, but the inspector may be able to guess.'

'He'll have to do a lot of guessing,' said Colin. 'Because everyone in this case seems to have a very good alibi. Oh, there's something.'

Owen had seen it too, as he stirred the ashes with his finger. It was a small piece of paper that had not been completely destroyed. But it was brown from the heat of the conflagration. He carried it to the window.

'Just the end of a letter, with a signature. Not very plain. What do you make of it?'

Colin was just able to see the concluding words.

' — hope to get proof soon,' he said. 'The signature looks like Alan De — something.'

'Yes, it's Alan plain enough. I'll have to take care of this. May be something else.'

He resumed work on the ashes but found nothing else that had survived the flames. The portion of the letter he placed in his pocket-book and then he made a very thorough search of the room. It was so void of anything in the nature of letters that one was bound to conclude that the intruder had been engaged in the same task, with probably greater success. There was evidence in various places that things had been disturbed and replaced hastily, for an absence of dust in two places on the mantelpiece indicated that the spaces had once been covered by the bases of two vases, now some inches distant from their original position. The kitchen and bathroom were tidy and uninformative.

'Lord, if we had been an hour earlier,' moaned Owen.

'My fault,' said Colin.

'Not a bit, sir. I'd just like to know what all that burnt paper really was. I'll have to get back now, and report to Inspector Ogilvie over the telephone. Can I run you to the station?'

'No, thanks. I'm going to get myself as good a lunch as London can provide these days. Drop me anywhere you like. Scotland Yard will do.'

Colin subsequently had his lunch alone at the Savoy Grill, and he was glad to be alone for there was so much to think about. Ogilvie had more than hinted at murder, and how right he was. Here was proof that Simbourne's premonition of sudden death was not based on mere morbidity. Simbourne either suspected, or knew, that he had an enemy, and had taken precautions accordingly. But circumstances had been against him, and the tell-tale documents which might have brought his murderer to book were destroyed for ever. All that remained of them was that charred piece of paper containing a few words, and an indistinct signature. It was curious too that that signature had a queer familiarity. He knew no one of the name of Alan, and yet he was sure he had seen, or heard, a name like Alan Dev — For the second time his memory was letting him down. No, it wasn't. The name had been mentioned by

Rhoda's doctor sweetheart. It was the name of the first man who committed suicide at Alton. He still couldn't remember the full surname, but now he was certain it was the same man.

This discovery caused him to break out in a cold sweat. What a grim connection! And how significant those few words 'hope to get proof soon'. What proof? This was indeed a leaf out of Ogilvie's book, but, he was bound to confess, not due to anything but a stroke of luck. And was it a coincidence that Simbourne had referred to Grandison in such scathing terms? Was Grandison the nigger in the woodpile?

With this new link forged his one desire was to get back home, and an hour later he was in the train, still with his mind deeply occupied by what had emerged during his excursion. He felt he should have given prior place to the very useful cheque, but somehow the Alton mystery rose above such mundane considerations, and Rosita not least among the human personalities involved — Rosita, who seemed to be getting farther away from him rather than closer.

'My, you're back soon!' said Rhoda. 'Did you get the sack or something?'

'Something,' he replied. 'Take a look,' and then handed her the cheque.

Rhoda gave a little gasp of pleased surprise.

'Your firm must operate in the black market,' she said. 'You ought to be hectic with delight, but you look like a mute at a funeral. Anything wrong?'

'Yes. Rhoda, do you remember our discussing that young R.A.F. pilot who shot himself at Alton?'

'Yes.'

'Do you remember his name?'

'No. Can't say I do.'

'But I'm sure Neale mentioned it. Oh, but I think you weren't present on that occasion.'

'I wasn't. But it was in the newspaper at the time. No, I can't remember it.'

'Can you get on to Neale?'

Rhoda looked at her wrist-watch.

'Yes. He will be at the hospital.'

'Give him a ring, and ask him the name.'

'But why?'

'I'll tell you later. Go on — there's a dear.'

'All right. I'll try.'

Rhoda used the telephone, and after a few minutes delay she spoke to Dr. McKinnon.

'Oh, Neale,' she said. 'Here's Colin — all mysterious. Wants to know the name of that young R.A.F. pilot who shot himself at Alton a year ago. What's that? I can't hear you. Alec? Oh, Alan Devlin. I'll tell him. No, I don't know why. How are the poor patients? Have you killed any more yet? To-morrow? Of course I shan't forget. Yes, I know you're busy. Good-bye, darling!'

She gave a howl of laughter at something, and then turned to see her brother's tense expression.

'Now let me in,' she begged. 'It was the name you wanted to hear, wasn't it?'

'Yes. I was sure I was right.'

'What's it all about, Colin?' she asked seriously.

'I've made rather an important discovery. Charles Simbourne knew that man Devlin.'

288

'But why shouldn't he? They were both at Alton.'

'You miss the salient point. Devlin died months before Simbourne came to Alton, and they were in communication. Can't you see the sinister connotation?'

'I think I do,' said Rhoda. 'By jove, yes.'

'I must ring up Inspector Ogilvie.'

'Colin, tell me first. What has happened?'

Colin narrated his experiences as briefly as possible, and Rhoda gasped her astonishment.

'It — it does look like dirty work,' she said at the finish. 'I told you that Alton was a foul place. The sooner you get Rosita out of it the better.'

'Easier said than done,' he replied grimly. 'Now I must get on to Ogilvie. I'd better try police headquarters first.'

But police headquarters told him that Inspector Ogilvie was not available, and asked him what his business was. This he refused to disclose, feeling that it was not a matter to discuss over the telephone. He said he would ring again later, but after a few moments reflection he rang up Alton

Hall, and asked if Ogilvie was there. The hall porter said he wasn't sure, but would find out. What name should he give?'

'Police headquarters,' lied Colin.

'Hold the line, please.'

Ogilvie's voice was heard after a long wait.

'Oh, you're back,' he said. 'I heard from Owen — about your visit. Congratulations.'

'There's something else,' said Colin. 'I should like to tell you about it. Shall I come along?'

'If you can spare the time. Or shall I come to you?'

'No. I should like to get this off my chest. I'll come at once.'

'Good! Come straight to the writing-room.'

Rhoda watched her brother leave, and did not wonder at his eagerness, for at Alton there was Rosita, and she had a pretty good idea that Colin's haste was not entirely due to a desire to see Ogilvie only.

'Poor Colin!' she murmured. 'You're not very happy — when you ought to be.'

Colin wasted no time in getting to Alton. In the hall he ran into the colonel.

'Hullo, old boy!' said the colonel. 'I've been looking for you. You're just in time to make up a four — '

'Sorry, Colonel,' said Colin. 'I can't manage it just now. Some other time.'

'Pity,' said the colonel.

Colin went to the writing-room and rapped on the door. He was asked to come in, and he found Ogilvie and Sergeant Harris closeted together, with masses of papers spread over the table.

'You've lost no time,' said Ogilvie. 'Take a pew, and get your breath back. That was a good job you did with Owen, and I'm grateful to you. Pity we were too late. I honestly believe that you missed the murderer by not more than an hour. That's something I didn't quite expect. He must have got the key from Simbourne's clothing.'

'That's what I thought,' said Colin. 'But if he came from here — '

'That's the point. I acted on that information. There was some delay, but I got the message within an hour, and came

291

straight here. I was hoping to find that someone was missing.'

'And weren't they?'

'No one who is in the least suspect. The person who opened that flat and stole what was there was, I believe, a complete stranger to us. It adds complexity to the whole business. But we must start from a new angle, and I think we have a jumping-off point.'

'I was coming to that,' said Colin. 'Did Owen tell you what was written on the piece of paper which we retrieved?'

'Yes.' Ogilvie looked at Colin shrewdly. 'Did you draw a conclusion from that?'

'I did. I — good God, I believe you know!'

'That signature? Yes, it was written by the other man who was supposed to have shot himself. Is that what you came to tell me?'

Colin nodded and then laughed.

'I think I'll stick to my own profession,' he said. 'I really thought I was being smart.'

'Not so bad anyway. Look at all those depositions. Everything filters through to me. I should be an idiot not to spot obvious connections, or obvious inconsistencies. The professional has everything in his favour. But you have been a very great help. Now may I be frank?'

'Yes, of course.'

'It may hurt your feelings, but I must say it. I can't bind you to secrecy on anything you may know about this case, but I ask you most seriously not to be too confidential with Miss Paston.'

'Why not?' asked Colin sharply.

'My impression is that she is on the friendliest terms with Grandison, and I'm not keen that Grandison should know just how far we have got.'

'So you suspect Grandison?'

'I ought not to on the facts of the evidence, but I can't help myself. He's a very astute person, armed with a perfect alibi. There may be a flaw in it somewhere, but at the moment I am bound to confess I can't spot it. All I can hope for at the coroner's inquest is an open verdict.'

'You mean you can't establish murder?'

'Not as things stand. I can't even prove

that he was shot with the stolen pistol — only that he was shot with the pistol which was found beside him. I am trying to trace the origin of that pistol, but I doubt if I shall be successful.'

'What about the break-in at the flat, and the burnt papers?'

'All rather circumstantial, but no more convincing than that Simbourne may have shot himself. There is conflicting medical evidence on that point, with the balance slightly in favour of suicide. The coroner will be prejudiced in favour of suicide.'

'Why?'

'Murder is an unpleasant verdict to pronounce, unless the evidence is indisputable. But an open verdict will suit me very well, for it will mean that the investigation can continue.'

'I suppose Simbourne's family are against suicide?'

'Very much. I am seeing the younger son to-morrow. By the way, the father died this afternoon, so the younger son is now Viscount Simbourne.'

Colin gave him a swift glance, and

Ogilvie knew what was passing in his mind. He shook his head emphatically.

'The two boys were extremely good friends,' he said. 'It is in evidence that Charles was willing to forgo the inheritance in favour of his brother, but the conditions of the original deed of entail did not permit.'

'You expressed a wish that Grandison should not know how far you have got,' said Colin. 'But isn't he bound to know after the inquest?'

'Not at all. That would be most unwise — I think.'

From this remark Colin gathered that Ogilvie intended to keep a little secret ammunition in his locker, and that Grandison remained the chief suspect despite his 'perfect' alibi.

'I'll take heed of your warning,' he said. 'But I'm certain that Miss Paston is as innocent as —'

'Yes, of course. But Grandison is a dominating personality, and may know how to get information without appearing to want it. I haven't had cause to see her to-day. I hope she is quite well. I thought

— the last time I saw her — that she was feeling the strain.'

'She is. I think I'll try to see her before I go. But I'll be discreet in what I say.'

'Thank you.'

15

In the meantime Rosita had been battling with a violent headache — a malady unusual with her. It had been so bad that morning that she seriously considered calling a doctor, but Grandison, with his usual concern for her welfare, diagnosed its origin as nerves, due to all the worry which now afflicted them.

'As a young man I studied medicine,' he said. 'I know that kind of headache, and it's easily got rid of. I'll send you up something. It's quite harmless, and if you take it and lie quiet for an hour or two I guarantee it will do the trick.'

The 'something' was a long drink with a milk basis, and no unpleasant taste. She drank it and lay down on the bed, gradually falling into a sleep. It was dark when she woke up, and she saw to her surprise that it was past six o'clock. To her great joy the headache had entirely disappeared. After a wash and a change of dress she went downstairs. One of the first things she saw was a bill advertising the next concert. Across it was a gummed slip bearing the word 'cancelled'. As she stood staring at it Stockforth came up behind her.

'Hullo, Rosita!' he said. 'Better?'

'Oh, yes, thank you. Why is the concert cancelled?'

'It was G's idea. He rang down half an hour ago, and told me to find some cancellation strips and get them round.'

'But — but it will spoil the whole series.'

'You'd better go and talk with him. He's in his den.'

Rosita decided she would, and she operated the lift, and was soon outside Grandison's abode. From inside came the sound of magnificent music, which she recognised at once as Elgar's Violin Concerto. Thinking it was merely the radio she pushed the bell hard, and then a second time. But still the music continued — the violin in particular performing miracles of magnificent melody. She turned the door-handle and looked inside. It was the great radiogram, but it was supplemented by Grandison, who stood in the centre of the large lounge, before a music stand, playing his violin like a man in a trance.

'Oh, I'm sorry,' she said.

At last he saw her, and stopped playing, but the violin part of the concerto still continued, for it was all on the set of records which were on the machine.

'Practising?' she asked.

'Cheating. That's Yehudi Menuhin. I use him to show me the way. God knows what he'd say if he only knew. But by what other means can I play with a full orchestra, and Sir Edward himself conducting? I'd sell what soul I have left to play like that.'

He switched off the radiogram, and laid down the violin.

'How's the headache?' he asked.

'Entirely gone — thanks to you.'

'It was easy. Let me look at you. Yes, you look more like your usual lovely self.'

'Mark,' she asked. 'Why have you cancelled the concert?'

'What else could I do? How can you do

yourself justice in the midst of all this worry? The true artist is a hot-house plant, that must be tenderly reared or it will die. Music to me is something more than making money.'

'I know, but I'm quite capable of going through with the concert.'

'You're not. I know best. I've already telephoned to cancel the vocalist. I'll have to pay him, but what does that matter? Now sit down and relax. I'm just going to have a meal. You'd better stay and join me, for you can have had nothing to eat since breakfast.'

Without waiting for her response he used the telephone and told the kitchen to bring up food for two.

'Add a bottle of champagne — the best,' he said. 'And hurry.'

'I should be practising,' said Rosita.

'Not to-night. With the concert off there is no need. I want to talk to you.'

He drew up a comfortable chair, lighted a huge cigar and offered her a cigarette, which she accepted.

'I take it those damned policemen are still in the house?' he asked.

'I really don't know.'

'Suppose I can't blame them, but everyone here must be getting fed-up with questions which they can't answer. Do you realise the position, Rosita?'

'What do you mean exactly?'

'There are a lot of people in the town who would like to close us down. All along they have resented this fine old mansion being used for a club. I have to buy drink in the black market. Every club has to do that if it hopes to keep going. There's nothing illegal about it. I don't think they could close down the club, but they could cancel the drink licence, and that, would come to pretty much the same thing. This tragedy gives them a wonderful opportunity. At the inquest they will make the most of the unfortunate fact that we have had two suicides among our members. In fact the police are now doing their damnedest to show that Charles was murdered. Did you know that?'

'Yes.'

'Do you believe it?'

'I — I don't know what to believe.'

'Well, it doesn't matter very much. There will be enough mud splashed around to undo all the good that your concerts have done. I've a good mind to drop the whole thing.'

'You mean — sell the place?'

'Yes. Stockforth is ready to take it off me — at a price, and take the risk of what may happen to the club.'

'But — but what then?'

They were interrupted by the appearance of the waiter who was staggering under a huge tray and a bottle of champagne in an ice-bucket.

'Ah, Henry, that Buckingham table,' said Grandison. 'Bring it up here.'

The waiter laid down his burden and brought the table forward, with two ordinary chairs. The contents of the covered tray were spread over the table, and plates and cutlery laid.

'Shall I stay and serve, sir?' asked the waiter.

'No thanks. We can manage. I'll ring for coffee.'

'Very good, sir.'

The 'spread' was magnificent in every

respect, and Rosita, having eaten almost nothing in twenty-four hours, found herself ready for the repast.

'Better than eating with that pack of hyenas downstairs,' laughed Grandison. 'Help yourself, my dear. I'm not very good at that.'

For a time they ate in silence, and it was only when Grandison had opened the champagne and filled the two lovely Venetian glasses that he came back to his subject.

'Where were we?' he asked. 'Oh, yes — the future. Well, to tell you the truth I'm tired of the mob here — the drinking and gambling. I keep away from it all as much as possible. Since you have been here my mind has gone off in a different direction — towards the stars. You remember the man I introduced you to last week — Benjamin?'

'The man who was so complimentary?'

'Yes. He's quite an important person in the musical world. I ran into him when I was in London, and he put up a proposition which I told him I would consider. It concerns you, but I didn't want to tell you until I had had time to think about it. But for this distressing business I would have turned it down, but now I'm not so sure it would be wise. Benjamin rang up again this morning, and I told him I would let him know in a couple of days.'

'What is this proposition?' asked Rosita.

'He offers you a Continental tour on very generous terms. Paris, Brussels, Lyons, Nice, and so on. Twelve weeks in all. One concert a week at fifty pounds a week. If the thing is a success he will follow it up with a British tour, finishing up in London, on terms to be arranged.'

Rosita could scarcely believe her ears, and yet Grandison looked serious enough.

'When — when would the tour start?' she asked.

'In a fortnight, but the decision must be made at once, as the halls for the first part of the tour are booked.'

'And you? What about you?'

'The concerts will be under my management. I come in on the profits.'

'You mean you are putting money into it?'

'Why not? I know a good thing when I see it.'

'But — but I might be a terrible flop.'

'I've no fear of that. None at all. You've got over stage-fright. It's no more trying to play to thousands than hundreds. You can do it. You have everything the crowd likes — talent, looks, personality. We would give you plenty of advance publicity. The fees aren't large, but it would be a fine start. You'd have real musical audiences instead of what you get here. Like to think it over?'

'Does it mean you will come with me?'

'Oh, yes. We can take the car across, and Rupert. That would make us independent of Continental transport, which is most unreliable just now. One concert a week shouldn't be very taxing. It would give you time to see something of the world. You, of course, already have a passport, so we shan't have to waste time over that. Yes, it could be a good life — watching you climb to stardom. Now all this must be a big surprise for you.'

'It is. It's come so soon — so much quicker than I expected. How long can you give me to make up my mind?'

'I promised Benjamin to let him know in two days. He must fill the bill by then. He has a brilliant vocalist signed up, but of course it is you who will be the star.'

'This is overwhelming,' said Rosita. 'I'll tell you to-morrow.'

'That will do. If you decide to accept it will just about give me time to settle my affairs here.'

'Are you sure you want to finish with Alton?'

'Yes. Stockforth can have it — at a price, and all that goes with it. There's just one thing, Rosita.'

'What is that?'

'Will you forgive me if I introduce a personal note?'

'Of course.'

'That young man — Colin Fairbright, isn't he just a little bit keen on you?'

'We are very friendly.'

'Not more than that?'

Rosita was silent for a moment.

'It's all right,' he said. 'I had no right to

ask that. I did so only because I thought that in certain circumstances Fairbright might try to dissuade you from this venture. People in love can behave rather selfishly you know.'

'What makes you think he is in love with me?' she asked.

'My eyesight and my common sense. Why should he not be in love with you? I find it difficult to imagine any young man who wouldn't be. All I hope is that he will not behave in such a way as to influence your decision — and future career.'

'He won't,' she said.

'Good! Now we'll have some coffee.'

He pushed a bell, and very soon the waiter appeared with the coffee and some liqueurs on a tray.

'Paris,' mused Grandison, as he sipped his coffee. 'I can almost see you there, and the vast audience in raptures. We may get as far as Rome. Ever been to Rome?'

'No.'

'There's a city for you — really the centre of the musical world, for every Italian has music engraved on his heart, and worships at the shrine of beauty. We'll make all those dead Roman emperors turn in their tombs.'

'You're going a little fast,' protested Rosita.

'Yes, but somehow I feel that is our destiny. But in any case I'm burning my boats, even if at the last moment you decide not to accept. But I'll be patient.'

Rosita eventually took the lift to the ground floor, with her brain swimming. She had promised Grandison a decision within twenty-four hours, but already she was nearing that decision. To throw away such a chance as this would be madness, she argued. Certainly she had imagined such a situation, but not for years, for she was knowledgeable enough to realise that the road to stardom was long and arduous, and full of pitfalls and bitter disappointments. The pitfalls might still arise, but at least here was the chance of being launched under what appeared to be excellent auspices.

'Rosita!'

She turned in the corridor and came face to face with Colin.

'Oh!' she gasped. 'You scared me.'

'Sorry. Glad to see you about. Are you feeling better?'

'Yes, completely well. I had a touch of migraine or something. I suppose it is all this trouble about poor Charles. Thank you for ringing up. What have you been doing with yourself?'

'I had to go to London to-day to see the head of my firm. Rather a pleasant interview. The Board of Directors had voted me a bonus, and the old boy wanted to hand it to me personally, with appropriate bouquets.'

'How nice.'

'Feel like walking out in the fresh air?'

'It's very tempting, but I must practise. I haven't touched the piano for days.'

'The excuse isn't valid,' he said with a laugh. 'I see that the concert has been cancelled.'

'That's true, but it doesn't excuse me from practising. As a matter of fact it is more necessary now than ever.'

'But not quite so urgent.'

'More urgent. You see, Colin, I have had an offer to go on tour, and if I accept it means that I must put in an awful lot of work.'

'On tour?' he asked, wrinkling his brows.

'Yes — a Continental tour, starting in Paris. It came about through a man coming here from London to hear me play. He was impressed and this is the outcome. I have to decide within two days, or someone else will get the contract.'

'I see,' he said slowly.

'Aren't you going to congratulate me?' she asked, with a laugh.

'Yes — yes, of course. It's a tremendous compliment — so early in your career. I certainly never expected that.'

'You mean you didn't think I was experienced — ?'

'I thought nothing of the kind, and you know it. When — when are you expected to start?'

'In about a fortnight. We go to Paris — '

'We?'

'Grandison is in this too. He will attend to the business side. Someone must do that.'

'What about his affairs here?'

'He's prepared to sell his interest. He's mad on music — always has been. If the Continental tour is a success we are promised a British tour, finishing in London.'

He looked at her searchingly and saw that her cheeks were flushed and her eyes exceedingly bright.

'You talk as if you had already accepted,' he said.

'No. It's still open.'

'But you mean to accept — don't you?'

'Yes,' she said. 'I should be a fool not to. Where should I get another chance like this? I may fail, but it's up to me. Colin, don't look like that. Don't dishearten me.'

'God forbid! You've taken my breath away. Do come into the garden — just for a few minutes. I feel suffocated in here. Please!'

'All right — but only for a short while. Wait here, while I get a wrap.'

Colin collapsed in a seat the moment she had gone. Was this always to be his luck — to be silenced by unexpected events on every occasion when he made up his mind to unburden his heart? A twelve-weeks' tour in foreign countries! Before she could get back he would be on his way to Malaya. If she went away in a fortnight it would mean that he might never see her again! And where, exactly, did Mark Grandison come in? Was it merely business; love of music, or was he really behind this venture, backing it with his own money, for rewards that had little — perhaps nothing — to do with music? Rosita came back before his sombre cogitations had gone very far. She was wearing a short coat with a scarf round her head.

'Won't you need a coat?' she asked.

'No. I don't catch cold easily.'

'I should have thought that after years of life in the tropics you would have become a hot-house plant,' she said.

He led her to a sheltered part of the garden, where there was a seat in a pleasant alcove. The sky was clear and a large yellow moon swam above the adjacent cedar tree.

'So it looks as if I am going to lose you soon,' he said, after a silence.

'Yes, for twelve whole weeks.'

'I wish it was no worse than that. But as a matter of fact I have undertaken to cut my leave short by two months. It wasn't a condition of the bonus which was given me, but a request, owing to some unforeseen circumstances. I could do no other than agree, and shall be sailing in three months from now.'

'That's bad luck,' she said. 'I never anticipated that.'

'Would it have made any difference?' he asked, determined to go through with it now, no matter what happened.

'I don't see how it could,' she replied slowly.

'You mean that music comes first with you — before any other consideration whatever?'

She remained for a moment in a state of deep reflection, staring up at the dark cedar tree against the starlit sky.

'I suppose it does,' she said. 'I've never thought of it in that way — quite. But if I have some ability in that direction shouldn't I do my best to follow it up — to seize an opportunity which may not occur again for a long time?'

He picked up the hand that was nearest him, and closed his fingers round it.

'Rosita, don't you know what I'm driving at?'

For the first time since they had been seated she turned her head and looked straight into his eyes.

'Don't make love to me, Colin,' she begged.

'Why not?'

'I don't want you to — not now. I've got so much on my mind.'

'So have I, but it is chiefly you. I joined this vile club only to have an excuse to be near you. On the night when Charles's body was found I came especially to tell you just what you meant to me, but it was impossible in the circumstances. You must listen to me now, because I believe you are on the verge of taking a step which might separate us for ever.'

'Why should it? If I loved you, wouldn't you be willing to wait a little while?'

'Do you call three years a little while?'

'Lovers have waited longer — and not so long ago.'

'I know. But how great were the risks? Rosita I love you as I never believed it was possible for me to love anybody. To be parted from you for three years would be hell, and in these particular circumstances worse than hell.'

'What circumstances?'

'This tour. I don't like it.'

'Why not?'

She asked the question rather sharply, and he was given to feel that he had been caught on the wrong foot, but he was not in the mood to change his ground.

'I don't like Grandison,' he said.

'So — that's it?'

'Yes. Does it surprise you?'

'No, but it hurts a little. You don't seem to understand that ever since I have been here Grandison has treated me with the greatest consideration. He gave me a job when I had scarcely a penny in the world. He has helped me and encouraged me in a way quite impossible for you to understand. He is now giving me a chance to make something of myself. I don't ask you to like him, but at least you might try to understand him.'

'Rosita,' he begged. 'Don't take it so badly. I assure you that there's a lot you don't know about him. There is this business of Charles's death to be — '

'Are you suggesting that Mark — '

'Mark!' he ejaculated.

'I won't listen, any more than I would listen to someone trying to blacken you in my eyes. Colin dear — must we quarrel? You're my good friend. I like you enormously — perhaps better than anyone else in this world. Please — please don't strain that friendship.'

Colin was silent, for it was abundantly clear to him that he and Rosita were at a dangerous pass. A few angry words now might place between them an uncrossable abyss, and this at all costs must be prevented. He did not believe for a moment that she was anywhere near to loving Grandison, but who could tell how soon her unshakable regard for him would develop into something approaching love? With himself removed across thousands of miles Grandison would have all the running and in a field which offered few obstacles. Poor Charles knew

316

what he was saying when he gave that solemn warning. Here was a man who knew what he wanted, and was willing to sacrifice many smaller pieces in a long drawn-out game played with consummate skill and patience.

'I'll say no more,' he said. 'I appear to have said too much already. Am I forgiven?'

'You know you are. Colin!'

'Yes.'

'You are not going to let this prevent me from seeing you before — before I am due to leave?'

'I am not.'

'I'm glad of that. Oh dear, life is very complicated,' she sighed.

'We make it so ourselves.'

'Have you seen Inspector Ogilvie again?' she asked.

'Yes — a little while ago. He told me that Viscount Simbourne died this after-noon.'

'How very sad! Has there been any further development about that London flat, whose address we can't remember?'

Colin hesitated. He did not want to tell a deliberate lie, but felt that in the circumstances he should respect Ogilvie's wishes.

'Not — so far as I know,' he replied.

'And the inquest?'

'That was not mentioned, but I think it must take place very soon.'

'I shall hate that. I shall be called as a witness, and it will be horrible.'

'Not pleasant. I too shall be glad when it's all over. All we can do is tell the truth as far as we know it.'

'Yes, of course. Now, I must really go and do some practice.'

'I'll come with you as far as the side door.'

At the entrance to the music-room she lingered a moment.

'Thank you for loving me, Colin,' she murmured.

'And thank you for tolerating me,' he replied.

'Oh, Colin, Colin!' she almost sobbed. 'Please don't be so hard.'

The next moment she was gone, leaving him facing a closed door.

16

On the following morning Colin drove to the club again, with no definite object in view. He was depressed as a result of his last meeting with Rosita. Why, at parting, had he been stupid enough to have indulged in cheap repartee at Rosita's expense? All night it had worried him, and he wanted to apologise, but to seek her out for that purpose alone was not good enough. He nosed round the place and heard that the two police officers had not arrived.

'Perhaps they'll decide to give us a break,' said the hall porter. 'It's about time they did, if you ask me.'

A little later he ran into the colonel, who was carrying a bag of golf clubs, and was dressed appropriately.

'Hullo, Fairbright!' he said. 'Like to take pity on an old man? I hate playing alone. Of course I'm no damned good, so if you — '

'I'll come round with you with pleasure,' said Colin. 'Give me two minutes to get into some shoes and dig out some clubs.'

'Grand! I'll be doing a bit of putting on this green.'

The colonel's golf was most erratic, and consisted chiefly of punishing the inoffensive ball. He hit every shot as hard as he knew how with results that were at times most spectacular but to the detriment of accuracy, and as he talked the whole way round he was so exhausted at the end of two rounds of the short course that Colin was almost alarmed.

'You really should take it easier, Colonel,' he said.

'Easy! I've always worked hard and played hard. If I have to hit anything I love to take a solid whack at it. Beats me how you get that distance with so little effort,' he grumbled. 'Why the hell can't we get some caddies here?'

Colin knew that any offer to relieve him of his clubs would be fiercely declined, so he let the red-faced old warrior stagger

320

back to the 'nineteenth' carrying his own impedimenta.

'Didn't give you much of a game,' growled the colonel, but by gosh I enjoyed it. Can't be young for ever I suppose. Heard anything about the inquest?'

'No.'

'Queer business, don't you think?'

'Very queer.'

'There's one thing that's sticking out a mile. This place will stink by the time it's all over — whether it was suicide or something worse.'

'What's your opinion?' asked Colin.

'Can't make up my mind. Dammit! Charles was talking about packing up and going to Kenya. Why the devil should he suddenly do a thing like that? Yet if he didn't it's a bigger mystery than ever. Oh, let's have a drink or two.'

While they were thus engaged Colin heard that the representatives of the police had not turned up that morning, and it was then he remembered that Ogilvie had mentioned an appointment with the dead man's younger brother

— now Viscount Simbourne. It looked as if this appointment was taking place at police headquarters, and was the cause of Ogilvie's absence from the club.

'Did you know the new viscount — Charles's younger brother?' he asked the colonel.

'No. He never talked much about his family connections.'

'How did Charles win the V.C.?'

'Airborne landing on D-Day. They were badly shot-up, and two of his comrades were severely wounded. He himself had a foot injury, but he got one of the wounded men back to cover, and then went after the other. Unfortunately he and the second man were captured by the enemy, and Charles spent a long time in a prisoner of war camp. He was in a shocking state when at last the camp was over-run. In hospital for a year. A wild chap in some ways, but by gosh he had guts.'

Later Colin wandered to the car park. He had hoped to drop upon Rosita accidentally, but saw no sign of her. He was about to enter the car when he noticed that the off-side front tyre was almost flat. He looked for the foot-pump which was normally kept in the back of the car, but was unable to find it. Across by the private garages he saw a form lying under a large saloon car, with little more than the two legs visible. He guessed it was Rupert, the chauffeur, and walked across with the object of borrowing a pump. Rupert appeared to be engaged in tightening up something, for there were several spanners at a handy spot. He was about to call him when his gaze was attracted by the chauffeur's left shoe. The large sole of the boot was directly facing him, and in it was embedded a drawing-pin. It was a rather unusual drawing-pin in design and finish, and yet was not entirely new to Colin, for quite recently he had seen other pins absolutely identical. He knew too, in an instant, just where he had seen those pins, and that knowledge caused him to draw in his breath with a little hiss of amazement, for they had been in the door of Simbourne's secret flat, from which the name-card had been torn! Rupert's oily face now appeared from under the running-board.

'Morning, sir!' he said in his rough voice.

'Oh, good morning, Rupert! I've got a flat tyre and haven't a pump. Can you help me?'

'Surely, sir.'

Rupert scrambled to his feet, and wiped his hands on a piece of cotton waste. He opened the door of the car and produced a foot-pump from the back.

'Shall I come and put some air in for you?' he asked.

'Oh, don't bother. I can do that. I'll bring it back in a few minutes.'

'No hurry,' said Rupert.

Colin took the pump and was soon putting air into the half-deflated tyre, but his mind was elsewhere than on his task, and he put too much pressure in the tyre before he was aware of what he was doing, and had to let some out. Was this merely a coincidence? If it was it was a most remarkable one. Had the drawing-pin been of the class of which there existed millions it would have been a different matter. But he remembered noticing the very uncommon design of the drawing-pins left in the door, for it was only yesterday that he had seen them. Probably they were there now, in which case a closer comparison might be possible — provided he could get possession of Rupert's left shoe. But how was this to be accomplished?

He took the pump back, and then displayed an interest in the big car which Rupert had been busy with. It was a Mercedes-Benz, and it looked as if it had recently been driven at speed over wet roads, for it was splashed with mud from end to end.

'Useful car,' he said.

'Yes,' agreed Rupert. 'Very good.'

'Heavy on petrol, isn't it?'

Rupert agreed that it was, and then proceeded to attach a rubber hose to the nearby tap. Colin saw his intention, which was to hose down the Mercedes, and a great hope arose within him. But he dared not linger lest he should give rise to suspicion. So he thanked the chauffeur again, lighted a cigarette, and then walked slowly back to his own car. From there he saw Rupert sitting on the running-board of the Mercedes, taking off his shoes. Close by was a pair of gumboots. What he had hoped for had come to pass. Rupert drew on the rubber boots and then placed his shoes inside the car. He then turned on the tap and directed the jet of water on the dirty coachwork.

Here was a heaven-sent opportunity, but how to make use of it he could not think. To get the shoe Rupert had to be enticed away from the car — and out of sight of it. There was the telephone, but he could not see that that would help much unless he could get Rupert brought to the club, and that would mean finding a public telephone from which he could make the call. He knew of none close at hand that would enable him to get back and take possession of the shoe before Rupert got back. The alternative was to get someone in the club to collaborate with him, but he knew of no one whom he could trust, with the exception of Rosita. Having concealed from her his visit to the flat and the results of it, it seemed unspeakably mean now to invite her trust and confidence, without telling her everything — a course which seemed dangerous in view of her close association with Grandison. But precious time was passing, and there was no knowing what might happen if Rupert finished his car washing and got back into his shoes. He might see that tell-tale drawing-pin, and be quick to get rid of it.

Yes, it was Rosita or nothing. No use having qualms about it. He drove the car out of Rupert's sight, and parked it temporarily in a convenient place. Then he hurried into the club, and looked in the music-room. To his great joy Rosita was there, sorting over some sheet music.

'Trespassing,' she said, with a smile as he approached her.

'I know. Rosita, something has happened, and I want your help.'

She looked at him searchingly.

'What kind of help?' she asked.

'Can you find an excuse to bring Rupert here for a few minutes?'

'Rupert — the chauffeur?'

'Yes. Please don't ask me to explain now, but the matter is important and urgent. He's washing a car at the garages, and there's something I want to get, without his knowledge.'

'Is it to do with — Charles?'

'Yes. Will you do it?'

'How can I get him here?'

'Invent some excuse. He does odd jobs, doesn't he?'

'Yes, but what job?'

'The piano. You can scarcely move that by yourself. Ask him if he will come and move the piano — a little farther back. That's reasonable. Might improve the acoustics. Will you do it — now?'

'I — I don't quite like the idea,' she faltered. 'But if it will help — '

'I assure you it will.'

'All right. Which way shall I go?'

'By the side door. I'll go the other way. But don't let him put off coming with you until he has finished the job he is on. Please — please hurry. I don't want this to fail.'

Rosita nodded and went out by the side door. Colin thereupon hurried through the club, but was unlucky enough to run into Grandison as he left the music-room.

Grandison glared at him, and made a gesture as if to stop him. But Colin paid no attention and was soon outside the house. He turned up in the direction of the garages and saw Rosita approaching Rupert. Rupert stopped his work as she drew near him. There was a short conversation and then Rupert nodded and looked down at his gumboots. Colin held his breath. Was everything going to be ruined at the last moment? But no — Rupert apparently saw no need to change into his shoes, and followed Rosita towards the house. Colin waited until they were out of sight, and then hurried towards the Mercedes, flung open the door and seized the left shoe, with the drawing-pin embedded in it. Two minutes later he was at the door of his own car. He took the shoe from under his coat — pushed it under the car rug, and then drove off.

On reaching home he rang up police headquarters and asked if Inspector Ogilvie was there. As usual they wanted to know the nature of his business and he said it was private and very urgent. But on giving his name and address he was told to 'hang on'. Ogilvie came to the telephone a few minutes later.

'I've got something that appears to be important,' said Colin. 'It's an exhibit in the Simbourne case. Shall I come to you, or will you come to me?'

'As you wish,' said Ogilvie. 'But it would be a great convenience if you could come here as I am expecting a witness in a few minutes. But by the time you get here I shall be free.'

'I'll come,' said Colin.

'Good. I'll leave a message for you to be sent straight up.'

Rhoda had appeared towards the end of this conversation.

'What's all the excitement?' she asked.

'I've got to run over to police headquarters. May be late for lunch, but don't wait for me.'

'You certainly do move around these days,' said Rhoda. 'Are you now co-opted into the secret circles of the C.I.D.?'

'I've made a bit of a discovery. Up to now my discoveries have always been second-hand, but this one isn't. Can't tell you anything more now, old dear.'

'Oh — come!'

'No, really. I'm in a frightful hurry.'

He made the trip to Lincoln in record time, and at police headquarters he asked for Ogilvie, and gave his name. The sergeant in charge nodded and conducted him up a flight of stairs and into a room where Ogilvie and his big sergeant were seated at a large table.

'You certainly haven't lost any time, Mr. Fairbright,' said Ogilvie. 'Harris, get another chair.'

Colin occupied the chair and laid his brown-paper parcel on the table. Ogilvie gave a glance at it, and then waited patiently.

'It concerns yesterday,' said Colin. 'When Sergeant Owen and I called at the flat in London we found on the door two bits of what had been a name-card of the occupant. The card had been pinned down by drawing-pins, and two of the pins remained in the wood. I took that to mean that the intruder had torn down the card as he left. The two looser pins had come out, but the other two were in very tight. I didn't look for the missing pins, but I did notice that the two which remained were unusual in type. Well, this morning, by a complete accident I saw another pin which I am certain is absolutely identical with the two in that door.'

'That's interesting. Where is it?'

Colin untied the string round the brown paper parcel and produced the black shoe. He turned it sole upwards, and Ogilvie saw the head of the drawing-pin. His gaze met Colin's.

'Whose shoe is this?' he asked.

'It belongs to the chauffeur at Alton. His christian name is Rupert. I don't know his surname.'

Ogilvie's interest was now intense.

'The pin is certainly unusual. Quite new to me,' he said. 'You think the others are identical?'

'I'm positive.'

'Well, before we go any further, I'll have a word with Owen.'

He picked up the telephone and put through a priority call to Scotland Yard. Within a minute he was talking to

Sergeant Owen. Yes, Owen remembered the pins quite well.

'Then run along and get them,' said Ogilvie. 'Ring me back when you have them, and then send them by special messenger. I want them in my hands this evening.'

Ogilvie hung up the receiver.

'By jove, you're improving, Mr. Fair-bright,' he said. 'This is really important. I remember Rupert. He gave his evidence well. Harris, turn up that deposition. Let's see exactly what he said.'

Sergeant Harris went through the bulky file, and finally drew out the required document.

'Rupert Zanfeld,' he said. 'Age thirty-five. Displaced person from Latvia. Arrived in England September, 1946. Permit to work for Grandison granted November same year. He was the last person known to have seen Simbourne alive. Stated that he washed Simbourne's car and that he saw Simbourne depart in his car at approximately half-past nine on the morning of the tragedy. Believed that Simbourne was going to Manchester.

Seen by several witnesses that evening after eight o'clock. No proof of his movements during day. Excellent character. Well, we have only his word that Simbourne intended to go to Manchester. He may have lied about that deliberately. I'll admit he was not among my suspects. There's another bit of evidence too which arises entirely from his statement. He says he cleaned out the ash-containers in the car. We found lipstick on a cigarette-end, and that seemed to indicate that a woman had been in the car between the time when Simbourne left the garage and when he lost his life. But he could also have lied about the ash-trays if he thought it would serve to lay another red-herring.'

'What about yesterday?' asked Colin. 'What was he doing round about noon?'

'That I have no means of knowing. I got Owen's message a bit late, and so there was a considerable delay in my subsequent check-up. But he was certainly here about three hours after the burning of those papers — presuming Owen's calculation to be approximately

334

correct. It doesn't look as if that were possible.'

'It was,' said Colin. 'The car he was tinkering with when I saw his shoes sticking out was a Mercedes-Benz. It's capable of enormous speeds on good roads, and it was covered with mud — just as a car would be after a long journey at great speed.'

Ogilvie was very reflective for a few minutes. He lighted a cigarette and then offered his case to Colin.

'I'll just wait for Owen's report,' he said. 'He'll move quickly. By the way how did you contrive to get hold of this shoe?'

Colin told him, and Ogilvie's eyes twinkled with amusement. Sergeant Harris was more forthright.

'Good bit of work, if I may say so, sir,' he said. 'Now if he had made a habit of cleaning his shoes every morning he might have spotted that clue and saved himself from some awkward questions. Looks as if cleanliness sometimes comes before even godliness.'

'We checked up Rupert's papers, didn't we, Harris?' asked Ogilvie.

'Yes, sir. He had everything.'

A few minutes later Sergeant Owen came through. He was speaking from a telephone near the flat, and he stated that he had retrieved the two drawing-pins from the door.

'What are they like?' asked Ogilvie.

Owen gave a very detailed description, and Ogilvie, with the shoe in his hand, was satisfied.

'All right,' he said. 'Get them to me without delay. Thanks for your speed.'

Ogilvie hung up the receiver.

'The two things must be connected,' he said. 'I mean the murder and the break-in at the flat. Rupert could have been responsible for both, although at the moment I can see no motive of any kind. Simbourne had over fifty pounds in cash on his person, and was wearing a very fine gold wristwatch. That would seem to rule out robbery. Well, it's no use wasting valuable time in speculation as to motive. The thing now is to see Rupert.'

'Shall you need me?' asked Colin.

'I think not. Better to leave him to guess how we got possession of this shoe.

336

Harris, we'll get to Alton at once. I presume you have your own car, Mr. Fairbright?'

'Yes.'

'Then you can get home under your own steam. I'm very grateful to you for your valuable assistance.'

17

An hour later Rupert was brought to the room at Alton where again Ogilvie and Sergeant Harris were seated. The chauffeur looked as calm and self-possessed as ever as he took the vacant chair.

'Mr. Zanfeld,' said Ogilvie, in his kindliest voice. 'I should like you to tell me just how you occupied your time yesterday morning — say up to one o'clock.'

'Yesterday,' mused Rupert. 'I woke up at half-past six and attended to the central-heating plant. I do that every morning. It takes a good time to rake out the ashes and fill up with coke. I had my breakfast at eight o'clock.'

'Where?'

'In my room over the garages.'

'Go on.'

'I finished at nine o'clock. Then I washed down two cars. That took two hours.'

'What cars?'

'Mr. Grandison's and the shooting-brake.'

'You finished by eleven o'clock?'

'Yes. Mr. Grandison then told me that he had a job he wanted me to do. I went to his apartment and he showed me that one of the doors was scraping on the floor. It was due to one of the hinges being loose. I had to take the door off and re-hang it before I could make it right. I finished just in time for my dinner at one o'clock.'

'Was anyone there while you did the job?'

'Yes. Mr. Grandison was there most of the time.'

'What was he doing?'

'He was trying over some records on his big radiogram — two new Beethoven symphonies.'

'So you were employed on the premises the whole morning?'

'Yes, sir.'

'Did you go out in the Mercedes later in the day?'

'No. But Mr. Grandison went out in

the evening. He made the car very dirty and I washed it this morning.'

Ogilvie undid a small case and produced the black shoe.

'Do you recognise this?' he asked.

Rupert glanced at the article and then stared at Ogilvie.

'Yes. It is my shoe. I missed it this morning. I had put it inside the Mercedes while I washed the outside. How — how did you get it?'

'Never mind. Look at the sole of it and tell me if you can how that drawing-pin comes to be there?'

Rupert did this, and shook his head.

'I must have stepped on it somewhere,' he said.

'Obviously. But where?'

'How can I say? I might be anywhere. Often one does that sort of thing.'

'Have you ever seen any other drawing-pins like that?'

'I don't know, and I don't understand why you ask that, or why you took away my shoe.'

'This is an important matter,' said Ogilvie sternly. 'But I will ask you to wait outside while I check up your statement. Harris, take him out and find Mr. Grandison.'

Sergeant Harris returned with Grandison a few minutes later.

'I'm sorry to trouble you again, Mr. Grandison,' said Ogilvie. 'But I find it necessary to check up the movements of your chauffeur during yesterday morning. At what time did you first see him yesterday?'

'I think it was shortly after eleven o'clock. I walked over to his lodging and told him I had a job for him.'

'What was the job?'

'Only a door in my apartment which was giving trouble. It had dropped a little and was difficult to open and close.'

'Did he attend to it?'

'Yes — quite successfully.'

'How long was he on the job?'

'About two hours.'

'Was it necessary for him to take the door off its hinges?'

'Yes. He had to re-hang it.'

'Were you present all the time?'

'Most of the time. I think I went out

twice, for a few minutes on both occasions.'

'Did anyone help him?'

'No.'

Ogilvie looked at him sharply, and Grandison corrected himself.

'I held the door while he screwed it back,' he said. 'He was unable to do that alone.'

'I thought not,' said Ogilvie dryly. 'So he was in your apartment from approximately eleven o'clock until one?'

'Yes.'

'Did you take your car out last evening?'

'Yes.'

'Where did you go?'

'Into the town to pick up a parcel at the station.'

'You made the car rather dirty in so short a journey?'

'Did I? I didn't notice. But the lanes were rather muddy.

'I have an idea you don't believe me, Inspector,' said Grandison. 'But if you will ring up the parcels office at the railway station you will find that I signed

342

for a parcel there. Really, I fail to understand these curious questions.'

'That does not lessen the importance of the questions,' replied Ogilvie sweetly. 'Thank you, Mr. Grandison, that is all. Harris, I'll have that man in again.'

Harris knew his job, and went out with Grandison to return with the chauffeur, without permitting the two witnesses to engage in any conversation.

'Oh, Mr. Zanfeld,' he said. 'Did anyone help you with that job on the door?'

'No, sir,' replied Rupert.

'That's all, thank you.'

Rupert left the room, and Harris closed his note-book.

'Lying, sir?' he asked.

'Yes. Not a bad story, but Rupert slipped up about hanging the door alone. Grandison was smart enough to realise that, but had no opportunity to warn Rupert. I rather imagined this sort of thing would happen. Rupert has to have an alibi, and his one witness is Grandison. He also had to fill in the hours when he was on the road to London, so he pretends he washed two cars, but note

343

that those two cars were both owned by the business, and we have no means of checking that statement. But out of all this comes one not unimportant bit of information.'

'You mean collusion?'

'Yes.'

'Then what's the position, sir?'

'The position is that I can't prove murder — yet. But I want an open verdict at the inquest. After that — well, it's up to us. The inquest will take place the day after to-morrow as arranged.'

★ ★ ★

Colin found the coroner's inquest of the greatest interest. It was the first time he had attended such a ceremony and he was surprised at its comparative informality. The coroner was a stern-looking man who conducted affairs with the utmost gravity, and the witnesses were legion. At the last moment he was told, to his surprise, that he would not be called upon to give evidence, and as the inquest proceeded it became clear to him that the police had no intention of revealing all they knew. Not a word was mentioned of the finding of the scrap of paper at Simbourne's flat, nor of Colin's discovery in the sole of Rupert's shoe. Rupert was called, but his evidence was limited to the morning when he had seen Simbourne leave in his car.

It was Rosita who had to face the chief barrage, and Colin's heart went out to her. She was pale and nervous, but her answers were very clear and concise, but in regard to Simbourne's offer of marriage she seemed to have changed her ground a little. She said that Simbourne had not appeared to be greatly depressed by her refusal, but afterwards admitted that he was not the sort of man to display emotion, and that perhaps he had felt it more than he was willing to show. Colin could not help wondering whether in the meantime Grandison had been working on her.

The medical evidence was of a conflicting nature. There was no doubt that Simbourne had been shot at close range, but whether he could have inflicted that particular wound on himself was still in doubt. Of the three medical witnesses two thought it possible that he might have done so, while the third believed otherwise.

Grandison did some variations on Rosita's theme. He was certain that Simbourne had been bitterly disappointed by his rejection. In his own experience of Simbourne he had found him to be subject to fits of depression. He told how he had seen Simbourne near Rosita's bedroom door on one occasion — when Rosita was not in her room, and he referred regretfully to Simbourne's heavy drinking.

But this evidence was offset by that given by the young viscount, who had quite a different story to tell. He spoke with great feeling of his brother's past, and was of the opinion that his brother, despite a liking for drink, had a very balanced mind. He pointed out that Charles had been seriously contemplating settling down in Kenya, and that he had ample means to buy a farm and lead a happy life there. It might have been that he had hoped Rosita would go with him, as his wife, but he could not believe that this disappointment would have driven him to take his own life.

Finally, after many hours, the verdict was returned, after the coroner had directed the jury in a very eloquent and erudite summing up of the evidence. There was, he thought, insufficient evidence for a verdict of murder, and if they thought the evidence for suicide while the balance of Simbourne's mind was disturbed was not conclusive, their duty would be to return an open verdict. That verdict was subsequently returned. Inspector Ogilvie had got all he expected.

Colin tried to see Rosita afterwards, for there was much he wanted to say to her, but she was whisked away in Grandison's car as if that worthy feared she might be abducted. But he did manage to have a few words with Inspector Ogilvie.

'Did it go the way you expected?' he asked.

'Yes.'

'It doesn't mean the case is closed?'

'Far from it. Are you a fisherman?'

'To some extent.'

'Then you will appreciate that it is sometimes better to play a big and cunning fish for a while, rather than attempt to land him in one haul.'

'Do you mean Rupert?'

Ogilvie would say no more, and Colin was left to feel that the inspector knew very much more than he was prepared to divulge to any outsider. He found his car and only then did he realise that he was feeling far from well. He put it down to the crowded court, and the bad ventilation, but on reaching home the headache developed and compelled him to lie down on his bed. Early in the evening Mrs. Fairbright insisted on shoving a thermometer in his mouth.

'Goodness!' she ejaculated. 'You're over a hundred and one. You must have caught the 'flu.'

'Oh, nonsense.'

'Well, don't you dare move from that bed. If you're not better in the morning I'll call the doctor.'

'I'll be all right by then.'

But morning found Colin worse. His

temperature was still up, and every limb ached most painfully. His throat too felt like a piece of sandpaper. Mrs. Fairbright got her way, and the family doctor came along and quickly diagnosed the case.

''Flu,' he said. 'There's a lot of it about. Nothing to do but stay put — and I mean that.'

'You would,' growled Colin. 'I've never had 'flu in my life.'

'Well, you've got it now.'

Colin cursed his bad luck. More than ever he wanted to see Rosita for he was convinced that Grandison's influence over her was not to her good. In all probability argument would be useless, but at least he could try. The doctor's opinion was that within three or four days the worst ravages would pass, but this hope was not borne out. The sickness took a new turn. Colin was aware of a growing pain in his chest, and twenty-four hours later the doctor looked grave as he put away his stethoscope.

'What is it?' asked Mrs. Fairbright anxiously.

'Pneumonia.'

'Oh!'

After that the world seemed to fade out for Colin. Every night his temperature sailed up to dangerous heights, and was only checked by large doses of M and B, the effect of which was violent sickness. There were spells of delirium during which he talked all sorts of nonsense. But at intervals he was lucid.

'Did you telephone Rosita?' he asked Rhoda.

'No.'

'But I told you — '

'You didn't, Colin.'

'I — I thought I did. Rhoda, telephone her and tell her why — why I haven't been to see her. How long have I been in bed?'

'Ten days.'

'Oh, no. It's only three or four days. There was something I wanted you to tell the inspector — something — '

'Please, Colin,' begged Rhoda. 'Don't excite yourself. All that is over. You're very ill and must lie quiet. The doctor said that on no account — '

'But this is important. Did you

350

telephone Rosita?'

'You have only just asked me that. I'll go down and telephone her now, if you will only lie quiet.'

'Yes — yes. Please do,' he murmured.

Rhoda wet-eyed went downstairs and was successful in speaking to Rosita. Rosita gave a little gasp as she heard the news.

'I'm so sorry,' she said. 'Could I see him if I called?'

'I don't quite know. I shall have to ask the doctor. You see, at times he's not conscious.'

'I'll call to-morrow and take a chance,' said Rosita.

She carried out this promise, but in the meantime the doctor had forbidden any visitors whatsoever, and when Rosita called it would have been useless in any case, for Colin was literally fighting for his life. Rosita seemed to be tremendously moved.

'All I can do is write, now,' she said. 'For I am leaving Alton to-morrow. I'm terribly — terribly sorry. Will you give him all my love and tell him I'll write and let him know my whereabouts and how things go with me?'

Rhoda nodded. It surprised her that Rosita was leaving, but she did not ask any questions, for her mind was too full of her personal trouble. What happened to Rosita could not matter very much to Colin in his present condition. Things were at a crisis and the next day or two must decide that issue. So she packed Rosita off and went back to the sick room, where poor Colin lay in extremis.

18

During the next few days it was touch and go with Colin, and then there came a change for the better, and soon the doctor gave it as his opinion that the worst was over. Nothing happened to cause him to change his mind, and Colin found himself emerging from a kind of dream, the details of which were never very clear.

'A nice time you've given us,' said Rhoda. 'You ought to be ashamed of yourself.'

'I am,' replied Colin weakly. 'Pull the curtains a bit more, and let me see the garden.'

He gave a little sigh of joy as Rhoda did his bidding. Spring was on the way, and the prunus and almond trees were showing small pink buds in the bright sunshine. Further afield he could see little clumps of early bulbs in full bloom, and there was much birdsong. To him it was like being born again.

'My first real illness,' he said. 'Can't say I like it. When shall I be able to get up?'

'What a question for a man only just risen from the dead. The garden's looking lovely isn't it?'

'Wonderful. Rhoda, tell me about Rosita.'

'But I've told you. She said she would write.'

'Did she say where she was going?'

'No.'

'You should have asked her.'

'I was distracted at the time. You were desperately ill and mother and I could think of nothing else. Don't you think she'll keep her promise?'

'Yes, of course.'

'You don't sound very confident. If I were you I should forget all about her.'

'Why do you say that?' he asked sharply.

'Well, isn't she rather a strange person?'

'In what way?'

'Going off with Grandison the way she did.'

'She had her living to get.'

'Weren't there other ways of getting it.

That man has a terrible reputation. There are many people who still believe he had something to do with Simbourne's death, and was clever enough to get away with it. Yet she goes off with him — '

She stopped as from below came the double ring at the bell which usually heralded the postman's arrival.

'Mother's not up yet,' she said. 'I must go down.'

She left Colin for a minute or two and then came back with a letter in her hand.

'Talking of angels,' she said. 'This may be what you are so anxious to receive. It bears the Paris postmark.'

Colin took the letter and recognised at once the bold handwriting. A new light gleamed in his eyes, but he made no attempt to open it.

'Am I right?' asked Rhoda.

He nodded his head.

'At least she kept her promise. Now I must see about breakfast. No help this morning.'

When she had gone Colin slit open the envelope and extracted a letter, to which was attached a cutting from a Paris newspaper. He raised himself a little higher on the pillow and started to read the letter. The opening phrases dealt with his illness and her unsuccessful attempt to see him. They rang with sincerity and anxiety and she prayed that he was getting better. She had given her first concert before a big and appreciative audience, and enclosed the cutting from one of the most important French newspapers. She admitted being shockingly nervous until she started to play, but after that all was well. On the following Tuesday she was due to play in Brussels, and she begged him to write to the Hotel Royale and give her some good news about himself. It had been hard to leave without seeing him, but there had been no way out of it, and he had been in her mind every hour of every day. Would he send his letter by air mail that she might get it the sooner. It would make all the difference in the world to know that he was getting better. Perhaps, in a few weeks she might be able to fly back and see him, while still keeping her engagements. She mentioned Grandison only once. He had been most kind and considerate to her, and was an excellent manager. She was overjoyed by the reception at her first concert. It made such a difference to have a good send-off. But how she wished he might have been there to share her undoubted success.

Colin then read the newspaper cutting, and was not surprised that Rosita felt gratified. The eminent critic referred to her as 'a newcomer in the field of musical interpretation whose progress all lovers of pianoforte music would watch with the keenest interest and delight. Her performance was of quite outstanding quality'. Colin was finding it hard to blame her for taking the step to personal advancement. All along she had made it plain that music was her first love — that she believed she had a mission, and that Grandison was a providential accessory to the divine plan. It was not impossible that she was right and that Grandison was innocent of the villainy attributed to him by some. But in that matter he had grave doubts. He could not but believe that Rosita was so blinded by the call of music that she failed to recognise any ulterior motive on the part of her champion.

He lost no time in writing back — a long careful letter assuring her of his recovery, and of his joy at the possibility of her and him meeting again before he was due to go back to the scene of his work. It was significant that not once did he mention Grandison, for to do so without making clear his suspicion and dislike of the man would have been impossible. He gave the letter to Rhoda and asked her to send it by air mail, and after that he felt much better.

The days passed and his quick progress astonished the doctor. He waited for another letter but none came. Disappointed as he was he made excuses for her, but soon he realised that if he wrote out of turn she would not be likely to get the letter before she left Brussels, so instead he sent a telegram, asking for her next address. To this there was no reply.

Now he was able to sit in the garden in the ever-increasing sunshine, and whenever the post came his heart thumped with expectation. But the silence continued, and he began to imagine all sorts of ghastly possibilities. Then, one afternoon, he was surprised to see a car coming up the drive. Out of it stepped Inspector Ogilvie. Colin, got up from his chair and walked to meet the inspector.

'I was in the neighbourhood,' said Ogilvie, 'and thought I would call. I heard you had been ill. How are things?'

'I'm almost fit again. It was very good of you to drop in. Can I offer you a drink?'

'No, thanks. I can't stay more than a few minutes. Do you know where Rosita is?'

'No. I wish I did.'

'You knew she had gone on a tour with Grandison?'

'Yes. I meant to have told you that, but I was suddenly bowled over with 'flu and then pneumonia. How did you know?'

'It was my business to know. She went to Paris and then to Brussels.'

'I heard from her while she was in Paris, but nothing since.'

'Hm!' grunted Ogilvie. 'I was hoping

you would know what her programme was. I thought I could rely upon our French colleagues, but they let me down.'

'You mean you had Rosita under observation?'

'Not Rosita exactly, but her companions. That case is not closed by a long chalk.'

'I see.'

'I should have liked to have kept Grandison in this country, but I had no grounds for holding him. The position is a bit sticky, and what I fear most is that he may lose himself in some South American state. I suspect that tour was simply a ruse to get out of the country.'

'But the concerts were genuine, weren't they?'

'So far as I can discover. But it's strange that he seems only to have booked Paris and Brussels, and that was done through a Frenchman who cannot now be found.'

'Good God! I'm sure Rosita never knew that. She mentioned all sorts of other engagements.'

'Did she give you any address after Brussels?'

'No. I wired her to ask her to do so, but got no reply.'

'If you should hear later will you let me know?'

'Of course. Inspector, is she in any danger?'

'Difficult to say. It depends upon what her relations are with Grandison.'

'Relations! There are none except a business arrangement.'

Ogilvie shook his head.

'What's in your mind?' asked Colin.

'I suggest that Grandison wouldn't have taken the girl with him if he hadn't been in love with her. There are reasons why he wanted to hide himself. Why should he act as he has done unless he was sure he could rely upon Rosita? It scarcely makes sense, does it?'

It was Colin's turn to shake his head. What Ogilvie was suggesting was hateful, and yet there was a lot of commonsense in it.

'You mentioned 'companions',' he said. 'Who else is with them?'

'The chauffeur — Rupert.'

'Then — then Rupert must be in his confidence?'

'Very much so.'

'Did they take the car with them?'

'Yes. That, I think, was the excuse to take Rupert.'

'Can't you trace them by the car registration number?'

'That raises an interesting point. The car which they took over was sold in Brussels ten days ago. Grandison apparently had the sense to realise that it was dangerous to ride about in it. You see, it all goes to bear out my conviction that he is really on the run, and has no intention of ever returning to this country.'

'Yes, I — I can see that now,' agreed Colin, much moved by these revelations. 'What about Stockforth, his late partner, doesn't he know where Grandison is bound for?'

'He may do, but I rather doubt it. I've questioned him twice and he swears he knows nothing about Grandison's past. Well, I am hoping to hear soon that contact has been made again. I'll let you know if I hear.'

'Thank you,' said Colin.

The inspector left a minute or two later, and Colin was left with his sombre thoughts. Slowly the days went by and not a word came from Rosita. Then the doctor came with a suggestion which Colin seized upon instantly.

'A change of air would do you the world of good,' he said. 'It would set you up finally. The weather is changing again and it looks as if we shall soon be shivering in a north-east wind. Why not take the car and find some enduring sunshine. There's Switzerland, or the French Riviera — '

'What about money? You can't take more than a few miserable pounds.'

'That could be arranged. There's a special allocation for persons in need of convalescence. Your bank would give you a form and I should be pleased to sign it. On the continent one can still get almost unlimited petrol. Think it over.'

Colin did think it over, and the idea appealed to him very much. To get into the car and drive across France into the sunshine was a prospect which did him good even to think of it. On the following day he walked into the town and saw his bank manager. The requisite form was produced and Colin filled it up.

'Better ask for more currency than you need,' advised the bank manager. 'Then if they cut the amount you may still have ample.'

A week later the permit was issued, and he found himself in possession of two hundred and fifty pounds' worth of traveller's cheques. A few more days sufficed for him to make arrangements for the transport of the car across the channel, and all the time his strength was flowing back like a river in full spate. Rhoda watched his feverish interest and undisguised impatience to be off, and came to the conclusion it was not all due to motives of health.

'It's Rosita,' she said to her mother. 'He can't get her out of his mind.'

'I know,' replied wise Mrs. Fairbright, and left it at that.

At last the day of departure came and

Colin checked up everything in the car.

'On this occasion,' he said. 'I appear to have forgotten nothing.'

'But you have,' replied Mrs. Fairbright. 'You haven't told us where we are to send any correspondence.'

'I'll wire you when I land up somewhere. Look after yourselves you two.'

A couple of quick kisses — so unusual with him — and he was on his way.

19

On the following night Colin reached Paris, and found himself a small hotel off the Champs Elysée. After a good but very expensive meal in a nearby restaurant he went out into the streets, and found Paris very different from what it had been when last he was there — before the Second World War. There was a noticeable slowing down of the old tempo and a great diminution of road traffic. The newspapers were even smaller than the British, and the men were even worse dressed than their compatriots on the other side of the channel. His desire was to find the place where Rosita had given her first concert, and he asked the first gendarme he saw. He learned that he was miles away from it, but that he could catch a bus which actually passed the place by waiting in the queue opposite. He waited and ultimately got aboard the overcrowded vehicle.

Twenty minutes later he got off immediately opposite the large concert hall. It was but dimly-lighted and when he stepped inside the vestibule he saw that only the booking-office was open. There was no concert that evening, but a bill announced a concert for the following evening. Two persons were booking seats and Colin waited until they had finished their business. Then he went to the grille and smiled at the girl behind it. She did not return the smile but asked him if he wished to purchase tickets.

'No, thanks,' he said in French. 'I wanted some information — about a pianist who appeared here some weeks ago. Her name was Rosita Paston. I am a friend of hers.'

'What is it you wish to know?'

'Do you know where she is appearing this week?'

'No — I regret. She was a very fine pianist, but I do not know where she went.' A man entered the booking-office behind her, and she spoke to him in voluble French. He peered at Colin through the grille.

'I will come round, m'sieur,' he said.

A few moments later he emerged from a side door, and bowed to Colin.

'So you are a friend of Madame Paston?' he asked.

'Yes. I came from England yesterday. She wrote and told me she had given a concert here.'

'That is so. She was a most talented artiste. I understood that she was going on to Brussels, but that was weeks ago.'

'Do you happen to know where she was due to appear — after the Brussels concert?'

'No. Her manager was not very communicative. I was anxious to book up madame for another concert in six weeks' time, but he would not commit himself. He just said he had certain arrangements for madame, but would think over my suggestion. I am afraid I went behind his back a little and approached madame herself, but she was satisfied to leave the whole matter to Mr. — Mr. — '

'Grandison.'

'Yes, that was the name. A very dominating gentleman.'

'I agree,' said Colin. 'Well, I am sorry to have troubled you.'

'Not at all. If you are a friend of madame you might tell her when you see her that we should be glad to see her again.'

'I will,' promised Colin.

Within twenty-four hours Colin found Paris a very expensive place for a man with but a limited amount of sterling, and he decided to linger there no longer. He dallied with the idea of going to Brussels and raising questions there concerning Rosita, but ultimately he accepted the improbability of succeeding where Ogilvie had failed, and Brussels was well off the route that appealed to him — that route which went south to the sunny Mediterranean, for overnight the sky had become full of clouds, and now it was drizzling with cold rain.

'Which is the best route to the south?' he asked the waiter at the hotel.

'There are many ways, m'sieur. Some go by the Rhone Valley, others over the Alpes Maritimes. Speaking for myself I should go by Clermont Ferrand and Issoire.'

'I don't know those places.'

'All the more reason why you should go. It is a little further but you would enjoy it. You go by Fontainebleau to Moulins, and then westward to Clermont and across the Sevennes to Le Puy and Mende. I was born at Mende. It is a lovely place still, and the road to the coast runs through the beautiful Gorge de Tarn to Nîmes and Arles. It is all unspoiled country and at this time of the year supremely beautiful. It is the way the nightingales come on their way to England. From Arles it is but a short journey to Marseilles, and so to the pleasure grounds of Europe. I wish I were there.'

Colin got out his maps and looked up the route. It looked interesting, and the waiter's enthusiasm was markedly sincere. After lunch he got out the car and very soon Paris was behind him. The roads in the main were straight and empty, and the rain pelted down. But by late evening he had passed through the rain-belt, and had reached Moulins, where he bargained for bed and breakfast, determined to conserve his precious francs.

The following morning brought blue skies and warm sunshine. He made an early start and now found himself in completely new country. At Clermont Ferrand he commenced the long climb to the higher altitudes, and very soon the hotel waiter's enthusiasm was justified. He made no attempt to hurry for the scenery was incomparable. At a quaint little village he was served a magnificent lunch for quite a reasonable charge, with excellent wine thrown in. It was market day, and the place was packed with carts, ancient cars and what not. Everyone seemed to know everyone else, and he felt very much a stranger in a strange land. He listened to snatches of conversation, but found it difficult to follow all the local patois. But it was all a marvellous contrast to the life which he had lived recently, and he lingered there in the sunshine for a long time.

Late that evening he arrived at Mende, which he found to be a town of quite appreciable size, living by what means he knew not. The main hotel was a modern structure, and here he was warmly welcomed by the proprietor who spoke English, and insisted on doing so even when Colin ventured to address him in his somewhat halting French. He learned that Mende was a considerable touring centre in the summer season, from which one could make short excursions to the innumerable places of scenic interest in the neighbourhood. Colin was tempted to stay awhile, but the real south was calling him, and now he was on the verge of it.

The doctor had been right. Already he felt miles better, with so much to engage his attention. Nîmes and Arles were veritable treasure stores, and at the latter place he found it impossible to go on and after driving the car through streets that were no wider than alleys he found himself in an old Roman Forum, part of which was incorporated in a hotel, which appeared to be beseeching him to come inside. There he booked a room for the night, but actually he stayed there two days, admiring the wonderful Roman antiques which abounded everywhere.

From where he indulged in the expensive luxury of a telephone call, and heard Rhoda's voice as clear as a bell.

'Where are you?' she asked.

'Arles.'

'Where?'

'Arles. A-R-L-E-S, in the south of France.'

'Never heard of it. Is it nice?'

'It's marvellous. To-day has been like an English summer. Any letters for me?'

'Only two bills. Where are you going next?'

'I don't know. Somewhere along the coast. I'll wire you when I feel like settling down for a bit.'

Mrs. Fairbright had half a minute on the line.

'Oh, Colin dear,' she said. 'Are you all right?'

'As good as new. This is a wonderful part of the country. Warm and sunny and lazy.'

'Expensive?'

'Until you know the ropes. I really am doing well, so don't worry.'

'Bless you. Do let us hear frequently.

The weather is vile here. You're well out of it.'

Colin thought so too, when on the next day he drove to the coast and made his way through Marseilles. Now the palm trees, olives and mimosas were in full display, and through the umbrella pines he got glimpses of the blue Mediterranean. He had never driven on that part of the coast before and every moment was sheer joy. He came down to the sea at Ciotat, parked the car outside a small café, and took a seat under a striped umbrella.

'Any beer?' he asked the waiter who came to him.

'*Oui*, m'sieur. Iced Lager.'

'Splendid. Make it a large one.'

At the next table was a bronzed man of about thirty years of age. He wore shorts and heavy walking boots, while beside him was a colossal rucksack. He looked English and he was obviously interested in Colin's car, the G.B. plate of which was in full view of him.

'From England?' he asked.

'Yes. You too presumably?'

374

The bronzed man nodded and stared at the brilliant blue sea.

'Grand sight, isn't it?' he said. 'I've been dreaming of this for years. Always wanted to walk from coast to coast and here I am.'

'Come over here and have another drink,' said Colin.

The bronzed man nodded and shifted himself and his rucksack to Colin's table. The waiter came with Colin's iced lager in a towering glass.

'What are you drinking?' asked Colin of his companion.

'That stuff looks pretty good to me.'

Colin nodded at the waiter and a second huge glass was speedily brought.

'Here's to the sunny Riviera,' said the bronzed man, and took a long gulp. 'Gosh, that's good,' he said. 'I had a thirst I wouldn't have sold for five quid. My name's Stafford — Hugh Stafford, late major of the Armoured Corps.'

'Mine's Colin Fairbright.'

'Army?'

'No. I was caught up in Malaya, but managed to get as far as India. Went back to Malaya after the Japs threw in their hand, and am now on leave. How long have you been on the road?'

'Three weeks. I was demobbed five weeks ago.'

'Which way did you come?'

'Down the Rhone Valley. Trouble with this sort of travelling is clean linen. Every few days I have to stop and get my laundry done. But it's the best way to see the country. Lord, but it's expensive these days. Fortunately, I have a brother in Paris and was able to borrow some money from him. Going far?'

'Haven't made up my mind. I'll probably stay at Cannes for a bit. Where do you plan to finish up?'

'Nice I think. One can live reasonably cheap there. But I'm breaking my journey at Bandol. That's not far from here. Lovely little spot. Haven't been there since — since I had a honeymoon. That was nearly ten years ago. Know Bandol?'

'Only by name.'

Stafford gave a curious little sigh.

'Seems longer,' he said. 'Twice as long.

So much has happened since then. I guess I'm a bit crazy to come back.'

'Why?' asked Colin.

'Always a risk in coming back to a place where you have been sublimely happy. I had a wife then, and a home, and hopes — '

He stopped and took a long drink from his glass.

'You see, Angela — my wife — was killed in an air-raid while I was in training. There — there was absolutely nothing left. Just a vast hole in the ground. No home, no Angela — nothing — nothing. Forgive me talking of my personal affairs, but all this brings it back so vividly. Have another drink?'

'Well, just a short one — for the road. A vermouth — plain.'

'Good idea. Hey, garçon!'

'How far is Bandol from here?' asked Colin.

'About ten miles.'

'Then have a ride for a change. You must be fed up with that rucksack, and I have to pass the place.'

'You mean that?'

'Of course.'

'Thanks. I will.'

A few minutes later Stafford pushed the large rucksack in the back of the car and took the seat next to Colin.

'Nice after you've been travelling rough,' he said. 'I think you'll like this place where I'm going. So you play golf?'

'Yes. I brought the clubs as I had plenty of room.'

'I used to play a lot. There's a marvellous course up at Mont Agel, above Monte Carlo, but the scenery up there is so gorgeous a chap simply can't keep his eye on the ball. I call this a disgusting way to finish up a walking tour. It was all your fault.'

Colin laughed and set the car moving. Stafford seemed to get excited as they drew near to Bandol. Colin could see him out of the corner of his eye twisting his brown hands together. At last they came to the little port, passed the cluster of buildings and proceeded along the promenade, where the palms and mimosa were brilliant in the sunlight.

'Steady!' said Stafford. 'It's near here. I

remember that villa. Just about a hundred yards from here.'

Colin slowed down, and came almost to a stop. He heard a low gasp from Stafford, and glanced at his distorted face. A moment later he found the reason. The war had reached Bandol and on the left was a hideous scar — a ghastly gap in the line of buildings, and some piled heaps of rubble. Colin stopped the car and Stafford almost fell out of it.

'It was here,' he said. 'That's part of the garden — where we used to sit — Angela and I. I meant to spend a few quiet days here, remembering — recalling — '

'Come back,' said Colin, in a low voice. 'Let's get on.'

'But — '

'I'll drop you somewhere farther along the coast. You don't need to do any more trudging — not to-day.'

Stafford hesitated for a few moments and then climbed back into the car. Colin drove on at once, and soon pretty little Bandol was left behind. That evening they reached Cannes, and stayed at one of the smaller hotels along the front.

'Jolly good of you to give me that lift,' said Stafford. 'To be frank I was a bit tired of walking.'

'I was glad of your comapany. See you later.'

In the days that followed Colin became very attached to his companion. Like so many others caught at an early age in the web of war he was uncertain about the future. He had been in an insurance office, and his job was still open to him — after he had taken his leave, but he couldn't see himself again in that occupation.

'It must be something active,' he said. 'But I'm not going to think about it. What about a spot of golf?'

'It's a question of golf clubs. But doubtless the 'pro' would fix you up.'

'But you've got a whole bag full, and I don't use many clubs. We'll make do.'

'Just as you like.'

What followed was surprising. Despite his illness Colin found himself in excellent form. He had not asked Stafford's handicap in view of the informal nature of the game, and he

380

realised that his companion was at a disadvantage in playing with borrowed tools, but the way Stafford went round that course was miraculous. He hit everything straight up the fairway, and did a long series of 'fours' that took Colin's breath away. When it was all over Colin, who had pencilled down Stafford's score, found that he had gone round in two strokes under bogey.

'Why didn't you tell me you were a professional?' he asked.

'I nearly was, but my father objected and pushed me into that office. But I was a bit lucky on that round.'

'I couldn't see any sign of luck. Next time we play I want four strokes from you. Do you play any more games?'

'Quite a lot. You see my father was an Oxford double-blue, and sport with him was a religion. He used to coach me at tennis and golf, and he had the patience of Job. He needed it too for in those days I was plumb lazy.'

The days they spent at Cannes were full of sunshine and fun. Stafford was the most excellent companion — ready to go anywhere or do anything which seemed to appeal to Colin. There was a noticeable absence of English people at Cannes. Most of the villas were closed, and the hotels were doing badly. Every day Colin bought all the French and foreign newspapers that he could lay hands on, and spent hours reading through the advertisements — a process which puzzled Stafford.

'Are you looking for a job?' he asked.

'No. I'm looking for some mention of a certain musical genius who is doing a European tour. I've lost touch with her.'

'Oh, it's a 'her'.'

'Yes. Her name is Rosita Paston, and she plays the piano divinely.'

'I can't imagine anybody giving a concert in this town. You couldn't fill the village hall.'

'That's true. But there's Nice, Milan and such places. I merely want to find out where she is.'

'An old friend?'

'Not very old. I met her in peculiar circumstances, and then, like a fool fell ill and lost touch with her.'

'You can't very well blame yourself for falling ill. Colin, do I smell a romance.'

'What you smell may turn out to be a tragedy. The trouble is I feel so damned helpless, and all the time someone else may be making the running. But let's go and have a bathe.'

Colin had wired his address at Cannes, and that afternoon he received a letter by air mail. As he feared there had been no communication from Rosita. The two letters which Rhoda had re-addressed were of no importance. The strange behaviour on the part of Rosita was the one dark cloud on his mental horizon. In the fortnight which had passed since he left home all his old abundant health had flowed back. The weight which he had lost had been regained, and he thought he felt better than ever before.

'I was lucky meeting you, Staf,' he said. 'Apart from your companionship which I value very much, you're keeping me fit. All this golf and swimming is just what I needed. I hope you're not going to run out on me — yet.'

Stafford looked reflective, and Colin realised that he had struck an unexpectedly important note.

'I was going to mention that, Colin,' said Stafford. 'The fact is I'm using up more money than I expected. You see, I scarcely bargained for staying in a first-class hotel.'

'Then let's get out and find a cheaper one.'

'I've been trying, but they're still beyond my immediate means.'

'Then let's get on to Nice, and find a garret,' laughed Colin. 'But better still, let me lend you some money. You see I got some extra sterling on the score of being an invalid. Don't laugh. At any rate I wasn't up to scratch. I've got enough money to see me through nicely, with a bit to spare.'

Stafford shook his head.

'It's generous of you, Colin,' he said. 'But at home I've put a seal on the little money I possess. I have already borrowed a hundred pounds from my brother in Paris, and that I shall pay him when he comes to England. I've got to get through with what money I have. I really think we had better split up, because you don't look the sort of chap who could exist in a fifth-rate hotel.'

'You find the hotel and I'll show you how wrong you are.'

'That's a bet. Ready to go to Nice, to-morrow?'

'Yes.'

20

At Nice on the following day Stafford found his fifth-rate hotel. It had no hot water in the bedrooms, and the scant furniture was broken-down and ugly. But it did possess a lovely little garden, and as it was on high land one could see the old port and the sea beyond over the roofs of the houses below. Their fellow guests all seemed to be displaced persons, living on their wits, and Colin was sure that one night they would get their throats cut. Here they committed themselves to bed and breakfast only, resolving to take the main meals at one of the thousand restaurants in the sprawling town. But after a couple of days they discovered that their humble hostelry could provide better and cheaper main meals than they could get anywhere else. Moreover, there was Beatrix — the half-Italian waitress, who looked as if she might have sat for Botticelli, and who spoke English with the most alluring accent.

'Do you think she's really only eighteen?' asked Stafford.

'Why not?' asked Colin.

'But she's so matured.'

'So would you be if you had to work half as hard as Beatrix. She's always working when we get up, and is still working when we go to bed. By the time she's forty she will be a hag.'

'I'll bet she isn't,' retorted Stafford. 'She's absolutely perfectly formed. Given the right clothes she could wipe the floor with all those Hollywood synthetic beauties who earn a thousand quid a week. Do you know that she's got rather a 'pash' on you.'

'Don't be absurd.'

'It's true. I've seen her cleaning your shoes. She handles them as if they were gold. Mine she merely spits on.'

'Don't. You ruin my illusions.'

'You'll finish up by taking her to the cinema, and having a knife stuck in your back by that Italian waiter.'

Colin laughed. He liked Beatrix well enough, but there was someone else he liked far better, of whom he dared now scarcely think, because of the long silence that had taken place, and seemed likely to be maintained. He still bought masses of newspapers, but that magic name never appeared.

In the meantime here was Nice, packed with people, despite the absence of those who had made the place — the British, soaked in sunshine and brilliant with flowers. Nice had its problems too, but life on the whole was joyful. Stafford took him to the golf course at Mont Agel — or rather he took Stafford in the car. It proved to be a very expensive day, for the green fees were heavy, and the price of the lunch was heavier still.

They came down from the higher altitudes to the cleanest little town in the world, and had some drinks at the café outside the Casino. Afterwards they dined at a small restaurant, again at great cost. But Colin was delighted to be able to change a travellers' cheque at black market rates, which reduced the day's cost.

'Let's be hogs and go to the Casino,' he

said. 'I used to be lucky at roulette.'

'Believe it or not,' said Stafford, 'I've never played roulette in my life.'

'Then it's time you did. It may teach you never to play again.'

'Can't afford to lose much.'

'You needn't. You can get a lot of fun for a pound or two.'

They produced their passports and paid for a day ticket. Despite the wonderful sunshine outside the place was packed with persons of all nationalities. The majority were in ordinary lounge suits, but there was a smattering of evening-dress. They bought their chips and lined up at one of the tables where every seat was occupied. Stafford had no idea of the game, and Colin gave him a few instructions.

'Don't waste your money on long odds,' he concluded. 'Keep to the even chances. It's your only hope of winning. And watch your stake, or one of these ghastly-looking females may claim it if it wins.'

Stafford, after much reflection, put a hundred-franc chip on red, and the spinning ball finally came to rest in No. 23. The croupier raked in the losers and doubled Stafford's piece.

'Shall I let it stay?' whispered Stafford.

'Don't ask me. It's your money.'

Stafford decided to let both pieces stay where they were, and again red won. The croupier threw in two more chips.

'Now what?' asked Stafford excitedly.

Colin, who had lost both his bets, had no advice to offer, so Stafford let the four pieces stay. Red won for the third time, and Stafford saw the pile raised higher. Colin who had made his first win, saw the nice heap of chips in front of Stafford.

'Is that all yours?' he asked

'Yes. Three times in succession.'

'Then collect some of it you ass. It can't go on for ever.'

'*Faites vos jeux, messieurs!*' called the croupier.

'Go on, pick it up,' urged Colin.

Stafford reached over and picked up his pieces, but in doing so the bottom piece slipped and dropped on to a single number.

'*Rien ne va plus!*' called the croupier.

390

'You'll have to let it lie,' said Colin.

The ball dropped into a slot, but the wheel continued to revolve for a few moments. Then it stopped and Colin saw that No. 24 had come up. It was the number on which Stafford had dropped his piece.

'Good God!' he ejaculated. 'Of all the luck!'

'Have I won?' asked Stafford.

'You wait and see.'

The croupier paid out the lesser odds and finally pushed chips to the value of 3,500 francs across to Stafford. In his enormous surprise Stafford forgot the stake.

'It's marvellous,' he said. 'You told me never to back a single number. Shows you know nothing about it.'

The wheel had been spun again and it stopped very quickly.

'*Vingt-quatre, noir pair et passe!*' chanted the croupier.

'My hat, you've done it again!' gasped Colin. 'Get your money and come and have a drink. I feel quite faint.'

'Not me,' said Stafford. 'I'm only just beginning.'

391

'Staff, be sensible,' begged Colin. 'You have had the most fantastic luck. Cash in while the going's good.'

'Oh, have a heart. I haven't enjoyed myself so much in years.'

'Well, put away five thousand and gamble with the balance. I'm going to try the other table. This one is too crowded.'

Colin moved to the opposite table, where some big gambling was taking place. He stood behind a seated man — one of the few in evening dress, and watched him scattering big bets everywhere. Whether he was winning or not it was difficult to say, but in front of him were piles of bone chips — many marked 5,000, and these he tossed about with complete abandon. Whenever he won a large sum he passed the croupier a couple of hundred francs. Colin had small luck on that side of the table so he moved round it, and then, for the first time, he saw the face of the big gambler. Instantly he forgot all about the game, for the man in immaculate evening-dress was no stranger to him. He was Rupert — Grandison's chauffeur!

Colin moved behind a very tall man lest he should be seen and recognised. His heart was thumping madly, and all his interest in the game had completely vanished. What was Rupert doing there — dressed like a duke? Had he left Grandison's employ, and come into a fortune? Or had his association with Grandison been closer than had been suspected? It was a little significant that Grandison had retained him after he had decided to make that tour with Rosita. It was significant too that Grandison had served as Rupert's alibi in the Simbourne case. And if Rupert was here, why not Grandison too — and perhaps Rosita?

He stood and watched Rupert playing, and it soon became obvious that he was losing heavily, for the great pile of counters grew less and less. But he displayed no emotions of any kind, whether his stakes were gathered in by the croupier's rake, or whether masses of chips were pushed across to him. All the time the question uppermost in Colin's mind was what his next move was to be.

To reveal himself to Rupert was unthinkable, for Rupert would undoubtedly lie if it suited his purpose, and then warn Grandison who, if it suited his interest, would promptly place himself outside Colin's reach. But at any moment Rupert might cease playing and leave the casino. Finally Colin detached himself from the crowd and went over to where he had left Stafford. He found that Stafford had now got himself a seat, next to the croupier, and in front of him was a big stack of chips.

'Staff, how is it going?' he asked.

'Fine. I can't go wrong. Have you given it up?'

'Yes. Something has happened. I may have to leave at any moment now. If so I'll come back for you?'

Stafford looked up at him.

'Anything wrong?' he asked.

'Yes, and no. Can't explain now.'

'Then I'll come with you. After all, we can come here another day.'

He gave the croupier some chips, and then crammed his pockets with the rest. Colin looked back at the other table and saw Rupert still sitting there. Stafford stood up, smiled at the croupier and then joined Colin.

'Where do I cash in my winnings?' he asked.

Colin led him to the nearest *caisse*, and watched him hand in great piles of chips. He had them in all his pockets, and the sum total was considerable. Then Colin paid in his own diminished store.

'I seem to have lost a couple of thousand francs,' he said. 'Well, what is the final result with you?'

'I'm over twenty thousand up. That's about forty quid. Enough to enable me to live at a higher level for a few weeks. You'll like that, won't you?'

'I'm not so sure. I'm not so sure — Oh, here comes the man I have been watching. I've got to get my hat. Come on quick. I can't afford to lose sight of him. That's the fellow — the dark man in evening-dress. He must have a hat or coat here. I must get to the car and watch him when he comes out.'

Stafford, mystified, went with Colin to the *vestiaire*. They quickly got their hats, and Colin managed to hide himself while Rupert tendered his *vestiaire* ticket. Then they hurried out, and found the car where they had left it — in the main avenue not far from the casino entrance. He sat at the wheel facing the casino.

'Here he comes,' he said. 'If he passes us get out and see if he has a car here.'

Rupert came up the avenue on the other side of the drive. Colin kept his head low, and finally Rupert passed the car, without even glancing at it. Stafford then got out.

'Crossing the street,' he said. 'Yes, he's going to a car further up. Looks like a Delage. It's facing this way, so he'll have to come past us. Coming out now.'

'Come inside then.'

Soon Colin saw the Delage through his driving mirror. It was a luxurious saloon, and it passed him at a crawl. Immediately it made the turn at the bottom Colin set his own car in motion. It was now almost dark and a myriad lights were twinking over Condamine and on craft afloat in the delectable little harbour.

'Wonder which way he'll go,' said Colin.

The Delage swung to the left at the bottom of the hill.

'Hurrah, he's going our way!' said Stafford. 'But what's the idea exactly? Are you a detective in disguise?'

'That fellow in the boiled shirt may lead me to someone I am anxious to meet.'

Stafford gave him a sharp glance.

'Not the pianist by any chance?' he asked.

'Yes.'

'I see.'

'You don't — quite. His name is Rupert Zanfeld, and he is — or was — chauffeur to a man named Grandison. It was Grandison who persuaded Rosita Paston to give a series of concerts abroad. She promised to keep in touch with me, but after one letter there has been a most mysterious silence. I want to know why.'

'Couldn't you have asked him while you had the chance — Rupert I mean?'

'He might have lied. He and Grandison are mixed up in a murder. Rosita believes them to be innocent, but I don't. They were successful in getting out of England, but there's a gentleman at Scotland Yard who wants to locate them.'

'But why, if they want to lose themselves, should they take this girl — Rosita — with them?'

Colin winced.

'It doesn't seem to make sense, does it?' asked Stafford.

'It does to me. Grandison is in love with Rosita, but she doesn't know it. She has no idea of the sort of man he really is. My hat, he's putting up a pace.'

They had entered a straight stretch of road and the big Delage was now tearing ahead at enormous speed. Colin put his foot down hard and Stafford held his breath. In front of them was a wide charabanc and the road now curved a little. As Colin made to pass it a car came from the other direction. It was a perilous situation, but Colin gave the car the last ounce of acceleration and shot through the narrow gap, to miss the oncoming car by a few feet. The infuriated driver of the car shook a clenched fist out of the window.

'My God!' ejaculated Stafford. 'We'll finish up in the local morgue.'

'Sorry, but this is a chance which may not come again.'

'I agree absolutely,' replied Stafford grimly.

'I'll get him yet. He can't keep up that pace on the curly bits of road. Just close your eyes, and leave it to me.'

'I don't believe you'll see him again. He's gained too much on us.'

'We'll see.'

They were now on the 'curly' section of the road, with Colin attempting to straighten it out by cutting all corners, and skidding round most. He was driving dangerously and knew it, but so much seemed to be at stake. Then again came a long straight stretch, and for a brief instant Colin saw a red tail-light far ahead of him. Then it vanished.

'That was him,' he gasped, treading on the accelerator. 'Goes in for fast cars, the swine. Last time it was a Mercedes. Hang on!'

At the end of the straight stretch there

was no car in sight — only a series of double S bends, which Colin negotiated with considerable skill.

'No use, old man,' said Stafford. 'Pity his rear number plate was so badly lighted.'

'It wouldn't have helped much. I believe I've lost him.'

'I'm certain you have. Where are we?'

'Only a few miles from Nice.'

'Easy with the pedal. You're just asking for trouble. Lots of traffic ahead.'

Colin was compelled to slow down, and a little later he gave up the chase for good.

'Never mind,' said Stafford. 'We may see him again.'

'By visiting the casino every day?'

'Why not? It was a good friend to me.'

'All the more reason why you should keep away from it.'

Colin finally garaged the car near their hotel, and he and his companion went to the little garden and ordered some drinks. It was Beatrix who served them. To Colin's surprise she was wearing new raiment, and had done her hair differently. When she brought the drinks she displayed her admirable teeth in a smile which enhanced her natural beauty of feature.

'Have a nice day — yes?' she asked.

'Very nice,' grunted Colin. 'At least Mr. Stafford did.'

'The fact is, Beatrix,' said Stafford. 'I won some money at Monte and Colin lost.'

'Ah, but next time Colin he win and you lose,' laughed Beatrix. 'I come with you, Colin, and show you all the winning numbers.'

'I'll bet you could too,' said Stafford. 'Oh, never mind about the change.'

Beatrix passed under the arch over which vines were scrambling, making great play with her hips.

'You should have encouraged her, Colin,' he said.

'She needs no encouragement. I'll bet she has a dozen lovers in the offing. Here's to your future success at roulette — which I venture to doubt.'

'You're disappointed aren't you.? Not about Monte, but being left at the post in that car chase?'

Colin nodded, as he stared at the lights in the sprawling city. He had built so much upon the result of that chase, and now it was ended in smoke. Stafford was watching him closely.

'You don't have to tell me you are in love with that girl,' he said.

'What girl?'

'Rosita, of course. Brazen Beatrix dresses up to allure you, and suffers a dreadful flop. I think you scarcely saw her.'

'I didn't. You're right, Staff. With me, it's Rosita or nothing. I've had opportunities but like a silly idiot I've missed them all. Now I've messed up the chance sent by Providence to get into the firing line again.'

'How could you help it? That Delage was twenty miles an hour faster than your old bus. But if we do see the damned thing again I'll know what to do.'

'What exactly?'

'Something to make it go a little slower. But what about making some inquiries in the town. For all you know Mister Rupert and the other chap may be staying here.'

'I was thinking of that,' replied Colin. 'Rosita may have played here some weeks ago. I'll start making myself a nuisance in the morning.'

On the following morning he and Stafford walked to the newspaper office in the main avenue and turned over the file covering the last month. This took some time but at last Colin was satisfied that the issues contained no reference to Rosita. Then he made inquiries at the Casino and some of the other public halls, all with the same result.

'What about the police?' asked Stafford.

'I can't see that it would help. People come and go in thousands, and even if I was successful in getting their co-operation it would result in too much public inquiry. No, I'm going to telephone to Inspector Ogilvie at Scotland Yard, and tell him that I have seen Rupert. He'll know how to induce the French police to work silently. At any rate it's worth trying.'

Later in the day he tried to do this, but the delay was so tremendous that he was compelled to give up the attempt.

'I'll write instead,' he said. 'And send it by air mail.'

He spent half an hour writing the letter, and then slipped it into his pocket to post.

'Good,' said Stafford. 'Now let's get over to Monte.'

'You merely want to gamble again.'

'How right you are. But if Rupert lost money yesterday isn't he quite likely to go over again and try to win it back?'

'He might.'

'We'll repeat yesterday's programme. Golf up at Mont Agel, then dinner in that little restaurant. This time you are my guest — and no argument.'

They carried out this programme to the letter, and reached the main avenue to the casino at about the same time as on the previous day. It was fuller of cars, and Colin was compelled to park at the top of the gardens.

'What a place!' said Stafford. 'I was always given to understand it was hell with the lid off. Why, you could eat your meals off the pavements. Oh, Colin!'

Colin turned his head from admiring

beds of flowers and saw Stafford pointing to a car.

'The Delage!' he ejaculated. 'But is it the same one?'

'I'm certain it is. I noticed that dent in the rear bumper. This, my lad, is where we came in. He must be inside — chasing the numbers.'

'It looks very much like it. This time he's not going to leave me on the road.'

'Any ideas?' asked Stafford.

'Yes.'

'Me too. Look! I came prepared.'

He produced from his pocket a tough yellow bag, and opened it for Colin to see the contents.

'Sugar,' he said. 'If I can get that into his tank he won't go very fast.'

Colin shook his head.

'That may stop him dead, and I don't want that to happen. There's a better and easier way.'

'What way?'

Colin looked down the almost deserted avenue. No one seemed to be interested in them or the car, and they might easily be mistaken for the owners of it. Casually he walked to the bonnet and raised it easily. It was the ignition side, and before him was a long row of sparking plugs, with the leads terminating in spring clips. He whipped off two of them and fastened them in such a way that they would not 'short'. Then he lowered the bonnet and clipped it down.

'That should do it,' he said.

'But will the car start?'

'Should do. If he notices that the engine's 'missing' he'll probably put it down to oil on the plug points, and if, as I believe, he has only a short journey to go, he'll probably put up with the bad running. We'd better move on.'

'The casino?'

'Yes — if you must.'

They found Rupert in the casino, and at the same table as before. On this occasion he was dressed in a lounge suit, but was playing the same bold game as before.

'You play if you want to,' said Colin. 'I'm going to watch him, from where he can't see me.'

Stafford took a seat two chairs away

from Rupert, and on the same side, while Colin stood in the background behind several punters. He was able to get a fairly good idea how Stafford was faring, for he could see Stafford's bets. At first he lost steadily — no matter what he did, but suddenly everything changed, and his amazing luck returned. The pile of counters in front of him grew larger and larger, and now his stakes were almost as large as Rupert's who was keeping the croupier busy all the time. Time passed and Colin grew restless. He began to walk round and round the table, and rather wished he had bought some chips so that he could play and kill time. But he was afraid to turn his back on the table lest Rupert should suddenly get up. So he continued his perambulating.

'*Le maximum a rouge!*' chanted the croupier.

Colin knew what that meant. Someone had backed the red for twenty-four thousand francs. He turned his head and saw the pile of counters on the red diamond, and then managed to get a glimpse of Rupert's face. It was as calm as ever. The wheel was spun, and finally the little ivory ball came to rest in No. I — *rouge*. The croupier pushed across a similar pile of counters, then gave a glance at Stafford and shoved the whole lot across with his agile rake. Colin almost yelled his surprise, for he had imagined that the bet was Rupert's. Stafford threw a few hundred franc pieces to the croupier and then shovelled his winnings into his pockets and got up. He joined Colin a moment later.

'I'll burst if I stay any longer,' he whispered. 'I've been wanting to do that all evening. All my winnings on one coup. Let's go and have a drink.'

'No. Rupert may leave. Cash in your ill-gotten gains, and come back to me.'

'Oh, I quite forgot why we came here. I'll be back in a minute. What a night!'

He was back with Colin a few minutes later, cramming large franc notes into his wallet, and as excited as a schoolboy on holiday.

'Is he still there?' he asked.

'Yes.'

'What a pity. To-night we've got to

celebrate somewhere. Wish I could send him a message that his grandmother is dying. But he's winning too and may stay all night.'

'However long he stays I stay too,' said Colin.

Another half-hour was to pass before Rupert left his chair and went to cash in his chips. Immediately Colin and Stafford went to the vestibule, and when Rupert was seen coming in that direction they went outside and found their car. Colin entered it and started the engine, but Stafford stood on the pavement looking towards the casino exit.

'Here he comes,' he said at last.

'Good. Come the moment you see his car move.'

'Lord I hope it works out,' muttered Stafford.

Shortly afterwards he nodded his head and dived into the seat beside Colin. Colin turned the car out into the open and saw the back of the Delage slightly ahead of him. He allowed it to draw away a little and then drove after it.

'Going the same way,' said Stafford.

'Yes. It will be interesting to see what happens when he comes to that straight stretch. He must know his engine is misfiring. Point is — will he stop and investigate the cause.'

But Rupert showed no sign of stopping, and when he reached the first straight stretch Colin saw him drawing away, but not at the great speed which he had put up the night before.

'Cross your fingers,' he said. 'Thank goodness it's pitch dark. He's not so likely to get out and look at his engine. I can hold him easily at this speed.'

'He may let something go — even yet.'

'I doubt if he can. But I dare not get too close in case he should suspect us and lead us on a wild-goose chase.'

At times Colin was compelled to step hard on the accelerator but always the Delage was kept in sight.

'It was about here where we lost him last time,' said Stafford.

'I'm going up a bit closer in case he dives off somewhere.'

It was as well that Colin did this, for about three miles from Nice the Delage suddenly cut across to the left-hand side of the road and then vanished.

'Where's he gone?' gasped Stafford.

'Must be a turning here. A private drive probably.'

He slowed down and then saw the 'drive'. It was a private one, leading down to a lighted villa, but there was no board of any kind to indicate the name of the villa. Colin got out of the car and stepped into the drive. In the moonlight he saw a white board. On it was painted Villa Lombrosa.

'So we've trailed him to his lair,' said Stafford.

'Yes — unless he is paying a social call.'

'What are you going to do about it?'

'I'm going to call.'

Stafford looked at him seriously.

'That may be dangerous if they are the sort of people you believe them to be.'

'But we are in a strong position. I want you to stay in the car. Give me a quarter of an hour, and if I'm not back by then go to the police, and tell them what has happened.'

'You think that's best?'

'Yes.'

'All right. It's now exactly ten-forty. I'll wait in the car until eleven o'clock. Best of luck, old man!'

'Thanks.'

Colin began to walk down the lighted drive. Very soon he came within full view of a splendid white villa, overlooking the sea.

21

On reaching the villa Rupert Zanfeld stopped the spluttering engine of the Delage, and got out and lifted the bonnet. The lights from the villa showed him the two detached ignition wires, and his brow became corrugated. He let down the bonnet and hurried across to the corner of the drive. Keeping concealed, he looked up to the main road, and saw two figures loitering by the villa name-plate. That, and the two disconnected wires were sufficient. He almost ran into the villa, passed through the luxurious hall and entered a room on the right of it. Pacing up and down was Mark Grandison. He swung round on Rupert.

'Where the hell have you been all this time?' he demanded.

'I looked in at the casino at Monte and — '

'Didn't I tell you to give the place a miss? You go about exhibiting yourself in public as if you were — '

'Shut up!' snapped Rupert. 'Let me talk for a change. I've been followed to-night. I didn't realise it until I got here. The car was behaving strangely, and I have just discovered that the engine has been tinkered with, to keep down my speed. Then I remembered that all the way home a car followed me, and never seemed to want to pass. I looked up the drive just now and saw two men. I believe they are coming here.'

Grandison's face was now purple with rage.

'You idiot,' he snarled. 'Now I'll tell you something. Karl telephoned from Paris an hour ago. There are details of you and me on all the Paris gendarmeries, and that means that in a day or so they'll be plastered over Nice and elsewhere. They include photographs taken years ago, but good enough to make us recognisable.'

'Good God!'

'You may well say that. Why in God's name couldn't you control your lust for gambling? You've brought about this situation — '

'You mean those two men may be policemen?'

'Who else could they be?'

'Well, what do we do about it — if they call?'

Grandison put his hand into his hip-pocket and produced a large automatic pistol.

'No better ideas than that?' sneered Rupert.

'Not at this moment. I need just a little more time to do anything. I'll get behind that screen, and you can entertain them here. Swear that you are the only person in the place, and show them that faked identity card. If there's any trouble — well, it will be just too bad — for them. You know what to say, and — '

He stopped as suddenly the bell rang loudly.

'Let Martha go,' whispered Grandison.

'But she may say you are here.'

'She knows I am out to everyone. S-sh!'

The woman who kept house for them was heard to move along the hall. Then there came the sound of a man's voice, and Martha was heard to say that monsieur must be mistaken. Some more inaudible conversation passed and finally Martha entered the lounge. She was a dark-eyed woman of about forty years of age, and was in Grandison's confidence.

'A young man,' she said. 'He wish to see a Mr. Zanfeld. I tell him no such person lived here. He then say he wish to see the gentleman who arrive in the Delage. What am I to say?'

'Did he give a name?' asked Grandison.

'Yes. He say his name is Fairbright — Colin Fairbright.'

Grandison gave a little hiss of surprise.

'That interfering young pup!' said Rupert. 'Well, what do we do about him?'

'See him,' said Grandison. 'We can't help ourselves. If we don't he may go to the police. It may be that he is only interested in Rosita.'

'Only interested,' sneered Rupert. 'It's a mighty big interest. What are you going to tell him?'

'I don't know. I want to think. Martha, tell the young man that Mr. Zanfeld will see him in a minute or two. Say nothing about anyone else in the house. Ask him into the library.'

'Yes, m'sieur.'

She left the room, closing the door behind her. Rupert now looked eagerly at Grandison.

'What do I say?' he asked.

'You have quarrelled with me and Rosita. I sacked you in Brussels, and you were fortunate to get employment by the owner of this place, who is at present away. You changed your name because it was not a very good name to use in France. You do not know where I am, but think I may be in Milan with Rosita, who had a booking there. If you play the part right we shall get the delay we need. In an hour or two the boat should be here.'

'I'll do my best,' said Rupert. 'Shall I see him here?'

'Yes. I'll get behind that screen.'

Rupert rang for Martha, and told Martha to show Mr. Fairbright in. While this was being done Grandison moved the screen further back and got behind it. A few moments passed and then Colin entered the room. Rupert was now calmly smiling.

'This is a surprise,' he said in his guttural voice. 'I am sorry the housekeeper said I wasn't in at first, but she knows me under another name. I was in a little trouble and — well — it was desirable.'

'So I should imagine,' said Colin. 'I happened to see you at Monte Carlo, and followed you?'

'But why? Oh yes, I think I understand. You are interested in that young lady — Miss Paston.'

'Very interested. Where is she?'

'I do not know. I parted company with her and Grandison in Brussels — after a quarrel.'

Colin looked at him with disbelief in his eyes.

'Then how do you come to be here?' he asked.

'I saw an advertisement in a Paris newspaper for a chauffeur, and I got the job. This villa belongs to my new employer. I drove him here from Paris, but a few days ago he had to go to Paris on business.'

'And while he is away you use his car?'

'I have to do that in order to buy petrol on the black market.'

'Where was Rosita due to appear after she left Brussels?'

'Rome. We were going by air, but as I told you there was a quarrel, and I left them.'

Colin took out his cigarette-case and lighted a cigarette. He offered the case to Rupert, but Rupert shook his head.

'Thank you,' he said. 'But I do not smoke.'

Colin then looked at the ash-container on the nearby table. In it were several cigarette-butts. Rupert saw these and smiled.

'The housekeeper,' he explained. 'She smokes all day when the master is away.'

'So you and she are alone in the villa?'

'At the moment — yes. The other servants come and go daily.'

Colin then decided to play a winning card. From his pocket he produced a small lace-edged embroidered handker-chief.

'I found this in the room where I was

kept waiting,' he said. 'It belongs to Rosita, and has her initials on it.'

'Oh, yes,' said Rupert. 'I found it in the car — Mr. Grandison's car — and meant to return it to Miss Paston. But I forgot.'

'I don't believe you,' said Colin.

Rupert succeeded in looking very hurt.

'Why should I lie to you?' he asked.

'That is what I am asking myself. Suppose you and I look over the villa?'

'But why?'

'Just to make sure that Miss Paston isn't here.'

'That is impossible. The housekeeper would never consent.'

'She might consent if she knew that the alternative is for me to go to the police.'

'Really, Mr. Fairbright, this is ridiculous.'

'Call the housekeeper.'

'I will not. It is more than my job is worth.'

'Very well. I propose to go to the police and tell them that I have cause to believe that Miss Paston is being held here against her will. They may also be interested to know why you have changed your name. That's all for the moment.'

Colin picked up his hat and made for the door. But before he could reach it a voice bellowed out behind him.

'Just a moment, Mr. Fairbright!'

He stopped and swung round. Grandison had emerged from behind the screen, and in his hand was the automatic.

'I thought you might possibly be on the premises,' said Colin.

'Very clever of you. Sit down!'

'I think I would prefer to stand if you've no objection.'

Grandison came closer, and looked at Rupert.

'Search him,' he said. 'He may be armed. Put up your hands, Mr. Fairbright.'

'Hadn't you better put that weapon down?' asked Colin. 'It may be loaded.'

'I assure you it *is* loaded. Rupert, what the devil are you waiting for?'

Rupert approached Colin, and Colin drew back a clenched fist. But he did no more than that for he saw in Grandison's eyes the maddest expression. Rupert went through his pockets and produced a number of things, one of which was most damning for Colin's future. It was the letter to Scotland Yard, which Colin had forgotten to post.

'What's that?' asked Grandison.

Rupert handed him the letter and Grandison's eyes blazed as he saw the address. He slit it open and read what Colin had written. His gaze switched from the letter to Colin's face.

'So you're nothing but a police spy,' he muttered. 'It's as well I took a hand in this.'

'What have you to fear from the police?' asked Colin. 'I thought you were found innocent — more or less.'

'You've made a big mistake in getting in my way. All along you have been a damned nuisance. But this is the end.'

'I shouldn't be so sure. What have you done with Rosita?'

Grandison regarded him with hateful eyes.

'You will never know,' he said. 'Now you force me to deal with you — most drastically. Rupert get some rope. Move man, for there is no time to waste.'

Rupert hurried out and Colin found himself facing the steady automatic which controlled the situation. Grandison's remark about Rosita troubled him deeply. The man seemed to be capable of anything. All his old self-control had gone, and he looked almost insane. Rupert lost no time on his mission.

'Bind his arms,' snapped Grandison.

Colin had to submit to this indignity, and as Rupert pulled the rope tighter and tighter Colin's thoughts went to Stafford. The allotted time was nearly exhausted, and he prayed that Stafford would not wait longer, for everything seemed to hang on his getting away quickly.

'Now march!' said Grandison, and pushed the barrel of the pistol into Colin's back. 'Rupert, lead the way — to the strong point.'

Rupert went to the wide casement window and opened it. Colin saw the moonlit garden — a series of terraces merging into olive trees, below which was the calm sea, forming a little bay. He was hustled along at the point of the pistol, and finally came upon a concrete construction which had evidently been built as a defence measure by the occupying German troops during the war against possible invasion. It was octagonal in shape, and there were embrasures through which machine-guns could be used. A key was in the steel door and Rupert turned this and pulled the door outwards. Colin was projected through it. He fell down two steps, and heard the heavy door clang behind him.

The light which came through the narrow fire-slits showed a number of wooden cases, a pickaxe, two shovels and some old camouflage netting. The walls were running with condensation, and the place alive with mosquitoes. He managed to get a glimpse of his wrist-watch and found the time to be exactly eleven o'clock. By this time Stafford should be making his departure. He prayed it was so.

Through one of the slits he could see part of the villa. It looked beautiful in the moonlight in that sub-tropical setting of large palms, mimosa, and tall agaves. The view seawards was equally impressive, for the woods ran right down to the sea beaches, and every bright star was reflected in the still waters. But every few moments the pinging mosquitoes worried him, and his sole defence against them was his breath, which he blew out explosively to prevent a landing on his face. All the same he believed he was being bitten incessantly.

But why had Grandison and Rupert gone to such lengths? Undoubtedly that unposted letter had been the prime cause, but in it he had merely told Ogilvie that he had seen Rupert in the casino at Monte Carlo. It looked as if some threat hung over Grandison of which he (Colin) was ignorant. The information contained in the letter seemed scarcely enough to warrant such drastic action. Then there was the handkerchief which he had found, and which seemed to indicate that Rosita had been at the villa. Why had Grandison not produced her, if she was alive and well? Could it mean that Rosita had gone the way of Charles Simbourne? If so — why?

He moved uncomfortably inside his

bonds, and wondered how long it would be before the police took a hand. What had Grandison meant when he said there was no time to waste? Was he planning immediate departure?

For a considerable time the silence was broken only by the low hum of the winged pests, and the shriller sound as they prepared to alight on his skin. Then he heard a different noise — the noise of approaching footsteps. They came closer and closer, and then the key rattled in the lock of the steel door, and a big body hurtled through it, tripped over the steps and fell heavily on the hard floor. The door was slammed immediately and locked. Colin looked down at the fallen man. It was Stafford. He had blood on his face, and like Colin, his arms were bound tightly to his body. He looked up at Colin and blinked.

'So — it's you,' he gasped. 'The swine got me before I could get away. I gave you a few extra minutes, and that was my undoing.'

'I'm sorry, Staf,' said Colin. 'It was all my fault. What is wrong with your hand.

426

It's covered with blood.'

Stafford laughed grimly.

'I had one crack at Rupert before Grandison hit me on the head with a pistol. If Rupert isn't lacking some teeth I'm a Dutchman. I caught him a real beauty. What is this place, anyway?'

'Old German defence point. About three feet of concrete all round and a steel door.'

'Not too promising is it? What happened to you?'

Colin told him briefly.

'Pity you didn't post that letter,' he said.

'You were in such an infernal hurry to get to the green tables. No, that's not fair. The blame for the whole thing rests with me. I shouldn't have got you involved in my sticky private life.'

'Rot! I'm enjoying it.'

'You don't give me that impression.'

'I certainly feel as if I had been kicked by a mule, but that crack I gave Rupert is exhilarating. Anything in these boxes?'

'I think they are all empty.'

Stafford now managed to get on to his

feet, and to occupy one of the boxes as a seat.

'Quite a situation, isn't it?' he asked.

'Predicament's the word. Your scalp looks pretty bad. Is it cut much?'

'Feels cracked.'

'Sit still, and let me look at it.'

'What's the use? You can't do anything.'

'Sit still anyway.'

Colin found the seat of Stafford's injury. The pistol had cut into his scalp, but not very deeply, and the blood had now ceased to flow.

'Not serious,' he said.

'Good. Colin, how did they know I was in the car?'

'I think Rupert must have seen us. Anyway, it doesn't matter. Damn these mosquitoes!'

'Is that what they are?'

'Yes, and all females I should imagine. If only we could get our hands free we might smoke them out, by setting light to some of that netting.'

Stafford blew at the insects, and then staggered to one of the slits and looked seaward.

'Lovely sight,' he mused. 'What wouldn't I give for a moonlight bathe. Just put me right. Hullo, what's this?'

He moved a piece of netting from a deep recess in the concrete wall and exposed a wooden box, stencilled on the outside.

'My hat!' he ejaculated. 'A box of German hand-grenades — unopened.'

'Are you sure?'

'Absolutely! It says so on the outside. If we could only get it undone we might be able to blow that door down.'

'And blow ourselves to pieces at the same time.'

'Not necessarily. We could build up a shield with these empty boxes. First gleam of hope, my lad.'

'Is it? With our arms bound so tightly that mine feel completely dead.'

'You know they weren't particularly brilliant.'

'What do you mean?'

'Crazy idea to put two bound men together, for it's wonderful what a bit of co-operation can achieve. Neither of us can do much for himself, but each can do a lot for the other. Come into the moonlight and let me have a look at those knots.'

'You'd need a marline-spike to undo them.'

'All my family have had remarkable teeth.'

Colin placed himself in the shaft of bright moonlight which came through one of the firing-slits.

'He certainly made a job of it,' complained Stafford. 'Lord, I wish these filthy mosquitoes would give a fellow a break. Now stand quite still and let me do my stuff.'

22

Up at the villa Grandison was busy packing several huge suitcases, and every few minutes he helped himself from a flagon of brandy which was on a table close to him. He looked troubled, as indeed he was, for he had much to be troubled about. Quietly the door opened and the dark handsome woman entered the room. Grandison gave a start as he suddenly realised she was close to him.

'Wish you wouldn't move like a cat,' he complained. 'Well, how is she?'

'Just the same. Only just conscious.'

'Did she say anything?'

'She asked for a doctor. I tell her she must sleep.'

'Sleep! She sleeps too much. I wish I knew what was wrong.'

'You ought to know,' said Martha with a shrewd glance.

'But I don't, and I dare not call — That must be Rupert.'

Rupert entered the room. He was slightly out of breath, and he gave a quick glance at the suitcases.

'What did you do with that car?' asked Grandison.

'Drove it further down the road — about half a mile from here.'

'Good!'

'Have you heard anything more?'

'Nothing.'

Rupert made a gesture towards the ceiling.

'What are you going to do about her?' he asked.

'She goes with us — of course.'

'You must be mad.'

'Why?'

Rupert turned to the woman appealingly.

'Bring him to his senses, Martha,' he growled. 'Personally I think she won't recover, but even if she did she'd be a perpetual danger. To take her would be stark madness, and I'm certain that Hans will be dead against it.'

Grandison turned on him furiously, but Rupert was not to be intimidated. He stood his ground and Grandison, on the point of striking him, withheld his hand.

'You — you don't understand,' he said drunkenly. 'Neither of you understand.'

'Make no mistake,' said Rupert. 'I've understood for a long time. You love her, and believe that you can go on for ever throwing dust in her eyes. But already she mistrusts you — '

'You liar! Why should she mistrust me? Haven't I given her everything — sympathy, appreciation, a career. There is an unbreakable bond between us, as you will see. This strange sickness cannot last much longer. In Barcelona I can get the drugs I need, and then I shall cure her, and all will be well.'

Rupert shrugged his shoulders, almost contemptuously, and turned to Martha.

'Talk to him,' he begged. 'He doesn't seem to appreciate the situation.'

Martha did so, but this time in German. She did not look much like a mere paid housekeeper as she laid down the law stridently. Were they to risk everything for the sake of this girl who had reduced Grandison to a drivelling

love-sick loon? She could tell Grandison
that it wasn't his name which Rosita
muttered in her semi-delirium but that of
the young Englishman. It was always the
same name — Colin — Colin — Colin.
Grandison stopped this harangue with a
howl of rage. He knew what he was
doing, and would take the cosequences.
As for Hans — Hans would have to toe
the line or damn well rot. If Hans knew
on which side his bread was buttered — .

The telephone bell stopped this wild
outburst, and Rupert went to the
instrument and picked up the receiver. It
was Hans speaking from a public
telephone in the town. Was everything all
right? Should he come to the villa at
once?

'Yes, the sooner the better,' said
Grandison to Rupert. 'But tell him to
stop the taxi some way from here. Say
— outside the Villa Hesperides, and then
to walk.'

Rupert put these instructions through,
and then had recourse to the brandy.

'I'm going upstairs,' muttered Grandison. 'Tell me when Hans arrives.'

He marched out of the room in his stiff-necked manner, but left the door open behind him. Rupert went across and closed it. He came back to Martha, who was searching for another glass to hold some brandy for herself.

'He'll ruin everything if he gets his way,' growled Rupert.

'Then he must not get his way. Can he do anything for her?'

'He could if he got that drug in time.'

'How long?'

'Four or five days.'

'Why can't he get it here?'

'He would have to go to a hospital, and produce his credentials. That's out of the question.'

They had almost finished the brandy when there was a ring at the door. Martha went into the hall, and then came back with a short, and rather corpulent man. He looked worried to death, and his great face was wet with perspiration.

'Hullo, Hans!' said Rupert. 'Any fresh news?'

'None since I last telephoned. What news of the yacht?'

'Should be here before sunrise. But something has happened to-night. A man who knew us in England paid us a visit. He was looking for the girl.'

'The pianist?'

'Yes. He threatened to go to the police unless we produced her, so we had to take action.'

'What action?'

'We're holding him, and a man who was with him. On him we found an unposted letter addressed to Scotland Yard telling them that he had seen me yesterday at Monte Carlo. Anyway they're safe. Now I've got to talk to you — about the girl. It's very important. Mark is completely out of his mind. He says he won't leave without her.'

Hans wiped the perspiration from his face.

'He — he can't be serious,' he said.

'You'll find he is. I've never seen a man so much in love. He makes me sick.'

'How much does the girl know?'

'Nothing. She is really a promising artiste and thinks of nothing but her profession.'

'What is the nature of her illness?'

'She's not really ill at all — simply under restraint.'

'What do you mean?'

'I was suspicious about a man who followed us from Paris to Brussels. I didn't want that damned music business to continue. Rosita was making a reputation, but she was advertising our whereabouts. It had to be stopped. I took steps to do that.'

Hans looked at him sharply.

'But could you fool Mark?' he asked.

'Yes. He never was as brilliant as he thinks. He's puzzled and dare not call a specialist.'

'What is it — a drug?'

'Yes, a beautiful one, on which I was engaged when everything went up in chaos. It can be detected in the blood but only with an electron microscope, and Mark hasn't got one.'

'How do you give it to her?'

Rupert smiled at Martha, and Martha shrugged her shoulders

'There was no other way,' she said. 'We had to stop those public appearances.'

'Of course.'

'And now we have to exert pressure on Mark. You must insist that he leaves Rosita behind.'

Hans sat for a moment stroking his flabby face. Then he looked up at Martha.

'Tell Mark that I am here and want to talk to him,' he said.

Martha left the room, and immediately Hans began to talk at great speed. It was no use risking a quarrel with Mark at this moment. The fool might even refuse to come with them, and for various reasons his presence was absolutely vital. No, the best thing was to pretend to see his point of view.

'You mean agree to take the girl?'

'Yes. Where is your imagination, Rupert? The oceans are wide and all sorts of accidents can happen. What better place for the permanent disposal of an inconvenient person? It could happen after we collected that chest at Barcelona. For that little operation Mark is rather necessary — eh?'

Rupert slipped out his hand and gripped Hans's fat fist.

'Agreed,' he said. 'Do we keep this matter to ourselves?'

'For the moment, yes. Martha is a dependable person, but it is never wise to allow too many people to share one secret. Ah, here is my old friend Mark!'

Grandison came forward and shook hands.

'Things appear to be urgent,' said Hans.

'Very urgent. We must be away before dawn.'

'Provided the boat arrives.'

'Lopez will not let us down.' Grandison glanced at Rupert. 'I suppose you have discussed Rosita?' he growled.

'Yes,' replied Rupert. 'I thought Hans should know the position as it is.'

Grandison switched his gaze to Hans.

'Out with it,' he said. 'What are you thinking?'

'I think it's a little dangerous, Mark. Can't you leave her here, with a nurse?'

'If I leave her here she will die.'

'But if she is as bad as that how can you possibly move her, and is she capable of making a long voyage in a small vessel.'

'Her trouble is functional. I lack drugs and medicines, but I can get them when we reach Barcelona.'

'And after that?'

'I can induce her to take the long voyage — for the sake of her health. I can arrange concerts for her at Buenos Aires and elsewhere. I have made up my mind.'

'Suppose she discovers the truth?'

'She will never discover that. In the Argentine we shall be married. Life will be different — for all of us.'

'In that case let us stop arguing.'

'So you agree?'

'Yes. Now what about the two men whom Rupert mentioned?'

'They can stay where they are. By the time they are found — if they are found at all — we shall be out of all danger.'

'Good! Now can I have some food. I haven't had a bite since I left Lyon this morning.'

'I'll see Martha about that,' said Rupert. 'Then I'll do some packing. What did you do with your baggage, Hans?'

'It's in the hall. Well, it's nice to be here.'

440

Upstairs in a great bedroom, magnificently furnished, Rosita lay with her eyes wide open, staring at the ceiling. Her cheeks were pale, and the flesh shrunken a little, but her mind was very active. Her thoughts were going back to the successful concerts which she had given, and all the hopes that had been aroused. Grandison had treated her with the greatest kindness and consideration, and she was looking forward to the next appearance at Lyon when the strange illness had overtaken her. While at practice she had fainted, a thing she had never done in her life, and two days later the same thing happened again. Then she began to run a temperature, and had to take to her bed. The temperature stayed with her, despite the frequent use of M and B, and Grandison had been compelled to cancel the next booking, with regrets that were clearly marked. After that life seemed to be an endless dream. She scarcely knew that she had been taken by car into the sunshine of the south, and put to bed by a strange woman in this palatial villa. She now knew the woman to be Martha — a distant relative of Grandison, who had found him the furnished villa, and taken on the job of nurse-housekeeper. Martha, like Grandison, treated her with kindness, and she was served with every imaginable delicacy — although she was unable to eat more than a minute portion of them.

In her more lucid moments she had asked to see an English doctor but the doctor never materialised. It puzzled her that Grandison who was so deeply disturbed by her condition failed to do what was so clearly required by the situation, but then she remembered that he had studied medicine in his younger days, and she recalled how, in the past, he had relieved her headaches with some kind of potion. It rather looked as if he were jealous of his medical knowledge, but all the same she would have liked to see a practising physician — to know exactly what was wrong with her.

There was another trouble too which had nothing to do with her health. Twice she had written to Colin, but had received no reply. That was a bitter disappointment in view of his expressed desire to hear from her regularly. But she had left Colin rather seriously ill, and now she feared that this silence could only be attributed to one cause — Colin's own state of health — or even worse. That stark possibility filled her dreams with terror, and her waking hours with morbid reflections. This tour which was to have been so pleasant a thing was ending in disaster. Perhaps Colin had been right — in a way — when he had begged her not to undertake it. Admittedly she had been swayed by ambition — by the promise of a short cut to success instead of the hard way by patient uphill work. Perhaps she had expected too much of life.

One morning after a horrid dream she had begged Martha to wire to Colin's mother, to inquire after him, and this Martha had undertaken to do. Rosita herself had dictated the message, but nothing came back. There were spells of great sickness when she was unable to take any food, and, strangely enough, it was after these bouts, and the fasting that took place, that she improved — until again she took food. She pondered over this, and in her confused mind was born a dreadful suspicion. It induced her secretly to dispose of her food for a day or two, and almost immediately she improved, although it brought about increased weakness. To counteract this she begged Grandison for grapes, and kept up her strength almost entirely by the use of this fruit.

Now she lay quiet, thinking of these things. Her evening meal had gone literally down the drain, and the last supply of grapes had been devoured. If, as she now believed, she was being poisoned, who was responsible? Certainly not Grandison. All along he had been her champion, sharing her triumphs and her woes. There was no doubt about his joy when on occasion he found her less stricken. There was Rupert — a very queer character. She had had the feeling that Rupert did not enjoy driving them about, and on one or two occasions she had found him sullen. But Rupert did not prepare the food. That was Martha's department. What had Martha to gain by ruining the business to which she and Grandison had set their hand? No, it made no sense. Nothing made any sense. She was weak and needed abundant food, but she was convinced that by taking it in that house she would rapidly sink again into helpless coma.

She decided to try her strength, and climbed out of the bed into a chair. There she sat for a few moments. Using the back of the chair as support, she pushed it off the persian carpet on to the polished floor. The effort was considerable, but she got as far as the door, and quietly opened it. The door of a room on the opposite side of the wide landing was slightly open, and from behind it came low voices. The voice she heard first was Grandison's.

'Are you sure the small boat is on the beach, Rupert?'

'Quite sure. I took it from the boathouse a little while ago and set it afloat. It is anchored in the sand on the foreshore.'

'Well, watch for the signal. You should see it from that window.'

'What is the signal?'

'Three flashes at two-second intervals. They will be repeated until you lower and raise the blind.'

'What about — her?'

'We can carry her down. We have the stretcher.'

'Without an explanation?'

'I shall explain to her. She will be glad to know she is going to England — by sea.'

Rupert gave a short laugh at the flagrant lie.

'Stop that!' rasped Grandison. 'You may find it comical, but I don't.'

'You wouldn't — my devoted half-brother. Well, you must have your way, and much good may it do you.'

Rosita gave a little gasp, and then retreated into her room and closed the door behind her. For the first time Rupert's real relationship with Grandison was established. It explained much, but not nearly enough. A feeling of great weakness swept over her, and only with the utmost difficulty was she able to climb into the soft bed.

23

Down in the concrete pill-box Colin and Stafford had accomplished the first part of their programme, but not without some damage to Stafford's teeth and gums. The tough rope which had bound their arms and restricted their circulation was now lying on the floor, and both of them were doing exercises to banish their numbness.

'Glory! I've just thought of something,' exclaimed Stafford. 'The grenades may not be fused. Without fuses they are absolutely useless.'

He walked across to the recess in the wall, and lifted the loose lid from the box.

'Saved,' he cried. 'Eight of them, and three are fused.'

He brought the whole box of grenades across to Colin, who knew little about such devilish things.

'All you have to do is remove that safety-pin, and let the lever go. That ignites the fuse, and after an interval of a few seconds off she goes.'

'Are they powerful enough to blow down that door?'

'I should think there is sufficient power to bust the lock, provided we can prop the grenade into the right position. Let's put them somewhere safe, and see what we can do to erect a platform and cover for ourselves.'

He placed the three fused grenades in a firing-slit at the far end of the place, and then began to arrange the numerous ammunition boxes, so that a shelf was formed up against the place where the lock was situated on the steel door.

'Just right,' he muttered. 'Now if we back up the grenade with those concrete blocks the explosive force should all go forward — just where we want it.'

'Suppose it doesn't?' asked Colin.

'My dear chap that is one of the laws of physics, as you ought to know. Of course we'll get some of the blast — '

'And a lump of concrete in our tummy.'

'I don't think so. If we lie flat on the floor with our faces on our arms we should be all right.'

Colin nodded. It sounded reasonable enough, but he hated the whole project. Yet the alternative was no less unattractive. He gave Stafford a hand with the very heavy concrete slabs which had presumably been left over from the construction of the place, and finally every bit of material in the pill-box was in use, except the heap of camouflage netting which Stafford reserved for cushioning any dangerous blast.

'That's exactly as we want it,' he said.

'It certainly looks professional enough. Are you going to use all three fused grenades?'

'No. One should do the job. We'll take the other two with us in case we meet with trouble. At least I will, for you don't appear to take kindly to them.'

'I don't,' admitted Colin. 'Frankly, I'd like to get this over.'

'Well, we're ready right now.'

'What am I to do?'

'Tuck yourself well under that netting, and leave a space for me. Once I remove the pin I'll have to take quick cover. There may only be five seconds delay.'

'Then I'll toss you to see who removes the pin.'

'No you won't. I've had a long experience with these things. Get yourself well down, and leave it to uncle.'

Colin did this, and Stafford took one of the fused grenades from the firing-slit.

'One last word,' he said. 'There'll be a hell of a noise, and a ghastly smell. They are bound to hear it up at the house, but we ought to be able to get up the drive before they can intercept us, and then, all being well we'll have the police here within half an hour. All ready?'

'Yes.'

'Here goes then. I'll snatch those spare grenades after the explosion. They're safer where they are — at the moment.'

Colin saw him move through the thin shafts of moonlight to where the improvised blast-wall had been erected. There was dead silence for a few moments, and then Stafford shouted 'she's off' and came running back to Colin. He burrowed like a rabbit under the netting, and Colin felt his heart thumping in his chest.

Then, almost immediately, there came a terrific report and a blinding flash of light. Things seemed to be raining down, and the air was acrid. Stafford was on his feet reaching for the grenades.

'Come on!' he cried. 'It's wide open. You're not hurt, are you?'

'No — no,' gasped Colin. 'Where's the door?'

'Right in front of you. Mind that box. It all went like clockwork.'

Colin stepped out into bright moonlight and looked swiftly left and right.

'To the right,' whispered Stafford. 'More cover that way. Three lots of steps and then that long open bit in front of the house. Put all you know into it.'

There was no need for that piece of advice, for Colin suddenly saw a light appear at the villa, then another. He raced with Stafford up a long flight of steps, then down a path and up another flight. They raced neck and neck for a bit and then suddenly there came a most ominous sound, and bullets flew all around.

'Damn!' muttered Stafford. 'They've

got a tommy-gun up on the veranda. Never expected that. Duck man, duck — '

Colin ducked as another fusilade of bullets spattered the trees in his vicinity.

'They certainly mean business,' muttered Stafford. 'Phew that was a close one. A rifle has joined the tommy-gun.'

'Let's make a bid for it. I object to being a sitting target.'

'So do I, but we're as plain as pikestaffs in this rotten moonlight. We can't get across the open space without inviting sudden death.'

'Then let's double back and make an attempt up the other path. They may not expect that.'

'We can try. Follow me — hands and knees.'

For a while this stratagem was successful and they made good progress up the opposite side of the garden. But again they were pulled up by open spaces where even a cat would have been visible from the bedroom verandah where the tommy-gun was sited. Stafford raised his head for a split second, and at once a shot came from the man with the rifle, whose position was not clear.

'The rifleman is moving towards us,' whispered Stafford. 'There's probably another man on the other flank.'

'But there were only two in the villa?'

'How can you be sure? We've got to do something — and quickly. Plenty of cover in our rear. Let's make a dash for that little beach, and then round the bay towards the town. Next door there may be a villa with honest people in it. Agreed?'

'Yes.'

'Come on then.'

They began a swift retreat, using every inch of cover which they could find, until at last they found a made path which led down to the beach, on which the waves were lapping lazily.

'Look!' gasped Stafford. 'A small boat — afloat, and within a few yards of the shore. It's anchored. I rather like the look of that. Hope you can row a boat.'

'You give me a chance.'

They were running now as fast as the steep twisting path would allow, and not a sound came from behind. The last stretch was through a flowery avenue, at the bottom of which was a gay boathouse which had a narrow slipway to the sea. Crossing the sand they came to the anchor, and Stafford pulled on the rope. The little boat was drawn inshore, and Stafford threw the anchor inside and saw that it housed two oars and a boathook.

'Furnished complete,' he said. 'Nip in and I'll shove her off.'

Colin got into the boat and moved towards the stern. When he was seated Stafford gave the craft a shove and clambered aboard. He took the second oar, turned the bows round and commenced to row hard towards the right arm of the bay, where the olive trees came down almost to bare rock. Colin quickly got in time with him and the boat responded satisfactorily.

'Have to give that promontory a wide berth,' said Stafford. 'There are rocks sticking up like shark's teeth. Gosh, it's good to get some fresh air again. We'll see where we are once we get round that point. Nice can't be far away. But probably we shall save time by landing at the first convenient place, and running to the nearest gendarmerie. What was the name of that crook's den?'

'Villa Lombrosa.'

'That's it. We've got to get the police there in quick time, or they may make a break for it. What a night! Look at all that phosphorescent stuff in the water. I wouldn't mind swimming all the way to Nice. Oh lord!'

'What's wrong?' asked Colin.

'Two men — just arrived at the beach. Pull like hell. One of them has a rifle.'

Colin glanced at the beach which was now about a hundred yards in their rear. He saw the man with the rifle sprawl on the sand. Then there came a flash of light, a 'zip' in the water quite near the boat and then the sharp report of the weapon.

'Too close to be healthy,' muttered Stafford. 'But we should be out of range — '

There came two more flashes and a bullet ripped through the side of the boat, between Colin and Stafford. It was just below the water-line and it passed through both sides of the boat.

'Keep rowing!' said Stafford. 'I'll try to plug those holes.'

Putting his oar inboard he tore his handkerchief into pieces and plugged one hole, then the other, but not completely enough to stop the inflow of some water. Again he went to the oar, and again the rifle flashed three times. Two more bullets entered the boat and a big jet of water shot up near Colin's feet. There was no stopping that hole, for one of the seams had opened, and soon there were several inches of water in the bottom.

'Keep her going, Colin!' yelled Stafford. 'There may be a baler in the locker.'

But an examination of the small locker showed no such thing, and Stafford began to use his cupped hands at great speed. Colin, rowing for dear life, heard the rifle again, but the bullets went wide, for the distance had now increased greatly, and they were near the point beyond which was cover from the sniper.

'How am I doing?' asked Stafford.

'Just about keeping pace with the

water. I'd better stop rowing and lend a hand.'

'No. Better get out of range. That fellow's a crack shot. I can do a bit better.'

They were now almost round the point, with Stafford working like an automaton, when the rifle flashed. Colin heard a curious sound behind him and, to his horror, he saw Stafford clutch his chest and roll over into the water in the bottom of the boat.

'Staff!' he gasped.

'The — the swine got me. Just a stroke — or two — old man, and you'll be round — the bend.'

Colin took two strenuous strokes and then pulled in the oar and knelt at Stafford's side. He opened the coat and tore the shirt down from the neck. There was the wound, at the base of the right lung, with blood oozing from it. The dilemma was frightful. If he attempted to stop the flow of blood the boat would sink. If he gave his attention to baling out the mounting water Stafford might die.

'What — what shall I do?' he muttered.

Poor Stafford was beyond replying. He lay there with eyes closed, and the water almost covering his legs, and Colin realised that the brief dilemma had passed. The boat was slowly sinking, and the slight tide was taking it further away from the land. The only thing to do was to row for dear life towards the nearest possible landing-place, and to put up a silent prayer. But he soon found that his most strenuous efforts were now unavailing, with the boat so full of water. Swiftly he removed shoes and coat, and then calmly waited for the climax. It came a few minutes later. The boat sank under him, and he remained floating on his back with his arms supporting Stafford. Then he commenced to use his legs. It was not a great distance to land, but what with his burden and the ebbing tide he was soon aware that he was making no progress at all. The relative coldness of the water had brought Stafford to consciousness, and he became aware of what was happening.

'No use, Colin,' he said. 'You can't do it — old man. I — I think I'm done — anyway. Let go and save yourself.'

'I got you into this, and I'm not letting go.'

'Heroics all — very well. But you can't do — impossible. Be sensible, man. I've no one to worry — much.'

After that there was silence, except for Colin's splashing feet and his convulsive breathing. He knew he was losing the uneven battle and strange thoughts passed through his mind. His leg movements began to flag, and everything became misty and vague. Then suddenly he was aware of a moving green light which, in his distressed state of mind, puzzled him. It was comparatively close, and as he stared at it uncomprehendingly its speed decreased until it stopped altogether and became a kind of fixed star in the firmament. He was low in the water now, and the weight of his burden was almost unsupportable. Something flashed with great brilliance, and he found himself in a wide circle of light. Only then did he realise that the green light came from the starboard side of a ship, and that the intense white light was that of a searchlight. It gave him new hope — new endeavour.

He did not see the small boat leave the ship and was scarcely aware of it until it was riding near him. Someone shouted and now he saw two men — within yards. One of them leaned over and succeeded in getting a grip of Stafford. With that awful weight taken from him he felt better, but he stayed floating on his back until he too was manhandled into the ship's boat.

'Thanks!' he muttered weakly.

One of the two men was pointing to the wound in Stafford's chest, and was gabbling something in a foreign tongue. He recognised the language as Spanish, but missed the meaning of the words — The ship was a curious one — some sort of converted war-time vessel. As they came under her bows a man in white drill leaned over the railings and shouted an order. Colin saw Stafford hoisted aboard in a cradle, but he himself subsequently went by way of the steps. On board he was greeted by the man who had looked over the railing. He was a handsome fellow of about forty years of age, with black wavy hair and flashing eyes.

'I am Captain Lopez, and owner of this vessel,' he said in English.

'My name is Fairbright,' replied Colin. 'I am very grateful to you for saving me and my friend.'

'It was my good fortune. But how did you come to be in the water?'

'Our small boat capsized, and my friend was — injured. He needs immediate medical attention.'

'So I understand,' replied Lopez. 'How did he come to get that bullet in his chest?'

'We were fired at — from the shore. I will explain later, but in the meantime my friend may be in danger. Can you put us ashore at Nice?'

'Yes — a little later. I am on a mission but it should not take long. My mate will take you to the cabin where your friend lies. There you can dry your clothes. I will come to you later.'

He beckoned a long lean fellow who was standing by and Colin was escorted down some steps and along a passage to a

461

very luxurious cabin, in which were two beds, and some first-class furniture. On one of the beds Stafford was lying, and dripping water on to a waterproof sheet which had been placed under him. The cadaverous mate pointed to an electric fire and then pressed the switch on the wall. He then took a look at Stafford's wound, and shook his head as if he regarded the case as hopeless.

'Can you find some brandy?' asked Colin.

It was clear he did not understand English, so Colin tried the same question in French, at which he nodded and hurried away. Colin then removed his coat and drenched shirt, and placed them in front of the glowing electric-fire. He then managed to remove Stafford's coat, and was surprised at the weight of it, until he remembered the two grenades in the side-pockets. He removed these and pushed them under the pillow of the neighbouring bed. By the wash-basin in the corner were two clean towels. He wetted the smaller towel and commenced to cleanse the wound. It was then he discovered that it went clean through the body, and this he thought was more promising since it would not necessitate probing for a bullet. The mate came back with some brandy in a glass, and Colin raised Stafford slightly and got some of the brandy between Stafford's lips.

'Good!' said the mate, in French. 'He is reviving.'

Stafford's eyes opened, and he stared up at Colin, for a moment in amazement.

'Oh, you,' he murmured. 'Where — where am I?'

A sudden restarting of the propellor gave him his answer. A bell rang and the vessel began to move. One of the crew entered and spoke to the mate in rapid Spanish, and then Colin and Stafford were left alone.

'A ship!' muttered Stafford, and Colin winced as a little blood came from his lips.

'We were picked up by a kind of pleasure boat,' he said. 'The owner has promised to put us ashore at Nice, which isn't very far away. You got hit by a bullet — remember?'

Stafford nodded.

'Much pain?'

'No. Not too bad. Thanks, Colin. You were grand.'

'Nonsense! Now I've got to get the rest of your clothing off. You're making a glorious mess.'

As he proceeded to do this he gazed through the porthole. All he saw was sea, for the land was on the other side, but he suddenly realised they were going away from Nice.

'He has to make a call somewhere,' he said. 'I hope it isn't far or that gang will get away. One would have thought that in the circumstances he would have put us ashore without delay. You need a doctor. Staff, you aren't feeling too bad, are you?'

'No. I think I'll weather this.'

'That's the spirit.'

'What about yourself?'

'Nothing wrong with me — except tiredness. Have a drop more brandy?'

'Thanks!'

Within a very short time the vessel slowed down, and then stopped completely.

'Hasn't gone very far,' said Colin. 'May be putting a passenger ashore in a tender. Can't see anything from this side. If that's the case we shall probably put about and make for Nice.'

'Colin.'

'Yes.'

'We must be almost opposite the Villa Lombrosa.'

'That's true.'

'Then — '

'Don't say it,' interrupted Colin. 'That would be the rottenest bit of bad luck. I'm going outside to have a glimpse shorewards.'

He went to the cabin door and turned the handle. It resisted him and he shook the handle angrily.

'It's bolted!' he growled.

'That's — what I rather expected,' replied Stafford. 'We've had the bad luck to be rescued by Grandison's means of escape. Looks as if we are out of favour with the gods.'

Colin, almost completely naked, sat on the bed with clenched fists. If Grandison and Rupert had really engaged this vessel to take them to some place of safety, then indeed the future for him and Stafford was unpredictable, for they would almost certainly never dream of putting in at Nice. He jumped up and thrust his head outside the porthole with a view to overhearing any remarks or orders that might be passed. But all he heard were Spanish words which conveyed nothing to him. Time passed and there came silence. Then he became aware of sounds in the passage outside. People were coming aboard and entered the other cabins. He hurried to the door and listened near the keyhole. The lisping voice of Lopez was unmistakable.

'The lady in number eight,' he said. 'It is just suited to a member of the fair sex. Steady there! Easy with that stretcher. Now, Mark, I have something important to say to you — in my stateroom.'

Colin stole back to Stafford.

'There's a woman aboard — on a stretcher,' he said. 'It must be Rosita. What devilry has taken place? She must have been in the villa all the time. Where

466

are they taking her? What are they going to do with her?'

'Steady,' urged Stafford. 'There's many a slip, and that axiom may apply to Mr. Grandison as well as to us. They may think it is to their advantage to put us off at Nice, provided they think we are ignorant of what is taking place. Your best plan is to pretend that you are perfectly innocent.'

'You don't really believe that, do you?' asked Colin.

'I'm trying to believe it. Hullo, we're moving again.'

The vessel did a turning movement and Colin, through the porthole, saw the moonlit villa come into view on the hill above the lovely gardens. Now they really were making towards Nice, but soon their course ceased to be parallel with the coast, and they moved at great speed.

'We're going out to sea,' said Colin.

'Are you sure?'

'Yes. Our present course will miss Nice by miles.'

'Then the future lies in the lap of the gods,' said Stafford in a dreamy voice.

'What happened to my coat?'

'It's in front of the fire — drying.'

Stafford made a rapid movement and almost sat up.

'Shift it, man,' he gasped. 'I put those two grenades in the side pockets.'

'I know. I've taken them out.'

'Where are they?'

'Under that pillow?'

'Good! So we aren't completely helpless. Possibilities there, old chap. Great possibilities. Glory, I'm so tired — so tired.'

24

In the large and comfortable deck-cabin the Spanish captain-owner was entertaining the male members of his sinister passengers, despite the hour of the night. He regaled them with very fine sherry and enormous Havana cigars, and he noted their unmistakable relief at being on the open sea. His remarkable vessel — picked up after the end of hostilities, and cleverly transformed into a luxurious pleasure craft — was now showing her paces to his great pride.

'She is good for eighteen knots,' he said. 'She is now doing sixteen. Engines overhauled and everything in first-class condition. She is yours the moment the balance of the purchase price has been paid.'

'You shall be paid at Barcelona,' promised Grandison.

'In gold?'

'In gold.'

'Good.'

'You said you had something to tell me, Lopez,' said Mark, as he sniffed at the smoke of his excellent cigar.

'Oh, yes. Just before you came aboard I had the good fortune — if it was good fortune — to pick up two young men from the sea.'

Three pairs of eyes regarded him fixedly.

'One of them was quite well. The other had received a bullet wound, and their small craft had foundered.'

'Good God!' ejaculated Grandison. 'Did you find out their names?'

'The fit man was named Fairbright. The name of the other was not mentioned.'

Hans looked at Rupert, and Rupert looked at Grandison, whose face had turned almost scarlet.

'Why the hell did you do that?' asked Grandison of Lopez.

'Because it is the custom of the sea to pick up drowning men. I did not realise at the time that these two men might conceivably have troubled you. But when you mentioned the loss of your small boat their presence in the sea seemed to be explained. They were anxious to be put ashore at Nice, but I presumed that was not your wish.'

'By God! — no,' said Rupert. 'Those men are dangerous. One of them in particular.'

'Fairbright?'

'Yes,' said Grandison. 'We thought they had got away. The boat was floating when we lost sight of them.'

Lopez smiled.

'Then in fact my act was not so foolish after all?'

'He's right,' said Hans. 'Had they got ashore they might have had us intercepted. Now they can do no harm.'

Grandison nodded.

'Where are they now?' he asked.

'Locked in a cabin. I thought it wise to take that precaution.'

'Quite right,' agreed Grandison. 'But all the same this is an awkward situation. Is the wounded man seriously injured?'

'I haven't had a chance to find out.'

'Did you tell them you were picking up

passengers?' asked Hans after a moment's reflection.

'Certainly not.'

'Then they are not to know we are aboard?'

'I don't see how they can know. Their cabin is on the port side, and they could not have seen your arrival in the boat.'

Hans nodded in silence, but Rupert was staring at Grandison to find out his exact reaction to this unforeseen situation.

'What are you thinking, Mark?' he asked.

'I'm thinking what we're all thinking — how best to deal with them.'

'There's one way — and one way only,' said Hans.

Rupert caught the ugly gleam in his small round eyes, and knew what it signified.

'I agree,' he said. 'And the sooner the better.'

'Speak when you're spoken to,' snapped Grandison. 'I've no reason to love that interfering young pup, but —'

'There's no 'but' about it,' interrupted

Rupert. 'As soon as we are out of one trouble we're in another, and all because you have fed and fostered a passion for that girl. From the day when she came to Alton you've thought of little else but her. But she gives you nothing back — absolutely nothing. Now, within yards of her, is the man she really loves —'

'Stop!' roared Grandison. 'Who are you to criticise my actions? Without my help where would you be now? And you Hans — it was my money which enabled you to remain a free man. I agree that those two men are a danger. They must be got rid of, but not perhaps by the crude methods you would adopt. There are other ways.'

'What other ways?' asked Rupert contemptuously.

'I'll think of one.'

'You can think of nothing but that blasted girl, to whom you've had to lie all along. She thinks she is going to England. But wait until we get through the straits and steam in the opposite direction. What lie will you tell her then?'

Lopez intervened with a wave of his slim dark hand.

'Gentlemen, you will get nowhere this way,' he said.

'Agreed,' replied Hans. 'You must control yourself, Rupert. Mark is confronted with certain problems. I am sure he is capable of solving them satisfactorily.'

'I am,' snapped Grandison. 'But not to-night. It's very late and I've had enough for one day. Lopez, I should be obliged if you will keep that door locked on those two men until — until I have decided just how to act.'

'That is my fixed intention.'

'Good. Now I'm going to bed.'

He left the cabin and Lopez laughed as the door closed after him, and filled up the glasses from his considerable barrel of sherry.

'I presume there will be no slip at Barcelona?' he asked.

'No,' replied Rupert. 'His passport is good, and he has the stuff there.'

'Enough to pay me off, I hope?'

'Enough and to spare,' said Rupert. '*Gott*, I wish that girl were out of the way — also the others.'

'It could be accomplished without much trouble — I mean without spilling blood, which I find distasteful.'

Rupert gazed at the Spaniard's smiling face.

'You've something in your mind?' he asked.

'Well, one has ideas in emergency.'

'We should be interested to hear any good ideas — shouldn't we, Hans?'

'Most certainly,' agreed Hans. 'If you have any suggestion to make which might ease the situation you will find us attentive.'

The wily Spaniard re-filled his long glass, and gazed through it at the cabin light. Then he gulped the potent contents as if they were a mere noggin.

'I was born on a small island in the Balearics,' he said. 'A very delightful part of the world. I learned to sail a boat almost as soon as I could walk, and as a result I know every inch of those islands. Some of the very small ones are difficult of access and uninhabited. Most of these are without food or water. If our uninvited passengers were dropped there

I rather fancy that many days might pass before they stood a chance of being rescued, and by that time you would all be — where you wish to be, and out of all danger. I know just the spot to suit the circumstances.'

He stopped and saw that the bait was being taken.

'You refer to the two men,' said Rupert. 'What about the girl?'

'Why should she not accompany them?'

'Mark would never agree.'

'Could he not be *persuaded* to agree?' asked Lopez with a lift of his dark eyebrows.

'Not as regards Rosita,' said Rupert. 'He would rather die.'

'Perhaps that might not prove inconvenient to us — once we took aboard the chest at Barcelona. It seems to me that the moment the girl realises she is not going to England there will be trouble. Why should you countenance trouble, and entertain great risk, all for the sake of what has been called 'A rag, a bone, and a wisp of hair'? You see, my friends, it is he who is the chief stumbling block.'

'That's true,' said Rupert. 'But short of killing him I see no way out of this trouble.'

'A horrid word,' said Lopez. 'There is really no need for it. I think there is a better way. Suppose I tell him that I intend to drop the two men on the island. He is likely to agree to that, isn't he?'

'Yes,' said Rupert.

'Good! Then I whisper to the girl that the island is Majorca, and ask her if she would like to join them. Would she not be pleased to go to the young man you say she loves?'

'I'm sure she would.'

'We take her there secretly. Afterwards Mark discovers that she has gone. What will he do?'

'Order you to bring her back,' replied Rupert.

'Exactly! After some argument I consent, and he comes with us. The moment he lands we return to the ship, and resume our voyage at full speed. I think that would clear up matters most satisfactorily.'

'But the girl is ill,' said Rupert.

'Not so ill as she would have you believe. I have seen her and she tried to win my assistance. She is now suspicious of Mark, and very doubtful about his intentions. She told me she had eaten no food for days because she was certain she was being poisoned.'

Rupert met the Spaniard's long stare at him.

'She was in no immediate danger,' he said. 'I had to keep her quiet while she was at the villa. Mark is out of his senses. He doesn't consider me or Hans. But what did you tell her?'

'I told her she was mistaken.'

'She does not know about the presence of the two Englishmen?'

'No.'

'We shall have to think it over, Lopez,' said Hans. 'There is a lot of sense in what you say. When shall we reach Barcelona?'

'To-morrow night. I shall not enter the harbour, but stand off while you and Mark go ashore in the tender. Once the chest is aboard we can make for the island I have in mind — that is, if you are agreeable.'

The pair nodded in silence.

* * *

When Colin was assured that Stafford was really asleep he sought his own bed, and lay there for a long time thinking over the situation. By this time there was no doubt in his mind that Lopez and Grandison were hand in glove, although Lopez could scarcely have known of the connection between the men he had rescued and his prospective passengers at the time of the rescue. The locked cabin was significant enough, and the fact that they had long since left Nice behind them. But what were the intentions of this queerly assorted syndicate? How would they solve the knotty problem of their two unwanted guests? The obvious answer was not pleasant to contemplate. Here were he and Stafford caught like rats in a trap, with Stafford in a helpless state and he himself incapable of dealing with the situation. Lopez had promised to come to the cabin, but now the hour was late, and there seemed little hope that Lopez would keep his promise.

At last he fell asleep, and knew nothing more until he awoke and found it was broad daylight. The porthole gave him a view of a calm sunlit sea with land in the far distance. A sound from behind him brought his head round. It was Stafford, with his eyes wide open — surveying the unfamiliar scene. He smiled as their eyes met.

'Hullo, Colin,' he said. 'I was wondering what had happened. But now I remember. Where are we?'

'Somewhere along the coast — towards Spain I should imagine. How are you feeling?'

'Not so bad. Can you give me a drink of water?'

Colin got this for him, and held the glass while he drank it. Some of the fears of the night vanished as he gazed into Stafford's face. He did not look like a dying man. When he examined Stafford's wounds he found both punctures looking healthy. There had been but the slightest flow of blood during the night.

'I'll have to get you washed up,' he said. 'But first I am going to dress. My clothing is quite dry.'

Stafford lay thinking while Colin got into his creased clothing. Then his wounds were cleansed to his further comfort. Colin gave a glance at the top clean sheet of his bed.

'Since they won't provide a bandage I'm going to help myself,' he muttered.

He removed the sheet and swiftly tore two three-inch strips from the longer side.

'They may shoot you for that,' said Stafford.

'They may shoot me anyway. I'll have to raise you up a bit. Gently! I don't want that bleeding to start again.'

The bandaging was satisfactorily done, and Stafford slipped back into a prone position with a little sigh.

'Rotten being so helpless,' he complained. 'Together we might have done something.'

'I can't think what.'

'There are the two grenades. Oh, where are they?'

'Still under my pillow.'

'Better shift them. Someone may come and make the bed.'

'I can't see anyone coming and doing anything. But I'll move them just in case.'

He looked round and saw a bronze vase on top of the wardrobe. Reaching for this he placed the two grenades inside it and put it back where he had found it. As he did so he became interested in a gaudy Spanish flagon with an ornamental carved stopper.

'Empty,' he said, shaking it. 'I think we might use this.'

'How?'

'In the sea. Just a chance in a hundred. Any fisherman might be interested in a nice flagon if he found it floating. All I want is paper and pencil, but I haven't got either.'

'I have — in my coat — if the sea water hasn't ruined the paper. I used them at Monte to take down the numbers — remember? There's all that money I won too — in my wallet.'

Colin went to Stafford's dry coat and found the thick pencil and a soiled diary.

He tore several sheets from the diary, and sat down at the small table.

'Now,' he said. 'What shall I write — Inspector Ogilvie, C.I.D., London. Am prisoner on converted motor cruiser with Grandison and Rupert. Vessel off south coast of France, making westward. Captain — Señor Lopez. Now the date.'

'Good!' said Stafford. 'Now do another message to finder and enclose a couple of those five hundred franc notes. Mark it 'urgent' all over in large letters.'

Colin did this and rolled the whole into a cylinder which he pushed into the flagon. The long narrow neck kept the roll close under the cork, which he pressed home hard.

'Going to drop it now?' asked Stafford.

'Why not?'

'Wouldn't it be better to wait until after dark, in case the splash is heard and the trick is discovered?'

'It might, but time is everything. The flagon is as light as a feather. Not likely to make a sound that will be heard from the deck. I'm going to risk it.'

He took the flagon to the porthole, let

his arm down as far as possible and then dropped it. Scarcely a sound came back, and when he looked back he could see the flagon bobbing about in the wake of the ship.

'About as much chance as backing a winner in the Grand National,' he said.

Some time passed and then the unexpected happened. There was a noise at the door and into the cabin came Lopez, wearing a very fresh suit of white ducks, and carrying a roll of bandage and some medicated wool. He looked perfectly calm — even jaunty. He closed the door behind him, and Colin had a feeling that a guard was outside.

'Good morning!' he said. 'I came to have a look at your companion.'

'You've left it rather late,' protested Colin. 'He might have died.'

'He doesn't look like dying,' said Lopez, staring at Stafford. 'I saw him when he came aboard and satisfied myself that he was in no immediate danger. Ah, so you've been working on him?'

'I had to. He was bleeding. You can charge me with one damaged sheet.'

Lopez laughed.

'We'd better put on a real bandage,' he said, and rapidly unrolled the improvised one. He examined Stafford back and front and nodded his head. 'Another inch to the right and the result might have been different. Young man, you had a very narrow escape. Have you any idea who fired that shot?'

'A very good idea,' said Stafford.

'Perhaps you do not care to discuss it?'

'We do not,' interjected Colin. 'All we want is to be put ashore. You told me you would disembark us at Nice, but we must have passed Nice hours ago.'

'That is true,' replied Lopez calmly, as he applied the new bandage. 'I will be frank. There were good reasons why I could not put in at Nice — a long-standing dispute between me and the harbour authority. But you shall be put ashore once I reach Spanish territory.'

Colin regarded him with a suspicion he did not attempt to conceal.

'Is it necessary for you to keep us locked in?' he asked.

'For the moment yes. You must permit

485

me to know my own business best, señor. I would ask you to remember that but for my intervention by now you would both be dead.'

'We are grateful to you,' said Colin. 'But we do not take kindly to the idea of being penned up here.'

'There are many worse places, and it will not be for long. There are matters which apparently you do not wish to discuss, and I am in much the same position. It calls, I think, for a measure of respect on either side. What is your name?' he asked Stafford. 'I have to make an entry in my log.'

Stafford told him, and Lopez pencilled it in a little memorandum book which he took from his pocket.

'In a little while I will have some breakfast sent to you,' he said.

'Thank you, Captain,' replied Colin.

When he was outside the door Colin heard the key turn in the lock.

'Ingratiating scoundrel,' said Stafford. 'Glib with excuses. No doubt about what side he is on.'

'None at all. I was aching to blurt out

that I know why he locked the door, but it couldn't have done any good.'

'What do you think of his promise to land us in Spain?'

'I don't know what to think. But there's this about it. Had he wanted to murder us he could have done so quite easily.'

'That's true,' murmured Stafford. 'The whole thing is peculiar to say the least.'

It was half an hour later when the breakfast arrived. The man who brought it knew not one word of English, or pretended not to. On the large tray was a fine assortment of fruit, abundant coffee and some eggs on toast. Colin had an appetite like a horse, but Stafford had to be content with a little fruit and the majority of the hot milk. The man who had brought it tidied up a bit, but did not attempt to make Colin's bed. All the while the boat slipped speedily through the calm blue sea.

Stafford fell into a sleep soon afterwards, and Colin turned his mind to personal things. Chief amongst these was Rosita. It was exasperating to know that she was only a few yards away, and yet ignorant of his nearness to her. What was the nature of her illness? Where were they taking her, and for what purpose? Between them Stafford and he had a great deal of ready cash. Would it be possible to bribe one of the crew to slip a message to her? No, there would be no guarantee that the message would really be delivered. The man might accept the money and the message and promptly place Lopez in possession of the fact. All they could do was to await Lopez's pleasure.

25

It was in the early hours of the following morning that Colin was awakened by some sound, to realise that the vessel was no longer moving. He got up and stole to the porthole. About a mile away were the lights of a large town, and between the ship and the town he could see in the moonlight a small boat moving away from the ship. Someone was going ashore. Could it mean that Lopez was landing his passengers? It might be Marseilles, or it might be a Spanish port. But it seemed unlikely that Grandison would use the ship merely to get to Marseilles. How he wished he had awakened earlier so that he might have been able to see exactly what persons were in the boat.

A long time passed, and some of the lights in the distant port were dimmed. Then he saw the boat again, making towards the ship. As it came closer he saw two men at the oars, and two passengers.

A little later he recognised the passengers. They were Grandison and Rupert. With them was something which looked like a large chest. Then the boat disappeared round the stern of the vessel, and he saw no more. Five minutes later the engines started up and the ship began to move — in a south-westerly direction.

The next morning found Stafford considerably better. The pain in his chest was much diminished and he made a better breakfast. It was after the meal that Colin told him what had transpired during the night.

'Curious!' said Stafford. 'It might have been Barcelona. If it was then Mr. Lopez has failed again to keep his promise. I can't make head or tail of all this.'

'It would make sense if we knew the truth. My guess is that Grandison and Rupert are on their way to some distant place. Perhaps they had funds in Barcelona, and needed them before they left the Mediterranean.'

'You don't think that any — any harm has come to Rosita?'

'Good God! Why should — '

'I was wondering if the chest was in the boat when they left the ship. Whether they wanted to get rid of her without the knowledge of the crew. No, that's too fantastic. Forget it, old chap.'

But Colin couldn't quite dismiss it from his mind, and was sunk in misery all through the day. The food was brought regularly, and always by the man who spoke no other language but Spanish.

'I'm going to have this out with Lopez,' said Colin finally. 'Why hasn't he been here? Why hasn't he put us ashore? It can't worsen things to let him know that we know about Grandison and Rosita being aboard. I want to be assured that Rosita is safe — '

'Colin, don't do anything impulsive. In a few days I'll probably be on my feet again — '

'Nonsense! You can't work miracles.'

'But if you bring things to a climax now — '

'S-sh!' hissed Colin.

Stafford stopped as there came the familiar rattle of the key, and this time it was Lopez himself, wearing his ever-present, self-confident smile.

'Ah, there's a brighter look in your eyes,' he said to Stafford.

'Look here,' commenced Colin. 'I want to know — '

'My friend is concerned about me,' interrupted Stafford. 'He thinks I ought to get out into the sunshine. We get so little on this side of the ship.'

'To-morrow you shall have sunshine,' said Lopez. 'Now listen to me. We are bound for the Balearics, and late to-night I shall land you at Majorca.'

'You mean that?' asked Colin.

'Yes. I will be frank. Spain as you know is much divided, and I am not loved by the present government. Last night I hoped to land you at Barcelona, but I found that conditions were not favourable. To-night you will be free to go your own way. I shall be compelled to land you away from a town, but by morning you should be able to get help. Now I have a surprise. I have a young and beautiful lady aboard. You may perchance know her.'

Colin gave a start and stared at Lopez, for he had not dreamed that Lopez would mention this fact.

'I know her very well,' said Colin.

'She did not come aboard at my instigation. I would have you know that.'

'Did she fly here?' asked Colin.

'You English, and your humour! But we will leave the means of her arrival alone. What matters is that she knows you are aboard, and has expressed a desire to be put ashore with you.'

Colin could scarcely believe his ears, but Lopez appeared to be quite serious.

'I was under the impression that she was ill,' said Colin.

'She was — but not so ill as she pretended to be. Let us not go into details that do not matter. She is well able to walk, and very soon will be herself again. Señor Stafford is a different matter, but I will see that he has every attention until he is safely landed. I will leave you some blankets in case the night is chilly. After that all should be well with you. Well, are you not pleased?'

'Very pleased indeed,' replied Colin, a

little more heartily. 'At what time are we to be ready?'

'I think about one o'clock in the morning. I must ask you to stay here and be very quiet until then.'

Colin nodded and Lopez then left the cabin. As before the key was turned outside.

'What — what do you make of it, Colin?' asked Stafford.

'I don't quite know. What is your opinion?'

'It can only mean that he has brought pressure to bear on Grandison. You're quite sure it was Grandison you saw in the boat?'

'Positive.'

'Then Grandison and Rupert must have approved the plan. If their main object is to get away quite clearly they have to get rid of us somehow.'

'But I don't understand why Rosita is included.'

'Why not?'

'She is no danger to Grandison. She believes in the swine.'

'But you haven't seen her for months.'

494

'That's true. Oh, it's no use engaging in speculation. Within a few hours things may be a bit clearer. But somehow I can't believe we are really leaving. Oh, what about those two grenades?'

'Take 'em with you — until we get safely ashore.'

'I think I will.'

Waiting for the promised event was slow torture, but at long last the night came down, and then for hours the boat seemed to be going very slowly.

'What's he up to?' growled Colin.

'Lopez? If you ask me he daren't show his nose in any place where he is likely to be recognised. Shouldn't be surprised if he's a post-war pirate. Help me out of bed. I want to see how I feel on my own legs. Make it easier if I could walk down to the small boat.'

'I think you had better — '

'Don't argue. Lend me a hand.'

Colin did so very reluctantly, and Stafford took a few steps up and down the cabin, with Colin supporting him.

'You're quite crazy,' Colin protested.

'Everything is crazy. But I'm feeling all

right. Good enough for a short jaunt. You'll see.'

'Well, get back in bed and rest.'

The minutes and hours dragged on, but the moon had risen in a slight haze, and soon it became completely obscured. With visibility almost nil Colin came away from the porthole, and looked at his watch.

'Half an hour past midnight,' he said. 'I'll help you into some clothing, so that you'll be ready on time. My God, if he fails us I'll start breaking things!'

Soon Stafford was fully dressed and lying on the bed. Colin had retrieved the two grenades, and placed them with a grimace into his side pockets.

'You're squeamish with explosives,' laughed Stafford. 'So long as the safety-pins are in those things are as safe as an unlighted candle.'

'I've only your word for it. Lord, how slowly the minutes pass. There's still a quarter of an hour to go — even if Lopez is on time.'

'I don't think he can tell the time. Hullo! I believe the boat is stopping.'

A few moments later this fact was made clear. The last note of the engines died away, and the vessel was moving up and down on the slight swell. Then from outside there came a noise. The door was opened, and Lopez came inside the cabin. He nodded his head to see Stafford dressed.

'All is ready,' he said. 'The young lady is being got into the tender now. As little noise as possible, please. I have a stretcher outside — '

Stafford waved his hand.

'I can make it on my feet,' he said.

'Are you quite sure?'

'Yes. All I need is Colin's arm.'

'Then let us go.'

As they moved along the corridor Colin saw that the door of No. 8 cabin was open. He glanced inside and saw that it was empty. It really looked as if Lopez was telling the truth. In a very short time they were on deck, and Colin glancing down at the waiting tender saw Rosita, fully-dressed, sitting in the stern of the craft. His heart seemed to be banging at his ribs, and he waved a hand. She waved back just as the lamp which illuminated her was switched to the descending steps. Lopez held out his hand as Colin was about to descend.

'I must not leave the ship,' he said in a low voice. 'The men are reliable. I wish you luck.'

Colin shook his hand, and murmured a suitable response. Then, supporting Stafford, he went down the steps, and again the light revealed the lovely pale face of Rosita. They were helped aboard by the two men in the tender, and as soon as Stafford was made comfortable they moved away from the vessel. It was now not quite so dark, for there were some rifts in the cloud, through which the moonlight filtered. Colin left Stafford and edged along to Rosita. As he reached her she put out her hand and their fingers became entwined.

'Colin!' she said emotionally. 'I — I didn't dream this could happen. Oh, Colin, I'm so — so overwhelmed.'

'I too. There are millions of things I want to say — questions I want to ask. Most of them can wait until we get ashore. You've been ill, haven't you?'

'Yes. But now I'm getting stronger.'

'Is that why you never replied to my letters?'

'Letters? I got no letters. I think they were intercepted. It's a long and dreadful story.' Her glance went to Stafford. 'Who is your friend?'

'That, too, is a long story. I'll introduce you to him later, but now he must rest. The great thing is that I have found you. Look, there's the island.'

Rosita glanced to where a fitful ray of moonlight played on a rocky headland.

'Majorca?' she asked.

'Yes.'

'It sounds too good to be true.'

The oars creaked in the rowlocks and the tender pushed her way through the calm sea which lifted at intervals in a long and gentle swell. The night air was soft and scented, and the whole thing seemed unreal. Nearer and nearer came the land, and when they were close to it Colin saw that the boat was being directed to a tiny patch of beach backed by steep and rugged cliffs. All around were jagged reefs which the sea uncovered every few moments, and which called for great care on the part of the rowers. At last the keel grounded on fine shingle, and one of the rowers stepped into the sea, and manhandled the boat through a little causeway formed of flat-topped rocks, which finally gave dry access to the beach.

'We're there,' said Colin. 'You first, Rosita.'

Rosita stood up and was helped by the seaman to the beach. Then Colin gave aid to Stafford, who made the passage quite easily. The man who remained in the boat then handed out three blankets, a water jar and a tin of biscuits. Colin was a little puzzled by the last two items, but there was no time to ask questions, for almost immediately the two seamen shoved the boat off, and were soon rowing towards the stationary ship. Colin spread out the blankets.

'Better rest a bit, Staff,' he said. 'Rosita, this is Mr. Stafford whom I met while on my way to Nice. He knows about you.'

Stafford held out a hand and Rosita shook it.

'Are you — injured?' she asked.

'He was shot while we were escaping from the Villa Lombrosa,' explained Fairbright. 'It was one of your late companions.'

'Then it was you who was in the garden that night? I heard an explosion and later shooting. Captain Lopez told me he had picked you out of the sea, but he wouldn't tell me any more.'

'I fell into Rupert at Monte Carlo, and we trailed him to the villa,' said Colin. 'I was fool enough to call on Grandison to ask him where you were. To cut a long story short he captured both of us and locked us up in a pill-box in the grounds. We escaped but ran into an ambush and had to take to the sea. Stafford was shot just as we were getting out of range, and the boat capsized.'

'Colin is too modest to tell you that he saved my life,' said Stafford. 'Lopez promised to land us at Nice, but he changed his mind when those two ruffians came aboard.'

'There were three,' said Rosita. 'The third is named Hans. He came to the villa that night, for the first time. I had been ill for weeks — a strange, an inexplicable illness. I couldn't continue with the concerts so they brought me to that villa, which the woman Martha had rented for Grandison. Later I knew I was being poisoned, and so I secretly disposed of the food that was brought to me, and managed to keep alive on grapes.'

'The swine!' muttered Colin.

'It wasn't Grandison,' said Rosita. 'He did not know what was taking place. I am sure it was Rupert. He wanted to be rid of me, and Martha must have been in agreement. On the night when we left I overheard a conversation, and discovered that Rupert is Grandison's half-brother. That explained much that had puzzled me — Rupert's sullen attitude at times. They had never been like employer and servant. Then I remembered what happened to poor Charles Simbourne, and how Grandison had been Rupert's chief alibi. My faith in Grandison was shaken for the first time. I believe they killed Simbourne between them.'

'Inspector Ogilvie has always believed

that,' said Colin.

'Do you know where Grandison was making for on the boat?' asked Stafford.

'He swore he had chartered the boat to take me to England.'

'Did you believe that?' asked Colin.

'No.'

'Did you tell him so?'

'No. I was terrified but thought it best not to appear afraid. I just pretended to be much worse than I really was, in the hope that an opportunity would come to escape. I thought that Lopez would put in at some port, but he did not. At Barcelona Grandison and Rupert went ashore, but came back again.'

'What did they bring back?'

'A big chest.'

'Do you know what was in it?'

'No.'

'So Rupert is Grandison's half-brother,' mused Colin. 'Why did he find it necessary to pose as Grandison's chauffeur? Clearly he was in hiding, and probably in possession of faked papers. The death of Simbourne is directly associated with this business, and Lopez has undoubtedly been hired to get them out of Europe. Did you confide in Lopez?'

'Yes. I asked him if we were really going to England, and he said we were not, but begged me not to tell the others. I then asked him to help me get back to England. He would not give me an immediate answer, but later he came and told me that you were aboard, and that plans had been made to land you both at Majorca. He said that as Grandison and his friends did not wish you to know that they were aboard, they would not be present when the tender left. At shortly before one o'clock he came to my cabin, where I was waiting, and took me to the tender. He said there would be hell when Grandison discovered I had gone, but he would plead ignorance, and it might be assumed that I had jumped overboard during the night.'

'And I had persuaded myself that Lopez was about the last man in the world I would trust,' said Colin. 'Yet he kept his promise.'

'Probably to suit his own purpose,' said

Stafford. 'There were three extra mouths to feed, and always the risk that he might be held up and searched. That brings me to an interesting point. Why did the seamen leave us water and biscuits? If this is really Majorca we wouldn't need such things.'

Colin appreciated this point. It had been at the back of his mind during the conversation.

'I'm going to have a look round,' he said. 'You two stay here. I'll go over the rocks and find some high point. It's lighter now, and I ought to be able to have some idea where we are. There should be lights visible if it is Majorca.'

'Right,' said Stafford. 'We'll sample the biscuits while you are gone.'

They opened the tin and found it full of good quality biscuits of English manufacture. While they nibbled them Stafford talked of Colin — how they had met, and the pleasant excursions they had made.

'He's a grand chap,' he said. 'One of the grandest I have ever known. When I was completely done — after the shooting

— he could have saved himself by letting me go, but would he listen? With him it was all or none. It's good to see him so happy again.'

'Hasn't he always been happy?'

'Not really. Searching the newspapers day after day for some mention of someone, and never finding a word. I'm glad I met him and chummed up, because I think on his own he might have found existence a bit sticky. Now he sees fresh hope, and somehow I think the worst of his troubles are over.'

Rosita sat quite still. For a moment it looked as if she were going to say something, and then suddenly Colin came down the rocky cliff like a chamois.

'That dirty cheat!' he gasped. 'This is not Majorca. It's only a bit of an island — half a mile square, with ghastly caverns and not a scrap of vegetation anywhere — not even a drop of fresh water so far as I have been able to discover.'

'Just as I imagined,' said Stafford. 'But we must be in the Balearic group, so things aren't too bad — so long as the water lasts.'

Colin came and sat down by Rosita.

'I'm sorry to bring such bad news,' he said. 'All we can do is wait until morning, and then see if there is any other land visible.'

'At any rate it is better than the ship,' said Rosita.

26

Colin was finding the situation far from unpleasant. To be a free person offset all the other disadvantages, and he could not but feel that their stay on this barren rock would not be prolonged sufficiently to imperil their existence. The two grenades had proved to be a handicap, and before seeking sleep he took them from his pockets and buried them in the sand near a little outcrop of rock, with a view to destroying them the next morning. In a short time all three of them were asleep under their respective blankets.

During the night the sky cleared, and when the dawn came it was a thing to be remembered. The increasing light caused Colin to stir and open his eyes. The first thing which took his attention was not the wonderful phenomenon of the rising sun, but the face of Rosita within a yard of him. It was irradiated by the mystic light — calm and beautiful as the dawn itself.

Her long lashes lay on her rather pallid and thinned cheeks, but she was a sight for the gods, and he sighed as he finally removed his gaze.

Then he became aware of two things — both extremely important. To the south there was land. It looked like two islands, but might have been two parts of the same island, not more than ten miles distant. The other fact was even more exciting. Less than two miles away was the ship which he had so recently left, and it was bearing down on them. He sat up in his astonishment, and touched Stafford on the arm. Stafford opened his eyes sleepily.

'Oh, you — Colin,' he said. 'Where the — ? Of course, we're on the island. I was dreaming — '

'Look out there,' interrupted Colin.

Stafford's gaze followed the pointing finger, and he blinked at what he saw.

'The ship!' he gasped. 'That's an amazing thing. Why are they coming back?'

'God knows. Unless — '

'Unless — what?'

'Unless Grandison has discovered the trick that Lopez played on him, and won't stand for it.'

'You mean — Rosita?'

'Who's taking my name in vain?'

Colin turned his head and saw that Rosita was now wide awake. She threw off the blanket and shook her glorious head of hair. Then she saw the oncoming vessel.

'Isn't that — our boat?' she asked.

'It looks very much like it,' replied Colin grimly.

'Then why — ?'

'We've already asked each other that question.'

'Do you — think they have come back for me?'

'That's the only explanation that makes any sense,' replied Colin. 'It may have been convenient for Grandison for me and Stafford to be marooned, but not you.'

Rosita looked deeply distressed, and Colin shook his head in his dilemma.

'Colin, can't I run and hide?' she asked.

'What purpose would it serve? By this

time they must have seen us?'

'But I'm not going back — not to that ship.'

Stafford beckoned Colin closer to him.

'What did you do with the grenades?' he whispered.

'Buried them — back there in the sand.'

'Better get them. We may need them.'

'But if they come armed what earthly good — ?'

'It's a chance. Get them, Colin.'

Colin nodded and hurried to the spot where he had buried the grenades. He soon unearthed them and thrust them into his side pockets. When he came back Rosita looked at him curiously, but she said nothing. In the meantime the ship had stopped, and men were seen getting into the tender.

'Two — three — five — six,' counted Colin. 'They are not taking any chances. I think I saw Grandison's buffalo shape.'

The tender pushed off and as it approached the little beach the occupants could be recognised. There were Lopez himself, and two seamen at the oars, also

Grandison, Rupert and Hans.

'What's to be done?' asked Colin.

'No use starting an open fight,' muttered Stafford. 'If they have firearms they're bound to win. But if they take Rosita, you could go as far as the boat with her, and then pitch a grenade into it and blow it to pieces. That would prevent any of them getting back, unless they have another tender, which apparently they haven't.'

'But the two seamen may stay with the boat.'

'They won't stay long once they see that grenade arrive, and I'll bet neither of them will have the guts to pick it up and heave it overboard.'

Colin nodded his acquiescence somewhat reluctantly, and a few moments later the tender reached the rock causeway. Grandison and Rupert got out, and were followed by Hans. Lopez said something to the two seamen and then followed suit. All four began to approach the squatting figures when one of the seamen called to Lopez, and held something up in his hand. It caused Lopez to turn back, and brought Grandison and his companions to a halt.

'What's he left behind?' asked Stafford. 'Looks like a piece of rag.'

Colin made no reply. His hand had gone out instinctively to Rosita, and she took it and held it in a tight grip. Then the most unexpected thing happened. Instead of taking the object held by the seaman, Lopez gave the tender a shove and leaped aboard with the agility of a cat. The next moment the two seamen were rowing as hard as they could — away from the land.

'Great Scott!' ejaculated Stafford. 'They're quitting.'

Grandison, who now realised what was taking place, ran down the beach, and into the sea. He took a pistol from his pocket and fired a quick succession of shots at the departing boat. Lopez ducked for a few moments, and when the range was too great he stood up and with one hand on his heart made a stagey bow at the three infuriated men on the foreshore.

'He's dished them,' said Stafford, with glee in his voice. 'Now they're in a hell of a mess. Oh dear, I wish I dared laugh.'

'But why has he done it?' asked Colin.

'Remember that chest — brought aboard at dead of night? Mightn't that be the answer.'

'Yes. And his letting Rosita come with us. A very slick piece of work. But where do we stand now?'

'We'll soon know,' replied Stafford. 'The gang are talking things over. I wonder how many pistols they carry.'

'I don't think they will dare come here,' said Colin. 'Not after what has happened.'

But here he was wrong. The party by the edge of the sea stayed there for a few minutes, until the tender reached the ship, and the vessel turned and made away. Then Grandison left his companions and came trudging up the beach. Colin stood up as Grandison drew close to them.

'What do you want?' he asked.

'Rosita. I want to talk to her.'

'You can talk from where you now stand. She is as close to you as she ever wishes to be again.'

Grandison thrust his big head forward, hatefully.

'I want to talk to her — not to you,' he growled. 'What I have to say to her is private.'

Colin looked at Rosita.

'Do you wish to speak to him?' he asked.

'No,' she said, with deep emphasis. 'I never want to see any of them again.'

The effect of this upon Grandison was remarkable. He thrust out his hands appealingly, while the perspiration poured down his cheeks.

'Why have you done this to me?' he babbled. 'I thought only of your talent — your future. We were on our way back to England, but you trusted that scoundrel Lopez rather than me. He lied to you to gain his own ends, and you believed him rather than me. Everything I had was yours, and once you were quite well again we could have — '

'Shut up!' snapped Colin. 'You're merely upsetting her. Keep to your own part of the island, and leave us alone.'

Grandison stopped his queer drivelling,

and became once more his old browbeating, bullying self.

'Have a care!' he snarled. 'I've suffered you quite long enough. You have been the prime cause of all this trouble. I was willing to bury the hatchet, but if you want war you can have it, and the circumstances aren't in your favour.'

'If you take my advice you won't start any trouble,' said Colin. 'Now get going. We've nothing more to say.'

'But *we* may have much to say,' he raved, and gave a significant glance at the blanket which Stafford had placed over the biscuits and the jar of water, before he turned and went back to his companions. After loitering for a few minutes they made off over the lower rocks and became lost to view.

'I think he's a bit mad,' said Stafford. 'But there's no doubt he knows we have water and probably food, and very soon that party is going to get very thirsty. That's when the trouble will come.'

Colin was bound to agree. The position was indeed desperate, for they themselves had only sufficient water for a day or two, and about four pounds of biscuits between three of them. The immediate task seemed to be the erection of some signal which might be seen from neighbouring land, and equally urgent was the need to explore their surroundings and find the most suitable place for such a signal of distress. But of the three he was the only really fit person.

'A fire would be best — on a high spot,' he said. 'But there is so little inflammable material, and I've no matches to start a fire.'

'I've a petrol lighter,' said Stafford. 'It has been in the sea, but it may still work. Let's try.'

He produced the lighter, and after a few attempts the wick took fire. He let it burn for a few seconds to dry out the damp and then put it back in his pocket.

'You'd better go and get the lie of the land,' he said to Colin. 'You may find an inhabited island quite close to us.'

'Suppose that gang comes back?'

'Hide the water and biscuits. They're not likely to murder me just for fun.'

'It seems to be the only way,' said Colin.

'Leave me one of those grenades just in case of trouble.'

Colin took one from his pocket and Stafford hid it under the blanket, close to his hand.

'Colin, let me come too,' begged Rosita.

'Won't you tire yourself?'

'I feel miles better, and Stafford won't mind, will you?'

'Not I,' replied Stafford. 'I'll probably have a little nap.'

Colin and Rosita found a hiding-place for the water jar and biscuits and then climbed over the cliff and began their survey. Seen in the full light of the sun the island was a most uninviting place. Nowhere were there any trees, and the stark rock was folded into the weirdest shapes, forming long series of stagnant caverns. In some of the deeper depressions there had been water, but this had now dried up, leaving slime and weed. There were hundreds of lizards everywhere but no bird-life. Soon the whole expanse of ocean could be seen, and Colin thought he could make out five islands, all very small. The land which he had seen from the landing-place was the nearest, but whether it was one of the main islands or not it was difficult to say.

'That's the most likely source of aid,' he said. 'If we could only get a fire going to attract someone's attention. In the ordinary way I doubt if anyone would dream of coming here.'

'Isn't that some dried-up vegetation over there?' asked Rosita, pointing ahead.

'I believe you're right.'

They went forward and were rewarded by the sight of a brittle creeping plant, rather like ivy. Colin pulled on it and found it so dry that it broke easily in his hands. Nearby was a cave, which went in for an interminable distance.

'Quite a good spot,' he said. 'We can build a fire right on this site, and keep it going night and day. You sit down and rest while I make a start.'

'I don't need to rest. There's life in this lovely sunshine, and I've always had a weakness for bonfires.'

'But you'll ruin your hands.'

'What does it matter — now.'

'It does matter.'

But Rosita only laughed, and went on with the work of collecting the fuel. The pile grew larger and larger, and finally they made a reserve pile a few yards away. Then, at last, they rested and gazed at the empty blue sea.

'You are really feeling better?' asked Colin.

'Yes — physically and mentally. Colin, I wish I could feel that I wasn't responsible for all this.'

'But you're not.'

'Yes, I am. I should never have made that tour with Grandison. I should have known that there was something sinister about him. But I was carried away by the maddest ambition. I believed that all he cared about was music — '

'And wasn't it?'

Rosita shook her head.

'He changed after we left England. At times he embarrassed me and I began to realise that the music was a secondary consideration.'

Colin looked into her face.

'You mean — he made love to you?'

'No. He never got to that, but I saw it in his expressions. He thrust presents on me. I didn't want them, but it made no difference. Then I grew afraid and wanted to go home, but I had given my word, and it was all so difficult. Colin, I want you to know that he was never anything to me but a musical colleague. You mustn't think — '

'I'm not thinking anything — only thanking God that at last your eyes are wide open. He ruined your father — '

'My father!'

'Yes. I didn't tell you before, because I thought it would look as if I were trying to take an unfair advantage, and besides, I had not positive proof. But I am certain that he cheated your father out of his money, while he was staying there as a guest.'

'Oh, Colin. What a fool I've been.'

'No. He's clever. Clever enough even to get away with one murder — perhaps two. I dare say he did love you in his possessive way. Even now he hasn't lost hope.'

'Oh, that's preposterous!'

'Sorry. But loving you isn't very difficult, you know.'

She gave him one long look, and then raised his hand and pressed it to her lips.

'I thought this was a horrid place,' she whispered. 'But really it's the Garden of Eden.'

'With the old Adam forever reborn. You know I love you, don't you?'

'Yes, Colin.'

'And you?'

Now, without a word, she drew his head to hers, and kissed him on the lips. Nor did she withdraw for a long time.

'Nothing matters now,' she said.

'No, nothing matters now — but you and me.'

Later they went back to Stafford and found him idly making sand castles. He said he had seen nothing of the other party, and wanted to know what had happened to them. Colin swiftly outlined the new plan. They would establish a camp where the bonfire had been prepared, and set it going immediately. But could Stafford make the journey? It was only five hundred yards, but the going was bad.

'I'll make it all right,' said Stafford. 'That bullet did me no serious damage. Seemed to go clean through a lot of useless fat and leave all the vital odds and ends intact. We take the water and biscuits of course?'

'Yes. But we need something to drink from. That big jar is impossible to handle.'

Rosita then had an idea, and went down to the sea to put it into effect. She came back a few minutes later with three clam shells which she had scoured with sand and swilled out in the sea.

'For our daily rations,' she said with a smile.

'Excellent! How much water is there in that jar, Staff?'

'Less than two gallons.'

'Eight quarts — sixteen pints. Sixteen divided by three. H'm! We'll have to go careful. I could drink a couple of pints at this moment. But maybe by to-morrow we shall be out of this place.'

They started the journey a few

moments later, Rosita carrying most of the impedimenta, and Colin chiefly engaged in supporting Stafford. Every hundred yards or so they rested for a few minutes, but finally the prospective camp was reached.

'All right?' asked Colin of Stafford.

'First rate. I'll be as good as new in a week or two. Quite a spot this. Do we start the fire now?'

'Yes.'

Stafford handed the petrol lighter to Colin. It sprang into flame at the second attempt, and Colin ignited the most inflammable corner of the big pyre. Colin wanted smoke, and he got plenty.

'That's a great sight,' he said. 'Now we'll have some rations.'

About half a pint of water was poured into each of the shells, and each of them took two biscuits.

'At two meals a day we shall last five days,' said Stafford. 'After that we'll pray for a thunderstorm.'

For some time they sat over their frugal repast and watched the great column of smoke and sparks ascending. Then Colin bade the others rest, and went on gathering more fuel. Later he was joined by Rosita who swore she felt fresh again. But the heat of the sun, added to the radiation of the bonfire, was terrific, and soon they were compelled to take shelter in the mouth of the ugly cavern.

'I wanted sunshine,' said Stafford. 'But now I wish some clouds would blow up. Old Lopez seems to have vanished completely. Nothing but sea and sky and blistering heat. Do you propose to keep the fire going all night?'

'Yes. It may be even more effective then, provided we can get a good blaze. Somebody ought to see it, and come and investigate.'

27

With the going down of the sun the stars began to blaze up like suspended lamps. There was no moon yet, nor would be for some hours, and no sound but the moan of the sea. Grandison and his companions were reclining on a patch of sand not very far from the place where they had landed. All day they had searched for water, and anything which appeared edible, but without success. Rupert had indeed opened a live clam and tasted it, only to spit it out with an expression of disgust. Now they had given up all hope of living off the island, and all of them were approaching desperation. Rupert and Hans talked at intervals but Grandison was silent. It was still hot. The rocks about them seemed to be radiating the fierce heat which they had gathered during the day, and Grandison had removed his coat and was sitting with his shirt-sleeves rolled up, staring fixedly at the sea. After a while a little breeze was felt and Grandison reached out for his coat, and put it on, while Rupert watched him through his half-closed eyes. Then suddenly Grandison thrust a hand into his coat pocket and swung round to face Rupert.

'You've got it,' he snarled. 'You've taken my pistol.'

'You're crazy,' replied Rupert. 'Don't tell me you've been fool enough to lose it?'

Grandison switched his gaze to Hans, and Hans shook his head miserably.

'It was in my pocket when I took off my coat. Rupert, you're lying. Give me that pistol.'

'I tell you —'

Grandison rose to his feet, his eyes blazing with fury. He gave a half leap at Rupert, but Rupert was as agile as a cat, and eluded him. Grandison then picked up a stone as large as his fist.

'I'll scatter your poor brains —' he fumed.

In a flash Rupert produced the pistol, and cocked it, with the business end pointing at Grandison's huge chest.

'Steady, Mark!' he said. 'I took the pistol because you have lost your grip on things. By to-morrow we shall be half mad with thirst, and up there — in their new camp — those people have water and food. You said so yourself.'

'That's true,' croaked Hans. 'Why should we sit here and do nothing, while they have —?'

'They won't give it up.'

'Who says so?' asked Rupert, waggling the pistol. 'We're three to one. The girl doesn't count, and the other man is sick. There will be no fighting. We'll take what we want. What do you say, Hans?'

'Yes,' replied Hans. 'I'm with you. Gott, why did I ever get myself mixed up in this? I was better off when I was on my own.'

'Ungrateful swine!' fumed Grandison. 'You begged me to take care of you because you were suspect. Who was it who sent you money and saved you from starvation —?'

'Money? Whose money?' snapped Hans. 'It belonged to all of us, but you took charge of it. Now you've lost everything, and all because of a pretty face. How much does she really know, eh? Suppose we had the luck to be rescued from here how much could she tell? Rupert was right all along. It's a pity he didn't finish her off while he had the chance.'

Grandison gave what was almost a howl of rage, and sprang at his tormentor, seizing him by the throat with his powerful hands. Hans gurgled and his eyes began to bulge from his head. Rupert shouted to Grandison to desist, but he was deaf to all entreaty. Finally Rupert went forward and pressed the barrel of the pistol into Grandison's back.

'Drop it!' he said. 'Or I'll shoot.'

Grandison threw aside the limp and almost lifeless form of Hans and turned round on Rupert.

'I understand now what he meant when he said 'finish her off,' he muttered. 'That strange illness that I couldn't diagnose. It was what you wanted — the end of the concerts and the end of her. You were responsible for that. You were poisoning her — you and your friend Martha. You can't deny it, can you? You can't deny it.'

'Why should I?' asked Rupert. 'We could have left that house in England long before we did, but you found it attractive because of her. She turned your blood to water. You used to be a man, but what are you now? A snivelling spineless toad, without even the guts to put an end to those who threaten your life — and mine. It's as well someone has the courage —'

Grandison's hand had closed on the heavy stone which he had previously brandished. The pistol was still directed at him, but he did not appear to be aware of it. Suddenly he raised the stone, with full intent to smash Rupert's scalp, but the pistol flashed twice and Grandison dropped the stone and fell back.

'You brought that on yourself,' muttered Rupert, and thrust the pistol into his pocket.

Hans came crawling across the sand, gasping for breath.

'You — you've killed him,' he gurgled.

'If I hadn't he'd have killed me. It's best this way.'

Hans looked at Grandison, whose breathing was still obvious.

'He isn't dead yet,' he said.

'We can do nothing. What's the matter? Are you turning yellow too?'

'I need water as much as you.'

'Then why waste time?'

'Give me a few minutes to get my breath. He — very nearly strangled me.'

'You shouldn't have opened your mouth so wide. I'll go and see if that fire is still burning. Back in a few minutes.'

28

Up at the little camp the fire was burning furiously, having been heavily replenished with fuel. The party had eaten their second issue of rations, with no noticeable benefit for it seemed to leave them thirstier and hungrier than before. But the blazing fire had a comfort all its own.

'Unless the adjacent land is occupied by completely blind people the bonfire must be seen,' said Stafford. 'What about another little drink, and let the future be what it may?'

'No,' replied Colin. 'Once we let the rot start we are finished. But you are in a privileged position. A sick man needs nursing, and I vote —'

'Oh, no, you don't,' said Stafford. 'I was only trying out your discipline. You get full marks.'

'But seriously —'

Colin stopped as from a distance there

came the unmistakable sound of two shots.

'That's queer!' said Stafford. 'Can it possibly mean that our signal has brought help?'

'I've been watching the sea all the time,' said Rosita. 'I'm certain I should have seen any boat approaching.'

'In the darkness?'

'But I should have seen it before it grew dark — you too, There was absolutely nothing in sight.'

'Then it must be the gang,' said Colin. 'I wonder if they can have quarrelled —'

'Sounds like wishful thinking to me,' sighed Stafford.

Colin stood up and walked round and round the fire, looking in every direction. At last he came back and joined the others.

'Strange that they should waste two rounds of ammunition,' he said.

They sat in silence for a few minutes, and then Rosita turned her head to Colin.

'There's someone coming,' she whispered.

'I heard nothing.'

'I'm sure there is. My ears are particularly keen. I — there it is again.'

'She's right,' said Stafford.

Colin nodded his head in agreement. The sounds were slight, and it was difficult to determine from which direction they came.

'Friends or enemies?' he asked in a low voice.

'Better assume they are enemies,' said Stafford. 'Rosita, you had better get inside the cave. There's no knowing what may happen with neighbours like that.'

'I'll be all right,' replied Rosita.

'Please,' begged Colin. 'You can stand guard over the water and biscuits. I imagine they are the bones of contention.'

'But what about you, and Stafford?'

'We may be able to persuade them to go away. Quick, here they come. Rupert and the fat man. Can't see Grandison. Go now, darling.'

Stafford stared at the sound of the endearment, and as Rosita withdrew he scrambled to his feet.

'One thing I won't be, and that's a sitting target,' he muttered. 'Give me the grenades, Colin. I've had more practice than you.'

'What are you going to do?'

'Make them realise that we are not completely helpless.'

Colin passed him the two grenades. One of them he slipped into his side pocket. The other he concealed in his right hand. The oncoming men were now within twenty yards — Rupert with the pistol in his hand.

'Stop!' yelled Colin. 'What do you want?'

'Water,' replied Rupert.

'We've no water to spare.'

'Think again,' said Rupert. 'You can bring the jar of water out here, or we'll come and get it.'

'I shouldn't do that if I were you,' said Stafford. 'If you take another step forward I'll blow you to kingdom come.'

He then pulled the safety-pin from the grenade, but kept the lever down. Hans immediately caught Rupert by the shoulder and attempted to restrain him, but Rupert was built of sterner stuff, and swept his companion aside.

'I'm coming,' he said. 'If you throw that bomb it will be the last thing you do on this earth. I'll shoot the whole three of you. Understand?'

'I understand. Come on if you want it.'

'Wait!' screamed Hans. 'We can settle this without violence. All we need is a drink of water. Rupert, put the gun down, and —'

Rupert stopped him with a look of withering scorn, and then stepped out boldly towards Stafford. Stafford moved swiftly to place the bonfire between himself and Rupert, and then rolled the grenade down the gentle incline. It went straight for Rupert, who leapt forward and picked it up. In a split second it was flying away behind him. Colin saw it fall, and for a moment he thought it was a 'dud.' But suddenly there was a roar and a dense cloud of smoke. Stafford now had the second grenade in his hand, but Rupert was only three yards away with the pistol pointing straight at Stafford's chest.

'Hold it, Staff!' shouted Colin.

Stafford gave one look at Rosita, who

had emerged from the mouth of the cavern, and was covering her eyes with her hand, and then pushed the pin back through the lever. Rupert struck it from his hand with the pistol and then kicked him violently on the shin, causing Stafford to crash to the ground. It was then that Colin went mad. He went for Rupert in a 'rugger' tackle, flooring him completely. The next moment the two were clasped in each other's hands, and the pistol was lying away from the pair — in Rosita's direction. She swept down on it, and reached it just before Hans got there.

'Get back!' she screamed. 'Back, or I'll shoot you —'

Hans, quivering like a jelly, turned on his heels and ran. The next moment the pistol was pushed into Rupert's back.

'Don't — don't shoot,' he cried, and took his hands off Colin's throat.

Colin rose and took the pistol from Rosita.

'Get up!' he said to Rupert.

Rupert, bloody and dusty, rose to his feet. He looked round for Hans.

'Your friend has chosen the better part of valour,' said Colin. 'You had better follow him, because we have no intention of parting with either food or water. Get out!'

Rupert backed away, and then turned and was soon out of sight. Stafford had now recovered, and was liking the new situation.

'I believe we've got the only gun they possessed,' he said. 'That makes us top dogs. Rosita, you saved the situation. Here goes the second grenade just as a celebration.'

He removed the pin and hurled the grenade as far away as he could. Like the first it exploded with a terrific bang.

'Thank goodness!' said Colin. 'I hate those things. How is that shin of yours?'

Stafford rolled up the leg of his trousers and displayed a nasty cut.

'Painful,' he said. 'But it will pass off. Only two rounds left in the pistol, but enough to deal with any emergency. I still don't understand about Grandison. Can they have murdered him?'

'We'll go and see in the morning,' said

Colin. 'Now we had better do watches. I'll take the first spell. Shall we say two hours at a time?'

'Suits me,' said Stafford. 'Can't help admiring the swine — the way he picked up that grenade. If Hans had been half as tough this affair might have ended differently. Wake me if there's any movement, Colin.'

'I will.'

He was sound asleep in a few minutes, but Rosita did not sleep. She was content to sit up with her head resting against Colin's shoulder, and watch the flames of the fire. After the passage of two hours she was still awake, and Colin made no attempt to wake up Stafford.

'Let him rest,' he said. 'He's a great chap. Why don't you try to get some sleep?'

'I'm all churned up inside — so many new sensations — some horrid, some lovely. And I hate myself a little for being the cause of all this strife.'

It was in the early hours of the morning that something happened. From a distance there came a low droning, which increased as the moments passed.

'A ship?' asked Rosita excitedly.

'No. It's in the sky. It must be a plane. Yes, I can see the navigation lights. She's coming this way. Look, there she goes in a wide circle. She must have seen the bonfire.'

'But she's going away?'

'What else can she do? But at dawn she may come back.'

'Or not.'

'Or not,' he repeated. 'But one can at least hope. You look lovely with the firelight on your face.'

'I'm grimy and dishevelled, and fiendishly hungry — but happier than I have ever been before. Oh, Colin, life can be wonderful in certain circumstances.'

'I've discovered that too,' he replied. 'I feel like — '

'Some watcher of the skies when a new planet swims into his ken. Or like stout Cortez — ' she quoted.

'So you remember that?'

'Yes. You quoted it to me on the night when we first met, but I confess I looked it up afterwards. How long ago it seems, and yet it might have been only last night. I think I'm going to sleep, Colin mine.'

Two more hours must have passed before Colin, coming to full consciousness in the hush of the dawn, realised that there was something on the sea which had not been there before. He rubbed his eyes as the growing light revealed the thing unmistakably. It was a vessel of naval type swinging lazily at anchor.

'Rosita!' he gasped.

She opened her lovely eyes and blinked at him — then smiled.

'Look!'

'A ship!' she gasped.

'Yes. It's come. Like a fool I fell asleep and exposed us all to danger, but now — Up you get. Staff! Wake up, and see what Father Christmas has brought you.'

They rose to their feet and Colin shook Stafford into consciousness.

'My — my turn,' he muttered. 'Why, it's light.'

'Yes, but look out there, and you'll see a sight for sore eyes.'

Stafford sat up and gave a shout of joy, while Rosita and Colin waved their arms to attract the attention of anyone who might have been aboard the vessel.

'There goes a small boat — to the ship,' gasped Stafford. 'They may be leaving. Fire the pistol — do something.'

Colin seized the pistol and raised it in the air, but there was no need to fire it, for from behind the cavern a form came to view. He wore a pair of flannel trousers with a blue shirt, open at the neck.

'Good morning — all!' he said.

'Inspector Ogilvie!' ejaculated Colin. 'My goodness, you're a welcome sight.'

'So are you,' said Ogilvie, and came and gripped Colin by the hand, and then Rosita.

'This is my friend Stafford,' said Colin. 'He had the misfortune to stop a bullet, but is now recovering. Was it you in the plane which flew overhead last night?'

'No. But the pilot got in touch with me. He saw your fire and the Spanish representative at Majorca put a vessel and men at my disposal.'

'Grand! The gang — three of them — are on the island.'

Ogilvie shook his head and pointed to

the boat which was making towards the ship.

'They're in that boat,' he said. 'Two live men and one corpse.'

'You mean Grandison is dead?'

'Yes. But he was just alive when we found him, and was able to make a statement.'

'Who killed him?'

'The man known as Rupert. He was actually Grandison's half-brother. The other man is not related, but like them he was a fugitive from justice. All three are Germans, and have been wanted for a long time by the War Crimes Commission. They used various spurious names, and were on their way to the Argentine when you upset things a little. The ship which they commissioned was intercepted yesterday and taken into port, and Señor Lopez, who seems to have outwitted them is now in jail. A picturesque scoundrel that. He stole the ship which he pretended to own, and really intended to go to the Argentine — but alone. On board we found a nice little hoard of gold and jewels, to the value of a quarter of a million pounds.'

'Do you mean you got the message we sent in a flagon?' asked Colin.

'No. That was ingenious of you, but it must be still floating around. I got on to Lopez's track by other means, and found that he had been in communication with Grandison. From bits and pieces we built up a picture, and I got help from France and Spain. Lopez told me you were here and the plane confirmed it. I see the boat is on its way back, so we had better make our way down to the beach.'

'There's Stafford. I doubt if he can — '

'You speak for yourself,' interrupted Stafford. 'I'll be on that beach as soon as any of you. Well, what are we waiting for?'

29

Half an hour later the three of them, with Inspector Ogilvie, were sitting under an awning in the bows of the swift vessel, partaking of coffee, eggs and bacon, and what not. Stafford looked comfortable in the long chair which had been provided for him, and ate almost as heartily as the others.

'You said that Grandison — or whatever his real name is — made a statement before he died,' said Colin. 'Did he refer to the death of Charles Simbourne?'

'Yes. It was Rupert who did that, but Grandison played a part. Simbourne was lured to a place — near where his body was found — by a false message purporting to come from a man he once knew. Grandison really was in London as he stated. It was Rupert who was the killer. Grandison was merely the planner. Between them they killed the other man at Alton — Alan Devlin, and made it look like suicide.'

'But why?' asked Rosita.

'That's another story. It goes back to the war at a place called Wallensee, where Grandison was the Camp Commandant, and his half-brother was in charge of the hospital. It was packed with prisoners of war, and among those prisoners were Simbourne and Devlin. Terrible things took place there, and Simbourne and Devlin swore that if they ever got out alive they would bring the half-brothers to book. Just before the Allies overran the camp Grandison and Rupert ran for their lives. Grandison had foreseen defeat and had managed to get that trunk of valuables to Spain. How he managed to get to England I don't know. But it was a bold and clever move, because the last place one would expect to find him was England. His half-brother had separated from him, but they kept in touch and finally Rupert came to England as a displaced person. Hans was an old friend, from another camp, and he succeeded in getting to France, where he lived in hiding for a long time, because he knew that he would be indicted if he were caught. All of them had powerful friends in the Argentine.'

'But what I don't understand is why Devlin didn't recognise Grandison and Rupert when he came to live at Alton, and give them away at once,' said Colin.

'It wasn't as easy as that. At Wallensee, apparently, neither Devlin nor Simbourne came into direct contact with the two officials. They were mere names to them, got through comrades who were beaten to death or subjected to hideous medical experiments. It was Devlin who first got on the right track, and he came to Alton to prove his suspicions, and kept in touch with Simbourne who was on the Continent. Simbourne believed that Devlin had been killed because his association with Wallensee had been discovered, and so Simbourne also came to Alton, to find out for himself. I believe that at the time of his murder he was on the brink of furnishing proof.'

'The papers which were destroyed in his London flat?'

'Yes. He too must have come under suspicion, and suffered the same fate as his friend. It was then that Grandison decided to change his address, so he used Rosita's musical ability as an excuse. Of course he had no intention of coming back to England.'

'But he must have been mad to have believed he could deceive Rosita for ever,' said Stafford.

'I think he was a little mad. Actually, Rosita, you were his undoing. He believed that you were his destiny. That through you he could live down the past. But Rupert had no such delusions. He saw the danger from the start, and meant to avert it.'

Rosita nodded her head.

'I've been a fool,' she murmured. 'But you can have no idea how persuasive he could be, and I was drunk with ambition. I can't understand why I never detected that he was a German.'

'I can,' said Ogilvie. 'For he fooled me too. His mother was English and, unlike his half-brother, all his youth was spent in this country. He spoke English even better than he spoke his father's tongue. Well, it's all over now, and I must say the ending is most satisfactory.'

'Are you going to re-open the Simbourne case?' asked Colin.

'I think not. It will be better to hand Rupert and Hans over to the War Crimes Commission. That is what they dread more than anything else, and it's what Simbourne would desire if he were alive.'

* * *

Ogilvie was called away a little later, and the little party sat on in the sunshine watching the lovely coast of Majorca growing nearer and nearer.

'What are you two planning?' asked Stafford, as he lighted a cigarette.

'You'd be surprised,' said Colin. 'Or would you?'

We do hope that you have enjoyed reading this large print book.

Did you know that all of our titles are available for purchase?

We publish a wide range of high quality large print books including:
Romances, Mysteries, Classics
General Fiction
Non Fiction and Westerns

Special interest titles available in large print are:
The Little Oxford Dictionary
Music Book, Song Book
Hymn Book, Service Book

Also available from us courtesy of Oxford University Press:
Young Readers' Dictionary
(large print edition)
Young Readers' Thesaurus
(large print edition)

For further information or a free brochure, please contact us at:
Ulverscroft Large Print Books Ltd.,
The Green, Bradgate Road, Anstey,
Leicester, LE7 7FU, England.
Tel: (00 44) **0116 236 4325**
Fax: (00 44) **0116 234 0205**

DEATH CALLED AT NIGHT

R. A. Bennett

Jimmy Ellis believes his parents have died in a car crash when as a young boy he is taken to live with relatives in Australia. The years pass happily, then the nightmare comes. Terrifying images flit through his mind in the dark — all through the eyes of a child, a witness to grisly events seventeen years before. He begins to delve into the past, and soon he finds himself on the trail of a double murderer — a murderer who is prepared to kill again.

THE DEAD TALE-TELLERS

John Newton Chance

Jonathan Blake always kept appointments. He had kept many, in all sorts of places, at all sorts of times, but never one like that one he kept in the house in the woods in the fading light of an October day. It seemed a perfect, peaceful place to visit and perhaps take tea and muffins round the fire. But at this appointment his footsteps dragged, for he knew that inside the house the men with whom he had that date were already dead . . .

THREE DAYS TO LIVE

Robert Charles

Mike Harrigan was scar-faced, a drifter, and something of a woman-hater. With his partner Dan Barton he searched the upper reaches of the Rio Negro in the treacherous rain forests of Brazil, lured by a fortune in uncut emeralds. Behind them rode three killers who believed that they had already found the precious stones. And then fate handed Harrigan not emeralds, but the lives of women, three of them nuns, and trapped them all in a vast series of underground caverns.

TURN DOWN AN EMPTY GLASS

Basil Copper

L.A. private detectiv
plunged into a bizar
voodoo and murder
ful singer Jenny Lu
him in fear for her
the lonely Obelisk
the sinister Legba,
the crossroads, wi
straw sack. But M
beneath the supe
apparently motivele
ing crimes is an ing
a multi-million doll